# Summer Breeze

# Catherine Anderson

## Summer Breeze

DOUBLEDAY LARGE PRINT HOME LIBRARY EDITION

A SIGNET BOOK

This Large Print Edition, prepared especially for Doubleday Large Print Home Library, contains the complete, unabridged text of the original Publisher's Edition.

SIGNET
Published by New American Library, a division of Penguin Group (USA) Inc., 375 Hudson Street, New York, New York 10014, USA
Penguin Group (Canada), 90 Eglinton Avenue East, Suite 700, Toronto, Ontario M4P 2Y3, Canada (a division of Pearson Penguin Canada Inc.)
Penguin Books Ltd., 80 Strand, London WC2R 0RL, England
Penguin Ireland, 25 St. Stephen's Green, Dublin 2, Ireland (a division of Penguin Books Ltd.)
Penguin Group (Australia), 250 Camberwell Road, Camberwell, Victoria 3124, Australia (a division of Pearson Australia Group Pty. Ltd.)
Penguin Books India Pvt. Ltd., 11 Community Centre, Panchsheel Park, New Delhi - 110 017, India
Penguin Group (NZ), cnr Airborne and Rosedale Roads, Albany, Auckland 1310, New Zealand (a division of Pearson New Zealand Ltd.)
Penguin Books (South Africa) (Pty.) Ltd., 24 Sturdee Avenue, Rosebank, Johannesburg 2196, South Africa

Penguin Books Ltd., Registered Offices:
80 Strand, London WC2R 0RL, England

First published by Signet, an imprint of New American Library, a division of Penguin Group (USA) Inc.

First Printing, January 2006

 REGISTERED TRADEMARK—MARCA REGISTRADA

ISBN: 0-7394-6293-8

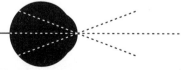

This Large Print Book carries the
Seal of Approval of N.A.V.H.

*To my grandson, Liam Ross Anderson, the newest addition to our family, who has filled our hearts with love and our lives with joy.*
*See you soon, little kiwi.*

**Joseph Simon Paxton, Sr. (1824–1866)**
**Dory Sue Jesperson Keegan (1831–1920)**

**Ace Keegan**
(1855–1932)
married ▼1885
↓
**Caitlin O'Shannessy**
(1863–1952)
▼
**Little Ace Keegan**
(1888–1976)

*KEEGAN'S LADY, 1996*

**Joseph Paxton, Jr.**
(1858–1953)
married ▼1889
→
**Rachel Hollister**
(1867–1954)

*SUMMER BREEZE, January 2006*

**David Paxton**
(1860–1949)
→
**Story Yet to Come!!**

**Esa Paxton**
(1867–1933)
→
**Story Yet to Come!!**

**Eden Paxton**
(1867–1954)
married ▼1890
→
**Matthew James Coulter**
(1859–1943)
→
**Story Yet to Come!!**

**James Matthew Coulter**
(1901–1986)
married ▼1920
→
**Sarah Beth Johnson**
(1902–1989)

**Harvey James Coulter**
(1942–)
**married**
♥1967♥
→
**Mary Ann McBride**
(1946–)

---

**Jake Coulter**
(1969–)
**married**
♥2001♥
→
**Molly Sterling**
(1972–)
→
**Garrett Coulter**
(2002–)
**Cheyenne Coulter**
(2005–)

*SWEET NOTHINGS*
January 2002

---

**Zeke Coulter**
(1970–)
**married**
♥2003♥
→
**Natalie Patterson**
(1973–)
→
**Chad Coulter**
(1992–)
**Rosie Coulter**
(1999–)
**(both adopted)**

*BRIGHT EYES*
June 2004

---

**Tucker Coulter**
(1970–)
→
**Story Yet to Come!**

---

**Isaiah Coulter**
(1970–)
**married**
♥2005♥
→
**Laura Townsend**
(1973–)

*MY SUNSHINE*
January 2005

---

**Hank Coulter**
(1971–)
**married**
♥2003♥
→
**Carly Adams**
(1975–)
→
**Hank Coulter, Jr.**
(2004–)

*BLUE SKIES*
January 2004

---

**Bethany Coulter**
(1974–)
**married**
♥2000♥
→
**Ryan Kendrick**
(1970–)
→
**Sylvester Kendrick**
(2001–)
**Chastity Kendrick**
(2004–)

*PHANTOM WALTZ*
July 2001

# PROLOGUE

*March 15, 2005*

Dust billowed up from inside the trunk. Tucker Coulter waved a hand in front of his face and coughed. When the sting cleared from his eyes, he brushed the grit from his dark hair and squinted to see in the dim light of the attic. Either his mother's memory was failing her or he'd opened the wrong camelback trunk. Instead of six baby books, one pink and five blue, he had unearthed what appeared to be a wedding gown gone yellow and fragile with age.

Bewildered, he carefully set the dress aside, hoping that the baby books might be underneath it. No such luck. Instead, he found a thick green tome with gold lettering on the front that read, *My Diary*. His mother's, possibly? Curious, Tucker picked up the book and turned to the first page. In a flowing, feminine cursive someone had written, *My Diary, Thursday, April 27, 1882.* Below was written a name, Rachel Marie Hollister. Tucker had never heard of the woman. Nevertheless, his curiosity was piqued. It wasn't every day that he came across a diary dating back well over a hundred years. Eager to read more, he flipped to the next page. The ink had faded over time, and in the attic twilight, it was difficult for him to make out the words.

*Today is my fifteenth birthday, and this diary is my present from Ma and Pa. I am going to write in it every single day and keep it in a safe hiding place so Daniel and Tansy will never find it.*

Tucker smiled in spite of himself. He guessed that Daniel and Tansy had been Rachel's brother and sister. Having come from a large family himself, he could sympathize with a young girl's need for privacy. He leafed farther ahead to skim over other entries, impressed by Rachel's perfect spelling and syntax. She spoke of attending school and frequently mentioned her teacher, Mr. Pitt, whom she described as being older than dirt and quick to mete out corporal punishment. It sounded as if Rachel's brother,

Daniel, had gotten his knuckles whacked on an almost daily basis.

Tucker found himself smiling again when he came across a passage about Rachel's dog, Denver, who had eaten her new kid boots. Tucker felt as if the years had fallen away and he'd stepped back into another era. It all seemed so real and immediate to him, as if Rachel Hollister had written the words only yesterday.

Impatient to learn more, he skipped ahead again. The next entry chased the smile from his lips. Not only had Rachel's spelling taken a sudden turn for the worse, but the tone of the diary had become gloomy and sad.

*Monday, December 17, 1888. I am always so lonely at t'is time of year. I cannot 'elp but t'ink of Cristmases past—of t'e wonderful smells of Ma's baking, and Daniel's excitement about going out wit' Pa to find a perfect tree.*

Tucker frowned in bewilderment. The errors in the script weren't so much misspellings as they were deliberate omissions of the letter H, which Rachel had painstakingly replaced with an apostrophe. *Strange.* She'd clearly realized, even as she wrote the words, that she'd left out the letter.

*I miss t'em so muc'. I yearn to string berries and popped corn for our tree wit' Tansy again, and o', 'ow I wis' I mig't 'ear Pa's voice one more time. I am now twenty-one, soon to be twenty-two. It's been almost five years since t'ey left me and almost as long since I've been able to leave t'e 'ouse. T'ere are days when I'm so lonely I fear I may lose my mind, but I dare not try to leave.*

For the life of him, Tucker couldn't imagine being trapped inside the house for five years. Had Rachel Hollister become agoraphobic? It certainly sounded that way. He read a few more lines, then closed the book and pushed to his feet.

"Mom?" he called as he descended the narrow drop-down stairway from the attic to the garage. "Hey, Mom?"

Mary Coulter opened the fire door that led into the kitchen. Dressed in gabardine slacks and a cheery pink blouse, partially covered by a white bib apron, she was everyone's picture of a contemporary grandmother, pleasantly plump but still beautiful, her short, curly brown hair only lightly touched with gray. "Did you find your birth certificate?"

Winter doldrums and a bout of depression had convinced Tucker to take a vacation, and he needed the document to get his passport.

"No, I opened the wrong trunk." He held up the book. "Instead of our baby books, I found this diary. Who was Rachel Hollister?"

Mary's blue eyes clouded with bewilderment. "Rachel who?"

"Hollister. This is her diary. The first entry dates clear back to 1882."

Mary pushed the door wide to let Tucker into the house. He went directly to the table and opened the dusty old tome. "Come look at this, Mom. It's fascinating."

"Oh, *my*." Mary's round face creased in a smile. "I had forgotten we even had that. It's Rachel Paxton's diary."

"According to this, her last name was Hollister," Tucker corrected.

Mary wiped her hands clean on her apron as she leaned over the book. "Hollister was her maiden name. She married Joseph Paxton, your great-grandma Eden's brother."

Tucker remembered hearing stories about Eden Coulter. "Dad's grandmother, the one with the fiery red hair and hot temper?"

"That's the one." Mary laughed. "I wish I had known her. If the stories your father tells me are true, she was quite a lady. Sadly, she died in 1954, when your dad was only twelve, and I never got to meet her."

"I never knew my great-grandma Eden's last name was Paxton."

"Eden took the name Coulter when she married your dad's grandfather, Matthew James Coulter." Mary ran her fingertips lightly over the faded handwriting and smiled wistfully. "Goodness. It gives you a strange feeling, doesn't it? To think that this was written so long ago."

Tucker hooked his boot around the leg of a chair to pull it away from the table, motioned for his mother to sit down, and then took a seat beside her. "How on earth did our family end up with Rachel's diary?"

Mary glanced up from the book. "All of her family were slain, and she was the only Hollister left. When she passed away, one of her children sent the diary to Eden as a keepsake because so many of the entries were written by her brother."

"By Joseph? It was Rachel's diary, wasn't it?"

"Yes, but after Joseph and Rachel married, the diary became a joint effort. You know how you kids are always asking your father and me how we met and fell in love?"

Tucker hadn't asked for years because he'd heard all the stories a dozen times. But he nodded anyway.

"Well, Joseph and Rachel told their story in this diary. He recorded his side, and she recorded hers." A distant expression entered Mary's eyes. "I attempted to read it once, but with five kids constantly interrupting me, I finally gave up. It's fascinating reading, as I recall, a he said, she said kind of thing, very sweet and romantic, but very intriguing as well with a murderer still at large."

Tucker wasn't into romance, but he loved a good whodunit. "A murderer?"

"Yes. As I said, Rachel's entire family was killed by a sniper. They were picnicking along a creek, as I recall, and the man came upon them unexpectedly and just opened fire.

Horrible." Mary shuddered. "Only Rachel survived."

Tucker leaned closer to read the entries. "Did they ever catch the guy?"

Mary shrugged. "I don't even know if it was a man who committed the slayings, actually. I had three of you boys still in diapers when I tried to read this, and I've forgotten most of it. All I clearly recall is the night Rachel and Joseph met. It stands out in my mind because he broke into her house, and she almost shot him."

"You're kidding." Tucker had been skimming the passages while his mother talked. "This is so incredible. I can't believe it's been in our attic all these years. Won't Bethany love it?" Tucker's only sister Bethany was the genealogy buff in the family. "Once she gets her hands on this, we'll have to fight for a chance to read it."

They both fell quiet. When they reached the bottom of that page, Tucker turned to the next. Soon they each had an elbow propped on the table, and the kitchen had grown eerily quiet around them, the only sounds that of their breathing and the ticking of the clock.

"Ah, look there," Mary whispered. "Joseph

Paxton's first entry. See the difference in the handwriting?"

Tucker nodded. The masculine scrawl definitely wasn't Rachel's. The passage was dated Friday, March 22, 1889, and Tucker was hooked after reading only the first paragraph.

*I write this after the fact and speak from experience when I say that there isn't any explaining what makes a man fall in love. I liken it to a hornet nailing me between the eyes. I never really thought I'd want to give up my Friday nights in town, playing cards and wetting my whistle with good whiskey. All that poetic stuff about getting lost in a woman's eyes was for my older brother Ace, not for me. I figured I was smarter than that.*

Those sentiments struck a familiar chord with Tucker. All of his brothers were happily married now, but he had no intention of following in their footsteps. Maybe, he thought whimsically, he had inherited his aversion to marriage from Joseph Paxton.

"What relation was Joseph Paxton to me, exactly?" Tucker asked his mother.

Pressing a fingertip to the page to keep her place, Mary frowned at the distraction. "He was your great-great-uncle."

Joseph went on to write:

*All the same, I figured if I ever did fall in love, the lady of my dreams would be someone really special, as pretty as sunrise, sunset, and everything in between, and with a disposition as sweet as fresh-dipped honey. Instead she was totin' a shotgun when first we met, and the little hoyden damned near killed me.*

In Tucker's mind, it was no longer the year 2005 but a blustery March day in 1889.

# Chapter One

*March 22, 1889*

Exhausted from pulling a calf and disheartened because he'd lost the heifer, Joseph Paxton rubbed the heel of his Justin boot on a clump of grass to rid it of barnyard muck, then reached into his shirt pocket for a pack of Crosscuts. Damn, but he was tired. Under the best of circumstances, hanging and skinning a beef wasn't his favorite task, but it had been a downright dismal undertaking today, every flick of the knife blade reminding him that the Grim Reaper had won another battle. Over the next week, he would be hard-pressed to cut up and preserve the meat. There weren't enough hours in the day as it was.

That was the way of it when a man started his own cattle operation. Days were long, nights were short, and come hell, high water, or Election Day, good meat couldn't be left to spoil. Joseph hoped things would be easier next spring. This year's heifers would be seasoned mothers by then and less likely to have trouble dropping their calves. He would also have the proceeds from the fall cattle auction in his bank account, enabling him to hire more help. As it was he had only two wranglers on the payroll, and both of them had already drawn their week's pay, left for town, and wouldn't be back until Sunday night.

Leaning against a fence post just outside the barn, Joseph struck a Lucifer on the side seam of his Levi's, cupped his hands around the flame to block the wind, and sighed in contentment as he lighted a cigarette. Buddy, his two-year-old sheepdog, brought to Joseph by his mother via stagecoach from San Francisco, flopped down beside him. The breed, which was long-haired, compact, agile, and highly intelligent, had, according to Dory Paxton, first been introduced to California by Basque sheepherders and had quickly become popular as cattle dogs as well.

Mindful of the fact that the animal had put in a hard day, Joseph fished some jerky from his hip pocket. Intelligent amber eyes filled with expectation, Buddy caught the offering in midair, swallowed without chewing, and then pushed to a sitting position to beg for more. Not for the first time, Joseph marveled at how pretty the canine had become, the white markings on his nose, chest, belly, and feet striking a sharp contrast to his thick red-gold fur. Judging by pictures Joseph had seen, the dog most closely resembled an English collie, the exceptions being that his coloring was different, his nose shorter and less pointed, his body a bit smaller. No matter. All Joseph cared about were results, and the dog could flat herd anything, cows mainly but sometimes even chickens.

"That's all I've got on me, you shameless glutton. You'll get nothing more until we call it a day."

Joseph fleetingly wished that he could eat supper in town as he normally did on Friday night, but with calving time fully upon him, he couldn't leave the ranch for fear another heifer might go into labor.

"There'll be no tasty meal for us at Roxie's place tonight, if that's what you're hoping," he informed the dog. "It'll be warmed-up beans and cornbread, and it's lucky we'll be to have that."

At mention of the pretty restaurant owner,

Buddy's ears perked up, and Joseph could have sworn the dog grinned.

"You'd best watch your step with that lady," Joseph warned. "All that special grub, and her lightin' up the way she does when we walk in?" He shook his head. "Not many restaurant owners save scraps for a dog and let him eat off a plate in front of the paying customers. Could be she's thinking the way to our hearts is through our stomachs."

Buddy worked his jaws, making a low, growling noise that sounded a lot like talking. So far Joseph hadn't been able to make out any actual words, but he was glad of the dog's responses. Otherwise, he might be accused of talking to himself, and only a crazy man did that.

"Mark my words, that woman has marriage on her mind. Many a confirmed bachelor has met his waterloo over a supper plate." Joseph narrowed an eye at the shepherd. "Chances are she doesn't even like dogs. Females can be treacherous creatures, pretending to be sweet when they're actually not. If she has her way, you could end up sleeping in a drafty doghouse with naught but a bare bone for company."

Buddy whined, dropped to his belly, and crossed his white paws over his eyes. Over the last few months, the dog had become quite a ham, somehow taking his cues from Joseph's tone of voice. His repertoire of acts included sitting up with his front paws held together in prayer, playing dead, rolling over, and lying down with his eyes covered to convey abject misery or dread.

Joseph chuckled and turned to study his newly constructed house, which sat about a hundred yards away. Roxie would undoubtedly insist upon painting the clapboard siding, and she'd want to pretty it up on the inside as well with lacy curtains, braided rugs, knickknacks, and all manner of other nonsense. *No how, no way.* She was a pretty lady, but Joseph wanted no part of locking down with one woman for the rest of his natural life. Just the thought made the bottoms of his feet itch. He liked things fine the way they were, with only him and Buddy calling the shots.

"Maybe it's just as well that calving season has come on so hard and fast. It'll give Roxie a chance to set her sights on someone else."

Gazing across his ranch, Joseph wondered

if he would ever grow accustomed to the fact that it belonged to him. He'd purchased the place only last August. Two full sections of rolling pastureland stretched out on all sides almost as far as he could see, giving him the feeling that he owned the whole world. In truth, the Bar H, better known as the Hollister ranch, lay to the north, and just south of the house was the boundary line of the Circle Star, Patrick O'Shannessy's place. Still, Joseph had plenty of elbow room with the sparsely forested foothills of the Rockies on the western horizon providing limitless open range. A man could saddle up his horse and ride for days without seeing another soul. Joseph had called the ranch Eden after his younger sister, but the name would have been fitting regardless. Finally having his own spread was his definition of paradise.

In the beginning, Joseph hadn't been sure if he could adjust to living alone. He'd spent nearly his whole life surrounded by family, a loving mother, an infuriating and spoiled little sister, and three brothers, one his elder, the other two younger than him by a couple of years. Before settling in here, he'd never come home of an evening to an empty house, let alone passed the night without hearing another human voice.

It had been difficult at first, but with Buddy to keep him company, Joseph had grown used to the solitude after a time. When he hankered for conversation, he could always visit with his hired hands, Bart and Johnny, in the bunkhouse or ride over to his brother Ace's ranch, only a short distance away. Joseph's two younger brothers, David and Esa, still lived there with Ace and his wife, Caitlin, who always seemed pleased to see Joseph when he dropped in for a cup of coffee. Joseph tried to go as often as possible. His nephew, Little Ace, was fourteen months old now and growing like a weed. Since Joseph had no plans to marry and have a family of his own, he wanted to enjoy his brother's children as much as possible.

In his peripheral vision, Joseph caught movement and pushed wind-tossed strands of blond hair from his eyes to get a better look. A horse and rider were slowly approaching. Tossing down the cigarette and grinding it out under the heel of his boot, he pushed away from the fence post and unfastened the holster strap of his Colt .45.

Not that he expected trouble. He'd just learned the hard way at a very young age that a smart man always made ready to defend himself when strangers approached.

Sensing Joseph's sudden wariness, Buddy bounded to his feet, sniffed the air, and let loose with a low growl.

"A fine watchdog you are," Joseph scolded.

Concerned at the way the rider slumped forward in the saddle, Joseph struck off to meet the man halfway. When he'd walked about a hundred yards, he recognized him as being Darby McClintoch, the foreman at the Bar H. Joseph had first made the old fellow's acquaintance when they worked together to mend a section of fence that ran between the two properties. Midway through that day, they had shared a patch of shade while they ate lunch. Since then, they'd run into each other only occasionally, a couple of times at the Golden Slipper on a Friday night, other times while out riding fence line or dogging a stray cow.

Joseph had almost reached the oncoming horse when Darby suddenly pitched sideways and fell from the saddle, his right boot hooking dangerously in the stirrup as he hit the dirt. Fearful that the gelding might bolt if startled, Joseph motioned for Buddy to drop and stay. Then he cautiously continued forward, saying, "Whoa, boy, whoa."

The buckskin snorted and tossed his head but didn't sidestep.

"Good boy," Joseph crooned as he covered the last few feet to grab the horse's bridle. "Oh, yeah, you're a steady old gent, aren't you?"

Giving the gelding a soothing pat, Joseph quickly wrapped the reins over the saddle horn with just enough tension to keep the horse from moving. Then he circled around to work Darby's boot loose from the stirrup.

"Darby?" Joseph's first thought was of the old man's heart. Darby was seventy if he was a day. "What's wrong, old friend? You feelin' poorly?" Dumb question. A wrangler by trade, Darby had spent most of his life on the back of a horse. For him to fall from the saddle, something had to be very wrong. "Can you talk to me?"

"Back shot," Darby gasped out as Joseph touched his shoulder. Dust had collected in the countless wrinkles of the old man's face and dulled the nickel-plate shine of his thick silver hair. "Near about—my right kidney."

"Back shot?" The hair at the nape of Joseph's neck tingled. He cast a quick look behind him to scan the horizon. When he was satisfied that no one had followed the old foreman, he rolled Darby partway over to have a look. "Oh, sweet Christ," he whispered when he saw the foreman's blood-soaked shirt. "Who did this to you, partner?"

"Dunno," Darby said weakly. "I was up—at the north end of the Bar H, lookin' for a heifer—that's due to calve." His chest jerked, and a grimace drew the skin over his cheekbones taut. "Thought I heard her—bawlin' up in the rocks. Rode that way—to have a look. Didn't see no tracks. When I turned back toward—the crick—some bastard shot me."

When the older man met Joseph's gaze, his green eyes glittered with pain. He made a loose fist on the front of Joseph's shirt. "You gotta go to the Bar H," he pushed out. "Miss Rachel—she's there all alone."

For the moment, Joseph had far more pressing concerns. Darby had lost a lot of blood. If he didn't get attention straightaway, he'd most likely die.

"First things first," Joseph replied. "You need patching up."

Darby shook his head. "No, you—don't under—stand. I think it was the same fella that murdered—Miss Rachel's folks. Now he's back to—finish the job."

Everyone in the valley had heard stories about the Hollister massacre. It had happened almost five years ago, a few months before Joseph and his brothers had settled in the area. The Hollister family had gone for a picnic one sunny June day at the north end of their property and been slaughtered like toms at a turkey shoot. Only Rachel, the eldest child, had survived.

"Ah, now," Joseph soothed. "You probably just caught a stray bullet, Darby. Someone out hunting, maybe."

"No, you gotta—listen," Darby insisted feebly. "Happened—in damned near the same spot. Too much to be—coincidence. He'll go after Miss—Rachel next."

A chill danced up Joseph's spine. Reason chased it away. The Hollister massacre had taken place way back in '84. So far as Joseph knew, not a lick of trouble had occurred since. It made no sense that a killer would lie low for so long, then suddenly start shooting at people again.

"No need for you to worry about Miss Rachel," Joseph said as he stripped off his shirt. "I'll ride over and make sure she's safe."

Darby shook his grizzled head. "Someone's got to—look after her 'round the clock. She's—in danger. I feel it—in my bones."

Joseph's bones were telling him that Darby's situation was by far the more urgent. "I'll look after her, Darby. No worries."

Darby's face had gone grayish white, and his green eyes had taken on a vacant expression. "Do I got your—word on it?"

"Of course you have my word on it." Joseph folded his shirt, worked it under Darby's back, and then used the sleeves to tie the makeshift bandage around the man's chest. "That's what neighbors are for, to help out in times of trouble."

Darby nodded and closed his eyes, seemingly satisfied with the answer. Taking care to jostle the foreman as little as possible, Joseph helped him back into the saddle. A travois would have provided a smoother ride up to the house, but Joseph didn't have one and couldn't spare the time it would take to make one.

"You steady on?" he asked the older man. "Grab onto the horn if you can."

Darby curled palsied hands over the base of the saddletree. When Joseph was satisfied that the old man could hold his seat, he loosened the reins and led the gelding forward. The house looked to be a mile away, and Darby moaned every time the horse took a step. Finally, the old foreman muttered a curse and lost consciousness, slumping forward with his head lolling against the horse's neck. Joseph made a fist over Darby's belt to keep him from falling and kept walking.

Once at the house, he made fast work of carrying the old man inside. After depositing his burden on the dark leather sofa, he hurried to the linen closet for rags to use as bandages. Until he could fetch the doctor, he needed to get the bleeding stopped, and the only way he knew to do that was to wrap the wound as tightly as possible.

Darby, still gray faced and unconscious, didn't stir as Joseph tended to him. When at last the bleeding had been staunched, Joseph quickly donned a fresh shirt, saddled Obie, his black stallion, and rode, hell-bent for leather, to fetch Doc Halloway.

Twenty minutes later, Joseph brought Obie careening around the last curve of Wolverine Road into No Name's town proper. Main Street, the community's only thoroughfare, swarmed with people. Lying forward along his mount's sweat-flecked neck, Joseph sped past the barber shop, nearly ran over a woman exiting the china shop, and brought Obie to a rearing halt in front of Doc's place. Buddy, who'd run neck to neck with the horse the entire way, barked shrilly and danced circles around Joseph as he alighted.

"Quiet!" Joseph scolded.

Tongue lolling, eyes bright with excitement, Buddy stood up on his hind legs and pawed the air. Brushing past the dog, Joseph looped the reins over the hitching post and cleared the boardwalk in one leap.

"Doc!" The door slapped the interior wall as Joseph spilled into the waiting room. "Doc? You here?"

Joseph had seen the waiting area only once, when Patrick O'Shannessy had been under the physician's care. A hanging shelf to the right held a clutter of thick, dusty medical books. Beneath it, four metal chairs with worn leather seats stood arm to arm along the chipped mopboard. Joseph veered toward the battered oak door that led to the examining rooms.

"Doc!" he yelled, rapping with his fist. "You in there?"

Joseph was about to burst through when the door swung open. Stooped with age, Doc Halloway peered up at Joseph through thick, askew lenses rimmed with gold. The strong smell of disinfectant surrounded him.

"Why in tarnation are you hollering so loud? I'm not deaf, you know."

"Sorry, Doc. I've got an emergency."

"Hmph." Doc pulled a white handkerchief from his pant pocket, gave it a shake, and wiped his mouth. His thinning, grizzled hair was all astir, giving Joseph cause to wonder if he'd caught the doctor napping.

"What kind of emergency?" Doc cast a disapproving look at Buddy, who'd dropped to his haunches at Joseph's heels. "I'm not a veterinarian."

As quickly as possible, Joseph related the details of Darby's injury. "I wrapped the wound as tightly as I could to slow the bleeding, but he's in a bad way."

Doc's kindly blue eyes darkened with concern. "Darby McClintoch, you say?" He shook his head and scratched beside his bulbous nose. "Nice fellow, Darby, minds his own business and as loyal as they come. Who on earth would have reason to shoot him?"

"That's for the marshal to figure out."

"True enough, I guess." Doc jerked up one red suspender strap as he shuffled around a padded examining table. He advanced on a set of drawers along the far wall, which were capped by a crowded countertop that looked remarkably dust free compared to the surfaces in the waiting room. "Did the slug go clear through?"

"No, sir. Went in at an angle on his right flank. I'm hopeful that it missed his kidney and lung."

"Any pink foam on his lips?"

"No, none that I saw."

"Coughing?"

"No, sir. But he was in a lot of pain before he passed out."

"Could be the bullet busted a rib. Damn it." Doc opened a black bag and began collecting items from the shelving over the counter, vials, bandages, and wicked-looking steel instruments. "Means I'll have to dig for the slug. Makes my work a lot easier when the lead goes all the way through." He tugged up the other suspender strap. "Ah, well, I was thinking just this morning that nothing exciting has happened around here for nigh onto a week. Man should be careful what he wishes for. This is the kind of excitement none of us needs."

Impatient to be going, Joseph shifted his weight from one boot to the other. "Is there anything I can do to help you get ready, Doc?"

"You can hook my horse up to the buggy. He's around back."

"It'll be quicker if you ride double with me."

"Never ride astride. Bad case of lumbago."

"But Darby's in a real bad way. Every minute counts."

"If you got the bleeding stopped and the slug hit nothing vital, he'll hang on until we reach him. If not—" Doc sighed and rummaged through another collection of vials until he located one that held something blackish-red. "Well, suffice it to say I'm no miracle worker. Last time I walked on water was when I got drunk in Dodge City and pissed my pants."

Joseph was in no mood for jokes. "I was hoping—" He broke off, not entirely sure now what he'd been hoping. He only knew that arguing about Doc's choice of transportation would waste precious time. "I'll go hook up your buggy and bring it around front, then."

"Fine," Doc muttered as he pawed through his bag. "Just fine. I'll meet you on the boardwalk."

Confident that he could overtake Doc's buggy in no time, Joseph loped up the street to the marshal's office before leaving town. He found his brother, David, kicked back in his chair, his dusty calfskin boots crossed at the ankle and propped on the edge of his desk, his brown Stetson tipped forward over his eyes.

Joseph slammed the door closed with a sharp report that shook the wall. With lazy nonchalance, David nudged up the brim of his hat to pin Joseph with an alert, sky blue gaze.

"What are you doin' here?" he asked. "I thought you'd given up Friday night gaming until calving seasons ends."

"You see any cards in my hand?" Joseph crossed the bare plank floor. A wanted poster lay faceup on the desk blotter, sporting the sketch of a bearded, craggy-faced stagecoach robber. "I've got a situation out at my place. Darby McClintoch has been shot in the back."

David sighed. "Well, that puts an end to my nap, I reckon."

He flexed his shoulders and rubbed the back of his neck as he dropped his feet to the floor and sat forward on the chair. His starched blue shirt fit snugly over his well-muscled shoulders, crisp creases marking the fold of each sleeve clear to the cuff. The shine of his freshly shaven jaw rivaled that of the badge pinned to his left breast pocket.

"How bad is the old fellow hurt?"

"It's bad," Joseph replied. "Doc's on his way out there now. I thought you might like to be there, just in case Darby comes around again. Maybe he can shed more light on what happened. Might be that he took a stray bullet. Some folks are running low on meat at this time of year, and a few men may be out hunting."

David slipped into his lined sheepskin jacket and then stepped over to lift his Henry from the rifle rack. "Did Darby tell you anything?"

Joseph quickly related what the old foreman had said. "It doesn't seem likely to me that the Hollister killer would wait five years before trying to finish what he started, but Darby seems convinced of it."

A thoughtful frown pleated David's forehead. "Give me five minutes to saddle my horse. We can ride out there together."

"Make it three minutes," Joseph countered. "I want to beat Doc there. He'll be needing boiled water and an extra pair of hands during surgery."

Joseph just hoped old Darby wasn't dead when they got there.

## Chapter Two

Icy gusts of wind buffeted the two-story house. With every creak and groan of the weather-beaten structure, Rachel Hollister's nerves leaped just a little. If she allowed her imagination to get the better of her, it was easy to believe that she'd heard a stealthy footstep or a floorboard giving under someone's weight. To distract herself and hold the collywobbles at bay, she hummed "Oh! Susannah," reminding herself between refrains that no one could enter her living area without first tearing away the barricade over the archway that had once opened into the dining room.

Long, golden hair still slightly damp from her bath and curling in wild abandon around her face, she sat in her mother's reed rocker near the stone fireplace, a wool blanket draped over her shoulders, the toes of her embroidered carpet slippers propped on the edge of the hearth. The hem of her muslin Mother Hubbard nightdress rode high on her shins, allowing the heat of the flames to warm her bare legs.

Hissing softly on a marble-topped table beside her, an ornate metal parlor lamp with a hand-painted glass dome provided light for her to crochet, one of her favorite pastimes when she didn't have her nose in a book. She was presently working on an Irish lace collar, a delicate creation she planned to give away. Though she could no longer attend Sunday worship services, her elderly ranch foreman, Darby, sometimes did. According to him, Hannibal St. John, the new pastor at No Name's only church, always welcomed donations for the poor. Since Rachel had little else to do, it made her feel useful to address that need in whatever way she could. Keeping her hands busy also saved her sanity.

Over the winter, she had made countless pieces, little pretties to adorn tabletops and garments, along with several pairs of wool stockings for women and children. Indeed, her output had been so considerable that Darby had been teasing her of late about opening a shop and selling her work for a profit.

Rachel frowned slightly, wishing that were possible. She routinely made butter and cheese, which Darby had no trouble selling at Gilpatrick's general store, and the chickens brought in a little egg money as well, but those small infusions of cash weren't nearly enough to offset the lost income of the Bar H. With her father and all the wranglers five years gone, Darby was hard-pressed to handle all the ranch work by himself. Out of necessity, he had cut back the cattle herd to only a few head, and the beef profits had diminished accordingly.

For a time, Rachel had tried to bring in extra money by hiring out as a seamstress, but she'd been in direct competition with Clarissa Denny, who owned the dress shop in town. Later, Rachel had turned to crochet, needlepoint, and embroidery, hoping to sell her creations on consignment at a few of the shops on Main Street, but eventually the items had been sent back to her, via Darby, yellowed and dusty from sitting untouched on a shelf. Nowadays, people who could afford fancywork preferred store-bought items.

Or so Rachel told herself. The only other

explanation for her abysmal failure to sell her work—that being reluctance among the townsfolk to purchase things made by a crazy woman—was wholly depressing and better ignored. She couldn't change the attitudes of others, after all, and fretting about it only upset her. As if she *chose* to live this way? As deeply as she yearned to feel sunlight and a soft breeze on her face again, she couldn't breathe and eventually lost consciousness if she went outdoors. Two deadlocks and a thick bar on the front door were all that made her feel safe.

Looking on the bright side, the wolves weren't scratching to get in yet. The ranch made enough to cover expenses and see to her needs, with a little left over for extras. Except for yarn, thread, an occasional bit of fabric, and a weekly dime novel or two, Rachel was careful about her spending. The only other luxuries she allowed herself were scented soap, some extra flour and sugar each month for baked goods and candy, and additional lamp fuel because she detested living like a mole. Light, and lots of it, was her only respite from the darkness, a substitute of sorts for the sunlight she so sorely missed.

With a sigh, she set her crocheting in the basket at her feet and got up to stir the beef stew simmering on the Windsor range. Darby would be along shortly, expecting his supper to be set out for him in the wood safe. She should stoke the cooking fire and get the cornbread in the oven. The old fore-man was nothing if not punctual when it came to mealtimes.

Keeping to Darby's schedule was difficult for Rachel sometimes. With her windows boarded over, inside and out, she couldn't tell daylight from darkness, and it was easy for her to lose track of time. Sometimes, if she strained her ears, she could hear the rooster crowing to herald the dawn, and at other times, if she concentrated, she could discern the difference between a morning and afternoon breeze buffeting the house. But overall, she existed in a limbo, the only structure to her days imposed by Darby's growling stomach.

The thought made Rachel smile as she added wood to the firebox and adjusted the stove damper. Her arrangement with Darby was more than fair, preparing his meals her only contribution. In return for tasty cooking and a middling wage, he worked the ranch and saw to her every need. Thanks to him, she never wanted for anything—unless, of course, she counted conversation. Darby turned loose words like a poor man did hard-earned pennies.

Rachel guessed that Darby's quietness resulted from the solitude of his occupation, riding the hills with only cattle for company his whole life long. He occasionally mumbled a short sentence to her through the door or wood safe, but that was the extent of it. Consequently, her yearning for conversation was only satisfied when she dreamed of her family, her mind recreating life as it had once been, with her parents and siblings talking and laughing over a meal or shouting to each other from different parts of the house.

Her thoughts drifting, Rachel set to work on the cornbread. It always cheered her to bake. She suspected it was partly due to the colorful bags and containers that peppered the counter. A man in a dark suit and top hat, wheeling a barrel, was imprinted on the Gold Medal flour sack. The Royal Baking Powder crock provided a lovely splash of crimson. Her speckled enamel saltshaker added a touch of blue, one of her favorite hues. The cornmeal sack, emblazoned with a cornstalk laden with partially shucked ears of field corn, lent green and yellow to the spectrum, along with GARNER MILLS scrolled across the top in bright red.

But it wasn't only the colors that made her enjoy baking. She loved the delicious smells that filled the room. They reminded her of days gone by when her family had still been alive. Oh, how she missed those times— with her fourteen-year-old brother, Daniel, forever up to mischief, her five-year-old sister, Tansy, running from room to room, and their mother always scolding. Rachel's dog, Denver, had contributed to the confusion as well, his brown eyes alight with affection, his tail wagging. Her pa had complained about the animal being allowed inside the house, but in truth, Henry Hollister had been as guilty of spoiling Denver as everyone else in the family.

As Rachel clipped sugar from the cone into a mixing bowl and crunched it into fine granules, she drew the memories close, a warm cloak around her heart. Life could be tragic. She would be the last to argue the point. But it could also be wonderfully rich.

One had to hold tight to the good things and try not to focus on the bad.

When she had whisked the dry ingredients together, she fetched milk and eggs from the icebox, melted some lard, and soon had a batch of bread in the oven. That done, she decided a hot peach cobbler for dessert would be lovely on such a windy March day. Darby had a sweet tooth, and regrettably, so did she, a weakness evidenced by her ever-increasing waistline. Her reflection in the water closet mirror told her that she wasn't actually fat yet, but in another few years she would be. The long walks and horseback rides that had once kept her trim were no longer possible, and the relentless boredom of her existence fueled her appetite. Homemade chocolate drops had recently become her favorite treat.

After collecting the lamp from the table and lifting the bar on the cellar door, Rachel descended the four wooden steps to collect a Mason jar of last year's peaches. Minutes later, she was back upstairs, sipping the extra juice she'd drained off the home-canned fruit while she mixed the cobbler batter. Darby would show up soon. By the time he finished his supper and brought his dishes back from the bunkhouse, the dessert would be cool enough to eat.

The cornbread was done to a turn by the time the cobbler was ready for the oven. While the dessert baked, she sat at the dining table to resume reading *The Adventures of Huckleberry Finn*, a fascinating novel that was, in her opinion, every bit as good as *The Adventures of Tom Sawyer*, heretofore her favorite—except, of course, for *Jane Eyre* and *Little Women*.

Dimpling her cheek with a forefinger, Rachel searched for her place on the marked page, and within seconds she was transported to the damp banks of the Mississippi, the blackness of night closing around her with only the light from Jim's lantern to penetrate the darkness.

Some minutes later, the smell of the cobbler jerked Rachel back to the present. "Consternation!"

She leaped up and ran to the stove, praying with every breath that she hadn't burned the dessert. Grabbing a cloth to protect her hand, she hurriedly drew the pan from the oven and sighed with relief when she saw that it hadn't scorched.

"Praise the Lord," she said. "When will I learn not to read while I'm baking?"

After adjusting the stove damper, she dusted her hands. En route back to the table, she glanced at the wall clock. *Five after six.* It wasn't like Darby to be late. She wondered if Poncho, his old buckskin gelding, had gone lame again. Rachel hoped not. Darby fussed over that horse as if it were a child.

Resuming her seat, Rachel found her place in the book, wishing as she started to read that she were actually there on the island with Jim and Huck. The thought no sooner took hold than she scoffed at herself. If she couldn't step out onto her own porch without succumbing to mindless fright, how could she possibly contemplate grand adventures on the fathomless, churning waters of the Mississippi?

Joseph pulled back on Obie's reins, bringing the stallion to a halt in Rachel Hollister's back dooryard. David drew up beside him, his sorrel snorting and stomping its front hooves. A moment of silence ensued as both men squinted through the deepening shadows of twilight to peruse the large, two-story house. Every window had been boarded up, and not a sliver of light seeped out through the cracks.

"If this don't beat all," Joseph muttered. "I heard she had boards over all the windows, but I had to see it to believe it."

David shivered and turned up the collar of his coat. "You sure we shouldn't go around front? Seems like poor manners to knock at a lady's back door."

"You heard what Darby said. She lives in the kitchen at the back, boarded off from the rest of the house."

"You suppose she'll answer if we knock?"

Joseph swung off his horse and dropped the reins to the ground, confident that Obie would stand fast as he'd been trained to do. "There's only one way to find out."

As Joseph crossed the short expanse of frozen, grass-pocked earth to the wide, covered back porch, which was about two-thirds the width of the house, he marveled at the strangeness of someone who chose to live this way. Since coming to No Name four years ago, he'd heard stories aplenty about Rachel Hollister, all with one common theme: that she had bats in her belfry. But this went beyond crazy. The woman lived in a hidey-hole, cut off from the world.

Studying the modified rear exterior of the house, Joseph heard rather than saw David coming abreast of him. The back door looked to be four inches thick, constructed of oak planks that only a battering ram might penetrate. To the left of the door, next to a boarded-up window, a large iron wood box had been set into the wall. Joseph had a similar setup at his place, a wood safe that could be filled from the outside and opened from inside the kitchen. He guessed that Darby normally kept the box stocked so Miss Hollister never had to venture outdoors for firewood.

Hoping that they might be invited in out of the cold, Joseph stomped his boots clean on the porch as David mounted the steps behind him. When they stood shoulder to shoulder before the door, Joseph glanced at his brother before raising his fist to knock.

When Rachel heard footsteps on the porch, she closed her book, thinking Darby had returned. She almost parted company with her skin when someone started pounding on the door. Not Darby. He only ever rapped on the iron wood safe to let her know he was home.

"Miss Hollister?" a man called out.

Rachel leaped up from the chair and fell back a step. No one ever came to call on her anymore. Her last visitor had been Doc Halloway, and that had been well over four years ago.

"Wh-who is it?" she asked in a voice gone thin with anxiety.

"Joseph Paxton, your neighbor," the deep voice replied. "I own the spread just south of here."

Rachel vaguely recalled Darby's telling her that someone had bought the land due south of her ranch, but the name Paxton didn't ring a bell. She whirled and ran for the gun case that stood between her night table and the armoire. Her hand went straight for the Colt breechloader, a 10-gauge shotgun with shortened barrels that Darby claimed would stop an enraged grizzly dead in its tracks. At close range, all you had to do was point and pull both triggers. Rachel had no desire to shoot anyone, but it only seemed prudent to have the weapon ready, just in case.

Muscles jerking with fear, she spilled a few shells from the ammunition drawer when she jerked it open. *Hurry, hurry.* She broke open the shotgun barrels, shoved a cartridge into each chamber, and snapped the weapon closed again. In the otherwise silent room, the rasp of Damascus steel seemed deafeningly loud.

On wobbly legs, she turned to face the barred door, braced the butt of the shotgun against her hip, and yelled, "State your business!"

She heard boots shuffling on the porch planks. *More than one man?* Her blood ran cold. *Oh, God. Oh, God.* Where was Darby? Had these men harmed him? The old foreman was never this late unless something detained him.

"This isn't the kind of news I want to shout through the door," the man replied. "The marshal is with me, if that eases your mind any."

*The marshal?* Rachel's heart skipped a beat.

"Can you open up for a minute, ma'am?" another man asked. "This is David Paxton, the marshal of No Name. I give you my word, we mean you no harm."

Rachel curled her forefinger over the triggers of the shotgun, prepared to start blasting if they tried to come in. "State your business through the door. I can hear you just fine." She swallowed to steady her voice. "My foreman will be along at any moment. If you prefer to speak face-to-face, you can wait a bit and talk to him."

Another silence ensued. Then the first man said, "That's why we're here, Miss Hollister, to bring you news about your foreman. Along about three this afternoon, he rode in to my place, looking for help. He's been hurt."

"Hurt?" Love of Darby had Rachel taking a hesitant step toward the door. Then she caught herself and drew to a stop. She was a woman alone, miles from the nearest neighbor. It would be sheer madness to trust two strangers. "How was he hurt?"

Rachel had grown up on the ranch and knew all the dangers. Darby could have been cut by barbed wire, thrown from his horse onto rocky ground, or kicked by a steer, to list only a few possibilities. Unfortunately, he might also have been bushwhacked by two thieving ne'er-do-wells.

She heard a low rumble of male voices. Then the man who called himself Joseph Paxton finally said, "He was at the north end of your property, tracking a heifer, Miss Hollister. When he left the rocks and headed back toward the creek, someone shot him in the back."

*Shot?* The word resounded inside Rachel's mind, and black spots began to dance before her eyes. She knew the place the man described. She saw it in her dreams every night. *Not again, God. Please, not again.* A strange ringing began in her ears, and she could no longer feel her feet. Images of her family flashed before her eyes—of her little sister, Tansy, chasing butterflies—of her father, sitting on the creek bank and playing his fiddle while her mother danced on the grass—and lastly of her brother, Daniel, golden hair gleaming in the sunshine, his grin mischievous as he wrestled with Rachel for the last drumstick in the picnic basket.

She made her way to the table and sank onto a chair. Dimly she heard Joseph Paxton speaking to her, but she couldn't make out the words. It was as if she had water in her ears. *Darby, shot.* She couldn't wrap her mind around it. And to think that it had happened in exactly the same place where her family had been killed. *No, no, no.*

A foggy darkness encroached on her vision. Rachel had experienced it before and knotted her hands into tight fists, determined not to let it happen again. Not *now*, with two strangers on her porch. But the blackness moved inexorably closer, a thick, impenetrable blanket determined to enshroud her.

## Chapter Three

"Well, hell." Joseph kicked a piece of stove kindling that lay near Rachel Hollister's woodpile. "That got us nowhere fast."

His breath fogging the frigid air, David hunched his shoulders inside his jacket. "It's worrisome, the way she went quiet all of a sudden." He gave Joseph an accusing look. "I knew we shouldn't talk to her through the door. You're supposed to break news like that gently."

"She wouldn't open the door," Joseph reminded him. "And tell me a gentler way to say it. I told her that he was hurt before I told her that he was shot."

"You're too blunt by half, Joseph. She may have a deep affection for that old man. With ladies, especially, you need to sugarcoat things."

"How can you sugarcoat such news?" Joseph demanded. "If you're so damned good with words, why don't you do the talking next time?"

"Thank you, maybe I will."

Joseph kicked at the kindling again. "Like you're such a charmer? I don't see you with a gal on each arm every Friday night."

"Saloon girls," David countered with a derisive snort. "Like your popularity at the Golden Slipper is a measure of your charm? I haven't seen you with a decent young lady in a good long while."

"The same can be said of you."

*Impasse.* Neither of them was in the habit of keeping company with respectable young women. Their older half brother, Ace Keegan, the closest thing to a father either of them could clearly remember, had always spoken strongly against it. When a man trifled with a proper young lady, he'd better be prepared to marry her, end of subject. That was the Keegan and Paxton way.

David sighed and toed the kindling back toward Joseph. "I just hope she's all right, is all."

"Anyone who boards herself off from the world like that isn't all right. Alive and halfway rational is the most we can hope for."

"With her family getting killed and all, maybe she's just scared half out of her wits."

Joseph considered that suggestion. "Could be, I reckon." Thinking of what had happened to Darby, he felt a chill inch up his spine. "And maybe with good reason."

Before stopping at the Hollister house to speak to Rachel, Joseph and David had ridden to the north end of the Hollister ranch to have a look around. They'd found the place where Darby had been ambushed, and in their estimation, the shooting couldn't have been an accident. The direction of the hoofprints left by Darby's horse bore out that Darby had been riding toward the creek when the shot was fired. The prominence of rock behind him would have blocked a stray bullet. Someone had been hiding in those rocks and deliberately taken aim at the old man's back.

"So now what?" David asked.

Joseph knew his brother was referring to the shooting, but he didn't have all of his thoughts about that in order yet. "The lady will need firewood to get her through the night. I'll start with that, I reckon."

As they loaded their arms with split logs,

David asked, "Where you planning to spend the night? In the bunkhouse?"

"Too far away," Joseph replied with a grunt. "On the off chance that Darby's right about her being in danger, I need to be close enough to hear if anyone comes around."

Arms filled, Joseph made for the porch, his brother only a step behind him.

"Where will you sleep, then? It's colder than a well digger's ass out here, and there's no windbreak that I can see."

They shoved the wood into the box. On the way back to the pile for kindling, Joseph said, "Darby says Miss Rachel lives in the kitchen, boarded off from the rest of the house. That must mean all the other rooms are unoccupied." He stacked slender pieces of pitch-veined wood on the crook of his arm. "I'll just slip in through a downstairs window and find a spot somewhere inside to shake out my bedroll—preferably as close to the kitchen as I can manage so I can hear if there's any trouble."

As they retraced their steps to the house, a cow lowed plaintively, the sound faint on the evening breeze.

"You think going inside is a good idea?"

David asked as they dispensed with their burdens. "The lady's a mite skittish."

Joseph dusted off his hands and straightened his Stetson. "What other choice is there? I'm as happy as a ringtailed possum to play Good Samaritan, David, but I'm not angling to get a bad case of frostbite while I'm at it."

David chafed his arms through the thick sleeves of his coat. "I can't say I blame you. It's not fit out here for man nor beast."

"I'll knock on the door again and explain that Darby sent me over to look after her. If she knows I plan to sleep somewhere in the house, it shouldn't alarm her to hear me coming in." Joseph flashed his brother a sarcastic grin. "You want to write me a speech so I sugarcoat everything enough to suit you?"

"I would if I had paper. You're nothing if not plainspoken, and that's a fact."

"Yeah, well, flowery speech has never been one of my strong suits." Joseph narrowed an eye at his brother. "Come to think of it, maybe you should be the one to stay. You were born with a lump of sugar in your mouth."

David threw up his hands. "Oh, no, you

don't. Darby asked *you* to watch after her, not me, and you're the one who gave him your word."

Joseph had never gone back on his word in his life, and he didn't plan to start now. That didn't mean he couldn't toy with the thought. There were better ways to spend a Friday night than playing nursemaid to a crazy woman.

David collected his gelding and mounted up. Joseph thought about asking him to stop off at Eden and bring him back a jug of whiskey before he headed home, but he already knew what his brother's answer would be. Now that David wore a badge, he was as puritanical as a preacher about the consumption of spirits—and practically anything else that Joseph thought was fun.

"Well," David said in parting. "Good luck. If nothing else, it should be an interesting night."

Sleeping on a cold floor with only hardtack and jerky in his belly wasn't Joseph's idea of interesting, but he couldn't see that he had a choice.

David rubbed his jaw. "I don't have a good feeling about this, big brother."

The comment brought them both full circle to that unsettling moment when they had realized Darby's shooting had been no accident. "Me, either," Joseph confessed. "My theory of a stray bullet was a lot easier to swallow."

"Only it wasn't a stray bullet," David said. "No how, no way could it have been an accident."

The words hung between them in the cold air like ice particles. David stared solemnly at the house. "As much as I hate to think it, she truly may be in danger."

Joseph hated to think it a whole lot worse than his brother did. He was the one who'd promised to protect the woman. "I'm sorry if my frankness put her in a dither," he offered by way of apology. "I know you wanted to ask her some questions."

David turned his gelding to head out, then settled back in the saddle and didn't go anywhere. "Maybe she'll feel more like talking tomorrow."

Joseph doubted it. Insanity didn't normally right itself overnight. "Maybe." Interpreting his brother's reluctance to leave as a sign that he needed to talk, Joseph asked, "In the meantime, what's your gut telling you?"

"That I'm flummoxed. Darby's so drunk on laudanum he can't tell me much of anything, and she refuses to talk. How can I make sense of this mess with nothing to go on?" David rubbed the back of his neck. "What if the shooting today actually is connected to the murders five years ago? We didn't even live in these parts then, and Estyn Beiler, the marshal at the time, never figured out who did it."

"Estyn Beiler was a piss-poor lawman." Just saying the man's name made Joseph's lip curl. "He was so caught up in his own shady dealings that he never did his job. You're dedicated, David, and you're a hell of a lot smarter than he was. I'm confident that you'll get to the bottom of this."

"Without even a suspicion to go on?"

Joseph reached inside his jacket for his pack of Crosscuts. "Ah, now. For the moment, forget the incident five years ago and start with the obvious question. Who might want Darby McClintoch dead?"

"Nobody that I can think of. He comes into town for a couple of drinks every now and again, but he never causes any trouble. He doesn't play cards, which rules out the possibility that he took someone's money and made an enemy. As far as I know, he never goes upstairs with any of the girls, either, eliminating all likelihood of a jealous lover. He's a quiet, inoffensive man, not given to discussing politics or religion, which can cause hard feelings. He just sits at a corner table, enjoys his drinks, and then goes home."

"Okay, then." Joseph offered his brother a smoke. The faint low of a cow reached them again. "Chances are the shooter has nothing personal against Darby."

"Which leads me right back to the incident five years ago and a big, fat nothing in clues." David accepted a cigarette and leaned low over the saddle horn so Joseph could give him a light. As he straightened, he said, "This whole thing is giving me a headache. My thoughts keep circling back on themselves. I have no idea where to start."

Joseph puffed until his Crosscut caught and then waved out the Lucifer. "Start with all the rumors and cast a wide net. A lot of folks hereabouts think that Miss Rachel's great-aunt Amanda Hollister might have killed the family. There was real bad blood between her and her nephew, Rachel's father, Henry. Near as I recall, it had to do with his inheriting the ranch and Amanda getting cut out of the will without a dime."

"That's the story I heard, too," David agreed.

"If Rachel had died with everyone else in her family that day, who stood to gain?" Joseph asked.

David squinted against an updraft of cigarette smoke. "Amanda Hollister. As the only surviving relative, she would have gotten this ranch lock, stock, and barrel and all Henry's money, to boot."

"So there you go, a prime suspect." Joseph spat out a piece of loose tobacco. "She definitely had motive. Maybe she's been keeping her head down the last five years because all the evidence pointed so strongly at her."

David thought about it for a long moment. Then he said, "Too obvious. In the short time I've been marshal, I've learned that the obvious answer is seldom the right one."

"I hear you. The woman would have had to be crazy to think she could get away with it. But maybe craziness runs in the family." Joseph hooked a thumb toward the house. "Folks blame Rachel's strangeness on her getting shot in the head, but maybe she was a little off-plum before it happened."

"Maybe." David exhaled smoke and flicked away ash. "Sort of like red hair running strong in the O'Shannessy family?"

"Yep. Only with the Hollisters, it could be lunacy." Joseph studied the glowing tip of his cigarette. "There again, we could be sniffing up the wrong tree. It's no secret hereabouts that Jebediah Pritchard hated Henry Hollister."

"Jeb's spread is just north of here, isn't it?"

Joseph nodded. "And rumor has it that his tail has been tied in a knot for going on ten years. Something about the flood back in seventy-nine altering the course of Wolverine Creek, leaving him high and dry without running water."

"I remember that, now. The original boundary description between the Bar H and his ranch included the creek and some rock formations. During the flood, the stream moved but the rocks didn't. Jeb wanted Henry Hollister to do a boundary line adjustment to follow the creek, and Henry refused because he would have been forfeiting several acres of prime grazing land."

Joseph pursed his lips. "If I recollect the stories right, Pritchard dynamited the creek a few months later, trying to redirect its course back onto his property. Evidently he didn't know what he was doing and only created a wide spot in the stream."

"Beiler never proved it was Pritchard," David observed.

"Who else had reason to care where that section of the creek flowed? It was Jeb. I'd bet money on it."

Jebediah Pritchard was a mean-natured, hostile man with an irrational streak rivaled only by his cowardice and body stench. His three grown sons, Hayden, Cyrus, and Alan, were apples that hadn't fallen far from the tree. When Joseph encountered a Pritchard in town, he stayed upwind and watched his back.

"I thought Henry Hollister channeled water from the creek into a big pond on Pritchard's property," David said. "That strikes me as being a fair compromise on Henry's part."

"More than fair. But what if Hollister had up and died, and his heir wasn't as generous? Pritchard would have been left with only a well to water his stock and crops. Maybe he decided to get rid of the whole

Hollister family with the hope that he could convince Henry's aunt to sell. She'd already purchased a smaller spread on the other side of town, and she was getting up in years. She might have been glad to take the money and have the responsibility of this ranch off her hands."

Warming to the possibilities, David inserted, "Only the bullet glanced off Rachel Hollister's skull, and she didn't die like he'd hoped."

"Exactly. And even worse, she woke from the coma crazier than a loco horse, and never stepped foot outside from then on. Pritchard could never get another shot at her. I've heard tell that he's tried to buy this place several times since the massacre, but Darby's always refused out of hand, knowing Miss Rachel wouldn't agree. That being the case, what's Pritchard to do? He's back to where he started, needing to get shut of Rachel. Only he can't get at her without getting rid of Darby first."

David flashed a grin. "You ever contemplate becoming a lawman? You think like a criminal."

"No, thanks." Joseph chuckled and bent

his head to grind out his cigarette under his heel. "I like ranching just fine."

"Any other suspects you can pluck out of your hat?"

Joseph considered the question. "All the neighboring property owners, I reckon. Couldn't hurt to question a few of their hired hands as well. This is prime ranchland. With Darby out of the picture, Miss Rachel would go broke in no time and be forced to sell, leaving someone to pick up this place for a little bit of nothing."

"You've just pointed a finger at yourself, big brother."

Joseph laughed again. "I reckon I did, at that. That's the trouble with casting a wide net. A lot of people fall under suspicion. Take Garrett Buckmaster, for instance. Even though his land is across the road and a little to the north, I believe he's made a couple of offers to buy this place over the last year. He strikes me as being a decent man, but he has no running water at his place, either. Stands to reason you should look at him real close."

David pinched the fire off his cigarette and tucked the butt into his pocket. "I guess I'll be a mite busy tomorrow."

"You mind having some company? I'd like to go along when you question everyone."

"Who'll look after Miss Rachel?"

"You can ask Ace to come over and spell me for a while."

David lifted a shoulder. "I'm not chomping at the bit to face Jeb and his boys alone. They're a shifty lot."

"That settles it, then. I'll ride along with you."

David tugged his hat low over his eyes. With a nudge of his heels, he set his horse to moving. "Tomorrow, then," he called over his shoulder.

Joseph watched his brother ride off. Then, whistling under his breath, he headed for the bunkhouse, where he hoped to find a lantern. He needed to put up his horse for the night and do Darby's chores, the first on the list milking those cows that were bawling so persistently. Making his way through an unfamiliar barn and barnyard would be easier with light to see by.

Joseph had just ripped away the outside boards from what he guessed to be a bedroom window at the front of the Hollister house when he felt something nudge his leg. He glanced down to see his dog standing there.

"What in Sam hill are you doing here? I thought I told you to stay home."

Buddy gave an all-over wag to convey his pleasure at being with his master again. It was difficult for Joseph to scold when he felt equally glad of the company. "All right," he said gruffly. "I'll let it go this time. But after this, when I tell you to stay put, I expect you to stay put."

Buddy worked his jaws and made the growling sound.

"Don't give me any sass," Joseph replied. "Who's the boss of this operation anyhow, you or me?"

*Shit.* The window was latched closed from the inside. Joseph pushed on the lower sash with all his might, but nothing happened. Resting an arm on the exterior sill, which was rough with peeling paint, he considered his options. To get inside, he would have to break the glass. Given the fact that it was colder than a witch's tit outside, he decided that it would be worth the expense. When Darby was back on his feet, Joseph would replace the pane, no harm done.

Decision made, he drew back his elbow

and struck the glass. The thick leather of his jacket sleeve protected him from the shards. A few more elbow jabs finished the job.

"Back," he ordered his dog. When Buddy had retreated to a safe distance, Joseph brushed the fragments from the outside ledge, then swept the ground with the edge of his boot, piling the glass off to one side of the window. "I don't want you getting your paws cut."

The window had been boarded up on the inside as well, Joseph realized as he groped the opening. *Madness.* One layer of wood over the windows wasn't enough to satisfy the woman? Standing at ground level, Joseph couldn't butt the planks with his shoulder to break them loose. Fortunately, he always carried a few tools in his saddlebags.

Within moments, Joseph had set to work with a crowbar to loosen the one-by-fours from the inside casing so he could knock them free. He winced at the racket each time a board fell into the room, but there was no way to do this quietly. He had forewarned Rachel Hollister of his intention to enter her house, so hopefully she wouldn't be too alarmed by the noise.

When the window opening had been divested of barriers, Joseph fetched the lantern, his bedroll, and his saddlebags from where he'd placed them on the ground. After thrusting all his gear through the window, he turned for his dog.

"Come here, you willful mutt. Let's get in out of this dad-blamed wind."

Buddy made the growling sound that Joseph found so endearing. He gathered the silly canine into his arms and gave him a toss through the window. Agile and sure-footed, Buddy was soon bouncing around inside the room, his nails clacking on the floor. Bracing a hand on the sill, Joseph swung up, hooked a knee over the ledge, and eased himself through the opening. A musty, closed-up staleness greeted his nostrils.

After locating his gear, Joseph struck a match and lighted the lantern. The lamp's golden glow illuminated a bedroom that looked as if its occupants had departed only that morning. A woman's white nightdress had been flung across the foot of the made-up bed, which was covered with a blue chenille spread and ruffled shams that matched the tiny flowers in the wallpaper. The armoire door stood ajar to reveal a man's suit and several white shirts, the remainder of the rod crowded with a woman's garments.

Upon closer inspection, Joseph saw that a thick layer of dust coated everything. He guessed that this must have been Henry and Marie Hollister's bedroom, and he felt like an interloper. A Bible on the night table lay open, a thin red ribbon angled across one page. Recalling the family's tragic end, he could almost picture Mr. and Mrs. Hollister rising to greet the day, never guessing that it would be their last.

"Come on, boy," he said to Buddy. "I'm getting the fidgets."

Joseph's fidgets worsened when he stepped out into a long hallway. A small parlor table, standing against the end wall, sported a vase filled with yellowed, disintegrating flower stalks. Judging by what remained of the leaves and the faded blossom pieces that littered the tatted doily, the flowers had once been irises. It gave him chills to think that Marie Hollister had probably cut the flowers and put them in water right before she died.

Holding the lantern high, Joseph continued along the corridor. He considered calling out to identify himself, just in case all the noise of the breaking glass and falling boards had upset Rachel Hollister. But what more could he possibly say? Before coming inside, he'd rapped on the door three times, once to introduce himself and tell her about Darby's injury, again to inform her that he'd done the chores, filled her wood box, and left two buckets of milk on the porch, and finally to tell her that he was going to enter the house by a front window. Even though she hadn't responded, he'd also explained his reason for being there, namely that Darby had asked him to come over and look after her. If all of that hadn't settled her nerves, nothing would.

He stopped briefly when he came upon what appeared to be a sewing room. The sewing machine was missing, but a half-made dress lay over a table, and an open closet revealed a nude dress form surrounded by lengths of lace and decorative trim looped over wooden pegs.

A little farther up the hall, he found a library. Tall rectangles of lightness in the pine-planked walls told him that several bookcases had been removed. Those that remained were only partially filled with what looked like tomes on animal husbandry and agriculture. Normally Joseph's interest would have been piqued, but tonight he hurried away, still unable to shake the feeling that the essence of the people who had lived here still lingered.

Deep in his heart of hearts, Joseph believed in ghosts. It wasn't something he'd ever talked about with anyone, but the belief was there within him. To his way of thinking, he couldn't very well believe in God and life everlasting without believing in spirits. So far, he'd never come nose to nose with a ghost, thank God, but there had been times in his life, like right now, when the hair on his arms had stood up.

He hurried to the end of the hall, his nerves leaping when Buddy suddenly growled. He tried to remind himself that Buddy *always* growled, but this was different, not a conversational sound but more a snarl of warning. What looked like a large sitting room opened to his right. Swinging the lamp high, he saw that some of the furniture was missing. It looked as if someone had absconded with the sofa, at least one chair, and a couple tables.

As Joseph moved on, his shoulder brushed against the wall, and a picture tipped sideways. The scraping sound startled him, and his skin felt as if it turned inside out. When he reached to straighten the frame, light washed over the photograph. A beautiful young girl stared back at him. Covered from chin to toe in dark muslin, her hair a cloud of light-colored ringlets around her thin shoulders, she looked to be about ten years old. She sat primly on a hassock, her folded hands resting on her lap. She had delicate features and large, expressive eyes, which he guessed to be blue given the lightness of her hair. Rachel Hollister, possibly? The younger daughter had never lived to see her sixth birthday.

Lamp still held high, Joseph stepped through an archway to his left and finally found himself in the dining room, which Darby had told him adjoined the kitchen where Rachel Hollister lived. A large window, which once looked out over the side yard, had been boarded up from the inside, the lace curtains over the planks gone dingy with age. A Louis XV sideboard graced one wall, the elaborate grape motifs on the doors reminding Joseph of the furnishings he'd seen as a boy in San Francisco. Surrounded by ten high-backed chairs, a long, marble-topped table, dulled by a layer of grime, sat at the center of the room. The ornate silver candelabra that had served as a centerpiece was draped with cobwebs, the once white tapers leaning this way and that.

Buddy scampered ahead of Joseph, his paws leaving prints in the film of dust on the fern-patterned burgundy carpet that stretched almost wall to wall. Clearly, the Hollister family hadn't lived a hand-to-mouth existence. This peeling, weather-beaten house had been a pretty grand place.

Joseph lifted the light higher. In the middle of the north wall was a boarded-over archway. He guessed that Rachel Hollister's hideaway was on the other side. After setting the lantern on the table, he tossed his gear on the floor. No way was he going to sleep in one of the bedrooms with ghosts as his bed companions.

The thought no sooner moved through Joseph's mind than the air exploded with sound and flying debris. Buddy yelped in fright. Joseph dived for the floor. When the dust settled, he was under the table, his Colt .45 drawn and ready, two overturned chairs providing him with scant cover.

*Holy shit.* Disgusted with himself for drawing his weapon when he knew damned well it was a woman shooting at him, Joseph slipped the revolver back into his holster and retrieved his Stetson, which had been knocked from his head. After putting the hat back on, he cautiously shifted position to see around one of the chair seats. Better to make a target of the Stetson than his head, he thought, and then promptly changed his mind when he saw the jagged hole that had appeared dead center in the boarded-up archway. The size of a prize-winning Texas pumpkin, it was well over two feet in diameter, the bottom edge a little over three feet from the ground, telling him that she'd probably fired from the waist instead of her shoulder. Only a shotgun had that kind of blasting power. If aimed anyplace near him, the gun would destroy the table, the overturned chair, his hat, *and* him.

Lamplight poured through the opening, lending additional brightness to the already illuminated dining room. With a shotgun-toting crazy woman on the other side of the wall, Joseph didn't count that as a blessing. Total darkness would have pleased him more.

Judging by the circumference of the hole, he felt fairly sure that Rachel Hollister had emptied both barrels. So far, he hadn't heard the telltale rasp and click of steel to indicate that she'd shoved more cartridges into the chambers. That was encouraging.

Once again, he thought about calling out to identify himself, but then decided it would be futile. If his earlier explanations hadn't satisfied her, telling her his name again wasn't likely to rectify the situation.

This woman wasn't messing around. She meant to kill him.

## Chapter Four

Ears still ringing from the blast, Rachel lay on her back, arms and legs sprawled, the weapon lying at an angle across her lower body. Her hip throbbed with pain. For a moment, she couldn't think what had happened. Then her spinning confusion slowly settled into rational thought. She'd been standing in the middle of the room, terrified by the sounds of someone breaking into her house and coming toward the kitchen. Heart pounding, she'd swung the gun toward the boards over the doorway. Then something heavy had struck the wall, she'd jumped in fright, and the next thing she knew, she was staring at the ceiling.

Pushing the weapon off her legs, Rachel struggled to sit up. When she saw the huge hole that the shotgun had blown through her barricade, her heart almost stopped for the second time in as many minutes. *Oh, dear God.* She scrambled to her feet and re-trieved the shotgun.

"Who's there?" she called, her voice shak-ing with fright. "Get out of my house, or I'll shoot. Don't think I won't!"

No answer. An awful dread squeezed her chest. What if she had killed him? She fran-tically tried to remember the name of the man who had knocked on her door. *Paxton?* The moment he'd told her about Darby be-ing shot, her head had gone muzzy, and then everything had turned black. Just be-fore that, it seemed to her that the other man had introduced himself as the marshal. *Oh, God. Oh, God.* What if he'd been telling the truth, and she'd just shot a lawman?

Afraid of the sight that might greet her eyes, she inched closer to the opening, the bottom edge of which hit her several inches above the waist, allowing her to look through without ducking. In all her life, she had never harmed anything, not even a spi-der. To think that she might have killed two men made her stomach roll.

"Mr. Paxton?" She cautiously poked her head through the hole to see into the other room. The silence that bounced back at her was ominous. "A-are you all right?"

\*     \*     \*

*Hell, no, I'm not all right,* Joseph thought angrily. The woman had almost blown him to Kingdom Come. He wished he could reach the lantern that he'd set on the table so he could lower the wick and extinguish the flame. As it was, the dining room was lighted up like a candle-laden Christmas tree, and all he had to hide behind was a chair seat.

How the hell did he land himself in fixes like this? If she opened fire again, he wouldn't even be able to shoot back. Crazy as a loon or not, she was a female. No man worth his salt harmed a woman. That wasn't to mention the difficulty he'd have explaining such a thing to a judge. *It was self-defense, Your Honor. When I broke into her house, she started blasting away at me.* Yeah, right. He'd end up swinging from the highest limb of a scrub oak.

At least he hadn't heard her reload the weapon yet. That was a comfort. He inched his head out from behind the chair again.

The sight that greeted his eyes made his breath catch. Then he blinked, thinking maybe his vision was playing tricks on him. Rachel Hollister was beautiful—the kind of beautiful that made men stop dead in their tracks to take a long second look and trip over their own feet.

Never having met a crazy person, Joseph had expected to see a wild-eyed female with matted strings of filthy hair, a skeletal countenance, and soiled clothing. Instead, she looked like an angel. A cloud of golden curls, ignited by the light behind her, framed one of the sweetest, loveliest faces he'd ever clapped eyes on. She had a small, straight nose, delicate cheekbones, a soft, full mouth, a pointy chin, and blue eyes, which, at the moment, were huge with fright.

"I mean you no harm, Miss Hollister. Please don't shoot again."

She jumped as if he'd stuck her with a pin. Then she vanished. Joseph figured she'd gone for more ammunition and muttered a curse under his breath. One second, she was asking if he was all right, and the next she was making ready to kill him again.

Buddy, who had been lying belly-up in front of the archway, chose that moment to recover from his fright and scramble to his feet. To Joseph's dismay, the dog reared up on his hind legs to hook his front feet over the lower edge of the hole, his snubbed tail wagging in friendly greeting. Rachel Hollister let out a startled squeak.

"Don't hurt him!" Joseph called. "He's harmless, I swear. Still just a pup."

"Go *away!*" she cried. "Get *out*, all of you! I don't want you here."

Joseph had gotten that message, loud and clear. Unfortunately, Buddy hadn't. The dog loved women, fat ones, skinny ones, and all shapes in between. Normally Joseph saw no harm in that. He liked females just fine himself. Only this one was armed, mad as a hatter, and trigger-happy.

The shepherd tensed as if to jump.

"Buddy, *no!*" Joseph cried, but the command came too late. With his usual agility, the sheepdog leaped through the opening. Joseph clenched his teeth and cringed, expecting to hear terrified shrieks, the snap of Damascus steel, and another shotgun blast. Instead, he heard a feminine yelp, followed by, "Go away! No! Bad dog! Get *off!*"

Soon after, a sputtering sound, interspersed by muffled protests, drifted to Joseph from the other room. Bewildered, he inched his head out from behind the chair again. He heard Buddy growling and could only hope Rachel Hollister didn't think the animal was threatening her. Joseph had come to love that silly canine more than was reasonable.

More sputtering. *What the hell?* Muscles tensed to dive for cover again if necessary, he crawled out from under the table, rose gingerly to his feet, and tiptoed to the hole. Shotgun shells scattered on the floor around her, Rachel Hollister knelt in the middle of the other room, the shotgun lying beside her. Buddy had his front paws planted on her slender shoulders and was licking her face. Rachel kept ducking her head, trying to gather the ammunition, but the dog was quick, agile, and determined to have his way.

Normally the sight might have amused Joseph, but he'd just come close to meeting his Maker.

"Buddy!" he called.

Rachel Hollister jerked and fixed Joseph with a fearful look. The dog wheeled away from her and trotted to the hole. Joseph snapped his fingers, and Buddy obediently leaped back through the opening, coming to land lightly on his feet in the dining room. When Joseph glanced back into the kitchen, Rachel Hollister had retrieved the gun and stood with the brass-plated butt pressed to her shoulder. He wasn't unduly alarmed because he knew she hadn't reloaded the weapon yet.

In Joseph's opinion, she was a mite small to be firing a 10-gauge shotgun, anyway, especially one with shortened barrels. Such a weapon had enough recoil to knock a grown man on his ass. She also seemed to be sorely lacking in weapon know-how. Most people realized that guns worked better with ammunition in them. He guessed maybe she was so scared that she couldn't think straight.

An urge to smile came over him. That gave him pause. Who was crazier, him or her? He decided his urge to smile was partly due to the two-inch ruffles that lined the yoke of her white nightdress and fluffed up over her shoulders like clipped wings, making her resemble a small bird about to take flight. Then again, maybe it was the lamp on the table behind her, which shone through the folds of muslin, clearly outlining her body. He hadn't seen anything so fetching since he'd paid a nickel to watch a peep show in his misspent youth.

She was trembling—an awful shaking that

made it difficult for her to hold the gun steady. Remembering the horror in her tone when she'd called out to ask if he was all right, he wondered if she had fired the weapon accidentally. Right before the blast, he'd tossed down his bedroll and saddle-bags. Had the thump startled her so badly that her finger jerked?

She didn't have the look of a killer. Joseph firmly believed in the old adage that the eyes were windows to the soul. He saw no meanness in Rachel Hollister's, only terror.

In that moment, his wariness of her abated. Now that he'd had time to assess the situation, he couldn't believe that she'd taken deliberate aim. She was just fright-ened half out of her wits, reacting without thought to anything that startled her.

Terrorizing females didn't sit well with Joseph. Unfortunately, looking back, he couldn't think what he might have done dif-ferently. He'd tapped on her door three dif-ferent times. Had she registered nothing of what he said?

He held her gaze for an endlessly long moment, waiting for her to look away first. The air between them turned electric, re-minding Joseph of the expectant feeling before a storm. When her lashes finally fluttered, he turned aside.

"If you mean to shoot me, Miss Hollister, you'd best reload your gun. Judging by the size of that hole, you already emptied both barrels."

In his peripheral vision, he saw her flick an appalled glance at the weapon. Joseph couldn't help but smile. He went to the table to douse his lantern and then shook out his bedroll, selecting a spot along the wall between the dining room and kitchen so he'd be able to hear any sound coming from the other room. As he arranged his pallet and blankets, a rattling sound told him that Rachel Hollister was trying to retrieve the ammunition that she'd dropped on the floor. A second later, he heard the telltale snap of steel. Oddly, knowing that she'd reloaded the weapon didn't worry him anymore. Unless she accidentally pulled the triggers again, he honestly didn't believe she would shoot him.

He took off his jacket and tossed it at the head of his pallet to use as a pillow. Then he removed his hat and set it on the floor next to his saddlebags. He sensed rather than saw Rachel Hollister return to the opening. He soon felt the burn of her gaze on him. Ignoring her, he sat on the pallet and toed off a boot.

Poking her golden head through the hole to stare at him, she cried, "What are you *doing?*"

"Like I already told you, ma'am, I promised Darby that I'd look after you, and I'm not a man to go back on my word. It's a mite too cold outside for me to sleep on your porch, and the bunkhouse is too far away."

"Well, you most certainly won't sleep *there.*"

"I won't?"

"No, you won't!"

Joseph toed off his other boot. Then, after pushing back the wool blankets, he pivoted on his ass and stretched out on his back, the jacket and his crossed arms pillowing his head. Buddy came to lie beside him.

Head angled through the opening, she stared at him with appalled disbelief. He studied her through narrowed eyes. "Do us both a favor, and keep your finger away from those triggers. Think of the mess it'll make if you blow a two-foot hole through me."

What little color remained in her cheeks drained away. "Mess or no"—she hooked a pointy elbow through the hole to better steady the gun—"I'll shoot if you don't get out of my house."

Joseph feigned a huge yawn, wondering as he did if he'd taken total leave of his senses. "You'd best pull the trigger then because I'm not leaving." He tugged the blanket to his chin. "I told old Darby that I'd stay, and that's what I mean to do. If the situation isn't to your liking, take it up with him."

Lowering her head and squinting one eye, she sighted in on him. As if she needed to aim? Joseph watched her with a curious detachment.

"You'd best get your chin away from that gun butt," he warned. "That shotgun will kick back on you like there's no tomorrow and bust your pretty little nose." He waited a beat. "Also—if it's all the same to you, that is—can you pull your aim wide to the left? Maybe then you won't shoot Buddy. His penchant for licking aside, he's a lovable dog, and he's never harmed a living soul. I'd hate to see him get hurt."

"I said you can't sleep there!" she cried.

"Why? You snore or something?"

"No, I don't *snore*!" The shrill pitch of her voice gave measure of her mounting frustration.

"Then I reckon I can sleep here well enough."

Light from the kitchen illuminated the side of her face. Joseph saw her mouth working, but no sound came out. Finally, she gave up on talking and disappeared. Shortly thereafter, he heard a commotion. It sounded to him as if she were tearing something apart.

Angling his upper body to see the doorway, he gazed curiously after her. He wasn't left to wonder what she was doing for long. She soon reappeared at the hole, a half dozen nails clenched between her teeth and a hammer in her hand. He watched as she set to work, nailing the slats of an apple crate over the opening. The sections of wood were barely long enough to span the distance and so flimsy as to provide little protection, but she furiously pounded them into place. Unfortunately, she lacked a sufficient number of slats to completely fill the hole, the result a sloppy crisscross with triangular gaps large enough to accommodate a man's fist. To curtain off her sanctum, she draped two bath towels over the lot, tacking them at top and bottom.

Joseph frowned in the ensuing dimness. A man could crawl through that two-foot hole, but not without making a good deal of noise in the process. With a loaded shotgun handy, she was as safe in there as a babe in its cradle.

Only a dim glow of light penetrated the linen towels. The illumination cast diamond patterns over the room. Settling back on his pallet, Joseph studied the shapes, acutely aware of every sound she made on the other side of the wall. Soft rustles, breath-less utterances. "Consternation" seemed to be her favorite byword, "drat" running a close second. She clearly wasn't pleased to have houseguests.

Joseph grabbed his saddlebags, thinking to fetch himself and Buddy some supper. His hand met with emptiness when he reached in the pocket. *Damn.* After a day of wrangling, he always replenished his trail supplies, but somehow or other he'd forgotten to do it last time. Thinking back, he recalled the reason: a heifer in the throes of a breech birth. He'd been out in the field with her until late and had been so exhausted when he reached the house that he'd fallen straight into bed.

*Well, hell.* Excuses wouldn't fill his stomach. More important, they wouldn't fill Buddy's. Joseph was accustomed to going hungry on occasion, but his dog wasn't. Sighing, he rolled onto his side and rubbed the animal's upturned belly. "Sorry, partner. I'll feed you twice in the morning to make up for it. I know you worked damned hard today. You should have stayed home with Esa. He would have fed you, at least."

Buddy's warm tongue rasped over the whiskers sprouting on Joseph's jaw. *Damn dog.* If there was anything he hated, it was a licker. He pushed at the shepherd's nose. "Stop it," he whispered. "You think I don't know where that tongue of yours has been?"

Buddy whined and nailed Joseph directly on the lips. He almost sputtered as Rachel Hollister had. Instead, he settled for rubbing away the wetness with his shirtsleeve and then changed the position of his upraised arm to guard his face. After a moment, the dog thrust his nose in Joseph's armpit, huffed, and went to sleep.

Joseph's thoughts drifted and circled until his eyelids grew heavy. Buddy snuggled closer, and their combined body heat made the bed cozy warm.

Rachel had turned her mother's rocker to face the archway. She sat poker straight on the chair, the shotgun balanced on her knees. A blanket draped around her shoulders, she stared fixedly at the towels she'd tacked over the crate slats. One question circled endlessly in her mind. *What in heaven's name am I going to do?*

She had no answers. She knew only that her world had been turned upside down. Nothing was as it should be—as she so desperately needed it to be. First and most alarming, her home was no longer safe. The hole in the barricade made her feel horribly vulnerable. When she thought about that man possibly crawling through, her skin shriveled, she broke out in a cold sweat, and she found it difficult to breathe.

He was there, just on the other side of the wall, a threat to her safety—and her sanity. She wanted him gone. Out, out, *out!*

But then what? She had no boards to repair the barricade, and she couldn't go into town to buy more. Darby always went to town and purchased what she needed. Without him, she was helpless, absolutely helpless. What on earth would she do if he died and never came back?

The question was one she couldn't answer, and it also filled her with guilt. What if

Joseph Paxton was telling the truth, and Darby had been shot? She loved that old foreman like a father. What kind of person was she to be worrying about boards when he might be dying?

Tears stung her eyes. She began rocking in the chair to maintain her self-control. *Squeak, squeak, squeak.* The whine of the chair came faster and faster until she realized she was pushing with her feet almost frenetically and forced herself to stop. *Darby.* He was much older than she was, and at the back of her mind, she had always known that she would outlive him. She'd just never allowed herself to contemplate the possibility that he might die any time soon. Darby was the closest thing to family that she had left. Oh, how she would miss seeing his craggy face through the peephole that he had installed in her door. And how empty her days would be if he never again tapped on the wood safe for his meals.

The wetness in her eyes spilled over onto her cheeks, creating cold, ticklish trails that made her want to scratch. Only she couldn't pry her hands from the gun. Why hadn't she shot Joseph Paxton when she had the chance? He'd known she couldn't do it, blast him. Even through the shadows, she'd seen the twinkle of amusement in his eyes.

This was all *his* doing. She never would have fired the shotgun if he hadn't made a loud sound and startled her. And just who did he think he was, tearing the boards off one of her windows and breaking the glass? She would never feel safe until the window was repaired and boarded up again.

Anger roiled within her. But before she could get a firm hold on it, worry for Darby assailed her again. If the old man truly was hurt, the least Joseph Paxton could do was apprise her of his condition. Had anyone fetched the doctor? How bad was the wound? And who was caring for the poor old fellow?

Rachel wanted to jerk the towels away from the opening and demand that Joseph Paxton give her answers. But was that even his real name? He'd come here with another man. For all she knew, they could be outlaws. The one she'd seen definitely had the look of a scapegrace. Men who wore sidearms were a dime a dozen in No Name, but there was nothing ordinary about the way he wore his, a pearl-handled Colt .45, strapped low on his thigh. Rachel had read

enough novels to know that a gunslinger
wore his weapon that way to minimize the
distance of reach, thereby maximizing his
speed at the draw.

She stared at the towels, which offered
her little privacy and even less protection.
*Darby.* She had to find out how he fared.
Only how? When she contemplated tearing
the towels away to confront Joseph Paxton
again, she started to shake.

He wasn't really a large man, she assured
herself. But he had a large presence, every
inch of his lean body roped with muscle, his
broad shoulders and well-padded chest ta-
pering to a slim waist and narrow hips. His
eyes were particularly arresting, an ordinary
blue yet razor sharp, giving the impression
that he missed nothing. In the lamplight,
they had shimmered like quicksilver.

A frown pleated Rachel's brow as she
tried to recall the rest of his face. Exposure
to the elements had burnished his skin; she
remembered that much. But she couldn't
for the life of her envision his features. He'd
worn a sand-colored Stetson with a wide
brim that dipped down in front. Perhaps
that was why. She could remember his hair,
which was as blond as her own, only as

straight as a bullet on a windless day. Shoulder length, if she recollected right, and tucked behind his ears.

The rapid creak of the rocker told Rachel that she was pushing too fast again. She brought the chair to a stop and then nearly jumped out of her skin at the sound of a low growl. The towels over the hole moved, and the next instant, a liver-colored nose lifted a bottom corner of the linen. *The dog.* She watched the animal's nostrils flare to pick up her scent. Shortly thereafter, another inch of white blaze on the canine's nose became visible.

"No!" Rachel cried softly. "Stop that."

But the reddish-gold dog kept pushing until the bottom of one towel popped free and a slat snapped. His head poked through. Rachel leaped up from the rocker. Leaving the gun on the sofa within easy reach, she advanced on the archway.

"Bad, *bad* dog," she whispered. "I don't want you in here. Away with you. Go on."

Rachel could have sworn that the silly animal grinned. And then he let loose with more growls, working his jaws so the sounds changed pitch, almost as if he were talking.

When she reached to push him back, he whined and licked her hands.

Rachel's heart sank. He was such a sweet, friendly fellow, and he truly didn't mean her any harm. He only wanted to say hello. She had always adored dogs. One of the great loves of her life had been Denver, a huge, yellow mongrel with soulful brown eyes. Many had been the time that Rachel wished the killer might have at least spared the dog's life. *Denver, her special friend.* The silly mutt had rarely left her side. In the end, his unfailing loyalty had been the death of him.

The thought always made Rachel sad. Unlike the other members of her family, Denver could have run and saved himself. Instead, he'd stayed to protect her and earned himself a slug between the eyes.

As though her hands had a will of their own, Rachel found herself fondling Buddy's silky ears. Dogs were wonderfully uncomplicated creatures. No subterfuge or pretense. What you saw was what you got. She liked the way his ears stood up, with only the rounded tips flopping forward. He only straightened them when she spoke or made a sound.

He was a handsome fellow, she decided.

A snow-white blaze ran the length of his muzzle, and the lighter russet spots above his amber eyes lent his face a pensive look. He was a sheepdog, she concluded, a breed that had proven useful in herding cattle and become popular with the ranchers hereabouts. Rachel had heard it said that most sheepdogs were uncommonly intelligent. Looking into Buddy's alert, questioning eyes, she had little trouble believing it.

"You're a pushy sort, aren't you?" she whispered, wishing that she could let him into the kitchen. As it was, he was about to destroy her makeshift repairs. He shoved with a shoulder and snapped another slat. *"Stop!"* she whispered. "You can't come in. Can't you tell when someone doesn't like you?"

"He's hungry."

Startled by Joseph Paxton's deep voice, Rachel jumped back from the opening.

"Whatever you fixed for supper smells mighty good," he went on. "I thought I had jerky in my saddlebags, but I was mistaken, and he's not used to missing a meal. I've spoiled him, I reckon."

Rachel retreated another step. The dog seemed to interpret that as an invitation. Before she could react, he jumped through the hole, breaking the remaining slats and jerking one towel completely loose. The next instant, she was being accosted by the friendly canine. Fortunately, he was an agile fellow and light on his feet. When he planted his paws on her chest, she barely felt his weight. He growled at her again, a *yaw-yaw-yaw* that sounded absurdly conversational.

It was impossible for Rachel to look into the animal's expressive eyes without wanting to smile.

"So you're hungry, are you? All I have is stew and cornbread, and I don't think that's good for dogs."

Buddy dropped to his belly, put his paws together as if he were praying, and then lifted his head to bark. The message was clear. Stew was very good for dogs, the more the better. Rachel was lost. Maybe it was the prayer position that did her in—or maybe it was the sweet, imploring expression on Buddy's face. She had never been able to turn away a hungry critter. As a girl, she'd loved to feed the wild animals and birds that visited the ranch. One year, her pa had built her half a dozen birdhouses for Christmas so she'd be able to watch the sparrows build their nests and hatch their babies the following spring. Oh, how Rachel missed the bird-song. With her windows boarded up, inside and out, she couldn't hear it anymore.

Just in case Joseph Paxton decided to climb through the hole after his dog, she retrieved the shotgun before advancing on the stove. With the weapon leaning against the wall within close reach, she set to work to feed Buddy. Thoughts of Darby once again assailed her as she filled a serving bowl with stew and added some crumbled cornbread. This was to have been the foreman's supper. Would he ever again tap on the wood safe and enjoy a meal that she had cooked for him?

She cast a considering glance at the damaged barricade as she set the bowl on the floor. Buddy didn't hesitate. With a happy growl, he began gobbling the food as if he hadn't been fed in a week.

Rachel straightened, gathered the blanket closer around her shoulders, took a breath for courage, and said, "I shall strike a bargain with you, Mr. Paxton. In exchange for information about my foreman, I'll feed you supper."

Surprised by the unexpected offer, Joseph sat bolt upright on his pallet. Surely he hadn't heard her right.

"I'm sorry. What did you say?"

"I said that I'm prepared to make a deal with you. Food for information about Darby."

Joseph ran a hand over his midriff. "I'm hungry enough to eat the south end of a northbound jackass, Miss Hollister, but I've already told you everything I can."

"That Darby's been shot, you mean?" Her voice went high-pitched. "Surely you can tell me more than that. Did you fetch Doc Halloway? Was he able to get the slug out? What is the prognosis? Does he think Darby's going to—*die*?"

Joseph had given her all that information earlier. "That's a mighty thick back door you've got. I guess you didn't catch a lot of what I said earlier." Resting his arms over his upraised knees, Joseph once again recounted the events of that afternoon, how Darby had come riding into his place, barely clinging to the saddle, and how Joseph had staunched the bleeding and gone for the doctor. "Doc seems to think he's going to make it. The bullet shattered a couple of ribs, but it missed the lung and kidney."

"What of infection?"

"Doc dressed the wound with honey."

"Honey?" she echoed.

"He swears by it. Says honey fights infection and has healing properties. He slathered all he could over the wound before bandaging Darby up, and he left some for my brother, Esa, to use when he changes the wrappings."

Silence. And then, voice quivering, she asked, "So your brother is looking after Darby?"

"Because I had to come over here, Esa volunteered." Actually, it had been more a case of Joseph's twisting his brother's arm, but he didn't think she needed to know that. Esa had a good heart, and he'd do right by the old man.

"Darby has it in his head that you're in some kind of danger," he expounded. "When he first got to my place, he kept telling me to forget about him and come straight here to make sure you were safe."

Another silence, a long one this time. After a while, Joseph grew concerned. "Miss Hollister? You there?"

He thought he heard her take a taut breath. "Yes. Yes, I'm here, Mr. Paxton." Another silence ensued, and then she added, "That's the first thing you've said all evening that makes me think you may be telling the truth."

That was a step up, Joseph guessed. Only what part of what he'd said had been to her liking? She gave a shrill little sigh that reminded him strongly of his mother. Dory Paxton was a great one for sighing.

"Well, now for your supper," she said. "That was the bargain, after all." He heard the faint clink of china. "I'll hand it through to you. Please stand well back, or I shall have to shoot you. I'm sure you're no fonder of that idea than I am."

Joseph grinned. "Have you shot a number of folks?"

"Not as yet," she informed him. "But don't take that to mean that I will hesitate."

His grin broadened. He was starting to like this lady. She had pluck. He was also starting to wonder if she wasn't crazy like a fox. Someone had shot Darby today, and both Joseph and David agreed that the bullet had been meant to kill. Wasn't it possible that Rachel Hollister had known for years that her life was in danger? Maybe David had hit the nail right on the head, and her hermitlike habits stemmed more from fear than lunacy.

Joseph lighted his lantern and then, honoring her request, stood well back from the hole in the archway to wait for his food. When Rachel appeared at the opening, he noticed that she didn't have to duck her head to look through at him, putting her height at several inches less than his own. He also noticed that she had small, fine-boned hands, her slender fingers gone pink at the tips where they gripped the bowl. Eyeing him warily, she thrust her arms through the opening.

"Here you go."

Not wishing to startle her, Joseph moved slowly forward, taking care to stop when the bowl was within reach. Even then, she was so skittish that she nearly dropped the dish before he could get a good hold on it.

"Thank you."

She retreated several steps, her gaze wide and wary. "You're welcome."

"I know that this is an uncomfortable situation for you," Joseph said as he carried his meal to the table. "You don't know me from Adam. But ask yourself this. Would Darby have sent me here if he didn't trust me?"

Standing some three feet back from the opening, she hugged her waist, the blanket tucked under her arms like the ends of a shawl. "I have no way of knowing if Darby actually sent you."

With a sweep of his hand, Joseph cleaned dust from the far end of the table and sat down facing her. "Why would I lie about it?"

"To gain my trust?"

Joseph fleetingly wished that his brother were present to handle this. A little sugar-coating was definitely in order. "If I meant you harm, Miss Hollister, I already would have done my worst, the devil take your trust." He inclined his head at the barricade. "Do you really believe a few boards would keep me out if I was bent on coming in?"

She stiffened. "You'd run the risk of getting shot."

"Not with an empty gun."

"It isn't empty now."

"But it was, and I knew it. What was stopping me, then, do you think?"

She only stared at him.

"And what stopped me from grabbing your wrist just now when you handed out the food?" He snapped his fingers. "I could have had you then, easy as anything."

She drew the blanket closer. "Are you threatening me, Mr. Paxton?"

"No, I'm making a point. You say you have

no way of knowing if Darby actually sent me? I think you do."

"Darby never so much as mentioned your name."

"Yeah, well, Darby's not much of one for small talk. We met at the south end of your ranch when the fence between your place and mine was in sore need of repair. We worked on it together. When it came time to eat, we shared some shade while we had lunch. Nothing notable happened. Maybe he didn't count it as being important enough to mention."

"You met only the one time?"

"We've run into each other a few times since."

"If he knows you only in passing, why does he trust you?"

Now there was a question Joseph wasn't sure how to answer. "I've got an honest face?"

She didn't smile.

Joseph was starving and wanted to dive into his meal. The stew and cornbread smelled so good that his mouth watered.

"You can learn a lot about a man by mending fence with him," he offered. "If he whines over the bite of barbed wire, you know he lacks grit. If he leans on his shovel a lot, you know he's lazy. If he picks the easier of two jobs more than once, you know he's inclined to be self-serving as well. If he neglects his horse—" Joseph broke off and sighed. "I can't say why Darby trusts me, Miss Hollister. Maybe he liked what he learned about me that day. Or maybe it's because he knows I come from good family. Only he can say."

"Good family? Do your folks live around here?"

"My older brother, Ace Keegan, owns the spread northeast of here."

"The piece of land that Patrick O'Shannessy sold?"

"That's right." Joseph glimpsed a thoughtful look in her eyes. "Ace married Patrick's sister, Caitlin. He also built the railroad spur into Denver."

"Caitlin?"

Joseph nodded. "Know her?"

"She's older than me, but we went to school together for a number of years."

"Did you now?" Joseph picked up a chunk of cornbread and took a bite.

Questions still lurked in her eyes. "How

can Ace Keegan be your brother? You don't have the same last name."

"We're actually only half brothers. When his pa died, our ma married my father, Joseph Paxton, senior. Back in sixty-five, he bought the piece of land that Ace owns now and moved our family out here from Virginia to make a fresh start. Unfortunately, things went sour, my ma took us boys to San Francisco, and none of us returned to No Name until four and a half years ago."

Light dawned in her eyes. "Joseph Paxton," she repeated softly. "I remember the name now." A frown pleated her brow, and her blue eyes sharpened on his face. "He was hanged."

Joseph winced, thinking that she'd picked a fine time to put all the pieces together. If she hadn't heard the entire story, which was a strong possibility, she might panic for certain. "*Wrongfully* hanged," he stressed, gesturing with the spoon. "My father was accused of squatting on the land he'd paid good money for and also of murdering Camlin Beckett, an upstanding citizen of No Name." Joseph's mouth went as dry as dirt. To this day, it wasn't easy for him to recall his father's death, let alone talk about it. "In truth, Beckett, Conor O'Shannessy, and a handful of others, including the town marshal, Estyn Beiler, were a bunch of swindlers, and my father was one of their victims. He just paid far more dearly than the rest."

Her eyes went wide, but she said nothing to indicate what she might be thinking.

"Four and a half years ago," Joseph went on, "all us boys returned to No Name to clear our father's name. But maybe you never heard about that."

She closed her eyes for a moment, and Joseph thought some of the tension eased from her shoulders. "I did hear about it. Darby isn't much for talking, that's true, but he told me about that. It was scandalous what Estyn Beiler and the others did to your father and family."

In Joseph's opinion, scandalous didn't describe it by half, but he was so relieved she'd heard the whole story that he didn't object.

She arched a delicate eyebrow. "Your brother, Ace Keegan—he's a gunslinger of some reputation, isn't he?"

"He gave all that up years ago."

She sent him a dubious look.

"Ace and Caitlin have a son now," he said,

hoping to distract her from that train of thought. "Little Ace. He's fourteen months old and cute as a button."

"And you?"

Joseph paused with a spoonful of stew at his lips. "Me, what?"

"You have the look of a gunslinger, too."

"I do?"

"Are you?"

He took the bite of stew. "This is down-right delicious, Miss Hollister. Darby's a lucky man if he gets to eat cooking like this every day."

"You didn't answer my question."

He spooned in some more stew, chewed, and swallowed. "What question was that?"

"Are you fast with a gun?"

"Fair to middling. Ace is the one that's fast."

Joseph couldn't see her feet, but he had a notion that she was tapping her toe. "Have you killed anyone, Mr. Paxton?"

Joseph decided then and there that honesty wasn't always the best policy. In self-defense, he had, in fact, taken human life. That wasn't something he wanted to talk about, especially not with a wary woman who might jump to wrong conclusions. "Do I look like a killer?"

"Yes."

Well, hell. He'd finally met someone as plainspoken as he was. Time to turn the tables. "It seems to me it's my turn to ask a few questions."

She looked genuinely surprised. "I am not the interloper in this situation, Mr. Paxton. You've broken into my home, and you refuse to leave. I'll ask the questions until I'm satisfied that you are who you say you are."

"Ah, but I wouldn't be here if Darby hadn't insisted on it." He took another bite of stew and studied her as he chewed. "Even doped up on laudanum, he was so worried about your safety that he was fit to be tied. Can you explain why?"

Her eyes went dark with shadows.

"That strikes me as being a little peculiar," Joseph pressed on. "Why would Darby instantly conclude that the attack on him today was somehow connected to the attack on you and your family five years ago?"

She closed her eyes and shook her head. "I don't know." Her lashes lifted. "I truly don't know."

Her face had gone as pale as milk, and

Joseph didn't miss the fear that had returned to her eyes. "There has to be a reason," he insisted. "He was scared to death for you and absolutely emphatic that your life might be in danger." He studied her closely. "What do you remember about that day?"

"Nothing." She swayed slightly on her feet and splayed a dainty hand over her midriff. "Darby was upset because he was shot near the creek." The pitch of her voice went so low he almost didn't catch her next words. "That's why he made a connection, I'm sure, because that's where it happened before."

Watching her, Joseph tensed on the chair. "Don't faint on me. If you fall, I'm not in there to catch you."

She passed a trembling hand over her eyes. "I'm fine."

Joseph knew better. She looked scared half to death, and his instincts told him that she was holding something back. Yet when he searched her gaze, he saw only frightened confusion.

"You must have some idea who killed your family," he insisted.

The clawing fear in her eyes gave way to anger. "If I did, I would have screamed it to the rooftops years ago, Mr. Paxton."

"I don't buy that. You have a suspicion, at least." Joseph honestly believed that was the only explanation for the way she lived. She was afraid of someone. She had to be. "I don't know why, but you're hiding something."

"I remember nothing. *Nothing,* do you hear? It was my *family* that died!" She made a fist over her heart. "My mother, my father, my brother, and my sister. I *loved* them." Her eyes went bright with tears. "If I had any inkling—even an unfounded *suspicion* of who killed them—do you honestly believe I would keep it to myself?"

Her question struck home for Joseph. He, too, had lost a loved one, and even today it still hurt him to think about that awful night. He'd been—what—eight years old? He couldn't even remember his father clearly. How much more horrible must it be for Rachel Hollister, who'd been sixteen or seventeen at the time? She would have vivid memories of each person's face and of the special moments she'd shared with them, particularly those last, precious moments right before they died. Naturally she would do everything within her power to see their killer brought to justice. He'd been wrong to imply otherwise.

"I don't mean to upset you," he said, his voice husky with regret.

She brushed angrily at her cheeks and whirled from the opening. A moment later, she passed by again, heading for the left rear corner of the room, the shotgun cradled in her arms. Joseph half expected to hear her start sobbing, but instead an awful silence settled over the house.

He finished his meal with one ear cocked, his gaze fixed on the hole. *No sound. No sign of movement.* When he'd cleaned his bowl, he left the dish on the table and crept over to the barricade.

Prior to this, Joseph had only caught glimpses of her sanctuary. The sight that greeted him was nothing short of amazing. Rachel had transformed the large ranch kitchen into a one-room home, grouping furniture to create different sections. The front of the room still served as a kitchen, the corner to his right had been set up as a parlor, and to his immediate left was her sleeping area, comprised of a double bed, a night table, a chest of drawers, and an armoire. Granted, each area was crowded, but they provided her with all the amenities of a tiny house.

Rachel sat with her back pressed against the headboard of the bed, the shotgun on the mattress beside her. Her eyes were squeezed tightly shut, her fragile jaw set. Joseph took a moment to study her, and what he saw made his heart hurt. No tears, no jerking of her shoulders. Body rigid, she just sat there, hugging her knees as if that were all that held her together. *Memories.* He saw them etched on her face, the grief they brought drawing the skin taut over her cheekbones. He had intentionally forced her to think about that day without considering how painful it might be for her, not just during the conversation, but possibly long after.

Too late, he knew that his brother David was absolutely right. Sometimes the truth went down a little easier if you sprinkled it with sugar. He had no talent for that, never had and never would.

Until now, he'd never thought of it as a serious failing.

# Chapter Five

Rachel's eyes burned as if they'd been soaked in lye. She had no idea how long she'd been sitting on the bed, only that she'd been there for hours, listening to the rumble of Joseph Paxton's snores. Her back felt as if the edge of a brutally sharp sword were pressing in just under her shoulder blades. She'd shifted and stretched, but the crick had taken up permanent residence. Quite simply, her body cried out for rest.

Unfortunately, Rachel couldn't bring herself to lie down and try to sleep. Instead, she stared at the hole. It was the proverbial chink in her armor, a weakness in the fortress that had saved her sanity these last five years. Now she felt exposed and vulnerable in a way that made her skin crawl and her nerves leap.

Oddly, the man who slept in the other room was no longer the focus of her terror.

His story about Darby rang true, and everything else he'd said rang true as well. He
knew things about the old foreman that only
a friend might—specifically that Darby
wasn't a talker and that he loved Rachel
deeply enough to die for her. Rachel was
also reassured by the fact that Joseph Paxton had foregone several opportunities to
harm her. It was true that he could have
grabbed her when she handed out his food.
He looked to be a strong man and quick on
his feet. There was also no denying that he
could easily dispense with the boards over
the doorway if he wished. With a couple of
waist-high jabs of a boot, he could enlarge
the hole, push through, and be on her. In
that event, only her willingness to fire the
shotgun would save her, and Rachel had a
feeling he knew the thought of killing someone gave her the chills.

What had stopped him from entering her
quarters? So far as Rachel could see, nothing, which had led her to conclude that he
was who he claimed to be and had been
sent by Darby, her beloved friend. The old
foreman never would have sent a scapegrace to look after her. Rachel knew that beyond a doubt. Darby was nothing if not pro-

tective of her. He was also an astute judge of character. In short, Joseph Paxton had come with the very best of recommendations, and she would be foolish to distrust him.

He snorted just then, an abrupt, raucous catch of breath that was so loud Rachel could have sworn it vibrated the walls. It had been so long since she'd heard a man snore that she'd almost forgotten what a comforting sound it was. As a young child awakening from unpleasant dreams, she'd been comforted by the low, rhythmic rumble of her father's snores, which had drifted through the entire house. It was a sound that said, "All is well." And it had always lulled her back to sleep.

Joseph Paxton's snores soothed her, too. Perhaps it was because she sensed that he was an alert, guarded man who slept with one eye open. Or maybe it was simply the sound of the snoring itself, which she'd known since infancy and come to associate with cozy warmth and safety.

His snores made her feel drowsy. Oh, how she wished she could stretch out on her soft bed and close her eyes. But with every creak and groan of the house, her heart

shot up into her throat. *Danger.* It lurked beyond her walls, a constant threat.

Joseph Paxton's presence didn't allay her
fears. Her father, Henry Hollister, had been a
strong protector, every inch of his frame
padded with steely muscle from a lifetime of
hard work. And yet he had failed to keep his
family safe. The danger had come unexpectedly and from out of nowhere, catching
him unprepared. No man, no matter how
strong and devoted, was impervious to a
well-aimed bullet.

Rachel shivered and rubbed her arms. Her
skin felt as if it were smeared with drying
egg white. *Oh, yes.* The danger was out
there. She had no idea where it lurked, only
that it might strike again if she let down her
guard.

That was the most awful part, the not
knowing. It had her jumping at shadows,
which went against her nature. Prior to the
slayings, she'd been a fearless girl, always
off and about, more tomboy than young
lady, much to her mother's dismay. One afternoon, a pair of rattlers in the barn had
sent all the hired hands scattering, and it
was Rachel who'd gone in to remove the
snakes. The men had teased her mercilessly

about her failure to kill the poor things, but she hadn't let that bother her. It had been her belief then, and still was to this day, that all God's creatures had a purpose and a right to live.

Perhaps that was why the murder of her family and dog still haunted her so—because the senseless violence was so inconceivable to her. Ever since she'd awakened from the coma, her world had been at sixes and sevens, a messy, untidy, chaotic, and askew reality interlaced with an awful unpredictability. And at the root of her confusion there was always a cloying fear—of the sunlight, of a breeze touching her face, even of the air itself—because she knew, deep down, that evil permeated everything beyond the safety of her walls.

Rachel couldn't say how she knew that. The conviction was simply there, hiding behind a black curtain in her mind. She had no clear recollection of the tragic events of that fateful afternoon, only a compilation of facts related to her by Darby, who'd grown concerned when she and her family had failed to return to the house and had finally ridden to their picnic place along the creek to discover the bloodbath, and by Doc Halloway, who'd been summoned to the scene by one of the other ranch hands and had, as a result, treated Rachel's head wound and nursed her back to health over the next few weeks.

Joseph Paxton had accused her of holding something back, of having memories of her family's murder that she'd chosen not to share. In a way, Rachel almost wished that were true. Knowledge would be far better than the blankness that stubbornly shrouded some parts of her mind. Doc Halloway maintained that Rachel must have been the first to be shot that June afternoon. A bullet from out of nowhere, and then only blackness; thus her inability to remember anything about the incident. Rachel had pretended to accept that because it seemed logical. She'd had no better explanation, after all. But deep down, she knew better.

Her nightmares told her that she had seen and felt and heard many things before the blackness had descended. The memories came to her in confusing rushes, blurry images flashing brightly and then going dark, all separate and disconnected but still so horrifying that they brought her bolt upright from sleep with a scream on her lips and rivulets of cold sweat streaming from her body.

Joseph was accustomed to awakening when the first faint light of dawn streaked the sky. But inside the Hollister house, no outside light filtered in. When he first opened his eyes the following morning, he thought for a moment that it was still night. Only the fact that he felt well rested told him otherwise.

He sat up and rubbed the back of his neck, his gaze trained on the barricade. Light still shone through the hole. He sat perfectly still and listened for a moment. He could hear the hum of Rachel's lanterns, but nothing else.

Always eager to greet a new day, Buddy fairly danced with excitement when Joseph's movements awakened him. The shepherd darted in to lick Joseph's face, then pranced to the doorway that led from the dining room into the hall.

Joseph pushed to his feet, hoping the dog would keep quiet for once in his life. But, no, the animal let loose with three earsplitting barks, followed by a series of happy growls.

"Quiet!" Joseph whispered, though he didn't know why he bothered. The dog knew the commands to sit, stay, and drop, but "quiet" wasn't in his vocabulary. Life was an endless celebration, and every incident called for at least one bark or growl to mark the moment.

Joseph escorted the sheepdog to the end of the hall and threw open Henry and Marie Hollister's bedroom door. "Go run off some of that mischief."

Buddy didn't need to be told twice. With three agile leaps, he was across the room and out the window. At a slower pace, Joseph followed, unbuttoning his Levi's as he went. After relieving himself through the opening, he refastened his fly and returned to the dining room. He wasn't surprised to see Rachel standing at the archway.

"I'm sorry if Buddy woke you. He gets a little excited first thing of a morning."

"I wasn't sleeping."

Joseph studied her face, taking in the redness of her eyes and the dark circles beneath them. He wondered if she'd sat up all night. She looked frighteningly fragile—like glass blown so fine that the slightest touch might shatter it.

"Would you like some coffee?" she asked.

Just the thought made his mouth water. "You don't have to bother."

"No bother. I need a cup myself." She turned away from the opening. "If you're hungry, I can make some breakfast, too."

Joseph was pleased to note that she didn't carry the shotgun with her to the range. He leaned a shoulder against the boards to watch while she built a fire in the box and stepped to the sink to rinse out the metal coffeepot.

"Running water?" Joseph had the same luxury at his place, but this house had been built a good many years before the novelty of indoor plumbing, which was still a rarity in these parts. "I'm surprised."

"Darby plumbed it in for me." She gestured at a closed door to his left. "He added on a water closet as well. I have a bathtub, a flushing commode, and a Mosley gas water heater from Montgomery Ward."

Joseph noticed a hand-cylinder laundry machine beside the range, the fill-up hose disconnected from the stove's water reservoir, the drain hose running from the machine to a hole in the wooden floor. That was a step up from his place. He had a fully equipped water closet, but he still did his laundry the old-fashioned way on the back porch. Last autumn, after getting his house finished, he'd thought about ordering a laundry machine, and he still might yet. But it wasn't one of those things that he felt he couldn't live without.

She noticed him staring past her at the door next to the range. It was barred shut with a thick pine plank. "The cellar," she explained. "It used to be Ma's pantry. Darby ripped up part of the floor, dug it out underneath, and built steps down into it. I needed a place to cure meat, make pickles and cheese, and store my home-canned goods."

As Joseph took in the details that he'd overlooked last night, he couldn't help but marvel. Darby had added every possible amenity to her confined living area, making sure that she had everything she could need or want. Even more amazing, she'd made it all pretty as could be with colorful rag rugs on the wood floor and curtains over the boarded-up windows, lace panels to the left on the back door, blue gingham to the right over the sink. On the kitchen table there was even a porcelain vase filled with silk and velvet geraniums. He guessed the fake flowers were from Montgomery Ward, too. Caitlin had ordered some a while back to brighten up their house during the winter.

"This is really something," he said.

Turning from the stove, she inspected the room with hollow eyes. "It loses its charm after a while."

She pushed at her hair, which had gone curlier since last night, little golden wisps springing every which way. Joseph wondered if it was as soft as it looked and found himself itching to touch it.

"If you'll excuse me, I need to get dressed," she informed him. "Then I'll start breakfast."

Joseph hated to use up her food. He wasn't an invited guest, after all. But until Ace showed up to relieve him later that day, he was stuck here without any rations of his own. "That'd be nice. I'll be sure to replace whatever I eat, plus extra to repay you for your trouble."

She gave him a curious look. "You're here at Darby's request to look after me. Providing your meals is the least I can do."

Joseph was pleased that she seemed to have accepted the situation at some point during the night. She wasn't exactly relaxed with him yet, but at least she was no longer jumping out of her skin.

"I'll replace what I eat, all the same," he insisted. "'Appetite' is my middle name."

Her soft mouth curved up sweetly at the corners. "Well, I'd best get to it, then."

"While you're getting dressed and fixing breakfast, I'll see to the chores. Did you ever empty the wood box and bring in the milk?"

"What milk?"

She truly hadn't registered anything he'd said to her through the door last night, he realized. "I milked both the cows last night and left the buckets just outside the wood box."

"Oh." She pushed at her hair again. "No, I didn't bring it in. I doubt I even can. Unless the buckets are in the safe, they're too heavy for me to lift."

"If you'll take the wood out, I'll put them inside for you."

She shook her head. "Just add the milk to the hog slop for now."

It seemed a terrible waste of good milk. "You sure?"

"I've enough aged cheese and butter to do me for weeks. Until Darby's back to sell the extra to Mr. Gilpatrick at the general store, there's no point in my making more."

Joseph hadn't planned on making frequent trips into town. Now he understood why Darby kept two cows and so many chickens, because the surplus milk and eggs brought in a small income. If Rachel depended on the money to meet her expenses, it might put her in a financial bind if she made nothing during Darby's recuperation.

"I can take your stuff to Gilpatrick's until Darby's back on his feet."

"That's generous of you." A ghost of a smile touched her lovely mouth again. "We'll talk about it. For today, the pigs will enjoy the milk."

An hour later, Rachel was still inside the water closet, unable to open the door to reenter the kitchen. It was madness. She knew that. But the kitchen no longer felt safe, and the water closet did. She wished she'd thought to come in here last night. With the walls all around her, she might have gotten some rest. Tonight, she promised herself, she would gather up her bed-

ding and create a makeshift bed in the bathtub.

First, however, she had to find the courage
to open the door and return to the kitchen.
Again and again, she grasped the lock to
turn it, but each time she lost her courage
and dropped her arm. *What if someone's
out there?* She knew it was an irrational fear.
Joseph Paxton had proven to her satisfac-
tion that he was there to help, not do her
harm, and he was probably already back in
the dining room standing guard.

Joseph shuffled his deck of cards to play
another round of patience, a one-person
game that irritated him to no end because
he so seldom won. As he dealt the hand, he
kept one ear cocked toward the kitchen,
wondering what on earth was keeping
Rachel. The coffee had been at a full boil
when he returned to the house and was still
boiling. If the pot didn't go dry, and that was
a big if, the stuff was going to be strong
enough to peel paint off walls. He'd thought
never to meet a woman who stayed in the
water closet longer than his younger sister,
Eden, but this one took the prize.

Was Rachel ailing? He recalled her pallor

and the circles under her eyes. He'd laid both off on exhaustion, but maybe she was sick.

"Mr. Paxton?"

Her voice was so faint that Joseph thought for a moment he had imagined it. Then she called to him again, slightly louder this time. He tossed down the cards and pushed quickly up from the chair. "Yo?"

"Are you back in the dining room?" she asked through the water closet door.

What did she think, that he was answering from outside? "Yes, ma'am, I'm here."

Long silence. Then, "Is there anyone in the kitchen?"

Joseph almost chuckled, but he could tell by her tone that she meant the question seriously. "No, ma'am."

"Would you look, please?"

Joseph poked his head through the hole and dutifully scanned the room. "Uh-oh. I lied. There is someone in your kitchen."

Alarm laced her voice when she replied, "There *is*?"

Joseph eyed his recalcitrant dog, who had taken up squatting rights on Rachel's bed. "Yep," he said. "He's a red-gold scoundrel with a white streak on his nose. At the moment, he's curled up on your sheets, letting fleas hop off, willy-nilly."

The water closet door came ajar, and her pretty face appeared in the opening. She studied the dog. Then she poked her head out to carefully examine the rest of the room.

When she finally emerged from the water closet, Joseph was stunned. Beautiful didn't describe the lady by half. With her golden hair in a swirling coronet atop her head, he could see the fine shape of her skull and the graceful column of her slender neck. Shimmering tendrils had escaped from her hasty coiffure to curl at her nape and above her dainty ears to frame the perfect oval of her face. Despite the ravages of exhaustion, she was absolutely lovely.

Though her outfit was everyday practical, Joseph suddenly felt scruffy. Fingering the stubble on his jaw, he skimmed her figure with purely masculine appreciation. Though he'd glimpsed her delightful curves through the folds of her nightgown last night, there was a lot to be said for a formfitting shirtwaist and a skirt with organ-pipe pleats at the back. The lady was made like an hourglass, with ample breasts and a small waist, enhanced by a wide belt. As she hurried across the room to rescue the coffee, Joseph's eyes shifted with every swing of her hips.

Grabbing a cloth to move the coffeepot away from the heat, she said, "Consternation! This coffee must be as thick as soup by now." She stepped to the sink for a cup of cold tap water, then returned to pour it inside the pot to settle the grounds. "If it isn't ruined, it'll be a miracle."

To please a woman so lovely, Joseph could have drunk kerosene and sworn he liked it. "I'm not fussy." The moment he spoke, he wanted to kick himself. His voice had gone gravelly with lust. He coughed to clear his throat. "I'm used to coffee made by sleepy cowpokes over an open fire. It's always boiled to a fare-thee-well."

"Mmm." She filled two mugs. Smiling shyly, she brought one to him. "Nothing smells quite so good as coffee on the crisp morning air."

Joseph remained at the opening, one shoulder resting against the boards. Half expecting her to request that he step back, he was pleasantly surprised when she walked right up to him.

"Here you are."

She smelled of roses, a faint, wonderful scent that drifted enticingly up to him. As he took the cup, his fingertips grazed hers. Joseph had heard of men being poleaxed by the sight of a beautiful woman, but he'd never heard tell of anyone's toes going numb.

His reaction to her troubled him. *Love 'em and leave 'em* had always been his creed. He liked women and particularly enjoyed the generous-natured ones, but that was as far as it ever went, a fleeting, mutual pleasure that began in the wee hours and ended long before the first cock crowed.

"Thank you," he said. "I can't wake up properly without a good cup of coffee."

She wiped her hand on her skirt, whether to remove the taint of his touch or to rub away a bit of moisture from the cup, he didn't know. Joseph wished that he'd thought to bring a clean shirt and razor. Around a pretty lady like her, a man wanted to look his best.

Without thinking, he took a big slug of coffee. *Fire.* The scalding liquid seared the inside of his mouth. He almost choked and spat. Instead, he managed to swallow. Bad mistake. He felt the burn clear to his go-nads.

"Are you all right?"

He'd singed all his tongue hairs and blis-tered the little thingy that dangled at the back of his throat. That wasn't to mention that his stomach was on fire. "I'm fine," he lied. "This is right fine coffee." It was the bit-terest coffin varnish that he'd ever tasted in his life.

Bewilderment filled her eyes. Then, as if pushing the questions aside, she hustled back to the stove, the back hem of her skirt trailing gracefully behind her. With well-practiced efficiency, she donned a pretty white apron with a spray of embroidered flowers curving up from the hem to border a large front pocket. Then she vanished into the cellar only to reappear a moment later with a slab of bacon, which she set about slicing.

"Don't cut yourself."

She glanced up. "No worries. In large part, I've spent the last five years perfecting my culinary skills, Mr. Paxton. Aside from needlework and reading, I haven't much else to do, and Darby's a man who enjoys his food."

Weren't most men? Joseph recalled the lecture he'd given his dog yesterday about bachelors who met their waterloo over a supper plate. Somehow, the warning seemed to have lost some of its salt this morning. If it ever happened that he followed in his older brother's footsteps and settled down with one woman for the rest of his days, he hoped she would be as easy on the eyes as Rachel Hollister.

And just what the hell was he *thinking*?

Joseph leaned his head through the hole and gave his dog an accusing glare. *Turncoat.* "Get off that bed, you spoiled mutt." *And don't go making yourself at home.*

This was a temporary situation. The moment that Darby got back on his feet, Joseph would be out of here faster than a cat with its tail on fire. "Come on!" He snapped his fingers. "You're a dirty cur. I'm sure Miss Hollister doesn't want your fleas."

"I haven't noticed him scratching," she observed from her work spot at the table. "And I truly don't mind his being on the bed. My dog, Denver, used to sleep with me all the time."

A woman after his heart. That thought didn't sit well, either. He took a chair at the table to drink his coffee. The purely awful taste made him feel better. A man would have to be out of his mind to tie up with a woman who couldn't make better coffee than this. Coffee was one of the mainstays of Joseph's diet.

Just then he heard Rachel spewing and sputtering. He craned his neck to see her bent over the sink, spitting and scrubbing her mouth with one hand, her other holding a coffee cup out from her body as if it contained poison.

"This is *horrible!*" she cried. She emptied the cup and advanced on the coffeepot. "How can you drink such awful stuff?"

Joseph thought it was a good remedy for what ailed him, namely a purely irrational, inexplicable, imbecilic attraction to a crazy woman.

Rachel was none too pleased when Joseph Paxton informed her that he meant to leave for part of the afternoon. He stood at the opening, ducking his hatless head to see through, his blond hair trailing forward over his sturdy shoulders.

"But one of my windows is wide open!" she reminded him. "And my wall has a huge hole in it! Surely you can't mean to leave me here alone."

"Of course I don't mean to leave you here alone. I told Darby I'd look after you, and I mean to see that you're looked after." He flashed her a cajoling grin. "Have a little faith."

Over the course of the morning, Rachel had catalogued his features, which were chiseled and irregular, his bladelike nose a little too large and sporting a knot along the bridge, his squared jawline accentuated just a bit too strongly by tendon, and his cheekbones just a shade too prominent. Only somehow the overall effect was attractive, especially when he spoke or grinned as he was now. His mouth was full and mobile, a distractingly soft and expressive feature for an otherwise rugged countenance that lent him a boyish appeal. She also liked his blue eyes. When they twinkled with warmth, she felt as if she'd just swallowed a dozen live pollywogs.

"While I'm gone, my brother Ace is going to stand guard," he explained.

His *brother*? Rachel had come to accept Joseph's presence in the dining room, and she was even starting to trust him a little.

But that was where her high-mindedness ended. If he had his way, every citizen of No Name would soon be traipsing through her house.

*"No."*

"Now, Miss Hollister, Ace is a champion fellow. You'll like him."

"I don't care how champion he is. I won't have him inside my house, and that'll be the end of it." She whirled away from the barricade and advanced on the sink to finish washing the breakfast dishes. "You tore the boards from my window, broke out the glass, frightened me into blowing a hole through my barricade, and now you're *leaving*?"

"I have important business to take care of."

"What important business?"

He took so long to reply that she glanced over her shoulder. All the laughter had left his eyes, and their usual sky blue had gone stormy dark. "My brother David is—"

"How many brothers do you *have*?" she asked, her tone waspish.

"Three. Ace, David, and Esa. David's the marshal who was here last night. Today he's going to question a couple people to see if he can find out who shot Darby. Since I'm as eager to find out as he is, I'd like to ride along."

Rachel returned her gaze to the plate in her hands. An iridescent soap bubble slid brightly over the white porcelain surface, caught at the fluted edge, hovered there in trembling splendor for an instant, and then vanished as if it had never been.

She closed her eyes, thinking of her little sister, Tansy, who had glided so brightly through life and then had vanished just as completely as the bubble. No one wanted her killer to be caught more than Rachel did. If there was a connection between the attack on her family and the attack on Darby yesterday, how could she, in good conscience, ask Joseph Paxton not to leave?

## Chapter Six

Jebediah Pritchard owned the spread that adjoined the Hollister ranch to the north. The Pritchard home was little more than a one-room shack, its shake roof sagging along the center pitch, the two front windows covered with tattered isinglass, and the porch littered with all manner of objects, most of which needed to be thrown on a garbage heap. A fat brown hen had made her nest in a washtub to the left of the battered front door, inarguable proof that the Pritchards bathed infrequently.

As David and Joseph rode up, Jeb came out onto the dilapidated porch. A short, beefy individual with grizzled brown hair, beady brown eyes, and skin darkened by sun and grime, he stood with his trunklike legs slightly spread, a shotgun cradled in one arm. The creases on his unshaven face were a slightly deeper brown where dirt and body oil had collected. His attire of the day was the same outfit that he'd been wearing for over a year, patched and faded dungarees over white longhandles that had long since gone gray with filth.

Content to let David do the talking since he was the one wearing the badge, Joseph relaxed in the saddle and lighted a cigarette. At least, he pretended to relax. He'd learned early on never to let down his guard around polecats or sidewinders.

"Whatcha want?" Jeb demanded.

Joseph exhaled smoke, thinking that that was a hell of a way to greet one's neighbors. Evidently Joseph and his brother thought alike, for David replied, "That's a downright unfriendly way to say hello, Jeb."

Silver-streaked, stringy brown hair drifting in the crisp afternoon breeze, Jeb leaned slightly forward to spew a stream of brown spittle through a gap in his decayed front teeth. The tobacco juice nearly struck the front hoof of David's gelding. "I'm never friendly to a man wearin' a badge."

"Ah, now."

"Don't you 'ah, now' me. I know why you're here, sniffin' around. It's because Darby McClintoch got hisself shot in the back yesterday. Well, I'll tell you right now, I don't know nothin' about it."

Joseph was pleased when David replied, "That's interesting. If you know nothing, Jeb, how is it you even know Darby was shot?"

"Got it in town from Slim Jim Davidson."

Slim Jim, the bootlack? Joseph dropped his gaze to Jeb's manure-encrusted plow shoes.

David glanced at Jeb's feet, too. "Got your boots shined, did you?"

"Hell, no. What do I look like, a Nancy boy? I seen Slim Jim when I dropped off my other boots at the cobbler shop."

Jeb's oldest son, Hayden, emerged from the house just then. His weapon of choice was a Smith & Wesson revolver. He wore the gun belt cinched tight at his waist, the holster hanging free. Stocky like his sire, he stood to his father's left, puffed out his chest, spread his feet, and planted his hands on his hips. He wore nothing over his faded red under-shirt, the tattered sleeves riding high on his thick, hairy forearms.

The stench coming from the porch grew stronger with Hayden's arrival. Soap and water being cheap, Joseph could only wonder why some folks refused to wash. Though he couldn't imagine it, he guessed there was some truth to the saying that a man stopped smelling himself after three days.

"What's this about the shooting?" Hayden fairly growled the question, displaying the inherent charm that ran so strongly in his family.

David shifted his weight in the saddle. "I just wanted to ask your pa a few questions."

"Why pester Pa?"

That inquiry came from inside the house. Boots thumped loudly to the door, and Cyrus, the next oldest son, came out. The very spit of Hayden and his father, Cyrus positioned himself at Jeb's right side.

"Pa's got no quarrel with Darby McClintoch," Cyrus exclaimed. "Neither does Hayden or me."

"Never said any of you did," David replied. "I'm just sifting through the flour for weevils, so to speak."

"Ain't no weevils around here," Cyrus assured him.

David smiled. "I'm sure not. I just dropped by to see if you fellows saw or heard anything yesterday. As a crow flies, the scene of the shooting isn't that far from here."

"Happened in the same place where Hollister got his," Jeb interjected. "Leastwise, that's what Slim Jim says."

"Slim Jim seems to know quite a few details," David observed dryly. "That's strange. I've kept a pretty tight lid on things."

Jeb's beady little eyes took on a dangerous glint. "You sayin' I'm lyin'?"

David sat back in the saddle, a clear sign to anyone who knew him well that he wanted fast access to his weapon. The blasting potential of a shotgun still fresh in Joseph's mind, he took his cue from David and tossed down his cigarette.

"I'm just amazed that Slim Jim knows so much about the shooting, like I said," David replied evenly. "Make what you want of it."

"Maybe you oughta talk to Doc," Jeb suggested. The brown hen chose that moment to leave her nest in the washtub. She clucked cheerfully as she hopped off the porch. "Doc was at the Golden Slipper last night, flappin' his lip about Darby to anybody who'd listen."

David's jaw muscle had started to tick.

"You never liked Henry Hollister, did you, Jeb?"

"Hated his guts, more like," Jeb shot back. "He was a selfish, connivin' bastard."

"How do you figure that?"

"Just was, that's all, and the devil take his black soul."

"Rumor has it that you had some kind of a boundary dispute with him."

"Dis-pute, hell. It was a flat-out war, and he only won 'cause he hired a highfalutin lawyer outa Denver to twist the facts all around."

"The facts as they actually were?" David asked. "Or the facts as you saw them?"

Pritchard came forward a step, his face flushing red with anger above his scraggly mustache and beard. "Facts is facts, and there's only one way to see 'em. Wolverine Crick marked my south boundary, and that damned flood in seventy-nine moved it. Way I see it, my property line should've moved with it!"

"Not according to the recorded deed that I read last night," David replied. "Your south boundary line description clearly states that the rock formation, once at the center of Wolverine Creek, is the permanent survey monument, with the boundary moving in a straight line, east and west from there, for a certain number of feet in each direction. The stream helped delineate that line, but it didn't legally define it. The rocks did."

"Fancy words! Hollister stole what was rightfully mine!" Pritchard jabbed his chest with a grimy finger. "My land, bought and paid for with my own sweat."

"A lot of folks think it was just the other way around, that it was you who tried to steal from Hollister by insisting that the stream marked your property line, even though it had moved and encompassed several acres of Hollister's prime ranch-land."

"Bullshit. It ain't stealin' to demand what's already yourn. I bought a place with runnin' water. Ain't right that the water's gone, leavin' me nothin' but a dry crick bed and thirsty cows. But Henry Hollister refused to set things right."

"He channeled water into a pond on your property."

"Well, whoop-dee-do. Wasn't that just grand of him?"

"Did you kill him?" David fired the question.

"Hell, no, I didn't kill him. But I can't say I'm sorry the bastard's dead. Put that in your pipe and smoke it. I celebrated when I heard what happened. Justice was served, if you ask me."

David's eyes narrowed. "And his wife and kids? You glad they're dead, too, Jeb?"

"The devil take the whole lot of 'em," Jeb volleyed back. "Too bad the oldest girl didn't die with the rest. Maybe then I could've bought that place. As it stands, you couldn't get her off that ranch with a wagonload of dynamite."

"Pa," Cyrus said, his voice cast low. "Watch what you say."

"Watch what I say, be damned. A man can't be thrown in the hoosegow for speakin' his mind."

From the corner of his eye, Joseph saw the youngest son emerge from the barn. Like his older brothers, Alan Pritchard wore a sidearm. There all similarity ended. Pale and flaxen-haired, he was a good fifteen years younger than Hayden or Cyrus, who were pushing forty. He was also the beanpole of the family, so thin that he barely cast a shadow standing sideways.

Gossip had it that Alan took after his

mother, who had died giving birth to him. Gossip also had it that shortly before Charlene Pritchard became pregnant with Alan, she had been sneaking off to meet a blond piano player at the Silver Spur, the oldest of No Name's two saloons. Jeb supposedly got wind of her shenanigans, came home reeling drunk, and beat her so severely that she went into early labor and bled to death.

For several reasons, not the least of which was Jeb's charming personality, Joseph believed the gossip. He could well imagine a woman sneaking off from Jebediah Pritchard to be with another man. He could also imagine Jeb using his fists and boots on his pregnant wife. Thirdly, Alan didn't have the look of a Pritchard. Normally, even when a child took mostly after its mother, there were slight resemblances to the father as well. Joseph suspected that Alan had gotten the blond hair and those long, graceful fingers that twitched so eagerly near his gun from his piano-playing papa.

Drawing gently on Obie's reins, Joseph backed the stallion up a few paces to better guard his brother's back. Alan might not be a Pritchard by blood, but he'd been trained up to think like one, and right now he looked to be spoiling for a fight.

"What's the fuss about, Pa?" Alan asked.

"The marshal here thinks I killed Henry Hollister." Jeb jutted his chin to spit again. "Thinks I shot Darby McClintoch, too, I reckon."

Alan's blue eyes glittered. "I'd shoot a man for insultin' me like that. Him wearin' a badge don't make me no nevermind."

"Your father would have to take both of us," Joseph pointed out with a humorless smile, "and he knows that'd be damned near impossible."

"How so?" Posture cocky and challenging, Alan advanced several steps. "There's four of us and only two of you. You may be fast like folks say, Paxton, but nobody's that fast. The odds is in our favor."

Joseph continued to smile. "Draw that gun, son, and you'll find out how fast I am."

"Don't go lettin' your temper get the best of you, Alan," Jeb warned. "He'll clear leather before you even touch your gun."

Alan curled his lip. "He don't look that fast to me."

Joseph sincerely hoped that Jeb got control of this situation. Alan appeared to be somewhere in his early twenties, no longer really a boy, but still too young to die. Joseph had enough regrets to haunt his dreams without adding another to the list.

"Don't be an idiot, little brother," Cyrus interjected. "Everybody in these parts knows his reputation. You got a death wish?"

Joseph remained relaxed in the saddle and kept his gaze fixed on Alan's. The most important part of a gunfight took place during the stare down. A large percentage of the time, the man who blinked first ended up walking away.

Alan blinked.

Holding his hands palm out, he made his way to the porch to stand with his father and brothers. In Joseph's opinion, this party was fast losing its shine. Knowing that his brother would sit tight and watch his back, he turned Obie and trotted the stallion from the littered yard. When safely out of pistol and shotgun range, he wheeled the horse back around, drew his rifle from its boot, and swung down from the saddle.

As David rode from the yard, Joseph kept a close eye on the Pritchards, ready to shoot if he had to but hoping he wouldn't. It was an old stratagem, drilled into both Joseph and

David by their older brother, Ace. *Never take your eye off the enemy unless someone you trust is watching your back.*

"That went fair to middling well," Joseph observed a few minutes later as he and David turned their horses onto Wolverine Road toward town.

"I didn't find out much of anything."

Joseph thought about that for a moment. "You found out for sure that Jeb Pritchard hated Henry Hollister's guts," he pointed out, "and that he's glad the man and his family died. Those were pretty strong words, if you ask me. He also said that he wishes Rachel had died with the rest of them."

David shook his head. "Can you believe that? What did she ever do to him?"

"She lived when the others didn't, and her existence is preventing him from buying the Hollister place."

"It's only land. To wish someone dead over it? If I live to be a hundred, I'll never understand how some people's minds work."

"Me, neither," Joseph agreed. "But there you have it, David. There are some folks in this world who have no respect for human life. They can kill and feel no remorse."

David nodded, his expression solemn.

"You catch that reference Jeb made to dynamite?"

"Yep. In my opinion, he's definitely the one who dynamited Wolverine Creek."

David removed his hat to wipe his brow. "We can't prove one damned thing. That's the problem. I can't arrest a man on supposition."

"Nope," Joseph said with a broad grin, "but you can sure as hell make him nervous." He let that hang there for a moment. "Here in a few days, I reckon you ought to go back. Keep him guessing and off balance. If he killed the Hollisters, he's become complacent over the last five years, thinking he got away with it. It must be unsettling to have a marshal in his dooryard again, asking if he did it."

"What good will it do to make him nervous?" David asked.

Joseph touched his heels to Obie's flanks to quicken the pace. "Nervous men make stupid mistakes, especially if they're dumber than dirt to start with."

Rachel had hoped to watch the dogs play through the peephole in her back door, but Ace Keegan sat on the back porch, his broad back and brown Stetson blocking her view of the yard. According to Joseph, Buddy had a brother named Cleveland that belonged to Ace and Caitlin, and the two animals romped nonstop whenever they got together.

Rachel had spent the first thirty minutes after Ace's arrival pacing in circles around the kitchen table, ever conscious of the gaping hole in her barricade. If someone sneaked in through the window that Joseph had broken, Ace Keegan would be none the wiser. Why wasn't he sitting at the side of the house to make sure no one got in?

Pacing, pacing. Rachel couldn't relax enough to sit down and pass the time reading. She thought about cooking something special for supper to make the hours go faster, but that would involve turning her back on the hole in her barricade. Not a good plan. She needed to be ready, with her shotgun close at hand, just in case something happened.

Rachel had paced to the point of exhaustion and was about to sit in the rocker to watch the barricade when she heard a strange sound coming from the front part of the house. A tinkle of laughter? The hair at the nape of her neck stood on end. Then it came again, a light, feminine giggle followed by footsteps, not the imaginary kind that so often set Rachel's heart to pounding, but real, honest-to-goodness footsteps.

"Raaaa-chel? It's Caitlin!" a feminine voice called out. "Caitlin O'Shannessy. When Joseph asked Ace to come over and watch the house, I couldn't resist joining him for a short visit."

*Caitlin?* Rachel could scarcely believe her ears.

"I won't come any farther, I promise, not unless you answer and say it's okay. I've got my baby boy with me."

This was unprecedented. This was *terrifying*. This was—oh, *God*, it was wonderful, too. *Caitlin.* Rachel hadn't clapped eyes on her in years and years. Except for Darby and Joseph Paxton last night, she hadn't seen anyone.

"Hello?" Caitlin called again. "Can you hear me, Rachel? I'm just here to visit for a bit. I won't come into your room or anything. But here's the problem. I can't come back with my baby until you say it's okay."

Rachel didn't have words. To hear a woman's voice—to know that a friend from childhood was only a few steps away—was almost overwhelming. Tears sprang to her eyes, so many that she could barely see.

*Caitlin.* As a girl, the redhead had often sported bruises, which she'd gone to great lengths to hide. Even so, everyone at school had seen the marks at one time or another. When asked about the injuries, Caitlin had always sworn that she'd had an accident, her explanations never ringing true. Her father, Conor O'Shannessy, had been an ill-tempered man with a heavy fist, an unquenchable thirst for whiskey, and little if any regard for his children.

"Hello?" Caitlin called again. "I'm just *dying* to see you, Rachel, and if it was only me—well, I'd be back there, lickety-split. But I have my little boy to think of. Joseph says you have a loaded shotgun. Little Ace, he's such a dear. I can't bring him back there until I know for sure that it's safe. Do you understand?"

Rachel tried once more to speak and simply couldn't. *Caitlin.* A ghost from her past, part of a world to which she no longer belonged but had never stopped missing.

"Okay, fine," Caitlin called. "Visiting is just talking, right? We don't have to see each other to do that. Although I must warn you, Little Ace is active. He's already squirming to get down. If I let him loose and he gets away from me, you won't shoot him, will you?"

Tears streaming, her throat closed off so tightly that she couldn't breathe, Rachel managed one choked word. "No." It came out so faint that she doubted Caitlin even heard.

"Well, then!" Caitlin said cheerfully. "He's down. And, oh, *dear*, he's off and running down the hallway. Don't be startled, please. He just *goes* as fast as his chubby little legs will carry him. He's— Little Ace, come out of there. Is there anything that he can get into in the rooms along the hall?"

The concern in Caitlin's voice had Rachel at the hole in her barricade, trying to re-member the contents of the rooms along the corridor. Was there anything that might harm a small child? The *sewing room*. It would be full of dangerous things. Rachel couldn't clearly recall what she had re-moved from the room or left lying about, but she knew that the child might find some-thing injurious if he were left to explore.

"Go get him, Caitlin!" she cried. "He's ei-ther in Pa's library or Ma's sewing room.

There are lots of bad things in Ma's sewing room. Scissors, maybe. And needles! I'm sure there are lots of needles."

Footsteps scurried up the hall. Then she heard Caitlin laughing. "You silly boy! What will your pa think if he sees you in that? It's a dress, sweetheart. Dresses are for ladies, not little boys."

Rachel recalled the half-finished dress that her mother had been working on when she died. It had been for Rachel, a graduation dress to mark the end of her school days. More tears sprang to her eyes. *Pain.* Over the last five years, she'd blocked out so many memories, unable to bear thinking of them. Beyond her barricade, the house was filled with them—memories that fairly broke her heart.

Rachel's hands were clenched over the jagged edge of the hole. The shards of splintered wood cut into her fingers and palms. Eyes closed, cheeks wet, she stood rigidly straight, every muscle in her body aching with the strain.

"Pa?"

Her eyes popped open, and there, standing at the other side of her barricade, was a toddler—a pudgy, raven-haired, sloe-eyed little boy with rosy cheeks and absolute in-nocence shining on his face. He wore a blue shirt without a collar, knickers that drooped almost to his ankles, and a grin to break Rachel's heart.

"Pa, pa, pa, pa, *pa!*" he shouted. And then he grinned, displaying pristinely white bot-tom teeth, with little ruffles along the edges. "Pa, pa, pa, pa, *pa!*"

"Little Ace, you get *back* here this instant!" Caitlin cried, and then there she was, hover-ing in the doorway, a mother intent on pro-tecting her baby. Her red hair was done up atop her head, just as Rachel remembered the fashion to be, only now long tendrils dangled before her ears and curls popped out almost everywhere. The latest in vogue? Or was the untidy look a result of mother-hood and too few minutes in the day?

"He knows his papa is on your back porch," Caitlin said breathlessly. "If you feel uncomfortable about this, I'll gather him up and go back outside."

The child chose that moment to lift his arms to Rachel, his plump face dimpled in a happy grin. "Pa, pa, pa, *pa!*" he cried.

And somehow Rachel's arms were reach-ing for him. He was birdsong and sunlight

and laughter and all that was lovely—
everything she hadn't seen in far too long—
a baby, toddling about, with skin so new it
glowed. *Oh!* The word echoed and re-
echoed in her mind, an exclamation of joy
she couldn't articulate. That inexpressible
joy was amplified a hundred times more
when soft, dimpled arms curled trustingly
around her neck.

"Pa?"

Rachel could barely see the child for her
tears. But she managed to nod and carried
him to her back door. In a voice tremulous
with emotions she couldn't separate or define just then, she said, "He's out there."

Little Ace was a smart boy. He saw the
hole and put his eye to it. Then he promptly
started giggling. "Pa, pa, pa, *pa!*"

"Yes," Rachel confirmed, "that's your pa."

The toddler poked his finger into the hole,
and then, as if mere pointing wasn't enough,
he twisted his wrist to drive his tiny finger
deeper into the depression. "Pa!" he said
proudly.

And Rachel got lost in his dancing brown
eyes. He was so soft and warm and dear, a
pint-sized miracle, and she never wanted to
let him go.

The peephole quickly became boring. He fastened a bright gaze on Rachel, grinned to display his new front teeth again, and said, "Hi!"

"Hi" was a lovely word, one that she hadn't heard or uttered in far too long. "Hi," she replied softly.

"I am *so* sorry. He can run faster than I can."

Rachel turned from the door. Framed in the hole of her barricade was the face of a longtime friend. "Caitlin," Rachel whispered.

"Yes, it's me. I hope you don't mind the intrusion. When I found out Ace was coming, I begged to come along. Joseph thought you might like the company because you'd mentioned knowing me, but my husband had an absolute *fit*." Her cheeks went high with color, and she flapped her wrist. "The shotgun had him worried. Ace is nothing if not protective, so he left me at home."

"So how—?"

"I hitched up the wagon and came on my own," Caitlin said with an impish grin. "He wasn't happy to see me, but he finally gave in after I promised to be careful." Caitlin rolled her eyes. "As if you'd shoot me. I kept telling him that we've known each other for years and *years*. I've never believed all those silly stories about you being—" Caitlin's blue eyes went wide, and she flapped her wrist again. "Well, you know."

"Crazy?" Rachel supplied.

"Well, there, you know how people talk. I never listened to a word of it. I used to come by once a week and knock on the door." She shrugged. "You never answered, so I'd just leave things on the porch."

Rachel's eyes went teary again. So it was Caitlin who had come calling so often in those early months after the tragedy. "The books," Rachel whispered raggedly. "You brought me *Tom Sawyer!*"

"Did you like it?

Rachel nodded, then laughed when Little Ace touched the wetness on her cheek. "It's one of my favorites. I never knew it was you who brought it. I heard you knocking, but I was afraid to open the door. Finally, the mystery of it bothered me so that I asked Darby to install a peephole, but after that you never came again."

"Oh, lands! I got married." Caitlin rolled her lovely blue eyes again. "And when I took on a husband, I took on every male in the family. Cooking and laundry and picking up.

It took me a full year to train all the bad habits out of them."

Rachel put the squirming toddler down. The child sped off like a pea from a slingshot, heading straight for Rachel's crochet basket.

"Little *Ace!*" Caitlin scolded. "That's a no-no!"

Rachel had no sooner rescued her fancywork than the child turned to the parlor table, his chubby hands reaching for the lamp. If asked, Rachel couldn't have described how she felt in that moment. She only knew that resenting the intrusion wasn't one of her emotions. "Oh, Caitlin, he is *so* precious."

"He's a little pistol, into this and into that, his feet going a mile a minute. He fills up my days, I can tell you that."

He had filled up Rachel's heart, easing the ache in empty places that she hadn't even realized were there. A baby. She'd lived so long within four walls, with only herself for company, that a little boy with dimpled cheeks was the best thing she could have wished to see, even better than sunshine.

Rachel carried the child to the kitchen,

opened the cupboard that held her pots and pans, and set Little Ace down in front of it.

"He'll pull everything out," Caitlin warned.

"Exactly," Rachel replied with a laugh, and even that seemed wondrous to her. It felt so fabulous to laugh. She took some large metal spoons from the flatware drawer and showed the child how to pound on the bottom of a pot. Little Ace loved that, and soon the kitchen resounded with noise.

"Oh, *my*. Perhaps I shouldn't have come," Caitlin said. "Your nerves will be completely frazzled." She chafed her arms through the sleeves of her green shirtwaist. "I took off my cloak before Ace boosted me up to climb through the window. Now I wish I hadn't. It's a bit chilly out here."

Rachel had a fire going in the stove and hearth to warm the kitchen, but she guessed only a little of the heat was escaping into the other room. "Would you like to come in?"

Caitlin took visual measure of the hole left in the barricade by the shotgun blast. "Do you suppose I can fit through?"

Rachel was trembling just at the thought. Since the day Darby had finished the modifications to her living quarters, no one besides Rachel had been inside. But this was

Caitlin. Even though she was four years Rachel's senior, they'd been educated in the same one-room schoolhouse and had played together in groups during recess.

"If you pull over a chair, it'll be easier to climb through," Rachel suggested. Rushing over to the table, she said, "I'll get a chair for this side and help all I can."

Within seconds, Rachel and Caitlin were giggling like schoolgirls. The hole wasn't quite so large as it had seemed in Rachel's imagination over the last many hours, and it had jagged edges to catch on Caitlin's clothing and hair as she twisted and bent into odd positions, trying to fit through.

"I'm stuck," she pronounced.

Rachel giggled and tugged on Caitlin's elbow, trying to get her loose.

"Is everything all right in there?" a deep, masculine voice called from the back porch.

Rachel nearly parted company with her skin, but Caitlin only laughed. "Yes, darling, everything's fine. Absolutely fine."

Hearing his father's voice, Little Ace scampered toward the door, pounding on a pot with every step.

"What in tarnation is that racket?" Ace Keegan asked.

"Not to worry, sweetheart." Caitlin tugged on strands of her hair that were caught on the wood. "It's only—*ouch*—Little Ace playing with Rachel's pots."

Suddenly—and unexpectedly—Caitlin spilled through the opening and sent Rachel scrambling to catch her. When Caitlin had both feet safely on the kitchen floor, she dissolved into laughter. As her mirth subsided, she said, "I can't believe I just did that." She looked over her shoulder at the hole. "Now the question is, will I be able to get back out?"

That was a worry for later. Rachel stoked the firebox in the range, put on a fresh pot of coffee, and dished up bowls of peach cobbler. Soon she and Caitlin were sitting at the table, and Caitlin was chattering like a magpie, telling Rachel all the news and tidbits of gossip that she'd missed out on over the last five years.

"Remember Beatrice Masterson and Clarissa Denny?" she asked.

"The milliner and dressmaker? Of course I remember them."

"Well," Caitlin said in a low, conspiratorial voice as she spooned up some cobbler, "they're in competition for Doc Halloway's favor."

"Truly?" In Rachel's estimation, both women were too old to be entertaining romantic notions, especially about a stooped, elderly gentleman like Doc.

"You didn't hear it from me, mind you. Normally I try not to carry gossip. It's just that there's so much you don't know about." She tasted the cobbler. "Oh, my, Rachel, this is delicious. May I have the recipe?"

"It's just a bit of this and a dash of that."

Caitlin took another bite. "It's better than mine." She washed the dessert down with a sip of coffee. "Now let me think. What else has happened?" She grinned mischievously and pointed at Rachel with the spoon. "Hannibal St. John, the new preacher."

"What about him?"

"Pauline Perkins carries a torch for him."

*"Pauline?"* Pauline had been a singularly homely girl, tall, rawboned, and hefty, with frizzy blond hair and as many pimples as freckles. Her father, Zachariah Perkins, published No Name's weekly newspaper, *The Gazette.* "Does the reverend return her fond regard?"

Caitlin let loose with a peal of laughter.

*"No,"* she said in a thin, breathless voice. "But Pauline won't leave him be. Last week—I have this on good authority, mind you—she cornered him in the church storage room and kissed him."

"When he didn't want her to?"

"Even worse, her mother, Charlene, caught them in the act and was absolutely beside herself. She accused Hannibal of compromising her daughter's reputation and demanded that he marry her."

Charlene Rayette Perkins was an older and heavier version of Pauline. Rachel had always been a little afraid of the woman because she wore a perpetual scowl and snapped at people when they spoke to her. "What did Hannibal do?"

"He refused, of course. Would *you* want to get stuck with Pauline?"

Rachel giggled and shook her head. "Lands, no. She used to push me down during recess. I never liked her very much."

"Well, her disposition hasn't gotten any sweeter. Hannibal is a very nice man. Handsome, too—very tall, with golden hair and kindly blue eyes." Caitlin winked. "Not that I'm given to looking, you understand. I have eyes only for Ace."

Rachel couldn't recall ever having seen Caitlin so happy. "Is he good to you, Caitlin?"

A soft, dreamy look filled Caitlin's eyes. "Good to me? He treats me like a queen. I love that man more than life itself, I truly do."

En route to Amanda Hollister's place, Joseph and David chose to bypass town by riding across open country through budding witches'-broom, newly blossoming clover, and more rocks than they could count. Spring was in the air, even though the March temperatures were still chilly enough to make both men shiver when the wind picked up. Joseph thought about tugging his coat free from the straps at the back of his saddle, but each time he started to reach for it, the breeze would slacken.

The sign over Amanda's main gate laid no claims to grandeur, stating only her name, followed by RANCH. As they followed the dirt road toward the house, Joseph took visual measure of the fenced pastures, trying to guess how large a spread it was.

"It doesn't appear that she has much land," he finally commented.

"A quarter section with open range," David replied. "When I went to the courthouse last night, I looked at her deed, too, along with other records of interest. I'm thinking the stories about her quarrel with Henry are true. She can't have been very happy about being left out of her brother's will. Two thousand acres, versus a mere one hundred and sixty? Even with open range for her cattle to graze, it's a big step down for a woman who worked most of her life on a larger spread that she hoped to partly own someday."

"You can bet her father didn't manage to increase his original homestead to encompass that much land without plenty of help from his kids."

"Amanda and her younger brother, Peter James, were his only children. Their mother, Martha, died in twenty-seven, when Amanda was eight and Peter was six. Their father, Luther, never remarried."

"So it was left to only Amanda and Peter to help their pa work the spread."

David nodded. "And according to what Doc told me, Peter inherited his mother's weak constitution, so the giant's share of the work fell to Amanda."

"But the old man left the ranch lock, stock, and barrel to the brother?"

"Yep. Even so, Doc claims that she remained loyal to the family and continued to work like a man, carrying much of the load because Peter was never very robust."

Joseph shook his head. "Peter—he was Henry Hollister's father. Right?"

David nodded. "And he only outlived his and Amanda's father by nineteen years. He was about sixty when he died."

"And he made no provisions for his hard-working sister in his will?"

"Nary a one. He left everything to Henry, consigning Amanda to live on her nephew's charity. She was sixty-two at the time, getting up in years and no longer able to work as she once had. I can't say that I blame her for petitioning Henry to grant her at least a monthly income from the ranch."

"But he refused."

"Flatly." David shrugged. "That was when she moved out and never spoke to him again. Doc says she had a small trust from her grandmother. She used that money to buy this place."

"What goes wrong in some families that they value the boys over the girls?" Joseph couldn't imagine it. "I'd never cut Eden off without a dime."

David grinned. "If there were anything for

us to inherit, I wouldn't, either. We're lucky, I reckon. There'll be no haggling in our family when Mom passes on. Everything she has came to her from Ace. It'll rightly go back to him."

Joseph mulled it all over for a moment. "It sounds like Henry Hollister was a selfish man." As Joseph spoke, he remembered the pain he had seen in Rachel's eyes and instinctively knew that Henry had been a kind, just man and a wonderful father. What had gone wrong in the family that a faithful, hardworking female relative had twice been denied her rightful inheritance?

"Maybe so." David pushed up the brim of his hat to meet Joseph's gaze. "Only, no matter what the provocation, what kind of person would kill her own flesh and blood? We've got to remember that it wasn't only Henry who died. His wife and two children went with him, one of them a little girl who wasn't yet six. Read between the lines when we talk with Amanda. Watch for any sign of insanity. Maybe you're right, and it runs in the family."

Even though Joseph had made the same observation last night, he bridled at the suggestion now. Rachel wasn't normal, living as she did. He wouldn't go so far as to say that. But she didn't strike him as being crazy, either. By hiding away, she'd found a way to feel safe, and now she clung to her seclusion like a drowning animal did to a log in a raging stream.

At a very young age, Joseph had learned to be a survivor, and so had everyone else in the family. His father's untimely death had left them without a breadwinner, and the land swindle had rendered them penniless. Supporting the family had fallen to Ace, an eleven-year-old boy, so their circumstances had grown a whole lot worse before they got better. In order to survive, they'd done whatever they had to do, just as Rachel was doing now.

When they reached the end of the road, Joseph saw that Amanda Hollister's house was as neat as a tumbler of straight whiskey. Green shutters bracketed the windows, and a veranda spanned the front of the house. Comfortable-looking wicker chairs flanked a swing, and several flowerpots were strategically placed to get sunlight. Nary a one hosted a plant that had sprouted any blooms yet, but that was Colorado for you. Spring didn't come until almost summertime, and summer died young.

As Joseph and David tethered their
horses to the hitching post that ran the
length of the front flowerbed, a man came
around the corner of the house. He had the
look of a ranch hand, his faded Levi's dusty
from working with livestock, his gray, collar-
less shirt stained with sweat. His honey
brown hair glistened like bronze in the sunlight, and his fine-featured countenance
creased in a warm smile.

"Howdy," he called out. "How can I help
you?"

Joseph and David flashed each other a
grin. After their reception at the Pritchard
place, it was nice to get a friendly greeting.

The man's arresting blue eyes dropped to
David's badge, and his eyebrows shot up.
"Oh, boy." He thrust out his wrists. "Cuff me
and get it over with. I've been found out."

David chuckled, and introductions ensued. The hired hand said he was Amanda
Hollister's ranch foreman, Ray Meeks.

"Have we met?" Joseph asked as he
shook Meeks' hand.

Ray squinted thoughtfully. "Not that I recall. I'm sure I would remember if we had."

"You look familiar, somehow," Joseph said.

Meeks shrugged and smiled. "We've probably seen each other in town at one time or another. You look sort of familiar to me, too." He hooked a thumb over his shoulder. "Miss Hollister is around back." He motioned for David and Joseph to follow him. "If you want to talk to her, I hope you don't mind a little dust. We're breaking some broncos, and she insists on supervising." Flashing a good-natured grin, he added, "God love her. She needs to leave the horse training to us men, but she won't hear of it."

Joseph had no idea what to expect. Given the fact that Amanda Hollister had motive to have killed Henry and his family—and also to want Rachel dead—he had a picture inside his head of a wicked old crone with calculating eyes and warts on her nose.

Instead, as they walked toward the breaking arena, Joseph saw that she was a much older version of Rachel, a small, fragile woman of about seventy, with delicate features, large, expressive blue eyes, a coronet of white hair that had undoubtedly once been blond, and a bad case of palsy that made her entire body tremble. She sat facing the corral in a wheelchair, head ducked to see through the rails, her divided riding skirt following the unladylike sprawl of her legs. Fists knotted, she pounded on the arms of her chair.

"Stop swinging that lariat at him, you damned fool! Make him afraid of it and you'll ruin him forever as a cow pony!"

Joseph seconded that opinion; the man *was* a damned fool. Chasing the terrified horse around the corral, the hired hand swung the rope like a whip, hitting the animal on its tender nose and rump. The poor, confused mustang flinched and darted, trying frantically to escape.

The sight made Joseph furious, and he wanted to put a boot up the man's ass. Sadly, there were more incompetent horse trainers than there were good ones, and it was the horses that paid the price. Too many greenhorns went into a corral thinking to mimic the technique of a good trainer, but taming a mustang wasn't that simple. Horses were large, very powerful animals and could be dangerous when cornered. Proper handling demanded a lot of experience, a host of little tricks, a measure of good sense, and a lot of compassion.

Amanda Hollister came up out of her wheelchair. Shaking so badly that it was difficult for her to keep her feet, she advanced on the rails. "Out of there. If you strike that animal again, I'll take a whip to you, I swear." She turned to Ray Meeks, her foreman. "Cut this imbecile his pay. I never want to see him on this ranch again."

Ray sent the trainer an apologetic look and motioned for him to exit the corral. Joseph caught the exchange and wondered why Meeks felt bad. When a man couldn't do the work that he'd been hired to do, he was damned lucky to get any back pay, and the apology was his to make.

Still oblivious to the arrival of guests, Amanda Hollister grasped a post to steady herself and took stock of the men who ringed the corral, some sitting on a top rail, others leaning against the fence. In Joseph's opinion, none of them looked highly energetic. At his place, a hired hand was expected to stay busy until daylight waned. It was Saturday, though. Maybe it was the men's day off, and they hadn't chosen to go into town.

"Does anyone here know how to tame a horse, or must I do it myself?" Amanda asked.

None of the men raised a hand. Amanda caught sight of Joseph just then. Without so much as a howdy-do, she said, "You've got the look of a horseman. Do you know anything about taming a mustang?"

Joseph shot David a wondering look, then plucked off his hat to give his head a scratch. "I know a little."

"Don't be modest, young man. How much is a little?"

Joseph almost grinned. Damned if he didn't like the old lady. She had a lot of sass in her frail old bones, and he admired that in anyone. "I've been working with horses most of my life."

"Well, don't stand there with your thumb up your butt. Get to work."

The next thing Joseph knew, he was inside the corral working with the mustang. Though relatively new to cattle ranching, Joseph knew horses and loved the animals as he did little else. As a fatherless boy in San Francisco, he'd hired out as a stable boy at liveries until Ace had mastered the fine art of gambling and started to rake in winnings. After seeing to his family's comfort, Ace had begun spending a portion of his winnings on horses, one of his stepfather's greatest passions. As a result, Joseph had finished out his childhood like a proper young Virginian, working with the animals when he didn't have his nose in a schoolbook.

The first order of business was to get the mustang to stand, and that was tricky business. Never striking the horse, Joseph swung the lariat much as his predecessor had, only with precision, technique, and a purpose in mind, namely to shrink the equine's radius of movement until standing was the only option left to it. An hour of hard work for both him and the animal ensued.

"That's enough for today," he informed Amanda Hollister as he swung a leg over a rail to exit the corral. "He's exhausted."

Back in her chair, Amanda inclined her head at the mustang. "Exhausted, yes, but not terrified. He's beginning to understand what you're asking of him." She turned amazingly clear and beautiful blue eyes on Joseph. "You're very good, young man. What's your price?"

Joseph dusted his Stetson on his pant leg, resettled the hat on his head, and said, "I'm not for hire, ma'am."

"There isn't a man here who holds a candle to you."

Joseph glanced at a nearby holding corral, milling with range-wild mustangs. "Wish I were available. I'd enjoy the challenge. But I have a spread and my own horses to train."

Her eyes sharpened with interest. "Where's your place?"

"Due north of the Circle Star."

"Nice property," she said. "You'll do well there if you put enough sweat into it."

Joseph nodded. She was familiar with the land, certainly. The Hollister place adjoined it to the north. "Sweat's cheap."

Her brilliant gaze came to rest on David's badge. "Marshal," she said by way of greeting as she thrust out a gnarled hand. "Dare I hope that this is a social call?"

David stepped forward to shake her hand. "I'd just like to talk with you for a bit if you can spare me some time."

"Time is a commodity in short supply around here, but I can spare you some." She smiled at Joseph. "One good turn deserves another. Maybe these yahoos learned something. I know the horse did. Please, come to the house. I'll put some coffee on and scrounge up some cookies."

She struggled to move her chair over the uneven ground, her trembling, arthritic hands barely able to grasp the wheels. Joseph grabbed the push handles. With a thrust of a leg, he got the chair out of a rut and soon had his passenger bumping along toward the house. Her voice shook as she talked. He wasn't sure if that was due to the rough ride or the palsy.

"I never got your names," she said. "Forgive my manners. You caught me at a bad moment."

"David Paxton."

She nodded and glanced around at Joseph. "And you, sir?"

"Joseph Paxton. We're brothers."

"I'm assuming that you know my name, or else you wouldn't be here."

"Yes, ma'am," David replied.

"Well, it's pleased I am to make your acquaintance." She settled in the chair. "So, Joseph Paxton, how many acres do you have?"

"Twelve eighty."

"Ah, two full sections. That's a great start. I only have one sixty here, but with the open range, I manage to keep the wolves from my door." She sighed and smiled. "As time wears on, you may be able to pick up more property, Joseph. In this country, you can eke out a living on two sections, but to do really well, you'll need a larger spread." She waved a blue-veined hand. "No worries. For every enterprising man, there's a lazy one, and lazy men can't make it in this country. It's a harsh environment and demands hard work."

Joseph's favorable first impression of this woman hadn't changed. He couldn't help but like her. He found himself wishing that he'd met her under other circumstances, that instead of asking her about the Hollister shootings and the attack on Darby yesterday, he could pick her brain about cattle ranching. He sensed that she had more knowledge in her little finger than he had in his whole body.

By the time she'd served them coffee, the three of them had moved past the awkward stage. Amanda settled back in her chair, gave David a questioning look, and said, "Well, young man, it's time to state your business. What can I help you with?"

David sat forward on the red leather sofa, propped his elbows on his knees, and steepled his fingers. "Have you heard about the shooting yesterday?"

"Shooting?" Amanda glanced at Joseph. "No, I can't say as I have. Did one of my boys cause trouble in town last night?"

"No, ma'am," David replied. "Darby Mc-

Clintoch was tracking down a stray heifer yesterday afternoon. He was at the north end of the Hollister ranch, between the rock promontory and the creek. Someone up in those rocks shot him in the back."

Amanda's face went ghastly white, and for a moment Joseph feared that the old lady might faint. Instead, she straightened her shoulders, raised her chin, and only closed her eyes briefly. "Darby," she said softly. Her lashes fluttered back up. "He's dead . . . ?"

"No, no, he's not dead," David rushed to clarify. "Not yet, at any rate. Doc patched him up and thinks he stands a fine chance of pulling through."

"Praise the Lord." Amanda passed a trembling hand over her eyes. "Darby and I go a long way back. He came to work for my father down south when I was just a girl. I hope he makes it. The world will be a poorer place without him."

David nodded. "He's a fine man. The problem is, Darby has no idea who shot him."

Amanda's gaze sharpened. "And you think I do."

It wasn't a question, and her eyes suddenly became guarded.

"I'm hoping you can give me some leads,"

David clarified. "It happened in almost exactly the same place where Henry and his family were attacked. Darby is convinced the two incidents are somehow connected."

"And since I was the prime suspect five years ago, you're back to pester me with questions again."

David held up his hands. "I'm not here to accuse you of anything, Miss Hollister. Just to see if you can tell me anything. Do you think Darby's right? Could there be a connection? And if so, do you have any idea who hated Henry enough to kill him?"

Amanda leaned forward on her chair to pick up her half-filled coffee cup. Her hands shook so badly that she almost slopped liquid over the brim before she could take a sip. "If I had any idea, do you truly believe I would have kept it to myself these last five years?" Her blue eyes fairly snapped with outrage as she returned the cup to its saucer with a clatter and clack. "I had problems with my nephew. Everyone in this valley knows that. But my problems ended with him. His wife, Marie, was a lovely person, like a daughter to me, and I loved those children like my own, Rachel especially. If I knew who opened fire on them, I'd hunt him down myself."

Joseph searched Amanda Hollister's face for any sign of artifice and found none. She had loved Marie Hollister and the children. There was no doubt in his mind about that.

"I totally agree that it was a heinous crime," David said. "And, please, don't take offense. I'm just trying to do my job. Someone shot Darby in the back. I have to find out who."

"So you start with the person who stood to gain the most by Henry Hollister's death?" Amanda rolled her chair back and wheeled it away from the library table where she'd set out the coffee and cookies. "Good day, gentlemen. You know the way out."

David shot to his feet. "Miss Hollister, please wait!"

"For further insult?" She struggled to turn the chair. "There isn't a piece of land on earth worth spilling blood over, marshal. Now, please, get out. You're no longer welcome under my roof."

## Chapter Seven

During the return ride to No Name, Joseph and David went back over their conversation with Amanda Hollister. David was of the opinion that her abrupt departure from the sitting room had been unduly defensive. Joseph's impression had been just the opposite, that Amanda Hollister was a fine woman who had been deeply offended by the implication that she might have killed members of her own family over a piece of land.

"Think about it," Joseph challenged. "She can't take a swallow of coffee without damned near scalding herself. How the hell could she have aimed a rifle at Darby yesterday and hit him in the back?"

"Maybe she hired somebody to do it."

"When it comes to killing, a smart person does it himself," Joseph argued. "Too much risk of being found out, otherwise."

"Maybe she's faking the palsy."

Joseph didn't think so, but he had to concede the point. "Maybe." He thought of Pritchard with his greasy hair and filthy body, a snake if ever he'd met one. "My money's still on Jeb, though."

It was David's turn to make a concession. "He's definitely capable of murder, no question there." He slumped in the saddle with a weary, frustrated sigh. "I guess from here on in, it's a waiting game. We've shaken things up. Now we'll see what falls out."

Joseph drew his watch from his pocket. It was going on four o'clock. "I need to get cooking. Ace has been at Rachel's place for over four hours."

"You heading straight there?"

Joseph clicked his tongue to quicken Obie's pace. "I have some things to take care of in town first, and then I need to swing by home to see how Johnny and Bart have been fairing, running the ranch without me."

"Isn't Esa overseeing things?"

Esa normally worked full-time as a hired hand at Ace's place and knew as much about ranching as Joseph did. "He's getting Bart and Johnny lined out each morning and trying to monitor their work. But taking care of Darby keeps him in the house most of the day. Can't hurt for Bart and Johnny to know that I'm still keeping on top of things. Johnny is on the lazy side. If there's an easy way to do a job, he'll find it. And Bart is too mild-natured to say much if the quality of Johnny's work falls off."

David shook his head. "Used to be that a man took pride in a job well done."

Joseph grinned. "Only when the boss is around. That being the case, I want to drop in on them as often as I can to keep them on their toes. I also need to check on Darby and pick up some stuff."

An hour and a half later, Joseph dismounted in front of Rachel Hollister's barn and led Obie into his stall. After rubbing the stallion down, he forked some hay into the enclosure, filled the trough with fresh water, and then measured out a portion of grain before turning his attention to the evening chores. He was pleasantly surprised to find that the horses had been brought in from the paddock and fed, the two cows were already in their stalls and had been milked, the sow was still standing in the trough, finishing her evening meal, and someone had recently scattered millet and cracked corn for the chickens. *Ace.* A fond smile touched Joseph's lips.

Shakespeare, Ace's black stallion, and two workhorses from the Paradise had been staked out to graze near the oak in Rachel's backyard. Joseph was puzzled by the presence of the two extra equines until he saw the buckboard parked at one side the house. *Caitlin.* She very seldom argued with her husband, but she had this morning, about coming to see Rachel. When Joseph had left, Ace was laying down the law, forbidding his wife from risking her safety by entering a house where a crazy woman might open fire on her with both barrels of a shotgun. Evidently Caitlin had taken the bit in her teeth, driven over here in the wagon, and somehow convinced Ace to let her go inside.

The thought made Joseph smile. There wasn't a man alive who could push Ace Keegan around, but one small redhead with pleading blue eyes got the better of him every time. Ace seemed content and happy. That was all that truly mattered, Joseph guessed. He was glad for his brother and equally pleased for Caitlin. With Conor

O'Shannessy as her sire, she'd had a horrible childhood and an even worse girlhood. It was high time she got to have her way the majority of the time and had a man who loved and cherished her as she deserved to be.

As Joseph climbed through the bedroom window, he heard voices coming from the rear of the house. Curious, he made his way up the hallway. As he drew near the dining room, delicious smells made his mouth water. *Fried chicken?* It was one of his favorites.

Ace sat at the dining room table, a plateful of food in front of him. He grinned and saluted Joseph with a half-eaten drumstick. Joseph was about to say hello when a burst of feminine laughter came from the kitchen. Amazed, he went to the barricade, bent his head, and peered inside.

Rachel's tidy world had been turned topsy-turvy. Little Ace was playing with an array of store-bought canned food, Van Camp's pork and beans, Campbell's soup, and some other stuff Joseph couldn't identify, the cans scattered around him helter-skelter. Behind him, an array of pots and pans littered the floor, with Buddy and Cleveland taking a snooze amid the debris. Caitlin and Rachel sat at the table having supper, but it looked as if they were doing more talking and laughing than eating.

"Well, I'll be. Is this an invitation-only party?"

"Joseph!" Rosy cheeked, her red hair attractively mussed, Caitlin sprang up from her chair. "You're late for supper. We didn't expect you to be gone so long."

Rachel came up from her seat more slowly and blushed when she met Joseph's gaze. "Caitlin came to call," she said, fluttering a hand at the mess around her. "We've had a lovely visit."

"I can see that." And Joseph truly could. Despite the blue shadows of fatigue under Rachel's eyes, she beamed with happiness. It made him feel good to know that he'd played a small part in making that happen by encouraging Caitlin to come calling. "I'm glad you enjoyed yourself."

"How is Darby?" she asked anxiously, her heart shining in her eyes.

Joseph chose not to tell her that the old foreman was running a slight fever. Doc had stopped by to check on his patient, and although he'd been concerned that the fever might worsen, he'd also stressed that it was to be expected. When a bullet invaded the body, it carried with it germs, and a fever indicated that the body was fighting off infection.

"He's doing as well as can be expected," Joseph settled for saying. "Esa made him some beef broth, and he kept that down. Doc stopped by and said the wound looks good. Darby's not quite ready to dance a jig yet, but I think he's on the mend."

Little Ace registered Joseph's voice just then and scrambled to his feet. Chubby legs scissoring, he came running toward the barricade, tripped over a can of pork and beans, and did a face-plant on the floor. Shrieks of distress ensued. Rachel reached the child first, Caitlin not far behind her.

"Oh, no, Ace, he's really hurt!" Caitlin cried. "He's bleeding. I think a tooth went through his lip."

Ace abandoned his meal to bolt toward the hole in the doorway. Such was Ace's momentum that Joseph feared his brother might plow right through the boards. Fortunately, Ace caught himself short, grasped the jagged edges of wood, and thrust his head through the hole. Peering over his shoulder, Joseph saw Rachel hand the screaming child off to Caitlin and rush to a kitchen drawer. A second later, she plucked out an ice pick and scurried to the icebox.

For the next five minutes, Little Ace was the center of attention while plates of food grew cold. In the end, it was decided that the tooth puncture wasn't all that serious.

When the child's lip had been iced and his mother had doled out enough kisses to soothe a mortal wound, Little Ace suddenly brightened, held out his chubby arms, and hollered, "Seff!"

"Yes, it's your uncle Joseph," Caitlin agreed as she set her son on his feet.

This time, Little Ace ran to the barricade without mishap. Joseph reached through the hole and scooped the child into his arms. "Hey, there, little man. Where did you come by those lungs of yours? My ears are still ringing." Joseph bent his head to nibble under the toddler's chin, which sent Little Ace into fits of giggles. "It looks to me as if you've had way too much fun today without me. Now I'm jealous."

From the stove, Caitlin asked, "Do you want butter or gravy on your potatoes, Joseph?"

"Both." Joseph made a gobbling sound and went after his nephew's belly. The child did an admirable job of fighting his uncle off, all the while lifting his shirt to accommodate the tickling. "Where'd your mama find you, under a cabbage leaf? I was never this ornery."

"The hell you weren't," Ace said from the table.

"I heard that!" Caitlin called. "Unless you want your mouth washed out with soap, Ace Keegan, you'll stop using words like that around your son."

About to take a bite of chicken, Ace said, "All I said was hell. That's not cussing."

"It's not a word that I want our son using," his wife replied. "Imagine how that will go over on his first day at school."

"He won't be in school for another five years," Ace protested.

"Yes, and I shudder to think what his vocabulary will be like by then if you don't get a handle on your language."

Joseph glanced at Ace, awaiting his comeback. Ace just shrugged and resumed eating his meal. Another mark on the chalkboard for Caitlin, Joseph guessed. Personally, he counted hell as being a byword and thought it was a hell of a note that a man couldn't say it when the mood struck.

After Ace and Caitlin left, which was no easy departure given the fact that Caitlin had to crawl back out through the shotgun hole, Rachel set to work tidying her living area. Concerned by the shadows under her eyes, Joseph watched through the opening from his position at the table, wishing he could help her. Mostly it was just busywork, though, putting little things precisely where they belonged, a knickknack here, a rug just there. Before leaving, Caitlin had picked up after her son and helped with the dishes, so the mess was mostly in Rachel's imagination, a result, Joseph felt sure, of her having lived in solitude so long, with little ever happening to disrupt the sameness.

"I want to thank you."

Joseph glanced up from petting Buddy to see her standing at the archway. Her shirtwaist sported spots, either from cooking, eating, or holding Little Ace when his hands were grubby. Even so, she looked beautiful. "Thank me for what?"

Smoothing a hand over the front of her skirt, she smiled and shrugged. "For making today happen. You encouraged Caitlin to come, and I'm ever so glad you did. It was lovely seeing her again."

Joseph could only imagine, and he knew that fell short. She'd been alone inside that kitchen for five long years. The thought boggled his mind. Minute after minute, hour after hour, day after day, with no company and no windows to look outside. If he had been cooped up alone that long, he would have lost his mind.

"I'm glad you enjoyed yourself."

She smiled again and tipped her head as if weighing his words. "Enjoyed? That only skims the surface. I can't tell you how much it meant to me. Little Ace is so darling."

Joseph rocked back in the chair. "You like children, then?"

A thoughtful look entered her eyes. Then she nodded. "Yes, I suppose I must."

It struck Joseph as being a strange answer until he considered the fact that Rachel had been little more than a girl herself when her family was killed, and she hadn't seen any children since to actually know if she liked them.

"Well, now that Caitlin's come over to see you once, I'm sure she'll be back," he said.

"When I take your eggs and cheese into town, I'll be asking Ace to stay with you. Chances are, she'll tag along."

"I hope so." Touching the jagged edges of wood, she added, "I only wish the way in and out were a little less difficult for her."

Ever since asking Caitlin to come visit Rachel that morning, Joseph had been considering that problem and had already taken the initial steps to solve it. Maybe he was wishing on rainbows, but it seemed to him that further modifications needed to be made to Rachel's hidey-hole so she might at least have occasional company. Living as she did was one thing. Even though the measures she had taken seemed extreme, he could understand her need to feel safe. But never to see anyone? There were surely people she trusted, Caitlin being one, who could drop by for coffee sometimes. Just one visitor a week would brighten her life immeasurably. Another thing that troubled Joseph was the constant darkness in which she lived. It was unnatural and couldn't be healthy. Rachel might resent his meddling, but after spending a night and morning in this aboveground tomb, Joseph itched to give her occasional glimpses of sunlight.

"I might could rig up something for you," he offered.

She gave him a curious look. "Like what?"

Still fondling Buddy's ears, he rocked back on the chair. "Has it occurred to you that your barricade didn't hold up very well under that shotgun blast?"

She paled slightly, a telltale sign to Joseph that the barricade's failings had not only occurred to her, but also troubled her deeply.

"I realize now that someone could shoot from the opposite side and do just as much damage, yes."

"Two blasts could make a hole damned near large enough for a man to walk through," Joseph expounded. "If the idea is to keep people out, you need something more than just boards."

"Like what?"

"A solid iron plate bolted to each side of every door, for starters, placed middling high where most people are likely to aim a gun. A shotgun blast can't penetrate iron. On the off chance that someone should try to blast his way in, that would slow him down considerably."

"Yes," she conceded, "I suppose it would."

"And I'm thinking about some iron bars, too, sort of like the cell doors in a jail, something made to fit over the outside of each door as added protection. You got a pad and pencil?"

"Yes." She disappeared for a moment and then returned with the items. Handing them through to him, she pressed close to the hole and watched as he sketched what he had in mind.

He gave her the drawing. "If I could find some long carriage bolts, I could sink them clear through the walls and anchor the barred doors on the inside of the house. In order to remove the exterior bars, a man would need a hacksaw, and it would take forever to cut through even one piece of the iron."

"That would surely increase my security," she agreed.

"And even better, the barred doors could be unlocked. Caitlin may want to come a lot. She enjoys gadding about when she can get away, and she's got only one other good friend, a gal named Bess."

Rachel's eyes brightened. "Bess Halloway, Doc's niece?"

"That's the one, only now her last name's not Halloway."

"Caitlin mentioned today that she'd gotten married."

Joseph nodded. "To Bradley Thompson."

"Do his parents still own the dry goods store?" Rachel asked.

"They do. Brad helps run the place now, and Bess is teaching. With two kids of her own, plus a full-time job, Bess is so busy— even with Brad's mother helping out—that she doesn't have much time for visiting these days. Caitlin could use another friend."

"I'd love it if she chose me," Rachel said with a dreamy smile.

Joseph took the notepad from her hand. "A barred door would simplify her coming and going. Here's what I'm thinking."

Sketching as he talked, Joseph quickly explained how Rachel's damaged archway barricade could be replaced with an extra-thick plank door, similar to the one that opened out onto the back porch. Then barred doors could be installed over both, and the front door of the house as well.

"You could give trusted friends like Caitlin keys to enter the house through the front door," he concluded. "Once Caitlin reaches the dining room, she could knock at the archway door, you could identify her through a peephole, and let her in, locking both the plank and barred door behind her."

"Oh, I never open my doors."

Joseph believed that it was high time she started, if only to allow a good friend like Caitlin to enter. "Ah, but with the added security of a barred door, you could look all around the dining room to be sure it was okay before you unlocked it. Then Caitlin could quickly slip inside, you could lock both doors behind her, and there you'd be, safe as two bugs in a rug."

"I might be able to handle that," she conceded. "It would be fabulous to have a friend come to see me, like a normal person does."

"It'd be safer than the setup you have now," he stressed, "with the added benefit of being able to have a visitor now and again."

She nodded thoughtfully.

"Even better," he went on, "with the bars as an added barrier, you might even feel safe enough to open the back porch door sometimes to enjoy a little morning sunshine."

"And hear the birdsong?" she asked wistfully.

"That, too." The incredulous yearning in her eyes made a tiny place deep inside Joseph's chest throb like a sore tooth. *Birdsong.* He'd not had time to consider all the thousands of things that had been stripped from Rachel's life—things that he and others took for granted. "Barred doors would be worth a try. Don't you think?"

She sighed and shook her head. "They would be lovely, but I could never afford to have them made."

"It won't cost a thing," Joseph assured her. "Do you remember Bubba White?"

"The blacksmith?"

"One and the same. I stopped by to see him this afternoon. He's got a huge heap of scrap iron left over from when he made rails for the spur Ace built from here to Denver. At present, the iron's rusting and creating an eyesore in front of the shop, and Bubba's wife, Sue Ellen, has been pecking at him to get rid of it. As a result, he's offering the scraps for free to anyone who'll take them off his hands."

"Really?" She frowned thoughtfully. "That would cut the costs, I suppose, but there'd still be Bubba's wages to pay. I don't have much extra money."

Joseph held up a finger to interrupt. "Ah, but you're overlooking one thing. A lot of people in No Name still care about you."

"They do?"

"Of course they do. They've just never known how they might help. Bubba's one of those people. When I told him the barred doors would be for you, he offered to donate his time to make them if I will handle the delivery and installation."

"He did?" She looked amazed. "How kind of him."

"It's not about kindness, Rachel. It's about being a good neighbor. According to Bubba, the attack on your family is the worst thing that's happened in these parts in all the years he's lived here, and he came out from Ohio back in the sixties when Colorado was still just a territory. There have been Cheyenne uprisings and the like, with greater casualties, I suppose, but at least that was during a war. What happened to your family was inexplicable, unprovoked violence that shocked the people in No Name to the core. They're as troubled as you are that the person who did it never was caught."

Dark shadows slipped into her eyes. "I figured everyone would have forgotten about it by now."

"Folks never forget something like that. Bubba is tickled pink to have an opportunity to do something nice for you. 'Some sunlight for Miss Rachel,' he said." Joseph flashed a grin. "In his estimation, it's a worthy cause, and he's more than willing to help me out. I can get everything made for nothing. All I need is a go-ahead from you."

"He actually said that?" Her face fairly glowed. "That it's a worthy cause?"

Joseph searched her eyes and saw the incredulity there. "People haven't stopped caring about you, Rachel."

"I figured they'd all decided I'm crazy."

That, too, but Joseph chose not to go there. "They care about you," he repeated. "Do you remember Sue Ellen, Bubba's wife?"

"Vaguely."

Joseph chuckled. "She's that kind of woman, sort of vague." He held up his hand. "Brown hair, about this tall, a fidgety little lady no wider than a toothpick."

Rachel narrowed her eyes as if to see into the past. "Does she have an eye twitch?"

"That's Sue Ellen. Her and Bubba have to be the most unlikely pair I've ever met, him so big and muscular, and her so itty-bitty. Before I left, she had him and their boy, Eugene, sifting through the scrap iron to find suitable lengths for your doors. I have a feeling she'll ride Bubba's ass until he gets them finished."

Rachel toyed with her collar. An expression of concern suddenly pleated her brow. "What if I can't bring myself to open the back door to let in sunlight? Will it hurt Bubba's feelings, do you think?"

The very fact that she cared about possibly hurting Bubba's feelings told Joseph more about her than she could know. "Nah. He's a tough old fart."

Her cheeks went rosy, and then she laughed. Joseph loved hearing that sound. He had a feeling that levity had been a commodity in short supply for Rachel over the last five years.

"You've a gift with words, Mr. Paxton."

Joseph figured that was her way of telling him he didn't. That was okay. He already knew that talking wasn't his strong suit. "Is that a yes, then?"

She thought about it for a moment and

then nodded. "If nothing else, ironwork over my doors will make me feel safer. I'll have to send the Whites some baked goods by way of thanks. A cake and some cookies, maybe."

"There's a plan," Joseph agreed. "But that's for another day. Tonight you need to get some rest."

Moments later, he heard her bustling about. Curious, he returned to the opening and saw her carrying bedding into the water closet. He almost hated to ask. "What are you doing?"

She emerged from the closet. "Making my bed in the bathtub." At his surprised look, she gestured at the barricade. "I couldn't sleep a wink all last night. I don't feel safe with that hole there."

Joseph thought about reminding her of how difficult it had been for Caitlin to crawl through the opening. "I won't sneak in on you or anything."

"It's not you," she assured him. "Well, maybe it is, just a little. I'm not used to having someone here. But mostly it's just the hole." She lifted her hands. "I can't explain except to say that it's part of my sickness.

Openness terrifies me. That's why I can't go outside."

"What happens when you try?"

She chafed her arms through the sleeves of her shirtwaist. "My heart pounds, and I can't breathe." She pressed the back of her wrist to her forehead, as if the mere thought made her breathless. "If I don't get back inside straightaway, I pass out."

Joseph couldn't imagine it. "What, exactly, are you afraid of out there, Rachel?"

She fixed him with a wide, bewildered gaze. After a long moment, she whispered, "I don't know."

Why, Joseph wondered, was this card game called patience? Frustration would be a better name. On his third fresh hand, he was already losing again. The cards just wouldn't suit up. Maybe it was his shuffling. Too much, too little. Hell, he didn't know. But he was bored to tears, and that was a fact.

For at least the tenth time in as many minutes, he stretched, rubbed the back of his neck, and thought about hitting the sack. Rachel had retired at least two hours ago. Only he wasn't sleepy. Accustomed to long hours of hard, exhausting work, his body hadn't been taxed enough today. All he'd done was take a ride with David and flap his jaw a little. He needed to do physical work and lots of it in order to sleep well at night.

He had just finished dealing a new row of cards when a bloodcurdling scream rent the air. He shot up from the chair like a jack from its box and reached the barricade in two long strides. There was no sign of any disturbance in the still brightly lighted kitchen.

"Rachel?" he called.

Buddy let loose with a volley of shrill barks and leaped through the hole in the barricade.

"Oh, my *God!*" Joseph heard Rachel cry brokenly. "Oh, my *God!*" And then she screamed again.

Joseph couldn't think how anyone might have gotten inside the water closet. He'd been in the dining room ever since Ace and Caitlin left. But something was horribly wrong.

Reacting instinctively, he backed up and gave the already damaged boards of the barricade several jabs with the heel of his boot. Then he started tearing at the wood with his hands. Within seconds, he was inside the kitchen. Buddy was clawing at the water closet door. Joseph ran over to try the knob. *Damn.* It was locked.

"Rachel?"

Between the dog's frantic barks, Joseph could still hear her sobbing.

"Answer me, honey. Are you all right?"

No response. Trapped in indecision, Joseph stood there for a moment. But then she whimpered again. He put his shoulder to the door. *Shit.* Tried again.

"Stop it! *Stop* it, *please!*" she cried.

Somebody was in there, Joseph thought. He took a step back and threw himself at the door, putting every ounce of his strength behind his weight.

## Chapter Eight

With one more thrust of his shoulder, Joseph heard the door casing split. He threw himself at the panel of wood one more time, and the door burst open.

Swathed in another white gown, her thick night braid falling forward over one breast, Rachel huddled in the bathtub, back to the spigots, her eyes huge as she stared up at him. In so small an enclosure, the single candle, set on a small parlor table in the corner, made the room as bright as day. Joseph scanned the area, saw no one, and relaxed his fists. Buddy leaped into the tub and began sniffing Rachel, as though to check for injuries.

"What?" Joseph asked. "You were screaming. What's wrong?"

Another whimper erupted from her. "N-night—m-mare," she choked out.

All that ruckus over a *dream*? Joseph

could scarcely believe his ears. "I thought someone was in here."

She shook her head wildly and pushed the dog's nose away from her face. "Only a n-nightmare."

Joseph turned to assess the damage. He'd flat torn the hell out of the water closet door. The entire casing had come loose, the top rail dangling. He didn't want to think what her barricade must look like. Easing his head out the doorway, he scanned the debris and said, "Well, shit."

"I'm s-sorry. I h-have bad d-dreams."

He raked a hand through his hair. "They must be all-fired awful." He glanced back at her. "What the hell did you dream about?"

She wrapped her arms around Buddy and pressed her face into his fur. "I'm not sure," she confessed raggedly.

If that didn't cap the climax. How could anyone scream that loud when she wasn't even sure what she was screaming about? Joseph felt his temper rising and tried to calm down. She'd scared the bejesus out of him, and after a bad fright, he always got fighting mad for a bit. That didn't give him license to take it out on her.

He left the water closet to assess the

damage to her barricade. "Well, that's catawamptiously broken all to pieces."

He heard movement behind him. Then a faint, "Oh, dear *heavens*, what have you *done*?"

The panic in her voice gave Joseph a really bad feeling, and when he turned to her, he forgot all about being pissed off. Her face had lost all color. Her eyes glowed like huge, wet ink splotches on a stark white sheet. Lantern light ignited the recalcitrant curls that had escaped her braid, the golden tendrils creating a nimbus around her head. Buddy paced in nervous circles around her, as if he sensed something was very wrong.

Even as Joseph watched, Rachel's chest started to catch. Her gaze still fixed on the mess he'd made of her barricade, she pressed a hand to the base of her throat.

"With a little bit of fixing, it'll be good as new. I promise."

Her lips were turning blue.

"You're not outside," he cajoled as he moved toward her. Waving a hand, he said, "Rachel? Honey, look at me." But her gaze remained fixed on the scattered boards behind him. "It's still only a hole, just a slightly bigger one than you had a few minutes ago.

That's nothing to panic over. I'm here. No one can hurt you."

A horrible rasping whine came up from deep inside her, and her eyes went buggy, like someone choking on a chunk of meat. She extended one slender hand, her fingers curled like claws. Joseph could see that she honestly couldn't breathe. This was bad. This was really, *really* bad. And he had no idea in hell what to do.

For want of anything else, he hollered at the dog to shut up. A lot of good that did. Buddy just barked more insistently, as if imploring Joseph to fix things. Joseph wished he knew how.

When he got within arm's reach of her, Rachel latched on to the front of his shirt, her fingernails scoring his skin through the cloth. Then her knees buckled.

"Christ." It was more a prayer than a curse.

"Sweet Christ," he said for good measure as he barely managed to catch her from falling. Feeling panicked himself, he scooped her up in his arms and hurried into the water closet. "You're safe, Rachel. See? Walls all around."

He sat on the commode seat, putting her

back to the doorway so she couldn't see the damaged framework. To his surprise, she hooked both arms around his neck, buried her face against his shoulder, and pressed rigidly against him, still struggling to breathe. Acutely aware of her feminine softness and warmth, Joseph hesitated to slip his arms around her. But then she shivered, and he instinctively embraced her, determined to ignore the reaction of his body and stay focused on her need to be soothed and comforted. Buddy whined and came to rest his chin on her knees.

"No worries," he whispered fiercely. "You've got me, and I'm a whole lot better than a wall. Trust me when I say no one will get through me, not with a shotgun or any other damned thing."

Joseph felt her lungs expand and took heart. He had never been one to blow his own trumpet, but sometimes necessity dictated. She desperately needed to feel safe.

Holding her tightly, he rubbed her back and kept talking. "Remember asking me last night if I'm fast with a gun?" All he got as a response was a labored whistle. "I was afraid to tell you the truth for fear you'd go into hysterics and swoon from sheer fright, but the truth is, I'm very fast." She took another breath. Joseph searched his brain for something more to say. "From the time I was about twelve, Ace insisted that I had to be good with a gun and made me practice every day. Practice makes perfect, as the old saying goes. After nineteen years of practicing, I'm so fast now that you can barely see my hand move when I go for my weapon, and I'm deadly accurate, to boot."

He listened to her breathing and gave himself a mental pat on the back. The whistles were coming less often, and he could feel the rise of her chest occasionally, which told him that her lungs were starting to work properly again.

Warming to his subject, Joseph went on to say, "I can go up against five men who are pretty damned fast and be the only one still standing when the smoke clears."

That was no lie. He had actually done it once. It was one of those memories that still haunted his dreams, a moment in time that he couldn't erase, a regret that he would have to live with for the rest of his life. He closed his eyes and buried his face in her hair. It was every bit as soft as it looked. The scent of roses clouded his senses.

"No one is going to hurt you," he whispered gruffly. "I'll kill any man who tries, Rachel." As Joseph made that promise, he realized he meant it with all his heart. In a very short time, this lady had gotten under his skin. Not a good situation. But that was a worry he would chew on later. "You've got my word on it. If anyone comes into this house, he'll be one sorry son of a bitch."

She made a mewling sound and pressed closer, as if trying to melt into him. "My walls," she said tautly. "I *need* my w-walls, Joseph. I know it's c-crazy, but I c-can't live without th-them."

Though he doubted that he would ever really understand it, Joseph was slowly coming to realize that she truly did need her walls. He guessed some things just had to be accepted whether you understood them or not. There was a sickness inside her head, pure and simple. Not insanity, like he'd thought at first, just a strange, obsessive need to have barricades all around her. He likened it to his obsession about never settling down to sleep along the trail without first checking his bedding for snakes. Even when he'd only just shaken out his blankets, he still had to look. Rationally he knew no snake could possibly be there, but reason held no sway. On some level, Rachel knew that her terror of open spaces was irrational as well, but knowing didn't lessen her fear.

When she was breathing evenly again, Joseph loosened his hold on her, but she clung to him like a baby opossum to its mother. "I thought I might see about fixing your barricade," he whispered. "Where do you keep your hammer and nails?"

"No, *no*. Please don't leave me."

Joseph heard her breath hitch again. He hurried to say, "I won't leave you, honey. A team of wild horses couldn't drag me away. I just need to fix your barricade, is all."

"No boards," she squeaked. "We have no boards."

When a woman couldn't breathe for panic, Joseph could get very creative. He would find something to cover that damned archway even if it meant ripping up floorboards in another room of the house.

Only Rachel wouldn't turn loose of his neck. At the mere thought of his leaving her, she was starting to grab for breath again. In all his days, he'd never seen the like. All of this over a hole in wall? What was it like when she stepped outside? Joseph decided he didn't want to know.

"I won't leave you," he assured her softly. "I'm here, I'm staying. Just calm down, Rachel."

It occurred to Joseph that he might be asking more of her than she could give. Buddy chose that moment to whine and nudge her leg.

"You've got Buddy worried about you," he observed. "He can't figure out what the problem is. Why do you feel afraid when you've got a sterling watchdog like him on duty?"

"Is he a g-good watchdog?" she asked.

Joseph considered the dog's worried face. He guessed Buddy was shaping up to be a fairly good watchdog. He just needed another year of maturity to make him more dependable. As it was, he sometimes grew too interested in food or playing to keep a really sharp eye on his surroundings, and when he fell asleep, he went completely off duty.

"He's the best," Joseph replied.

Hell, if he could brag on himself, he could brag on his dog. In Joseph's opinion, Buddy was the best at just about everything, watching out for danger included. He was just a little young yet. In a few more months, his talents would really start to shine.

"He has hearing like you wouldn't believe." That much was absolutely true. If Joseph touched the cornbread pan to grab a quick snack, the dog came running from any room in the house. "And, boy, howdy, does he raise sand when strangers come around." Sometimes Joseph still had to alert the silly mutt that strangers were approaching, but that was beside the point. "And he's loyal to a fault." Except around golden-haired ladies with big, frightened blue eyes who made stew that smelled too wonderful to resist. Then the dog was a turncoat.

Joseph's spine was starting to ache. He wondered how long she might cling to his neck. Surely not all night. Then again, maybe so. That's what a man got for bragging, he guessed: a woman who counted on him to protect her.

Evidently her muscles were getting cricks in them, too. She squirmed on his lap to get more comfortable. *Uh-oh.* Joseph stared at a curl poking up in front of his nose. Now that she was breathing okay again, a certain part of him, which he'd named Old Glory in puberty, was starting to notice all that warm softness. *This won't do,* Joseph thought. But he couldn't think of a way to rectify the situation. Her butt felt powerful good, and Old Glory had never heeded a single thought in Joseph's head. Nope, Old Glory just did his own thing, and sometimes, like now, that could be pretty damned embarrassing.

He felt Rachel stiffen and knew she felt the hardness. Given the way she'd lived the last five years, Joseph fleetingly hoped that she wouldn't realize the significance. Fat chance. There were some things a female instinctively understood, and a flagstaff poking her in the butt was one of them.

Her head came up, and Joseph found himself being pinned by an alarmed blue gaze. He couldn't think what to say, but, true to form, he opened his mouth anyway. "Don't let that worry you. Old Glory just stands at attention sometimes." Like *now,* with soft, warm, feminine flesh melting all around him. "In my younger years, I let him influence most of my decisions. Those days are gone forever. I finally figured out that he's got a nose for trouble, and I never pay him any mind."

Her cheeks went bright pink. Joseph was

glad to see some color come back to her face, whatever the cause.

"Maybe I should move."

She scrambled off his lap and back into the tub. On the one hand, Joseph was glad to be able to stretch and get the crick out of his spine, but he wasn't pleased to see her gaze shift to the doorway. She locked her arms around her knees, her fingers interlaced and clenched so tightly that her knuckles glowed white. Then she jumped.

"Did you hear that?"

Joseph tipped his head. "Hear what?"

"*That.*"

He listened again and heard only the wind buffeting the house, but the creaks and groans clearly terrified her. "It's just the house settling."

"No, no." Her pupils went large, the blackness almost eclipsing her blue irises. "A footstep," she whispered. "I just heard a footstep."

Buddy whined.

"There, you see?" she said. "He hears it, too."

Buddy was reacting to the fear in her, plain and simple. Animals could smell it. "It's nothing, honey, just an old house shifting in the wind."

She went quiet, but Joseph could tell that she hadn't relaxed a whit. He found himself wishing he had some of Doc's laudanum. That would relax her. As things stood, it promised to be a mighty long night, and she needed some rest.

A sudden thought occurred to him. "Buddy," he said, "go get my saddlebags."

Fetching the saddlebags was a trick that Buddy had learned out on the trail, a fairly easy one for Joseph to teach him, actually, because the dog knew all their food was in one of the pouches. The shepherd was nothing if not accommodating when it came to getting his treats. He sped off for the dining room.

It took Buddy an uncommonly long while to drag the bags back to the water closet. Joseph figured that the leather probably had gotten hung up in the archway where a few broken boards still protruded.

"Good boy!" Joseph said warmly when the shepherd reappeared, tugging the saddlebags behind him. "First things first." Joseph opened the side pouch, which he had replenished with rations, and pulled out two pieces of jerky. "There you go, partner."

Eyeing Rachel, Joseph opened another bag, found what he sought, and drew it out. Pulling the cork with his teeth, he took a swig, wiped his mouth with his shirtsleeve, and then passed the jug to his charge.

"What's this?" she asked as she grasped the bottle in a shaky hand.

"Ne'er may care," he said with a grin. "A remedy to cure what ails you. Have a snort."

She sniffed the contents and wrinkled her nose. "It smells like whiskey."

"I like 'ne'er may care' better, but whiskey's another name. Bottom's up."

She pushed the jug back at him. Joseph held her gaze and slowly shook his head. "Not an option, darlin'. You're as jumpy as a long-tailed cat in a room full of rockers. The way I see it, we've got two choices. I can go repair that barricade"—he paused and arched an eyebrow at her—"or you can put a brick in your hat and calm down."

She looked back at the jug. "You expect me to become intoxicated?" she asked in a scandalized voice.

"Think of it as getting happy."

"Ladies do not overindulge, Mr. Paxton."

"My name's Joseph, and sure they do when the circumstances call for it. For tonight, think of it as a medicinal remedy. With a few swigs of that under your belt, you won't care if every wall in the place blows down."

"Precisely why I don't choose to obliterate my good sense with drink."

Joseph pushed to his feet. "I reckon I'll see what I can do with that archway, then."

She gave him a glare, put the jug to her lips, and took two dainty swallows. Then she gasped, her eyes went watery, and she started whacking her chest.

"It'll pass," Joseph assured her. "The next swallow will go down like warm honey."

She eyed the jug askance. "I don't care to have any more," she said thinly.

Joseph leaned down to get nose to nose with her. "You'll drink that whiskey or let me go out there to fix the hole. Your choice. Your eyes look like they've bled onto your cheeks. You have to get some sleep."

She took another gulp of the whiskey. "How much do I have to drink?"

Joseph resumed his perch on the toilet seat. "That'll do for the moment."

She rolled her eyes and made a face.

"*Nothing,* not whiskey or anything else, will calm my nerves about that hole."

Joseph had a double eagle in his pocket that said otherwise, but he just shrugged, checked his watch, and winked at her. Holding the neck of the jug clenched in one fist, she remained in a tense huddle, one arm locked around her knees. Every time the house creaked, she wiggled like a Mexican jumping bean.

He liked her nightdress. It was different from the one last night, still a Mother Hubbard but trimmed with lace over the front and at the cuffs. With her knees drawn to her chest, the hem rode high on her shins, revealing shapely calves, trim ankles, and dainty feet, tipped by ten shell pink toes. In all his days, Joseph had never clapped eyes on such tiny toes.

When five minutes had passed, he asked, "How you feelin'?"

She jumped at the mere sound of his voice. "*Nervous.* It won't work, I tell you."

"Try three more swigs."

She lipped the bottle.

"Not sips, sweetheart, *swigs.* By definition, that means big swallows."

He saw her throat working, counted the

times her Adam's apple bobbed, and then watched her shudder down the burn. As she settled the jug beside her, Joseph noticed that her fingers limply encircled the neck now. That told him she was starting to relax.

"Now three more," he urged.

She narrowed an eye at him but obediently tipped the jug and took three more gulps. When she came up for air, her cheeks were flagged apple red. She swiped at her mouth with the sleeve of her gown. "Goodness, me."

Joseph grinned. "Feelin' any better yet?"

She fanned her face. "Is it hot in here to you? I'm stifling."

He couldn't very well open a window to let in fresh air. "It'll pass." At least she wasn't listening to the house settle now. "Here in a bit, you'll feel fine as a frog hair."

"Fine as a what?"

"A frog hair. And that's pretty damned fine."

She startled him by pushing suddenly to her feet. Grasping the front of the gown in both hands, she fanned the cloth. "I'm stifling, I say."

When she exited the tub, Joseph gave her a wondering look. "What are you doing?"

She bent over the sink, turned on the tap, and cupped cool water to her cheeks. When she groped for a towel, he tugged one from the rack and handed it to her. "Thank you," she mumbled into the linen. When she lifted her head, she added. "That's better."

"Good." She looked bright eyed and bushy tailed, which wasn't the effect Joseph had been hoping for. "You ever played poker?" he asked.

"Never."

"You aren't fixing to say that ladies don't play cards, are you? Caitlin does, and she beats Ace's socks off."

"She does?"

Joseph pushed up from the toilet. "Will you be all right while I run get my cards?"

She frowned up at him. "Where are they?"

The very fact that she would consider letting him leave the water closet told Joseph that the whiskey had soothed her nerves some. "On the dining room table."

"Will you hurry back?"

Joseph gave her a mock salute. "Yes, ma'am."

Within seconds he had returned with the cards. Rachel was back in the tub. She wiped her mouth and corked the jug before looking up at him. "It doesn't taste so bad after a while."

*Uh-oh.* Joseph retrieved the bottle and gave it a shake to check the level. He wanted her relaxed, not pie-eyed. He sat on the commode seat to shuffle on his knee. *Problem.* The rolled edge of the tub wouldn't hold the cards. Joseph eyed the interior.

"Is there room enough in there for you to sit at one end and me at the other if we cross our legs?"

She scooted around with her back to the faucets again. Joseph toed off his boots and crawled in, cards in hand. "I can sit at that end if you like."

"I'm fine."

He handed her the pillow. "Use this to cushion your spine."

He sat cross-legged facing her and settled back. "Okay," he said. "We'll start with five-card draw. It's a pretty simple game." Buddy reared up, hooking his white paws over the edge of the bathtub to eye them. After a moment, he gave a disheartened sigh and curled up on the floor. The dog knew it was time to sleep when he saw his master with playing cards in his hand.

Joseph began explaining the rules. A few sentences in, his student yawned. "You getting sleepy?"

She blinked and sat up straighter. "No, no, I'm fine. With that huge hole in my barricade, I shan't sleep a wink, I assure you."

He dealt the first hand of cards.

She gave him a questioning look. "I pair up the cards, you say?"

Joseph nodded.

"What do you do when you've got three?"

Joseph narrowed an eye at her. "Three what?"

"Three of the same card."

Three of a kind beat his two pairs, hands down. His only hope was to deal himself a third king. That wasn't impossible. He'd seen it happen a number of times. "You keep the three cards and discard the other two," he explained.

"Even if the other two make a pair?"

Joseph gave her another hard look. "You're funning me, right?"

She turned her hand so he could see it. Three aces and two tens. "I'll be a bungtown copper. That's a full house."

She smiled brightly. "Is that good?"

Joseph groaned and bunched that deal. "Beginner's luck," he assured her. "A full house, dealt cold? Never happen again."

Two hands later, Joseph was leaning forward over his crossed ankles, enjoying himself as he hadn't in weeks. "We need something to bet." He studied his cards and bit back a smile. A straight was surely better than anything she had. "It just doesn't feel right without a pot to win."

"I can't afford to gamble with money."

"How about tokens?" Joseph thought for a moment. "You got any hairpins?"

She laid her cards facedown between them and struggled to her feet, treating Joseph to a delightful glimpse of bare thigh when her nightgown rode up. She stepped from the tub to open a cabinet over the sink and returned with a tin of hairpins. Joseph doled out twenty to each of them and schooled her in the fine art of betting. She caught on fast.

"I'll meet your hairpin and raise you"—she pursed her lips as she studied her cards—"two, no, three."

Joseph kept his face expressionless as he eyed his straight. He tossed out three more hairpins. "Call."

With a flick of her wrist, she showed him her hand. Joseph gaped. When he finally found his voice, he said, "A royal flush?"

"Is that good?" she asked innocently.

The question told Joseph he'd been hood-winked, good and proper. "If you didn't know it was good, why'd you raise me three?"

Her dark lashes swept low, the tips gleaming golden in the candlelight.

"You've played before," he accused.

Her cheek dimpled in an impish grin. "Ma wouldn't let Pa gamble at the saloon, so he taught me how."

"I'll be." He shook his head as he watched her take the ante. "You're having the mother of all lucky streaks."

She giggled, a light tinkling sound that Joseph could have listened to all night. "Luck or know-how. It all depends on if you're winning or losing."

She looked too sweet for words in that lacy Mother Hubbard nightdress with her beautiful hair coming loose from the braid and forming shimmering ringlets around her slender shoulders. Joseph refused to allow his gaze to dip lower, even though he'd done his share of looking earlier. She was all-to-pieces beautiful, make no mistake. And she played poker. He couldn't believe it when she shuffled the cards with a flick of her wrists and started dealing like a pro. He just flat couldn't believe it.

He picked up his cards, arranged his hand, and said, "I'm in for one."

He tossed out a hairpin and discarded. She anteed and stayed, her lips curved in a smug little smile as she dealt him replacements. Joseph perused his hand. He had a full house, kings over deuces. If she had better, he'd gargle salt water while he whistled "Dixie."

He raised the bet by two. She paid to see his hand and raised her delicate brows. "Very nice." Her cheek dimpled again. "But it doesn't beat aces over sevens."

"No way." Joseph stared at the cards she laid down, faceup. "No *way*."

She giggled and collected the ante. "Your deal. Maybe we should change the game."

"Seven-card stud," he suggested.

In truth, Joseph didn't really care if he won. He just enjoyed playing. It was especially pleasurable when his opponent was so lovely to look at. *The perfect woman,* he thought. *Beautiful, a dog lover, a poker player, and a fabulous cook, to boot.* It just didn't get any better than that.

A prickle of alarm worked its way up his spine. He was coming to like this lady a little too much for comfort. In his recollection, he couldn't recall ever having felt this attracted to a female.

She reached over the side of the tub to retrieve the whiskey jug. The cork departed from the neck with a hollow *thunk*. She thrust the bottle at him. "Maybe you need a drink to change your luck."

Joseph guessed he could have one more swig. He didn't want to drink too much for fear that he would sleep too soundly. As unfounded as most of Rachel's fears seemed to be, she hadn't imagined that bullet in Darby's back. He needed to be on guard, just in case the old foreman had it right about her life being in danger.

After taking a swallow of whiskey, he handed back the jug and began the deal. When she saw her first two cards, she burst out laughing and bet three hairpins. All Joseph had so far was a four and a five. Even so, he didn't want to fold. He anteed and dealt her a card faceup.

"An ace?" She grinned and rolled her eyes. "Definitely worth another three tokens."

Joseph's pile of hairpins was dwindling at an alarming rate. She was flat kicking his butt. *His dream woman.* For reasons beyond him, the thought no longer alarmed him. When a man met a woman who appealed to him on so many levels, why run?

A few minutes later, Rachel had most of his hairpins, and her lashes were starting to droop.

"You're exhausted," he said. "We need to quit and get some shut-eye."

"Naturally you'd say that when I'm the biggest toad in the puddle."

Joseph just grinned. "You are, no doubt about it. How about a silly game to cap off the evening? You ever played Injun?"

She nodded. "One card each, on your forehead, face out, without looking?"

Joseph nodded, shuffled the cards, and dealt one to each of them. Without turning hers over to look, she pressed it to her forehead. It took all of Joseph's self-control not to laugh. She had a five. To his surprise, she started giggling so hard when she saw his card that tears came to her eyes. Joseph figured he was holding something pretty pathetic. But what were the odds that it could be worse than a five?

He tossed all his remaining hairpins onto the blanket between them. Still laughing, she met his bet. Then they lowered the cards.

"I don't believe it!" he cried. "No way.

You've won every hand so far. I dealt myself a *three*?"

Joseph went to collect his bedding. When he returned to the water closet, his poker opponent's head was lolling. When she heard his footsteps, she jerked erect.

"I think you need to stretch out, darlin'. The biggest toad in this puddle is going under."

"Don't leave me," she murmured as she turned in the tub, punched up the pillow, and drew the blankets over her legs. "If I wake up and you're gone, my heart will stop, I swear."

Joseph shook out his bedroll. "I'll be right here beside you, close enough for you to reach out and touch me. No worries."

She snuggled up to the pillow. "Promise?"

"Absolutely," he assured her. "Buddy and I will be right next to you."

Enough lantern light poured in from the kitchen to dimly illuminate the room. Joseph snuffed out the candle and settled on his pallet, Buddy curled up under the blanket beside him. Within seconds, he heard a faint, feminine snore and smiled to himself. The biggest toad in the puddle was out like a light.

# Chapter Nine

When Rachel first opened her eyes the next morning, ice picks stabbed her pupils and it felt as if someone were doing the double shuffle on her skull. Grasping the edge of the tub, she pulled herself up and slumped forward over her knees.

"Oh, *God*."

"Good morning, sunshine."

Joseph's cheerful baritone sent shards of pain lancing through her brain. She held up a hand to silence him. "Whisper. Please. It hurts." Even her own voice hurt. "Oh, God, help me. I'm dying."

"Nah," he assured her in a softer voice. "It's just the Old Orchard, taking its revenge. Drink this. It'll chirk you right up."

Rachel carefully turned her head and squinted one eye at the cup he proffered. "What is it?"

"My remedy. Mostly coffee, with a few

other ingredients guaranteed to make you feel better in about a half hour."

With shaky hands, Rachel accepted the cup and took a gulp of the contents. She sent him a questioning look. "It has whiskey in it."

"That it does. Nothing like some hair of the dog that bit you to set things right."

In thirty minutes, Rachel did feel some better. After leaning the broken water closet door against the shattered frame to afford herself some privacy, she managed to get dressed. Then she moved the broken door to one side to poke her head out the opening to survey the kitchen. To her surprise, the archway doorway was covered with something. The yawning hole that had sent her into a spell last night was gone.

"What is that over the archway?" she asked.

"The dining room table. I stood it on end and walked it over. By way of a barricade, it has its drawbacks, but it'll work for now."

Her skin still crawled as she emerged from the water closet. Joseph motioned for her to sit at the kitchen table and shoved a plate in front of her. She stared dismally at the two pieces of crisp, buttered toast.

"I can't possibly eat."

"You need to. It's part of the cure." He sat down across from her, looking so cheerful that she wanted to shoot him. "Just break off little pieces and wash them down with coffee. You'll feel better with some food in your stomach."

A sound in the other room made her jump. Joseph followed her nervous gaze. "It's nothing. Just the house creaking again. Let me worry about guarding the hole. You eat."

"How do you know eating will make me feel better?"

He winked and grinned. "Experience, darlin'. I've had a few too many tipples in my time."

Rachel broke off a tiny piece of bread and swallowed it with coffee. Her eyebrows shot up. "There's whiskey in this cup, too."

"Like I said, some hair of the dog. It'll help. Trust me."

In that moment, when Rachel looked into his twinkling blue eyes, she realized just how much she *had* come to trust him. If someone had told her two days ago that she'd soon be sitting at the table with a huge hole yawning in her barricade, counting on a stranger to protect her, she would have laughed. Only now it didn't seem ludicrous at all.

When she thought back, she knew she hadn't known Joseph long enough to feel this safe with him, and yet she did. His presence soothed her in some inexplicable way, filling her with a sense of well-being and security that she hadn't felt in a very long while. Even the sound of his voice was a balm to her frazzled nerves.

He gave her damaged barricade a long look, and then he drew out his watch to check the time. "Right about now, your horses are wanting out in the paddock, your cows are bawling to be milked, the hens are demanding breakfast, and that sow is looking in her trough, hoping to see some slop. If Ace comes over today, it'll be later, probably well after noon. I'll have to do the chores myself if they're going to get done."

Just the thought of being left alone made Rachel's heart catch. Evidently he saw the panic in her eyes. "I'm thinking about rigging up a door for your barricade before I leave the house. Would that make you feel any better?"

From the corner of her eye, Rachel could see the archway yawning like a giant mouth waiting to swallow her. The table had been a nice gesture on Joseph's part, but if he had been able to set it there, someone else could just as easily move it. "Yes. Yes, a door would make me feel much better."

"I'm thinking about borrowing an interior door from another room." He let his chair drop forward. "Here's the thing, though. In order to borrow a door and make it work, I'll need the whole unit, doorframe and all. It's liable to do a little damage when I start prying stuff loose."

It had been years since Rachel had ventured into any of the other rooms. A smidgen of damage elsewhere wouldn't matter a whit to her. "That's fine. I don't really care about the rest of the house."

"You sure? Sentimental meaning, and all that. If you ever get well, every nook and cranny will hold memories for you."

Remembering only brought her pain, and Rachel had given up on ever getting well. "I don't think I can handle your going outside unless something is over the hole."

"All right, then." He smiled and shrugged. "I'll need that hammer of yours, all the nails you have on hand, and a screwdriver if you've got one."

Rachel pushed up from the chair. Moments later, she returned to the table with an assortment of tools and a box of nails. Joseph pushed to his feet and went to fetch her shotgun. As he walked back to the table, he motioned to the chair she had vacated.

"I want you to sit right there while I'm gone," he said. "I'll be just up the hall, mind you, but sit right there, all the same."

As she lowered herself onto the chair seat, he handed her the shotgun. "You've got both barrels loaded, right?"

She nodded.

"Well, then. If anyone appears in that archway, point and fire." He leaned down to fix her with a twinkling gaze. "Just don't get spooked and shoot me."

Buddy squeezed through the gap between the lower end of the table and the wall just then. He bounded happily across the kitchen, smelling of fresh air, grass, and oak leaves, scents that Rachel had nearly forgotten. Joseph bent to pat the dog's head.

"Finished with your morning run, fella?" He pointed at the floor. "Sit."

Buddy promptly dropped to his haunches beside Rachel.

"You *stay*," Joseph said firmly. "No deciding different and following me this time, you hear? I want you to stay with Rachel."

Buddy flopped onto his belly, crossed his paws over his eyes, and whined mournfully.

The dog's antics brought a reluctant smile to Rachel's lips. She sent a nervous look at the archway.

"Listen to me." Joseph planted his hands on his knees, once again leaning forward to get nose to nose with her. "I came through your parents' bedroom window when I broke into the house. If I borrow their bedroom door, I'll be working between you and the only window in the house that isn't boarded up. No one will be able to get past me to pester you. I'll be just up the hall, only a few steps away."

A lump of dread filled Rachel's throat. She tried her best to focus on his words and be reasonable. But her fear had nothing to do with reason. She wished she knew how to explain that. Only how could she make sense of feelings that she couldn't understand herself? Her barricade was gone.

That was the long and short of it. It was *gone*.

"I'm sorry," she whispered. "I know I'm crazy. You can say it if you want. It won't hurt my feelings or anything."

He took the shotgun and put it on the floor. Then, with a weary sigh, he hunkered down in front of her. Taking her hands in his, he said, "What's crazy and what isn't? What's normal and what isn't? We all have a phobia about something."

"I'm sure you don't."

"Of course I do."

"What is it then?" she challenged.

His full mouth quirked at one corner. "For starters, I'm afraid of ghosts."

Rachel half expected him to suddenly snap his fingers, point at her, and say, "Gotcha." Then she searched his face and realized he was actually serious.

"Ghosts?" she echoed, the revelation so astounding that she forgot about the hole for a moment. *"Ghosts?"*

He nodded. "It's loony, I know. Most folks don't even believe in ghosts." He narrowed an eye at her. "Tell anyone, and I'll swear you're lying. I've never told anybody, not even my brothers."

A strange ache filled Rachel's chest. "Why are you telling me?"

His lips twitched again. "Now there's a question. Maybe because I know you'll understand and not laugh. And maybe because I think you need to know. You're not the only person on earth with irrational fears, Rachel. If that makes you insane, then all of us are off our rockers."

Tears sprang to her eyes.

"Don't cry. I'm trying to make you feel better, not worse."

Rachel smiled through her tears, for he had made her feel better. Joseph Paxton, afraid of ghosts. Imagine that. "I'm not crying."

He tugged a hand free to thumb moisture from her cheek. "If that's not a tear, what is it?"

"Maybe the roof sprang a leak." She dragged in a shaky breath. "Ghosts? I never would have thought it."

He shrugged. "I believe in God, and I believe in eternal life. How can I believe in those things and rule out the possibility of ghosts? To my way of thinking, I can't. That being the case, if there are good people and bad people in this life, it stands to reason that there must be good spooks and bad spooks in the next life, and it also makes sense that the truly bad spooks may remain true to character, not following any of the rules. So what if they just up and decide not to go to hell? I sure wouldn't if I could weasel out of it."

"So you believe the really bad spooks who are destined for hell sometimes stay here?"

His sun-burnished face flushed to a deep umber. "Yes, and the thought scares the be-jesus out of me."

Rachel couldn't feature Joseph as being afraid of anything. "Truly?"

He nodded. "I'm fine with things I can see. I've got my fists and my gun. I'm confident that I can defend myself. But how can you protect yourself from things you can't see or hit or shoot?"

Rachel totally understood that feeling. "I'm afraid of things I can't see, too," she whispered. She glanced past him at the hole and squeezed his fingers with all her strength. "Things I can't even name."

"I know," he said softly.

Her gaze jerked back to his. He was smiling sadly. As she searched his dark face, she realized that he understood her terror in a way that no one else ever had. Darby accepted her strangeness because he loved her, and he'd stood by her through all the bad times for the same reason. But he'd never really understood. More tears sprang to her eyes, the shimmers nearly blinding her.

"I know it's only a hole," she squeezed out. "In the old days, I walked through that archway dozens of times a day. I don't know why it frightens me so to have it uncovered now. It just does."

He brushed the wetness from her cheeks. "That's good enough for me."

It wasn't good enough for Rachel. She wanted to be well again. "When I was a girl, my absolute favorite pastime was to lie under an oak tree on a sunny afternoon and stare at the fluttering leaves until I fell asleep. I watched the clouds drift by, and I fancied sometimes that there were whispers in the wind. And I loved listening to the birds sing. Denver used to lie beside me, with his nose on my shoulder, and snore."

Joseph watched the expressions that drifted across her pretty face, and his heart ached because he could almost feel her yearning. "Denver, your dog?"

She nodded, tears glittering like diamonds on her pale cheeks. "He was my very best friend in the whole world." Her eyes fell closed. "In the end, he died for me." Her voice went thin and taut. "The man was on horseback, and Denver jumped up and sank his teeth into his leg. He wouldn't turn loose, so the man drew his revolver and shot him right between the eyes."

Joseph's insides went suddenly quiet—so quiet that even his heart seemed to stop beating for a second. "You remember that?"

Her lashes lifted. "I've seen it in my nightmares. Not a memory, exactly. Just a picture that moves through my mind and brings me awake, screaming." Her chin quivered. "There are so many horrible pictures, Joseph. But they just flash and then go black."

Joseph squeezed her hands. "You ever get a flash of the bastard's face?"

Her already pale countenance lost all remaining color. "No, I never see that part of him, and the things I do see don't string together." A distant look entered her eyes. "It's like my brain has erased his face."

Joseph wondered if she had known the man. He couldn't imagine anything more horrible than to look into the face of a friend who'd suddenly peeled away his mask to reveal a monster. His stomach turned a slow revolution. If that was the case—if Rachel had known the killer and counted him as a friend or trusted neighbor—was it any wonder that everything once dear and familiar now terrified her?

Holding both her hands in one of his, he pushed forward on his toes, grasped her chin, and trailed his lips lightly over her tear-streaked cheek. He meant to end it there, just a comforting show of affection, but somehow his mouth found hers, and what had begun innocently somehow became a searching kiss. Again that strange quietness filled him, as if everything within his body had gone still in anticipation.

Despite the saltiness of her tears, she had the sweetest mouth he'd ever tasted. It was also the most inexperienced mouth that he'd ever kissed. *Careful, Joseph.* After only a taste, he greedily wanted to plunder every tempting recess. Only the training of a lifetime held him back. This was her first kiss. He knew that, both rationally and instinctively. Yet she surrendered completely, her lips soft, slightly parted, and offering no resistance.

When Joseph drew away, she blinked and swayed on the chair. "Oh, my."

He almost chuckled. Not a wise move. He didn't want her to think he was laughing at her. "I'm sorry. I probably shouldn't have done that."

Her eyes slowly came into focus, the expression in them dreamy and slightly confused. "Why? It was very nice."

Better than nice, Joseph thought, and therein lay the problem. She wasn't a sporting woman at the Golden Slipper who flitted from man to man. She was likely to take a kiss very seriously, possibly even as some kind of commitment from him. He didn't want to give her the wrong impression and end up hurting her. She had experienced enough hurt in her young life.

"Yes, it was nice," he agreed. "Nice enough to get us both into trouble." He leaned in to kiss the end of her nose. "You're a lady from the tips of your toes to the top of your head, Rachel Hollister, and a lady isn't for the likes of me."

She tipped her head to study him questioningly. "Why is that?"

"Because I'm not the marrying kind." Joseph pushed to his feet. "You'll do well to remember that." He walked across the room to the archway. "I take my pleasure where I find it, and then I move on. I don't have it in me to love just one woman. I'm more what you might call a buffet man."

"A what?"

Joseph strained to shift the table. "A buffet man. I like to sample all the dishes and don't have a taste for any particular one." He angled her a warning look. "I love first helpings, but I rarely go back for seconds. I'm the same way with women. You understand what I'm saying?"

"That you're a scoundrel?"

He grinned. "There you go, a scoundrel. When it comes to kissing and that kind of thing, don't trust me any farther than you can throw me. Are we clear?"

"Perfectly clear. What are you doing?"

He managed to scoot the table off to one side so he could squeeze through. "No worries." He returned to collect the tools. "I'll move it back to cover the opening while I'm gone."

The noise that filtered into the kitchen told Rachel that Joseph was making grand headway on removing the door and casing from her parents' bedroom. She sat on the chair, where he had told her to sit, staring dry eyed at the upturned table, which hadn't budged from the archway. Buddy lay beside her, snoozing. She took comfort from the fact that he seemed to be bored with the whole business.

Finally, she heard footsteps returning to the dining room, interspersed by crashes, bangs, and muffled curses. "Rachel?" he called. "I'm gonna move the table now. Don't get scared and shoot, all right? It's just me."

"Me who?" she couldn't resist asking.

Long silence. "It's me, Joseph." Another silence. "Are you having me on?"

Rachel smiled. "I am, I suppose."

"Will miracles never cease? The woman cracked a joke."

The table grated across the floor, and a moment later Joseph's blond head poked around its edge. He flashed her a grin that made her stomach feel all squiggly. "Howdy. Long time, no see."

"Howdy."

He set to work on installing the doorframe, cussing almost constantly under his breath because the measurements of the archway weren't exactly the same as the doorway in her parents' bedroom.

"Can you make it fit?" she asked.

"Not snug," he confessed. "It's gonna be as loose as a fancy woman's nether regions." He froze and shot her a look over his shoulder. "Pardon me. I forgot for a second who I was talking to."

Rachel went back over what he'd said and couldn't make much sense of it. When he saw her bewildered frown, he chuckled, shook his head, and went back to work, muttering under his breath again.

When the door was finally installed, its swinging edge was an inch shy of touching the jam, and the top rail didn't stretch all the way across. It nevertheless provided a barrier. Joseph had hung it to open into the kitchen. He borrowed the niches and pine plank from the pantry door to bar it shut.

The instant the plank fell into place, Rachel let out a sigh of relief. "Thank you, Joseph."

He came to lay the tools on the table. "Better?" he asked.

"Much better." She felt safer now. "I can't tell you how grateful I am. I know it was a bother."

"Not a problem." He glanced at his watch and then tucked it back in his pocket. "Now here's the question. When I get back from doing the chores, are you going to be able to open up for me?"

Rachel thought about it for a long moment. Normally the very idea of opening a door sent her into a panic, but with Joseph standing on the other side, she thought she might be okay. "I think so."

He flashed her a teasing grin. "It'll be a hell of a note if you can't. I'm leaving Buddy here with you." He bent to scratch behind the dog's ears. "He needs to go out every now and again."

Thanks to Joseph's morning-after remedy, Rachel's headache and nausea were completely gone within the hour. With a door in the archway, she felt relaxed enough while he was off doing chores to follow her usual morning routine, emptying the wood safe, stoking the range fire, and starting breakfast, a workingman's meal of bacon, fried potatoes, biscuits, eggs, and gravy.

*A buffet man?* Every time Rachel remembered him telling her that, she grinned. He was far too kind a man to possess an inviolate heart. One day soon, when he least expected it, he would meet a lady who would make him forget all that nonsense about second helpings. She'd seen how good he was with Little Ace, a sure sign that he'd make a wonderful father. She also felt confident that he'd be an equally wonderful husband. He just hadn't found the right woman yet.

Rachel refused to let herself wish that she might be that woman. Her situation didn't lend itself well to getting married and raising a family. *Too bad.* She had truly enjoyed that kiss. His fingertips on her chin had made her skin tingle, leading her to wonder how it might feel if he touched her in other places. *Shocking* places. She had no idea where such thoughts had come from, but come they had, and now she couldn't push them from her mind.

Did two people actually *do* stuff like that? A part of Rachel couldn't imagine it, but another part of her thought maybe so. As a girl, she'd sometimes seen her parents caressing each other when they thought she wasn't watching, and though she'd never seen them touch each other in truly intimate places, thinking back on it now, she could remember their coming close. Her father, as she recalled, had been especially fond of touching, running his hands upward from her mother's waist almost to her bosoms and sometimes cupping her posterior in his palms to pull her hips snugly against him. Her ma had always giggled and given him a playful push, as if she hadn't liked it, but it was obvious that she actually had.

Rachel realized that her hands had gone still. She stared stupidly at the dry biscuit ingredients in the bowl, unable to remember what she'd already added and what she hadn't. *Lands.* There was nothing worse than biscuits made bitter with too much baking powder. Dampening a fingertip, she took a taste, trying to determine if the rising agent had already been added. It was hard to tell. To be on the safe side, she measured more in, stirred industriously, and took another taste. No bitterness. That was a good sign. She could only hope she hadn't used twice as much as needed.

Enough woolgathering! She'd end up ruining the entire meal. With determined concentration, she began cutting in the lard, trying her best to think of nothing but the biscuits. Only a picture of Joseph's face crept into her mind again. At some point over the last two days, she'd come to think that he was extraordinarily handsome in a rugged, sun-burnished way. His large, bladelike nose now seemed perfectly right for his face, and she barely noticed the knot along the bridge anymore. She also found his sky blue eyes to be wonderfully expressive and compelling. And his mouth, ah, she loved his mouth. For a man, he had full, beautifully defined lips, and they were fascinatingly mobile, the corners curving up and dimpling one cheek just before he smiled. They were also delightful to watch when he talked, shimmering softly in the light like polished silk.

Rachel realized that her hands had gone still again, and she sighed with frustration. *Enough.* They were just lips, after all. She had work to do after breakfast. If Joseph would take her homemade goods into town to sell them, she needed to make bread, some butter, and a new batch of cheese to start it aging. Otherwise, she'd find herself with nothing in her cellar to replace the blocks of cheddar that were coming ready to be sold now. Her cheddar cheeses were popular items at Gilpatrick's general store, and she needed the money they brought in.

So that was that. No more daydreaming for her this morning.

Cursing to turn the air blue, Joseph kicked an empty oilcan across the barn. What had he been thinking to kiss her like that? Sweet, innocent, decent young ladies were forbidden fruit. He *knew* that. But he'd gone after her anyway, conscienceless bastard that he was. Afterward, she'd looked at him as if he'd just hung the moon. If he didn't watch his step, he'd find himself with a ring through his nose.

Rachel was a sweetheart, and he had to admit, if only to himself, that he liked just about everything about her. Last night, for a fleeting moment, he'd even considered the possibility that she might be *the* woman. That was dangerous thinking, the kind of thinking that could lead him to make a decision he would come to regret.

No way. He liked his life just fine the way it was, and he meant to keep it that way. No fuss and folderol. No female drawers hung to dry over the edge of his bathtub. No grabbing the wrong soap and coming from the water closet smelling like a whore. No woman harping at him like a shrew when he stayed gone all night. Ha. Ace could have it. Joseph enjoyed his freedom.

From now on, that girl was totally off-limits, he lectured himself as he milked the cows. No more looking through her nightgown when she got between him and the light. No more salivating over the taut tips of her breasts when they pushed against her nightdress. No more doing that eye thing, either. He'd always laughed at men who talked about drowning in a woman's eyes. Now here he was, gazing into blue depths himself like some kind of mindless fool.

The lady spelled "trap" in capital letters. Now that he was away from her, he honestly couldn't think what had gotten into him. He felt sorry for her. Maybe that was it. She hadn't asked for the sorrow that life had dished out to her, and she certainly hadn't asked to live as she did. He couldn't be around her without wishing he could make things better for her.

That was it, he assured himself, as he left the barn with a can of chicken feed. He pitied her, and his feelings were all in a tangle. It had been a spell since he'd gone into town on a Friday night. He needed to visit Lucille again. Or was her name Cora? Damned if he could remember. It wasn't about names, after all, or even about being friends. He had needs that couldn't be ignored, and she took care of them, for a price. It was as simple and as awful as that.

Joseph stopped dead in his tracks. *Awful?* And just where had that thought come from? What was awful about two people scratching each other's itch? Nothing that he could see. So why did he suddenly feel guilty?

Shoving his hand into the can, he started throwing feed with such force that the hens squawked and scattered. *Damn it all, anyhow.* She was messing with his mind, making him find fault with himself, with how he lived his life, and with every other damned thing. Like his house, for instance. He'd liked it just fine before he met her. Now he found himself looking at her rugs and doilies and knickknacks, thinking his own place could use a woman's touch.

What was *that* all about?

# Chapter Ten

Thirty minutes later when Joseph shoved half of a fluffy, buttered biscuit into his mouth and decided it was equal to none, he knew exactly what his problem was. He'd found the perfect woman.

The realization did not make him happy. He didn't want a woman. Well—he *did* want a woman. What red-blooded man *didn't* want a woman? But he didn't want just *one* woman. He liked variety—plump ones, skinny ones, big-breasted ones and little-breasted ones, tall ones and short ones, bubbly ones and somber ones. *Always* plural.

Only when he looked at Rachel, he didn't think about variety. She was so darned pretty and nice. It almost didn't seem right that she also cooked like a dream, played poker, and loved dogs.

The woman was out to get him.

He chewed and glared at her butt. She

was bending over like that on purpose. He knew she was. What woman in her right mind opened an oven door to wash away a few drippings and pushed out her rump like that at a man? Nearly under his nose, give or take a few feet. It was almost an engraved invitation. *Come and get me.* Well, *he* wasn't harkening to the call. Down that path lay marriage, responsibility, and no more Friday nights in town.

He really, *really* needed a night in town. Calving season had kept him at home for going on a month now, and he was as horny as a three-pronged goat. *That* was why her butt looked so good to him, because any woman would tempt him right now.

He pushed another half of a biscuit into his mouth, chomped down, and bit his cheek. Pain radiated. "Damn!"

"Oh, *dear*! What's wrong?" Rachel and her rump raced over to the table. "Did I put in too much baking powder?"

"No, my tooth's just panging." He didn't know where that had come from. But as lies went, it was fair to middling. "The biscuits are fine."

She fixed him with worried blue eyes. He

wondered if she practiced in front of a mirror to look that sweet.

"I've got just the thing for that," she said, and raced off to the water closet. "Oil of Cajeput on cotton wool. I keep a few balls from the apothecary on hand. Every now and again, Darby gets a toothache."

Joseph finished his meal in stony silence. When he'd cleared all but two slices of bacon from his plate, he pushed up from the table, tossed the meat to his dog, and advanced on the sink.

"Just never you mind the dishes," she said. "Sit back down so I can doctor that tooth."

If this wasn't a fine predicament, Joseph didn't know what was. His teeth were fine, but unless he confessed to fibbing, he couldn't very well tell her that. Not knowing what else to do, he sat back down.

She came to hover over him and told him to open his mouth. "Which one is hurting?" she asked.

The scent of roses intoxicated him as she pressed closer and cupped the back of his head with a slender hand. "Naw her," he said. It wasn't easy to talk with his mouth open.

"What?"

One of her breasts was pushing close. He closed his mouth. "I'm not sure."

"Oh, well. That happens sometimes. Open wide, and I'll have a look."

He definitely had an ache now, but it was a long way from his head. Old Glory had gone rock hard and started to throb. He opened his mouth and tipped his head back. She bent to peer in, the pleated front of her shirt-waist grazing his jaw and then the soft, warm weight of her breast coming to rest against his shoulder. God help him, he'd never wanted a woman so badly in his life.

"There it is," she informed him. "Oh, yes, I can see the cavity. You might consider see-ing the dentist, Joseph. It needs to be filled, I think."

His eyebrows arched in surprise, but with her fingers in his mouth, he couldn't speak. A nasty smell filled his nostrils, totally oblit-erating the rose scent. It burned down the back of his throat.

"There you go," she chirped. "Bite down."

He brought his teeth down on the cotton wool, and pain exploded all along his jaw. He came up out of the chair so fast that he almost knocked Rachel over. "Ouch! Oh, *damn*!" He ran a finger into his mouth to scoop out the wool, then ran to the sink and started spitting. "What *is* that shit? *Ouch.* Oh, *damn!*"

"It only hurts for a moment."

Easy for her to say. It wasn't her tooth that was shooting pain clear through her gray matter and out the top of her skull. If he hadn't had a toothache before, he sure as hell did now. "You *knew* it was going to hurt? Why in hell didn't you tell me?" He gingerly prodded the tooth. A cavity? He'd always had perfect teeth. "If that doesn't beat all. I *do* have a cavity back there."

"You really need to keep the wool on it for a few minutes."

Joseph ran some water to rinse his mouth. The pain was finally lessening. "No, thanks. The cure is worse than the toothache."

"It really will help," she insisted.

Free of aches now—in *all* parts of his body—Joseph wiped his mouth on his shirtsleeve and turned to give her a wary look. Old Glory had shriveled up and dived for cover. "It's better already," he assured her.

She beamed a beatific smile. "There, you see? It works for Darby every time."

Accustomed to constant physical activity, Joseph couldn't stand to just sit, so he decided to help Rachel. Over his lifetime, he'd made bread and butter countless times, but he'd never made any kind of cheese.

"This is kind of fun," he said as he minded the large pot of milk heating on the stove while Rachel bustled around him. She had already added a quarter teaspoon of starter to the milk, and here in a bit they would let it ripen while they churned the butter. For now, the milk had to be heated to a certain temperature before she added the rennet to make it curdle. "What'll it taste like when it's done?"

She laughed lightly. "Well, now, it's my hope that it'll taste like cheddar cheese."

He chuckled. "I mean before it ages."

"It's not very good before it ages, just pressed and drained curd that's lightly salted."

Soon Rachel judged the milk to have reached the right temperature, and she added some rennet mixed with a little water. When it was stirred in, they set the pot on the counter by the sink. "It'll have to sit now for about forty-five minutes until the milk breaks clean."

Once again, Joseph found himself with nothing to do but twiddle his thumbs. William Shakespeare had hit the nail on the head, he decided. Dreams were the children of an idle brain. He couldn't keep his eyes off Rachel, and his imagination kept taking him places he didn't want to go. Would she surrender her mouth to him just as completely if he kissed her again? And what would it be like to unfasten that prim little shirtwaist to unveil those soft, full breasts?

In desperation, Joseph reached for the book that lay open on the table. "*The Adventures of Huckleberry Finn?*"

Rachel glanced up from the sink where she was lining a colander with cheesecloth. "Have you read it?"

Since his school days had ended, Joseph seldom read anything unless it pertained to horses, cows, or raising crops. "No, I can't say that I have."

"How about *The Adventures of Tom Sawyer?*"

"Nope."

She went to one of the bookshelves along the water closet wall and returned a moment later with a leather-bound novel. "You first meet Huckleberry in this story." She sat across from him, turned up the lamp wick, and lovingly opened the book, her graceful fingers caressing the pages as if they were old friends. "Let me just read a bit of it to you."

Joseph was glad of anything that might take his mind off Rachel and her tempting curves. Thirty minutes later, he was lost in the tale, envisioning the small town of St. Petersburg along the shore of the Mississippi River and laughing over Tom Sawyer's shenanigans, which frequently resulted in his receiving a licking from his aunt Polly.

"That darned Sid is a terrible tattletale," he remarked.

Rachel smiled and pushed the book toward him. "It's time for me to drain the curds and churn the butter. Why don't you read aloud to me while I work?"

Joseph took the book and rocked back on the chair while he found their place. Soon he was lost in the story again. As he read, he was dimly aware of Rachel bustling around the kitchen or occasionally coming to sit.

As punishment for skipping school to go swimming, Tom had to whitewash the fence around Aunt Polly's house. Only, being the smooth talker that he was, he convinced some neighbor boys to finish the job for him.

Time flew by on swift wings as the story

unfolded. Tom fell wildly in love with a girl named Becky Thatcher, the judge's daughter, and got his heart broken. Then one night, he and Huck sneaked off at midnight to the graveyard to perform a special ritual to cure warts. Convinced that the cemetery was filled with ghosts, the two boys were sore afraid of seeing one.

Joseph chuckled and glanced up at Rachel. "I guess I'm not the only one afraid of spooks."

She grinned. "Keep reading."

Within moments, Joseph's skin had developed goose bumps. Frightened into hiding by approaching voices, the boys accidentally witnessed a trio of grave robbers pilfering a grave. Only soon a fight broke out among the three men, and Tom and Huck witnessed something far worse: a murder. Terrified for their lives, the boys ran. Later they made a pact never to tell anyone of what they'd seen because they were afraid that the murderous Injun Joe might kill them, too.

"This is good," Joseph confessed when he stopped reading to give his voice a rest. "I didn't expect to enjoy it so much."

Rachel worked at the counter, pouring

curds into cloth-lined cheese molds. "I absolutely *love* that book, and *The Adventures of Huckleberry Finn* is even better, I think. Truly Twain's masterpiece."

Joseph went back to reading. A while later, Rachel took another turn as the narrator, and before they knew it, it was time for lunch. While helping to make sandwiches, Joseph marveled aloud over the story. "I haven't been back down south since I was knee-high to a tall grasshopper, but that story makes me feel like I'm actually there."

"Reading is one of my favorite pastimes," she confessed, her cheeks going rosy. "Books bring the world into my kitchen. I can feel the sunlight on my skin, feel the summer breeze in my hair, smell the flowers, and hear the birds sing. Without my books, I truly believe I would shrivel up and die."

Joseph was glad that she had had her books to sustain her, but it saddened him deeply that her only glimpses of the world came to her through the written word. He could tell by her tone that she yearned to feel the sun warm her skin again and that she sorely missed dozens of other pleasures that could only be found outdoors. In that moment, he would have given almost anything to make it possible for her to experience those things again. Sadly, he couldn't think how.

Ace showed up shortly after two that afternoon, ready to stand guard duty while Joseph went to town. Rachel's face fell with disappointment when Ace called through the back door that Caitlin hadn't accompanied him this time.

"We had church this morning, and Caitlin had plans for this afternoon," Ace explained. "She said to tell you that she'll try to come next time."

Joseph slipped out through the archway door. When Rachel had barred it behind him, he exited the house via the broken window to go around back to see his brother. Barking joyously, Buddy and Cleveland met in the side yard and tumbled to the ground in a blur of reddish-gold and white fur. When the dogs regained their feet, they raced away, taking turns nipping at each other's heels and knocking each other down. Joseph saw them sail over a pasture fence and then vanish in the tall grass. Knowing full well that they would return when they'd played themselves out, Joseph didn't bother calling them back.

"Howdy," Ace called from where he sat on the steps. "Nice weather we've got today."

Joseph nodded in agreement. "It is a beautiful afternoon. Spring is in the air." He gazed off across the tree-studded pastures that stretched as far as the eye could see, wishing that Rachel could come out to enjoy the sunshine. "It's shirtsleeve warm, and that's a fact. A mighty nice change, if you ask me."

"It being the Sabbath, Caitlin can't do any actual chores, so she's out hoeing her garden rows, getting ready to plant."

Joseph had lived in the same household with his sister-in-law long enough to know that she didn't think of gardening as work. The girl flat loved her plants. Every year at the first of February, she lined every windowsill in the house with her garden starts and could scarcely wait to transplant them.

"I keep telling her it's way too early to put anything out yet," Ace went on, "but she'll have her way about it, I reckon. Then along will come a frost to kill all her sprouts, and I'll have to buy her some chocolate drops to cheer her back up."

Joseph chuckled. "You spoil that girl rotten. No worries about the seed she'll waste, only about how sad she'll be if a frost kills her plants."

Ace just shrugged. "I can buy her a wagonload of seed and never miss the money. Anything that makes her happy is okay by me."

"She's happy, Ace. The woman thinks the sun rises and sets on your ass."

Ace barked with laughter, throwing back his head so sharply that he lost his hat. His black hair glistened like jet in the bright sunlight. "You do have a way with words, little brother."

"I've been told that a lot lately." Joseph went to sit on the steps to have a smoke before he hooked up the team to Rachel's buckboard and loaded all her commodities. Harrison Gilpatrick always opened the general store after Sunday morning services so churchgoers who came into town only once a week could replenish their supplies. "How's the boy's lip today?"

"Fine, just fine." Ace's eyes softened with warmth. "He's playing in the dirt with his ma and having himself a grand old time."

Joseph could well imagine that. "Little boys do love dirt."

The breeze picked up just then, trailing Joseph's hair across his face in a fan of yellow. He stared through the strands at the swaying branches of the oak tree, which were laden with new buds. Soon spring leaves would unfold and the field grass would darken, painting the ranch in different shades of brilliant green. Rachel would get to see none of it.

"What are you looking so gloomy about?" Ace suddenly asked.

Joseph sighed and shook his head. "Just thinking, is all. It's sad, seeing her live like that." He hooked a thumb over his shoulder at the house. "Day in and day out, never leaving that kitchen. She can't even look out a window to see the sunlight or watch a bird in the tree. I'm already going crazy after being in there with her for only a couple of days. I've been reading a book. Can you believe it?"

Ace drew out his own pack of Crosscuts and lighted one up. "You're growing right fond of her, aren't you?"

"It'd be a mite hard not to," Joseph replied with a sharp edge to his voice. "She's a nice lady."

Ace mulled that over for a moment. "No need to be so prickly."

"I'm not being prickly. Just don't go making something out of it. I'm fond of lots of women. It doesn't mean anything."

"I didn't mean to imply that it did."

Joseph caught him smirking. "What?" he asked, feeling inexplicably angry.

Ace held up his hands. "Nothing. You just seem mighty defensive all of a sudden. That's not like you."

Joseph tossed away his cigarette and jammed his hat more firmly onto his head. "I've got better things to do than listen to this."

Ace gave him a bewildered look. "Damn, Joseph. I haven't said anything."

"You can give a whole dissertation without saying anything. Do you think I can't read between the lines?"

Joseph stomped down the steps, ground out his smoke, and sent his brother a glare. "You know exactly what you're hinting at."

"No, I don't."

Joseph refused to dignify that with a reply and took off for the barn. He heard his brother following him. "You're supposed to watch the house," he grumped over his shoulder.

"I can see the damned house just fine from here."

Joseph went into the barn. When he emerged a few minutes later leading the two horses, Ace was waiting to help put them in the traces. As they worked in tandem to harness the team, Ace asked, "Are you falling for that girl, Joseph?"

That ripped it. "No, I'm not falling for her!" Joseph realized that he was almost yelling, and that only made him madder. "There you go, making something of it!" He jabbed a finger over the rumps of the geldings at his brother's dark face. "Don't even *think* it. You hear? You're the romantic in this family, not me. I take my pleasure where I find it, and then I move on. That's how it's always been, and that's how it'll always be."

"Boy, howdy, have you ever got a bad case."

Joseph bit down hard on his molars and made his tooth pang again. "I don't, either." He swung into the buckboard, gathered the reins, and kicked the brake release. "I'll see you when I get back. Hopefully you'll be talking better sense by then."

Joseph was almost a mile from the house before he realized that he'd forgotten to load the wagon. "Son of a *bitch*." He drew the team to a stop and just fumed for a moment.

*A bad case?* Ace always had known how to put a burr under Joseph's saddle. Well, he who laughed last laughed longest. Joseph Paxton, falling for a woman? Ha. Not in this lifetime.

Simone Gilpatrick was a buxom, sharp-tongued woman with black hair and glittery brown eyes. A lot of folks disliked her for being too bossy and nosy. She also had a reputation for being a gossip. Because Joseph normally shopped at the general store on weekdays when Gus, a burly, dark-haired employee, helped Harrison to man the counter, he seldom encountered Simone, and on those rare occasions when he did, he tried to ignore her.

"Good afternoon, Mrs. Gilpatrick," he called as he entered the building.

"The afternoon is waning," Simone retorted from behind the counter. "It being the Sabbath and all, it's lucky you are that we're still open."

Hooking his thumbs over his belt, Joseph skirted the baskets and barrels of grains and foodstuffs that peppered the plank floor, his boot heels scuffing as he walked. "Looks to me like plenty of people are still out and about. I reckon you won't close until the boardwalks are clear. You might lose some sales."

She sniffed and puckered her lips as if she smelled something bad. Joseph just grinned. Everyone in town knew Simone was greedy. If not for her kindly, fair-minded husband, Harrison, she would have jacked up all the prices and never felt a moment's remorse as she put the pennies in her till.

She gave him an inquisitive look. "So what can I do for you, Mr. Paxton? If you're here to bend Harrison's ear again about heifers and calving, he's busy cleaning shelves in back."

She wore a pale purple dress of shiny cloth that made her huge bosom look even more gargantuan than usual. Joseph wondered why on earth Harrison allowed her to wear something so unflattering. Then he wondered at himself for wondering. Harrison Gilpatrick was a quiet, peace-loving man who picked his battles and only bucked his wife when he felt he had to.

"I'm not here to visit today," Joseph assured her. "I've got some butter, eggs, and cheese to hawk."

Simone nodded. "I heard you were staying

out at the Hollister place with Miss Rachel.
Day *and* night, as I understand."

Joseph flicked her a sharp glance. There
was an underlying tone in her voice that he
didn't quite like.

"There's nothing improper going on. If folks
are saying otherwise, they're dead wrong."

She shrugged. "I've no control over what
other people say, Mr. Paxton. As for what's
going on out at the Hollister place, that's for
you to know and the rest of us to only wonder about."

She came out from behind the counter, her
manner brisk and businesslike. The shiny
dress, when seen from hem to collar, magni-
fied her plumpness until she looked like a gar-
ish barn door waddling toward him. "Where
are these commodities you'd like to sell?"

Joseph was still stuck on what people
were wondering about. "Now look here."

Simone arched an imperious black eyebrow. "Yes, Mr. Paxton?"

"Darby McClintoch, the foreman at the
Hollister ranch, is laid up at my place from a
bullet wound in the back."

"We heard about that. How is he doing?"

"Doc thinks he'll pull through. That isn't
the point." He followed the store propri-

etress through the maze of baskets and barrels. "Darby believes the attack on him may be connected to the Hollister massacre five years ago, and he's afraid for Miss Rachel's safety. That's why I'm staying at the Hollister place, to protect the lady."

"I see," she said, her tone dubious.

"Miss Rachel lives in a boarded-up kitchen," Joseph protested. "She hasn't opened the door to anyone in years. How can people think anything improper is going on between us?"

Simone swished out the doorway, her broad ass grazing the doorjambs on both sides. "Rachel Hollister is an unmarried young woman, Mr. Paxton, and you are an unmarried man who—if you don't mind my saying so—has something of a reputation for being a womanizer."

A *womanizer*? Joseph was starting to get the mother of all headaches. A womanizer chased anything in a skirt. A womanizer had no scruples. A womanizer would compromise a decent young woman without batting an eye. He had *never* consorted with decent young women.

"That isn't to say that *I* believe anything inappropriate is happening out there." She flashed him a syrupy-sweet smile that fairly dripped venom. "But you may as well know there has been a lot of talk."

And Joseph was willing to bet that her tongue had been wagging the fastest.

"No matter how carefully you slice the pie, Mr. Paxton, some folks are always going to scrutinize the pieces."

Joseph's temples were pounding by the time he joined her at the wagon. The self-righteous, judgmental old bitch. It made him furious to think that anyone in this dusty little town would *dare* to point a finger at Rachel Hollister. She was one of the finest and most proper young women he'd ever met.

"Some people forget the eighth commandment," he told her. "It's a sin to bear false witness against your neighbor."

Simone just lifted her eyebrows again. "Do you want to sell these commodities or not?"

Joseph had been pissed at Ace earlier. Now he wanted to do murder. He couldn't very well strangle the old biddy, so he did the next best thing. He got his revenge by haggling with her over prices.

"Four cents for a dozen eggs? These are from grain-fed chickens, and I know damned well they should go for six cents a dozen. You sell them for nine. I just saw the sign. That's a fair thirty-three percent profit margin for you."

"Go away."

Joseph nodded. "Maybe I'll just do that. I reckon I can stand on the boardwalk, cut your store prices by a penny, and sell out, lickety-split, making not only Miss Rachel's usual profit, but most of yours as well. Care to make a wager?"

Joseph got six cents a dozen for the eggs, eight cents a pound for Rachel's cheese, which was top price, and six cents a pound for the butter. As he drove the buckboard up Main Street, he grinned like a fool. Who ever said revenge wasn't sweet?

His next stop was at the sawyer's. Ronald Christian was a jet-haired man of medium build with friendly blue eyes. He wore patched but clean overalls, winter and summer, unless he was going to church, whereupon he donned a suit.

As Joseph swung down from the wagon, the little Christian boys came running out to greet him. Richie, a six-year-old, hugged one of Joseph's legs, and Donnie, a year younger, grabbed the other one. Joseph patted their ebony heads and smiled into their big blue eyes.

"Hello, boys. How are you doing today?"

Ronald emerged from the mill, an open-sided structure, essentially only a roof supported by poles. "Now, Richie, now, Donnie," he scolded. "Let go Mr. Paxton's legs. He can't walk with you hanging on him like that."

Joseph ruffled the boys' hair and then focused on their father. "Hi, Ron. I need some planks."

"What kind?"

"I don't much care. I just need them extra thick." He held up his hands to demonstrate. "Miss Rachel Hollister needs a new door."

Ronald nodded. "I heard you were staying out there."

Joseph could only wonder what else Ronald had heard.

"I was real sorry about what happened to Darby. How's he doing?"

"Doc has been dropping by to check on him regularly. So far, so good. He was running a bit of a fever last night. That's a worry. But Doc says it's to be expected."

"Bullet wounds are nasty business," Ronald agreed. "Always liked Darby. I hope he pulls through." He motioned for Joseph to follow him into the mill where he kept his stockpiles. "So what kind of wood are you looking for?"

"I don't rightly care. I just need really thick planks to build a barricade door, something stalwart to fill an archway."

Ronald led Joseph to the far end of the building. His boys swarmed over the stacks of wood like tiny ants, giggling, yelling, and seeming to be everywhere at once.

All of Christian's planed boards were no more than two inches thick. Joseph wanted stuff much stouter than that. He came upon a stack of roughly planed pine that hadn't yet been vertically cut.

"Those are perfect," Joseph said. "Can you plane them more smoothly at that thickness?"

Ronald stroked his jaw. "I can give it a try, but they won't be as smooth as regular planks."

"I can sand them down."

Ronald grinned. "You don't want boards, my man. You want quarter sections of trees."

Joseph nodded good-naturedly. "Can you fix me up with four of them?"

Diana, Ronald's wife, appeared just then. She was a pretty little woman with brown hair, gentle green eyes, and a slender build. Her gray dress was ready-made from Montgomery Ward and on the cheap side, but she looked Sunday perfect anyhow. She extended a slender hand.

"Mr. Paxton, it is so good to see you. It's not often we get buyers on Sunday."

"I stopped by in the hope that Ron would be out here working."

Diana smiled. "Normally I scold if he works on Sunday, but Garrett Buckmaster is building a new barn, and Ron's got to fill his order no later than Tuesday." Her expression grew solemn. "We were very sorry to hear about Darby, Mr. Paxton. It must be difficult for Miss Rachel. Darby is the closest thing to family that she has left."

Ronald glanced past Diana at his frolicking boys. "Richie, get down off there before you fall and break your neck!"

Diana rushed away to corral her children, leaving Joseph and Ronald to negotiate prices.

On the way out of town, Joseph heard Bubba striking his anvil. It seemed that most all of No Name's business owners worked on Sunday. After turning the team into the yard in front of the shop, Joseph set the brake, swung down from the wagon, and wandered into the building.

"Bubba?"

The huge, muscular blacksmith appeared from around a corner. His grizzled red hair lay wet on his forehead, and his bare, muscular shoulders glistened with sweat. The heat that radiated throughout the building almost took Joseph's breath away.

"Joseph. Hey."

"No rest for the wicked, I see."

Bubba chuckled. "No rest for the blacksmith on Sunday, anyhow. People stop by to place orders before going on to church, and I have my hands full, trying to fill them before they leave town in the afternoon."

Joseph nodded. "I won't keep you, then. I was just wondering if you've started on one of the doors yet, and if you think the idea will work."

"There wasn't much to it," he said, gesturing over his shoulder. "Just straightening and fusing the bars together. They don't look like much. In my opinion, they could use some paint."

"You mean they're done?" Joseph followed the blacksmith into the firing area. The barred doors lay on the ground near the forge. Bubba was right about the call for paint. The rusty iron didn't show well.

"These are *great*, Bubba. You must have been up working half the night."

"I did work for a spell after supper." He grinned and winked. "My Sue Ellen is tickled about me getting them done so fast. When she's happy, I'm happy, if you get my meaning."

Joseph chuckled. "Well, you tell Mrs. White that I appreciate her kindheartedness. Rachel will feel much safer with those bars over her doors."

"Me and the wife just hope she can start enjoying a little sunshine." Bubba leaned over to grab a bar in one massive fist. "I'll help you get 'em loaded up."

On the way out to the wagon, Bubba called over his shoulder, "Now that Sue Ellen knows about Miss Rachel missing the sunshine, she's got a maggot in her brain about building the lady a courtyard."

"A what?"

"A courtyard," Bubba repeated. "A walled-in yard with a barred gate and ceiling. You reckon Miss Rachel would enjoy something like that?"

It was a brilliant idea, in Joseph's estimation. A courtyard. A bubble of excitement lodged at the base of his throat. "I can't rightly say if she would or not, Bubba. She's skittish as all get-out about open places."

"Wouldn't be open, not really. Sue Ellen's talking about tall rock walls, with the ceiling bars set into the mortar and anchored by a final layer of stone. With a heavy iron gate that locks from the inside, it would be an outdoor fortress with walls on all sides."

"I don't know," Joseph said cautiously. "Let me see how she does with the bars over the doors first. No point in our going off half cocked, building something she won't use."

Bubba looked disappointed.

"It's a really grand idea, though," Joseph hurried to add. "Ever since I saw how she lives, I've been racking my brain, trying to think of some way she might enjoy the outdoors. I never would have thought of a courtyard. If Rachel feels safe with the bars and can open the regular door to let in fresh air, there's a good chance that she'll feel safe inside a courtyard, too."

Bubba wiped sweat from his brow. "I'm thinking fifteen feet wide, maybe twenty feet long." He swung a beefy hand toward the pile of rusting metal in the yard. "God knows I've got plenty of scrap iron. Just a little area where Miss Rachel can sit outside for bits of time and maybe even grow a flower garden to attract the butterflies and birds."

Joseph could already picture it. A lovely garden area with a bench and flowers all around, perhaps even a small tree. He wanted to hug Sue Ellen for coming up with the idea. If Rachel could gather the courage, she would be able to sit outside. Sunlight would filter down through the grillwork. She'd be able to feel the summer breeze in her hair. Even better, she'd be able to hear the birdsong again. Joseph knew, deep in his bones, that Rachel would absolutely love that.

"Bubba, your wife is a genius."

The blacksmith's freckles were eclipsed by a blush that suffused his entire face. "Well, now, don't tell her that. She's pesky enough as it is." He rubbed a hand over his sooty leather apron. "Truth to tell, though, I'm convinced it's a pretty good idea myself. This morning, Sue Ellen talked it up at church, and a number of folks have volunteered to bring wagonloads of rock. Everybody seems to have a rock pile from when their land was cleared. All we lack is the mortar, and Jake Lenkins, from out at the quarry, said he'll donate the mixings for that."

Joseph's throat had gone tight. He couldn't push any words out.

"I hope you aren't thinkin' it's none of our beeswax," Bubba said. "I tried to talk Sue Ellen out of it, but once she got the idea in her head, there wasn't any stopping her."

Joseph took off his hat, slapped it against his leg, and then plopped it back on his head. He didn't know if Rachel would ever find the courage to step from her kitchen into a courtyard. But did that really matter? What counted the most to Joseph was that Bubba and his wife had cared enough to come up with the idea. Maybe some people always scrutinized the pieces of pie. But there were others who were just wonderful folks who didn't give a care about gossip and only wanted to make nice things happen for others.

Rachel Hollister had lived in an isolated purgatory for five long years, and now the people of No Name meant to liberate her.

## *Chapter Eleven*

As Joseph left the blacksmith shop and headed for home, his mood had greatly improved. A courtyard for Rachel. He could scarcely believe that Sue Ellen White had already found people who'd volunteered to bring rock. Once it was delivered, all that would remain was for Joseph to start erecting the walls. He felt confident that his brothers would pitch in to help. An almost impossible dream—summer breezes for Rachel—might soon be a reality.

A dozen different plans took shape in Joseph's mind—how to design her flower garden, what plants to order, and the kind of bench to build. And birdhouses, maybe. They'd look cute, hanging from the ironwork over the courtyard, and a few birds might even nest in them. Wouldn't Rachel be delighted if she could watch the eggs hatch and the babies grow?

When Joseph reached his place, he was surprised to see a strange buggy parked in front of his house. Not Doc's, he decided. This one was newer and looked to be something a lady might drive. Joseph parked the buckboard just outside the barn because he wanted to gather some tools before he left for the Bar H. He circled the barn to check in on Johnny and Bart, caught Johnny sitting on his laurels in the shade with his hat pulled over his eyes, and coughed to wake the young man from his nap.

"Mr. Paxton!" the hired hand sputtered as he lurched to his feet.

"Is this what I'm paying you a fair wage to do, Johnny, napping before the day is over?"

"No, sir." Johnny clapped his hat back on his head. "I was just taking a break, is all. I don't know how I managed to drift off like that. Maybe just working too hard."

Joseph doubted that. "Don't let it happen again, or I'll dock your wages," he said sternly. He thumbed his hand toward a heifer out in the field. "You need to be riding the fence lines, looking for cows that are about to calve. Where's Bart?"

"Off doing that, I reckon."

"Well, get out there and help him," Joseph

shot back. "I expect a fair amount of work for a fair amount of pay."

The younger man dusted off his pants and went to collect his horse. Joseph gazed after him, glad that he'd stopped by and caught the hired hand lollygagging. It would be a few days before Johnny forgot the reprimand and napped on the job again.

Joseph watched until the hired hand rode from the barnyard. Then he decided to mosey over to the house and find out who'd come calling.

When he entered through the front door, he heard voices coming along the hallway that led to the back of the house. He'd built three bedrooms, just in case his two younger brothers ever decided to leave Ace's place. Joseph loved David and Esa, he truly did, and he wouldn't mind if they came to live with him, but he'd gotten enough of bunking with them as a boy.

He crossed the sitting room, which was open to the kitchen, and followed the voices to Darby's sickroom, the first door on the right. To his surprise, Amanda Hollister sat on a straight-backed chair beside the bed. With trembling hands, she was sponging Darby's flushed face. From the opposite side of the bed, Esa looked on, his expression concerned.

"How's he doing?" Joseph asked softly.

Amanda glanced up. Joseph was struck once again by her resemblance to Rachel. "Joseph," she said with a smile. "It's good to see you."

Given the fact that they hadn't parted on the best of terms yesterday, Joseph was surprised by the warm greeting. "It's nice to see you, too," he replied and meant it. There was something about this old lady that he instinctively liked. "What brings you over this way?"

Bright spots of color flagged her cheeks. "I'm tempted to say I came only to check on Darby, but the truth is, I also came to apologize. I was unforgivably rude yesterday. I shouldn't have gotten so defensive."

Joseph searched her blue eyes, which were amazingly clear, considering her age. "David and I understood." He glanced at Darby again. The old foreman looked to be asleep. "Is he still feverish?"

"He is, I'm afraid." Amanda dipped the sponge into a bowl of water on the nightstand. "Burning up, in fact."

"Doc just left a bit ago," Esa said. "He doped him up with laudanum so he can rest. The wound is inflamed and paining him something fierce."

"I hate to hear that." Joseph rested loosely folded arms on the wrought-iron foot of the bed frame. "What's Doc saying?"

"Mostly the same thing, that inflammation and fever are to be expected."

Joseph nodded. "Does he still think Darby's chances are good?"

Esa shrugged. "He didn't say. I take that to mean he's worried. Darby's no spring chicken, and this fever is taking a toll."

Amanda left off bathing the foreman's face. "No spring chicken, you say? Darby McClintoch has more steel in his spine than six younger men." Her eyes fairly snapped when she looked at Esa. "He'll make it through this, mark my words, and he'll go on to work circles around both of you for another twenty years."

Joseph hoped she was right. He wasn't sure how Rachel would handle it if Darby died, and he sure as hell didn't want to be the one to deliver the news to her.

Amanda tossed the sponge back into the bowl and struggled to her feet. She wore a tailored brown jacket and a matching ankle-length riding skirt. She reached out a frail hand to Joseph. "Lend me your arm, young man. I want to take a turn in the yard with you."

Joseph hurried around the end of the bed. Instead of merely lending her an arm, he encircled her back to better support her. She was none too steady on her feet.

After they exited the house, she slowed her pace and then came to a standstill near her buggy. "I barely slept a wink last night for thinking about your visit."

"Don't worry about it. It won't be the last time that David will be invited to leave someone's house, and me along with him. A badge has a way of wearing out a man's welcome in short order."

Amanda shook her head. "I felt bad about asking you to leave, but, in and of itself, that wasn't what kept me awake. Your brother came to me for help, and instead of trying to provide some, I took offense and ordered him out." She gazed for a long moment at the house. "I love him, you know. Darby, I mean."

"So does your great-niece. By all accounts, he's a fine man."

"That's not the way I mean," Amanda corrected. "I mean I *love* him. I have for years."

"Oh."

She smiled tremulously. "I see the questions in your eyes. How and when did we meet, and if I love him, why am I seventy and still not with him?" She drew away to lean against the buggy wheel. Her eyes went shadowy with pain. "Darby went to work for my father back in Kentucky when I was still just a girl. When my father pulled up stakes to come out west, Darby came with us."

"So you've known him almost all your life?"

"Oh, yes. When my father died, Darby stayed on to work for my brother. Over the years, he became like a member of the family, more than just a hired hand."

Joseph nodded to convey his understanding.

She shrugged. "As a girl back in Kentucky, I suppose you might say I was just a mite headstrong."

Joseph could well imagine that. Not many women her age threatened to take a whip to a man for mistreating a horse. "Never met a Kentuckian yet who wasn't just a little headstrong, and we all take the bit in our teeth when we're young, I reckon."

"I was more headstrong than most, and when I was sixteen, I made a terrible mistake." She drew a quivering breath. "A fast-talking, handsome young wrangler came to work on my father's spread, and I fancied myself in love with him. When I got in the family way, the wrangler showed his true colors and lit out for parts unknown. My father was a stern, prideful man. Rather than endure the shame of it, he sent me away to have my child in secrecy. My baby was given up for adoption, and no one at home ever knew about it, not even Darby.

"When I returned home, Darby seemed to sense that I needed a friend. It was a difficult time for me. My father was an unforgiving man. But Darby was always a support to me. He never said much," she added with a smile, "but that's just Darby. With a little maturity under my belt, I began to appreciate the man behind the quietness. He wasn't a slick-talking charmer, to say the least, but he was steady, and he was true, and I came to love him."

"How did your father react to that?" Joseph asked.

"He never knew. He would have objected, I'm sure. Darby's only assets were his horse and saddle, and my father would have wanted me to marry a landowner. No matter. The relationship was doomed from the start. When Darby eventually asked me to marry him, my answer had to be no."

Joseph frowned. "But why? If you loved him, why didn't you marry him?"

"I said no *because* I loved him," she said softly. Then she waved her hand. "It made sense to me at the time, Joseph. I was ruined—*tarnished* was the word for it back then. I believed with all my heart that Darby deserved better, someone pure and untouched."

"That's plum crazy."

She laughed and wiped her cheeks with palsied hands. "Yes, well, looking back on it, I realize that a woman can bring far more important things to a marriage than her virginity, and I deeply regret that I was such a misguided little fool. But there you have it. I did what I thought was right at the time—a great sacrifice for love. I was all of—what—eighteen? Girls can be very dramatic at that age, and I had no mother to set me straight. If I'd had a mother, maybe I wouldn't have gotten into such a pickle in the first place. But I didn't, and my father hated me for bringing shame upon my family and his good name."

"That seems mighty harsh."

"He *was* a harsh man. My mother's death nearly destroyed him. He was never the same afterward. But that's neither here nor there. When I first came home after my time away, he called me into the barn and gave me an ultimatum. In order to remain in his household, I had to give him my solemn oath that I would never speak of my shame to anyone. As a result, I wasn't free to tell Darby *why* I wouldn't marry him. I just said no and left him to draw his own conclusions." Her eyes went sparkly with tears again. "He drew all the wrong ones, of course, namely that I didn't return his feelings. It was the end of our friendship, along with everything else that had grown between us. He continued to work for my father and later followed us out here to Colorado, but he always steered clear of me. It hurt him to be near me, I suppose."

"Why are you telling me this?" Joseph asked.

She looked him dead in the eye. "So you will know, absolutely and without a doubt, that I didn't shoot Darby McClintoch. Your brother, David, needs to go after the real killer, not waste time trying to pin it on me."

That seemed a reasonable explanation to

Joseph. "You got any idea who might have done it?"

She sighed. "I can think of no one. Darby's as loyal and true now as he was fifty-two years ago. I honestly don't believe he's ever had an enemy."

"What about Henry, Rachel's father? Did he have enemies?"

"He had two that I'm aware of, myself and Jeb Pritchard."

Joseph admired her honesty. She was under suspicion for shooting Darby, and she knew it, but even so, she cut herself no slack. "I know why Jeb hated Henry. But I'm not real clear on why you did."

Amanda smiled. "I didn't *hate* Henry, Joseph. I was furious with him. There's a big difference."

"Okay, why were you furious with him, then?"

She closed her eyes briefly. "In truth, it wasn't so much anger at Henry that made me leave the ranch as it was anger at my father and brother. I worked like a man, back in Kentucky and out here, forever trying to regain my father's high regard. But until the day he died, I remained the *bad seed* in his mind, the one who'd fallen from grace. You can't know what it's like to live with that, day in and day out. Coming in from work at the end of the day and having your father and brother not speak to you over supper. Having your every idea shot down, not because it was flawed, but because it was *yours*. Henry was raised to look down on me. I was the wayward aunt, the one who wasn't quite up to snuff, the one who'd brought shame upon his family."

"So Henry knew about the child?"

"I'm not sure. He never actually said. It was his attitude toward me that rankled and hurt. I thought of his wife as a daughter and loved his babies as if they were mine. But he would never unbend toward me. It had been drilled into him all his life, I guess. I was the outcast. My father died and left me nothing. Then my brother died and left me nothing. I was getting up in years and facing possible poor health." She glanced at her hands. "The shaking had started by then. I asked Henry to grant me a monthly stipend from his inheritance—none of the land or buildings, just a small stipend so I might feel less a beggar when I could no longer work to earn my keep."

"And he refused."

She nodded. "Flatly refused. It wasn't about the money. He was a generous man. But he felt obligated to honor his grandfather and father's wishes. They had cut me off without a cent, and it wasn't up to him to change that."

In that moment, Joseph honestly couldn't blame Amanda for leaving and starting up her own small spread. He would have done the same.

"Henry wasn't a bad man," she went on. "He just clung to the opinions that had been drilled into his head from infancy. He was fair to a fault with everyone else. Jeb Pritchard, for instance. Henry bent over backward for that scapegrace. He just couldn't see his way clear to be equally so to me."

"I'm sorry," Joseph said. In his opinion, everyone was entitled to make one bad mistake. She had been paying for hers all of her life. "It was unfair of your father to hold it against you for so long."

She shrugged and smiled. "When is life ever fair? It was good that it all came to a head after Peter died. I needed to leave the family ranch and put the past behind me. I should have done it years before. I had a very small trust from my grandmother. I put it to work by buying a patch of land. My little spread isn't much, but it brings in enough of an income to sustain me until I die, and it's mine. I bend my head to no one now."

Joseph couldn't imagine her ever bending her head to anyone, but he kept that to himself. "So, in your opinion, Jeb Pritchard was behind the attack on your nephew and his family."

"I can't prove it, but, yes, I've always believed it was Jeb."

Joseph drew out his pack of Crosscuts. When he tapped one out, Amanda held out her hand. "Don't be selfish. I'll take one, too."

Joseph had never known a woman who smoked.

"Put your eyes back in your head. If a man asked you for a cigarette, would you stare at him like that?"

Joseph tapped her out a Crosscut. After she'd lighted up and exhaled, she said, "I worked shoulder to shoulder with men all my life, sweating with them, getting hurt with them, cursing with them. I guess I'm entitled to have a damned cigarette, if I want."

She was, at that. Joseph chuckled. "You're right. My apologies. I'm just not used to ladies smoking."

"I'm not *just* a lady, Joseph Paxton," she retorted. "I'm one *hell* of a lady, and don't you ever forget it."

"I won't," Joseph assured her. And he sincerely doubted that he ever would. Amanda Hollister was a rare gem. "There's one more thing I'd like to ask you, though. A little off the subject, I suppose, but it troubles me, all the same."

"What's that?"

"Why have you never gone to see your great-niece? You're the only family she has left."

Her eyes darkened with pain again. "I went. Right after she came around from the coma, when she was still at Doc's. I loved that girl like my own. Of course I went."

"What happened?" he asked.

Amanda took a shaky drag from the cigarette. "She took one look at me and started screaming."

When Joseph reached the Hollister place later, the first words from Rachel's mouth were, "How is Darby?"

The anxiety that he saw in her big blue eyes prompted him to lie through his teeth. "He's doing grand. Still weak, of course, but definitely on the mend. He's a tough old fellow."

Rachel beamed a smile, her shoulders slumping with relief. "Oh, I'm so glad. Did you give him my love?"

"I did. Won't be long before he's back over here so you can tell him yourself, though."

The way Joseph saw it, there was no point in worrying Rachel about Darby's condition when there was absolutely nothing she could do for him. The old foreman's chances were still good, after all. If he went into a sudden decline and it appeared that death was imminent, Joseph would have to level with her, but the situation hadn't come to that yet.

She was as pleased as punch when she learned that Joseph had gotten two cents more per dozen for her eggs, three cents more per pound for her cheese, and a penny more per pound for her butter.

"Lands, how did you do it? That woman squeezes a nickel until it squeaks."

Joseph felt a couple of inches taller than he had upon entering the house. "I threatened to set up shop on the boardwalk, undercutting her prices by a penny. She knew damned well that I'd get customers, cutting her out of any profit, so she quickly saw reason."

"Well, then." Rachel wrinkled her nose and looked at the coins in her hand again. "My *goodness*, such a lot! I can afford to do some shopping."

"Shopping, huh?" Sitting at the table, Joseph dangled a hand to scratch Buddy's head. "And what is it you're dying to buy?"

Joseph expected her list to include feminine items. Caitlin spent hours poring over the Montgomery Ward catalog, dreaming about this and yearning for that. Afterward, Ace sneaked behind her back to order every damned thing she'd wished for.

Rachel surprised Joseph by asking, "How much is Simone asking for flour? Did you happen to notice?"

"Two and a half cents per pound."

"That's highway robbery!" Rachel rolled her eyes. "Whatever is that woman thinking? We're not in a mining town where staples bring premium prices. How about dried peaches?"

Joseph struggled to remember. "Twelve cents a pound, I think."

"*Twelve?*" She came to sit at the table

with a pad and pencil. "Well, that settles that. I can't afford such nonsense. Salt?"

"Last week when I bought some, it was going for three cents a pound."

"You're *serious*? What do the Gilpatricks *do* with all that money?"

"Well, now, I can't say for sure, mind you, but today Simone was wearing a shiny, light purple dress that made her look like a schooner under full sail."

Rachel gave an unladylike snort of laughter and tucked a fingertip under her nose. "Pardon me." Then she snorted again. "A schooner? Oh, my."

"Imagine the cost of all that fabric. It takes more than a swatch to cover hips that broad. She can barely wedge them through a doorway. I thought for a moment she might get stuck. I was looking sharp for some lard so I could grease her up and pop her out."

She snorted again. "Enough!" Then she fell back in her chair, dropped her pencil, and laughed until tears squeezed from her eyes.

"Does she still poke her nose in the air?"

Joseph nodded. "And flares her nostrils. She also puckers her lips all up, like as if someone just stuck dog doo-doo in her mouth."

Rachel burst out laughing again, pressing a slender hand to her midriff and sliding into a slump on the chair. In that moment, Joseph knew beyond a doubt that he'd never clapped eyes on a more beautiful woman in his life.

The realization scared him half to death.

His ma had always told him that the very best things in life happened along when you least expected them. Okay, fine. But what if a fellow wasn't ready? He *liked* Rachel, and there was no question that he felt helplessly attracted to her. But a lasting and enduring affection for someone surely didn't come upon a man this quickly.

"What?" she asked, wiping tears of mirth from her cheeks. "You look so serious suddenly."

Thinking quickly, Joseph replied, "I was just thinking how crazy life can be sometimes." That much was true. "Here you are, pinching all your pennies to spend them at Gilpatrick's so Simone can squander them on dresses that make her look broad as a barn door. There's just no justice."

"I shouldn't have laughed," she said, still

struggling to straighten her face. "Someday I'll be old and fat, and I'll look like a schooner under full sail if I wear polished poplin. Especially *lavender*." She shook her head. "A dark color better becomes a hefty person."

"Lavender. Is that what that light purple color is?" Joseph couldn't imagine Rachel ever growing fat, but if she did, he felt confident that she would still be a fine figure of a woman. "You females have a fancy name for everything. What's wrong with light purple?"

"Purple is a deep color. Lavender is much lighter in shade."

In his opinion, purple was purple.

She began making out her shopping a list. "There's no hurry on any of this, mind you. The next time you go into town will be soon enough. I'm just getting low on a number of things." She glanced up. "When I'm finished, I'll draw up a bank draft to cover the cost. Would you mind depositing today's profit in my bank account?"

"Not at all."

She finished her list in short order and pushed it across the table, along with the coins that he'd brought to her. "That should keep me in staples for a spell."

He ran his gaze over the items. Her handwriting was fluid and graceful, as pretty as the lady herself, and she had perfect spelling. His eyes jerked to a stop on one item, "w'eat flour."

"What's this?" he asked.

"Wheat flour."

"You left out the H."

Her face drained of color, and she suddenly pushed up from the table. "I'll fill out that draft before I forget."

She returned to the table, opened a large red ledger, and bent to write. Moments later, when she handed him the draft, she said, "I think that will cover everything. You can re-deposit anything left over next week."

She'd written the draft for two dollars, which was plenty enough to cover everything she needed, with some extra. What troubled him was her signature, *Rac'el 'Ollister*. She'd left out both Hs. He angled her a searching look.

"How is your name spelled, Rachel?"

She pushed up from the chair and turned away, presenting him with her back. "My goodness, I didn't realize the time. I need to start supper."

Joseph followed her with a bewildered gaze. The set of her shoulders told him that she was upset about something, but he didn't know what. He went back to studying her list, and there, right at the top, she'd written and underlined *T'ings needed from town.* Again, no H.

Why did she avoid writing that letter? He didn't for a moment believe that she had misspelled her own name or the other words. Her spelling was perfect, otherwise. And she'd also replaced the missing Hs with apostrophes. In each instance, she knew very well that she had made an omission.

For reasons beyond him, she simply hadn't written it in.

Shortly after supper, Joseph heard the faint sound of David's voice drifting to them from the front of the house. Rachel jumped as if she'd been stuck with a pin.

"Did you hear that?"

"I did." Joseph pushed up from the table. "It's my brother David. But where the hell is he?" He stepped close to the archway door. "Ah, he's around the side of the house at the window, I'll bet." He sighed at the interruption to their reading. Tom Sawyer, Joe Harper, and Huck had just developed a distaste for "normal" society and run away to

Jackson Island, smack dab in the middle of the Mississippi River. "I'd better go see what he wants."

Joseph went to collect his jacket from where it lay on his pallet in the water closet. When he reentered the kitchen, he gave Rachel a questioning look. "Do you care if I invite him in?"

Rachel jerked her gaze to the door. "In *here*, you mean?"

Joseph didn't know what he'd been thinking. Of course she wouldn't welcome a male guest. It was just—well, she seemed so *normal* here inside the kitchen. It was hard for him to remember that she was terrified of almost everything beyond these walls.

"Never mind." He drew on his coat. "I'll only be a few minutes."

She wrung her hands at her waist. "You can have him in. He is your brother, after all, and the marshal, to boot. I'm fine with it. He's surely safe."

*Safe.* Joseph stopped and turned from the archway. He didn't want to push too much at her too quickly. "That's all right. I can have a cigarette while I'm out there."

"No, please. I'll enjoy having him come in

for a bit. Just bring him in through the window, if you don't mind. I feel better about lifting the bar on this door because it opens into the rest of the house."

Where there were walls. Here he was, dreaming about building her a courtyard, and just the thought of opening an outside door unnerved her. "Actually, David probably wants to talk about marshaling stuff. You'd find it boring."

"No, really, Joseph. I want you to bring him in. Please."

Joseph could see her pulse pounding at the base of her throat and knew the situation frightened her. But maybe this was something she needed to do.

"Are you sure?"

She nodded. "Yes. Bring him in. I'll put on some coffee."

Joseph grabbed a lantern and slipped out into the dining room. He heard the bar drop behind him. That alone bore testimony to her illness. He'd be right back, but she still needed her barricade secured for the few moments that he would be gone.

David had tethered his horse to a porch post and was smoking a cigarette when Joseph rounded the corner of the house.

"Howdy," he said.

Joseph peered at him through the darkness. "What brings you out so late?"

"It's time for me to visit my suspects again. I was wondering if you might like to ride along with me tomorrow. I'm hoping to visit several of the surrounding ranches to question the owners and their hired hands, plus Pritchard and Amanda Hollister. Ace says that he's wallowed out a spot on the porch step and doesn't mind coming over to sit for a spell."

Joseph chuckled. "If he doesn't mind, I reckon I can be away for a while. I'm willing to let you make a tour of the ranches alone to talk to the landowners and hired hands, but I think it best that you don't go over to Pritchard's place by yourself." He fell into a lengthy recounting of his conversation with Amanda Hollister. "In her opinion, Jeb killed Henry and the others and may have shot Darby."

"You think she's telling the truth?" David asked.

Joseph shivered inside his unbuttoned jacket. "That old woman loves Darby Mc-Clintoch. I'd go to the bank on that, and I think she told me true about her falling out with Henry as well."

David chewed on that for a second. "Well, then, I reckon Jeb bears watching. If he shot Darby, he'll come after Miss Rachel sooner or later. It's a good thing you're camping out over here."

"Actually, it's a little better than camping out now. You had supper?"

"Not yet. I keep late hours on Sunday, waiting for all the wranglers to leave town. Caitlin always saves something on the warmer for me."

Joseph clapped his brother on the shoulder. "We just cleared the table. Rachel boiled up some thick slabs of salt pork, floured them, and fried them to a turn. And there's mashed potatoes, home-canned corn, and apple crisp for dessert, plus fresh coffee."

"You shittin' me?"

Joseph flashed a grin. "I've got it really rough."

"And here I've been feeling sorry for you, having to stay over here with a crazy woman. If she cooks, you can't complain."

Joseph had lost the will to complain about much of anything. "Come on in. It's still a cumbersome entry, through the window like a thief."

Once inside Henry and Marie Hollister's bedroom, David apparently had second thoughts. As Joseph lifted the lantern to light their way back through the house, David said, "This is creepy. It looks like the people just left and will be back at any moment."

"I know. Time has stood still in most parts of this house. But the kitchen at the back is as normal as can be."

"You sure that woman wants me in there?"

*That woman?* Joseph pictured Rachel's sweet face and knew his brother was in for a big surprise. He led the way up the hall. "If she didn't want you in there, she wouldn't have invited you."

When Joseph tapped on the door, Rachel almost jumped out of her skin. Buddy scampered about and gave a happy bark. It was definitely Joseph, she decided. But even though the dog had identified the person on the other side of the partition, Rachel couldn't go on faith.

"Joseph, is that you?"

"Yes, sweetheart, it's me. Who else would it be?"

Rachel started to lift the bar, but then she froze. His brother, a complete stranger, was with him. She'd felt a lot braver a few minutes ago when she'd insisted on his being invited in. Joseph had been with her then. Everything had come to feel a little less scary with Joseph beside her.

She heard an unfamiliar voice say, "You sure she's okay with this?" And then she heard Joseph reply, "Of course she's okay with it. Would I have asked you in otherwise?"

Rachel lifted the bar, but she couldn't bring herself to actually open the door. She retreated a few steps, hugged her waist, and called, "It's open, Joseph. You can come in."

The door cracked open, and Joseph's blond hair appeared. His blazing blue eyes came next, questioning her before he pushed the portal all the way open. In the next instant, she had a guest walking into her kitchen. He was about Joseph's height, bundled up in a sheepskin jacket with the collar turned up. His Stetson covered him from the crown of his head down to just above his ears. Unlike Joseph, he had closely cropped hair. She couldn't tell the color. But then he nudged up the brim of his hat, and she saw his eyes. *Joseph blue.* And his face was similar, too. Not nearly as handsome as Joseph's, in her opinion, but he had the same high-bridged nose, prominent cheekbones, and strong jaw.

"Howdy," he said and then swept off the Stetson.

Rachel gazed up at him, wondering why on earth she'd felt so afraid. He was cute as a button. His face was still boyishly soft where Joseph's had hardened and become chiseled.

"Hello. You must be David."

David sent Joseph a wondering look. Then he flashed Rachel a broad grin. "Yes, ma'am, that'd be me."

Joseph dropped the bar, clapped his brother on the shoulder, and said, "Take off that jacket. Rachel, I promised him some supper. We have plenty left over, don't we?"

"Of course." She took David's coat. The chill of night clung to it. She ran her hands over the leather. It even smelled of the outdoors. "Please, David, have a seat at the table. The food is still warm, and you're more than welcome."

The two men sat while Rachel bustled around the kitchen, serving David up a plate. Joy surged into her throat, a wonderful warm feeling that soon suffused her entire body. She was serving a guest. And she wasn't having any problem with her breathing at all. He was a stranger, yes, but he wasn't, not really. He was Joseph's brother, Caitlin's brother-in-law. Rachel felt almost as if she knew him.

As David tucked into his meal, Rachel joined them at the table. Joseph had run out of things to talk about and fallen silent. When she sat across from him, he pushed *The Adventures of Tom Sawyer* toward her. "Read to us, darlin'. David's never heard this story, either."

"But we've already read the first part," she protested.

"But now we're at a *good* part," Joseph retorted. "Trust me, he'll like it."

Rachel smoothed the pages and started to read. In the relative silence, she heard David's jaw popping just as Joseph's did when he chewed, and a lovely calm settled over her.

Tom was sneaking off Jackson Island in the dark of night to return home and leave a note for Aunt Polly so she wouldn't think he was dead. Only when Tom entered the house, he heard his aunt and Mrs. Harper making plans for his burial. Tom returned to the island, and he and his friends decided to sneak back into town later so they could attend their own funerals before revealing that they were alive.

Rachel started to turn the page and realized that David had stopped eating. She glanced up, saw that he was staring at her, and asked, "Is the food gone bad?"

David jerked erect and went back to eating. Cheek puffed out with meat, he said, "No, ma'am. The food's delicious. I've just never heard of anybody attending his own funeral."

Rachel smiled and went back to reading. Once back in school, Tom and his friends were the envy of every pupil. But Tom still hadn't won back Becky's heart.

"Who's Becky?" David asked.

Joseph briefly synopsized the story up until that point and then motioned for Rachel to keep reading.

Tom Sawyer caught Becky reading the

schoolmaster's book, startled her so badly that she jumped in surprise and accidentally broke the book. Later that day, when the schoolmaster accused Becky of the crime, Tom stepped forward and assumed the blame. As a result, he received the punishment in Becky's stead and finally earned her fond regard.

"What a man won't do for love," David said.

"Quiet," Joseph said. "Let her read."

While David enjoyed Rachel's apple crisp for dessert, Muff Potter's trial began. The entire town had already convicted the innocent man. Tom and Huck were racked with guilt, for they'd seen Injun Joe kill the doctor with their own eyes and knew that Muff was innocent. Their guilt only increased when Muff thanked them for being so kind to him.

David drew out his watch to note the time. "This has been such a nice evening," he said. "But if I don't head on home, I'll be dragging in my tracks come morning. It's after nine o'clock."

Rachel closed the book. In the distant past, she'd once had to worry about time schedules. "It's been lovely having you," she told David. "I hope you'll come again."

David reached out to tap the book. "I'll be back. Just don't read any more without me."

"No way am I holding to that," Joseph protested. "Not unless you come back to-morrow night to hear more. I'm not waiting a week or something."

It was agreed that David would return the following evening for supper, only at an ear-lier hour so he might eat with Rachel and Joseph. Afterward, it was decided, they would take turns reading the story aloud.

Joseph saw his brother out, taking Buddy along with him for a run before bedtime. Rachel hustled about the kitchen while they were gone, doing up the last-minute dishes and putting the food in the icebox. She was just straightening the table when Joseph tapped on the archway door.

Swallowing down what she knew was irra-tional trepidation, she scurried across the room. Leaning close, she called, "Joseph is that you?"

"Nope, it's Injun Joe," he called back.

Buddy answered with a *yaw-yaw-yaw*. She giggled and lifted the bar, allowing

Joseph to push into the room, his dog squeezing through ahead of him.

"Well, now," he said, "that was fun. I think David's addicted to *Tom Sawyer*." He turned to secure the door. "Now that you're all buttoned up in here I'll collect my bedroll and sleep in the dining room again tonight."

"But no heat gets in there."

"As long as I've got a windbreak, I can sleep outside in the dead of winter. Buddy and I'll be fine." He cut her a meaningful look. "You and I bunking in the same room isn't appropriate."

That made no sense to Rachel at all. "But, Joseph, who will ever know?"

"I'll know," he replied.

"So sleep in the water closet, then. That's a different room, and it'll be warmer in there."

He cocked an eyebrow at her. "You still feeling nervous?"

For the time being, the barred door over the archway provided a sufficient barrier to make her feel safe. "A little, yes." That wasn't really a lie. She always felt just a little nervous. "I'll feel safer if you're in here with me."

"You sure?"

Rachel had never been more certain of anything in her life.

## Chapter Twelve

The following afternoon, David was none too pleased when Joseph confessed that he'd failed to divulge part of the conversation that he'd had with Amanda Hollister the prior day.

"Rachel took one look at her and started screaming?" David wheeled his horse around and gave Joseph an accusing look. "Here I just spent ten minutes bedeviling Jeb Pritchard, and now you tell me?"

"I'm sorry. I didn't think it was important when you and I talked last night."

"Not *important*? You know damned well what this implies, Joseph. Rachel saw something that day, possibly something she doesn't even remember, and it made her terrified of her aunt."

"It's hard for me to believe that," Joseph argued. "I know it's the obvious conclusion, David. But remember what you said? The obvious and easy answer is seldom the right one. There's something about that old lady. I just can't help but like her. And I can't wrap my mind around her being a murderer."

"Well, I can. She wants that ranch."

"For what reason? She's an old, palsied woman. She has no legal heirs. I know a lot of people are sentimental about land that's been in their family for a few generations, but so sentimental that they'd kill for it? I'm sorry. It seemed like a plausible theory in the beginning, but now that I've met Amanda, I just can't believe it of her."

"It's a good thing you aren't a lawman. I never knew you were such a softy."

Joseph gave his brother a narrow-eyed glare. "There's no need to get insulting just because we have a difference of opinion."

David laughed and shook his head. "There's nothing wrong with having a tender heart, Joseph."

"I don't *have* a tender heart. I'm a clear-thinking man who just happens to be a better judge of character than you are."

"Like hell."

Joseph leaned forward over his horse's neck. "Damn it, David, that old lady loves Darby McClintoch. I'd bet my boots on it. I saw her face as she was talking. You can't fake that kind of emotion and regret. She felt it with all her heart. Her palsy aside, how could she have shot the man she loves?"

David held up a hand. "All right, all right. So why'd you tell me about Rachel screaming and get me in a dither, then?"

Joseph swore and pulled out his Crosscuts. "Because there's more."

"More?" David huffed with irritation. "Well, spit it out, then. I need *all* the facts to solve this case, Joseph, not just the ones you decide to share with me."

"Rachel's a perfect speller," Joseph said. "You heard her reading last night. The girl's got an excellent command of the English language."

"How does that relate to her screaming when she saw Amanda?"

"If you'll shut up and listen, maybe I'll tell you." Joseph swallowed hard because he knew the conclusions that his brother would reach once the words were out. "Rachel can't spell her own name."

David nudged up the brim of his Stetson to pin Joseph with a searching look.

"She leaves out all the Hs. She signed a bank draft and spelled Rachel, R-A-C-E-L.

And she left off the H in Hollister as well. Even stranger, she knows she's leaving out the letters. She replaces them with an apostrophe, like we do in a contraction."

"Did you ask her why?"

"She refused to talk about it." Joseph swallowed again. "Why would she revile the letter H?"

"Because her last name starts with it, and Amanda *Hollister* killed her family in cold blood?"

Joseph rubbed his eyes. "I knew you'd think that, because it was my first thought as well. But it feels like I'm missing something. It's there, right in front of me, but I can't put my finger on it."

David sighed. "I'm sorry, Joseph. I know you like that old lady. But I'm going to have to question her again."

"I know it." And Joseph truly did. The evidence was stacking up against Amanda. David would be a piss-poor marshal if he ignored that.

"If it's all the same to you, I think I'll go alone this time," David said.

"Why? Don't you trust me to keep quiet?"

"It's not that," David replied. "I'm just thinking it'll be easier for you this way. Chances

are, it's going to get ugly, and for reasons beyond me, you're fond of the old lady."

After parting company with David, Joseph
rode into town to visit the blacksmith shop.
He found Bubba hard at work on the ironwork for the ceiling of Rachel's courtyard.

"So you decided to go ahead with the
idea, did you?" Joseph said.

Bubba grinned. "Folks will be showing up
out there with rock soon, so get yourself in
a mind to work."

"I haven't even gotten her barred doors installed yet."

"Well, you'd best get started, son. With
my Sue Ellen at the helm, things get done in
short order. Spring's coming on. Just look at
this pretty weather. She says every day that
we delay is one day less that Miss Rachel
will get to enjoy the sunshine."

"I really appreciate what all you folks are
doing," Joseph said.

Bubba went back to pounding a red-hot
bar on the anvil next to the forge. "Not doing
it for you. We're doing it for her. And we'll
see how grateful you are when you're working from dawn to dark, building those walls."

"I'm hoping to get my brothers to help." A

memory flashed in Joseph's mind of the first fireplace that he and his brothers had built out at Ace's place. Along had come a rainstorm, and the whole damned thing had toppled over. Hopefully they'd all learned a few things about working with mortar since then. "Those walls will go up in no time."

"I hope so, or Sue Ellen will be out there building them herself. That's how come she's so skinny, don't you know. The woman's a bundle of nervous energy. Never stands still."

For a time, Joseph and Bubba discussed the particulars of the courtyard design. In snow country, a covered back porch was a must, and Joseph didn't want Rachel's to be removed.

"Why can't we build around the porch?" Bubba asked. "The simplest way would be to encompass the backyard, the courtyard consisting of three stone walls, the house itself providing the fourth, with the porch inside the enclosure. If you build the rock wall shorter than the porch overhang, I can make grid work to stretch from wall to wall until we reach the overhang and support posts. From there, we'll span the distance with individual bars so we can place them around the posts."

"So the rock walls will attach to the house at each corner?"

Bubba nodded. "And the ceiling will come in under the overhang and be flush against the house. When she looks up, there'll be bars spanning from wall to wall, just under the porch roof."

"That'll work," Joseph agreed. And so it was decided.

Darby was sitting up in bed and sipping a cup of broth when Joseph stopped at Eden thirty minutes later. The old foreman's face crinkled in a weak grin when he saw his visitor.

"Joseph," he said. "Last time I recall seein' you, your face was floatin' around in a laudanum haze."

"Well, now, and howdy. No haze today, I can see. You look as bright eyed as a speckled pup." Joseph swept off his hat and grinned at Esa, who had taken up squatting rights on the chair beside the bed. "Your patient is a far sight better today, little brother. You're shaping up to be a damned fine nurse."

"Not to mention a wrangler," Esa countered. "I delivered two calves this morning, too."

"Any problems with Johnny?" Joseph asked.

"Bart says he's been doing better since you threatened to dock his pay the other day," Esa assured him. "Everything's good on all fronts."

"I wish I had two Barts," Joseph said with a sigh. "Sadly, they don't all have a good work ethic. What else has been happening around here?"

"Doc left about two hours ago." Esa grinned. "He thinks there's a good chance Darby might live. I have ten dollars that says otherwise, and Doc's a betting man, so now he's in town trying to get a pool going. If the majority of folks go with Doc's prognosis, I'll make a killing if Darby goes into a sudden decline."

Joseph chuckled. He was pleased beyond words to see Darby sitting up. "Seems to me like a conflict of interest, Esa. You're caring for the patient."

"Like I'd hedge my bet? I'll take good care of the old fart." He held out a hand to

Joseph. "Who are you betting on, Darby or the Grim Reaper?"

Joseph reached into his pocket and flipped his brother a gold eagle. "My money's on Darby. He's so stubborn, he'll live just to spite you."

Darby shakily set the cup of broth aside. "I've got an eagle. Can I bet on myself?"

"Hell, no," Esa protested. "You'd stay alive just to get a cut."

Darby held his stomach because laughing pained him. "God help me, if I survive, it'll be a miracle. This boy may poison my broth." Then he sobered and looked at Joseph. "How's my little girl doin'?"

"Good," Joseph said. "Except for her stealing my dog, she and I are getting along just fine."

"Your dog?" Darby's eyes filled with bewilderment.

Joseph encapsulated the events that had transpired since Darby's injury. "Buddy has fallen in love, I'm afraid. Miss Rachel's prettier than I am, she's sweeter than I am, and she cooks better than I do. I can't compete with all that."

Darby sighed, let his head fall back against the pillows, and closed his eyes. "Take good care of her for me, Joseph. Whoever shot me will go after her next."

"I haven't left her alone once," Joseph assured him. "When I have to leave, my brother Ace stands guard on the porch."

Esa stood just then and excused himself to go start something for supper. When Joseph had taken his brother's seat, he leaned forward to rest a hand on Darby's forearm. "Are you too worn out to talk about the shooting, partner?"

Darby's lashes fluttered. "I never saw who done it, if that's what you're wantin' to know. Wish I had. I'd strap on my gun and go after the bastard myself."

Joseph nodded. "David can't prove anything yet, but we've been out to Pritchard's place twice now, mostly just to make the old codger nervous, hoping he'll do something stupid and hang himself." Joseph paused, then reluctantly added, "Amanda Hollister is our other prime suspect."

Darby gave Joseph a sharp look.

"Don't get me wrong," Joseph hastened to add. "I've grown right fond of the lady, and I find it hard to believe she has it in her to kill anyone. It's just that all the evidence seems to be stacking up against her."

"What kind of evidence?"

As briefly as possible, Joseph recounted Rachel's terrified reaction to seeing Amanda shortly after the massacre and how Rachel could no longer bring herself to write the letter H.

"Rachel took to leavin' off the Hs right after her folks was killed," Darby revealed. "It struck me peculiar, but I had so much on my plate back then that her spellin' was the least of my concerns."

Joseph could well imagine.

"It was a hard time after Henry died," Darby went on wearily. "All the hands quit, thinkin' they wouldn't get paid, and left me with all the work. And let me tell you, there was a heap of it. On top of that, I had the girl to think of. She wouldn't come out from behind her bed. Just huddled there in the corner, day and night. I had no choice but to leave off wranglin' and set myself to the task of makin' her feel safe. She grew so thin she looked like a skeleton."

"Hell and damnation," Joseph said softly.

"That don't say it by half. I've never in all my life seen anyone that pale and skinny. She just sat in that corner, starin' out all wild-eyed and afraid. When I tried to leave her to do my work around the place, she'd cry and beg me not to go. It fair broke my heart."

Just thinking about it broke Joseph's heart. "I've seen all your handiwork, Darby. You created a whole world for her in that kitchen. It's nothing short of amazing." A lot of men—hell, most men—would have gone looking for another job where they could have been sure to see payday. "You're a good man, Darby McClintoch."

"Pshaw. She's like family to me. You stand fast with family, son, no matter how lean the times. Her and I got through it."

Joseph sighed. "Back to Rachel screaming at the sight of Amanda and leaving out all her Hs. David and I believe the latter may have something to do with Amanda bearing the Hollister name."

"You don't need to explain your reasonin' to me," Darby said. "If Amanda opened fire on the family and Rachel saw it, everything makes sense, don't it?"

Joseph relaxed back on the chair. "So you think we're on to something?"

"Didn't say that. I just see how you're thinkin' and can understand why."

"But you disagree?"

"Absolutely," Darby answered without hesitation. "I can tell you right now, son, you and your brother are tryin' to tree the wrong coon."

"Rachel screamed when she saw Amanda, Darby. She must have seen something when her family was killed—something that made her terrified of the woman."

"Maybe so. Rachel loved her aunt Amanda like no tomorrow. There has to be a reason why she screamed. I just know it had nothing to do with Amanda being involved in the killings." A distant look filled Darby's green eyes as he stared at the ceiling. "Only Miss Rachel can give you the answers you're seekin'. All I can tell you is what I know to be fact."

"And that is?"

"Amanda might have been furious enough to shoot Henry, but she loved Marie and never would've harmed a hair on those children's heads. Especially Rachel. She loved that girl like her own. Rachel takes after Amanda, you know."

Joseph had noticed that, yes.

"Before Rachel took to hiding behind her walls, she and Amanda were like two peas in a pod, both of them as pretty as can be and too spunky by half. Rachel drove her mama to distraction. Marie wanted to put the girl in fancy dresses all covered with lace, and Rachel always ruined them first thing, more inclined to be in the barnyard than the parlor. I think Amanda pretended in her mind that Rachel was her own daughter. She lost a child early on, back in Kentucky when she was real young. I don't think she ever quite got over it."

"Who told you about that?" Joseph blurted.

Darby gave him a long, inquisitive study. "I was there, son. Question is, who told you?"

"Amanda."

A slight frown creased Darby's brow. "Did she now? In all these years, I've never known her to speak of it."

"She swore a solemn oath to her father that she wouldn't," Joseph revealed. "He demanded her silence in exchange for allowing her to remain with the family."

Darby's eyes drifted closed. "That heartless old bastard. Is that why she never spoke of it?"

This was a fine kettle of soup, Joseph thought, with more secrets stirred into the mix than he could count. Darby knew about Amanda's child? It boggled Joseph's mind to think that two people who loved each other and should have been together might have been happily married all these years if only they'd been honest with each other.

"I hated that old son of a bitch," Darby said.

Joseph jerked back to the moment. "Who, Luther Hollister?"

"Yes. He didn't deserve Amanda as a daughter. Her little brother, Peter, was a sickly child. She was the only mother he ever knew, nursing him through one sickness after another while she kept the house and worked outdoors with the men every chance she got. Luther never gave her credit for one damned thing. She was such a fine girl. Loyal, clear to the marrow of her bones. But that counted for nothing when she got in trouble. He just washed his hands of her, like as if she was dirt. I honestly believe the only reason he allowed her to come back home was for fear of what folks might say. He didn't care about Amanda, not the way he should have, anyways."

"That's too bad."

Joseph studied the old foreman's weathered face. Darby was a good, honest man and firmly believed in Amanda Hollister's innocence. That probably wouldn't sway David, but it went a long way with Joseph.

"She loves you, you know," Joseph said softly.

Darby's lashes fluttered open. "Who does?"

In for a penny, in for a pound. "Amanda. She never stopped loving you."

"Aw, heck. Go away with you. That's pure nonsense. That girl never loved me. I just thought she did."

Joseph met the old foreman's gaze, saw the glimmer of hope in those green depths, and decided the poor man had been getting the small end of the horn long enough. "She wouldn't marry you all those years ago because she felt unworthy. 'Tarnished,' was the word she used. She believed that you deserved someone pure and untouched, so she refused your proposal. She couldn't tell you why because she'd sworn to her father that she'd never speak of it to anyone. But she never stopped loving you, Darby, not once in all these years."

Darby struggled up on his elbow, clenching his teeth at the pain.

Joseph grabbed the foreman's bare shoulders, which were amazingly well muscled for an old fellow's. "What the hell are you doing?"

"I got some—hash to settle," Darby bit out. "Damned fool girl. I knew—about the baby. What'd she think—that I believed she went off to finishin' school like her daddy said? She didn't come back finished. She came back skinny, with that little belly gone. In addition to bein' stupid, does she reckon I'm blind, to boot?"

Esa heard the commotion and appeared in the doorway. "What's going on?"

"I need my britches and boots," Darby said.

"You can't get up," Esa cried. "Doc said so. Two weeks bed rest, no less."

Darby flung his wiry legs over the edge of the mattress. Hugging his waist with one arm, he sent Esa a fiery look. "I don't care squat what Doc said. Get me my trousers, boy."

"Darby," Joseph tried, "you can't be doing this. You'll start that wound to bleeding again. There'll be time enough later to—"

"Don't talk to me about time. I almost died with that fever. What if it comes back? I have to talk to her *now*. So she'll know I love her back. I can't take that to the grave with me, son. I need her to know my feelin's."

As crazy as it would be for Darby to stand, let alone get dressed and try to ride a horse, Joseph could understand the old man's sense of urgency. That was sobering. A week ago, he would have thought him totally insane. But that was before he met Rachel.

Thinking quickly, he said, "If you're bent on talking to her, Darby, I'll bring her here."

The tension eased from Darby's shoulders. "I'm bent on it. I love that woman to the marrow of my bones."

"Fine, then. I'll go fetch her. You can't get up. You'll bleed to death before you get there."

Darby lifted his head. "You reckon she'll come?"

"I know it," Joseph assured him.

Darby sank weakly back onto the pillows. "Well, damn it, go get her then. I gotta give her a large piece of my mind."

David's horse was tethered to the hitching post in front of Amanda Hollister's house when Joseph rode in. He swung down from the saddle and looped Obie's reins over the horizontal pole, then ascended the steps two at a time to rap his knuckles on the front door. A few moments later, Amanda answered. She sat off to one side of the doorway in her wheelchair.

"Joseph," she said with a sarcastic edge in her voice. "Have you come to attend the inquisition?"

"No, ma'am." Joseph peered into the room and saw David sitting on the sofa. "I'm sorry to interrupt, little brother, but something important came up. Miss Hollister is urgently needed over at my place."

Amanda's face drained of color. "It's Darby, isn't it?"

"Yes, ma'am, but not in the way you think. The fever broke, and he's on the mend."

She placed a shaking hand over her heart. "Thank God. I thought he'd taken a turn for the worse."

"No, ma'am. But he insists on seeing you, straightaway. If you don't go to him, he'll try to come here. The effort's liable to kill him."

Amanda's eyes filled with tears. "You told him."

It wasn't a question. Joseph nodded and said, "Damn straight I told him. Someone needed to."

"You had no right."

"I know it, and I apologize. But I can't honestly say I'm sorry. He needed to know."

"Is he angry?"

Joseph considered the question. "Well, now, let's just say he'd be whipping wildcats right now if he weren't weak as a kitten."

Amanda rolled her chair back so Joseph could enter. "I trusted you."

"Yes, ma'am, I know you did." Joseph considered trying to explain his reasons for breaking her confidence, but the words just wouldn't come. "But there are some things a man has a right to know, and that's one of them. He knew about the baby all those years ago."

"He what?"

"He knew," Joseph repeated. "He never believed the story your father told about sending you off to finishing school. He knew you'd gone away to have a child in secret long before he asked you to be his wife."

A stricken expression came over Amanda's face. "Why did he never say anything?"

Joseph removed his hat and finger-combed his hair, thinking that she hadn't exactly been the epitome of forthrightness herself. But this wasn't the time for accusations. "I can't speak for Darby. You'll have to ask him why he never said anything. Will you go with me? If you don't and he tries to come here, it'll be on your head."

Riding alongside the buggy, Joseph escorted Amanda Hollister back to his place and sat in the kitchen while she made her precarious way along the hall to Darby's room. The instant Darby saw her in the doorway, he said, "Come in and shut that door, girl. I don't want everybody and his brother hearin' what I've got to say."

Esa glanced up from pouring Joseph a cup of coffee and whispered, "What's this all about?"

"Love," Joseph said with a broad grin.

"Love?" Esa came to sit at the table across from his brother. "They're old people."

"Just goes to show that love isn't only for us young folks, I reckon."

"He called her 'girl.' How crazy is that?"

Joseph thought about it for a moment. It was true that Amanda Hollister had left girlhood behind her well over a half century ago, but maybe in Darby's eyes she was still as young and beautiful as she'd ever been.

Just then they heard Darby's voice booming through the walls. "I never heard such a bunch of poppycock in all my born days! Unworthy? I oughta tan your fanny for even thinkin' it. You're the finest swatch of calico I ever clapped eyes on, and that's a fact."

"Don't refer to me as a swatch of calico! I don't like it, Darby McClintoch."

"The prettiest thing I ever saw in a skirt, then."

"There's a lot more to me than this skirt."

"Like I don't know it? I loved you with all my heart, and damn it to hell, I still do!"

Amanda's softer voice didn't carry through the walls. All they could hear was a low murmur.

"All these years, I thought you didn't love me back!"

Another murmur.

"And that was the only reason? Damn it, Amanda Grace, what were you thinkin'? You havin' the child never mattered a whit to me. I loved you then, I love you now, and all I can think about is the wasted years."

The front door opened just then and David stepped inside. "You got enough coffee to spare another cup?" he asked.

Esa swung to his feet. "Sure. Come take a

load off. The entertainment's above aver-
age."

Darby's voice rang out again. "Too *old*?
The hell you say. I'm not takin' no for an answer this time. As soon as I get back on my
feet, I'm marryin' you, and that's my last
word on the subject."

Joseph chuckled. "Church bells are gonna
be ringing in No Name."

"We don't have any church bells," Esa
pointed out.

"Then we'll all ring cowbells," Joseph retorted. "When two people wait this long to
get hitched, they need bells to mark the occasion."

David shoved his hat back to glare at his
older brother. "Have you plum lost your
mind? The woman may be a cold-blooded
killer. If I can prove it, she may hang."

Joseph shook his head. "Are you still
stuck on that? You're never going to prove
it. Darby says you're trying to tree the wrong
coon, that she couldn't possibly have done
it. That's good enough for me."

"So why did Rachel scream when she saw
Amanda?"

"I don't know," Joseph replied. "I'd venture a guess that Rachel doesn't even know

for sure. But I'm willing to wager every cent I've got that it wasn't because Amanda Hollister committed the murders or was somehow involved."

"You can't be sure," David shot back.

"Yes," Joseph replied. "I'm as sure of it as I've ever been of anything."

## Chapter Thirteen

Rachel sat at the table with her chin propped on her fist, staring vacantly at nothing. Joseph had been gone for hours, and she felt lonely. Over the last five years, she'd become accustomed to being alone. But this was different. The silence that had become such a mainstay of her life suddenly seemed almost deafening. She missed the sound of Joseph's voice. She yearned to hear his deep, silky laughter. Even Buddy had deserted her in favor of playing outdoors with his brother.

She had tried to read, but for the first time in her recent memory, her books brought little comfort. Crocheting and needlework held no appeal, either. In a very short time, she'd come to like—no, to *need* the company of others to make her world seem complete.

The realization frightened her. Darby was

recovering nicely, and he'd soon come home. When he did, Joseph would leave. There would be no more laughter in her kitchen, no more guests for supper, no more reading aloud long into the evening. She would once again be alone with the silence. The thought made her feel almost claustrophobic, which might have been hilariously funny if it hadn't been so sad. A claustrophobic agoraphobic?

Tears filled Rachel's eyes, and the next thing she knew, she was weeping without really knowing why. She only knew that she felt desolate and absolutely forlorn. And trapped. She felt so trapped. Her kitchen, which had been her safe haven for so long, was now also her prison. She needed her walls in order to breathe, but Joseph's intrusion into her life had awakened other needs within her, some of them needs she'd felt before, others completely new, mysterious, and indefinable, yet just as compelling.

She loved Darby. She truly did. And she looked forward to hearing his knocks on the wood safe again. But to go back to living her life around those three knocks a day? Rachel wasn't sure she could do it again, not after having Joseph and Buddy there.

They'd made her realize how barren her existence was, and now she wanted more, so very much more.

Rachel knew it was beyond silly to sit there in her dim kitchen, weeping over the things that were missing in her life, but that didn't make her want them any less. Even more horrible was her certain knowledge that they were all things she could never have or experience. She would grow old without ever knowing what it was like to be loved by a man. She would never hold her own baby in her arms. She would never know the joy of watching her children grow up and become productive adults. And when she grew old, she would have no one with whom to share her memories. In truth, she wouldn't even live a life worth remembering. The days and nights would blend together in a lantern-lighted, silent, empty blur.

And so she wept, her sobs bouncing back at her off the walls that she needed so desperately but had also come to hate.

When she heard Joseph talking to Ace out on the porch some time later, she dried her eyes, patted her cheeks, and leaped up from the chair to tidy her clothing and hair.

He would come inside soon, and she didn't want to look a fright. Nor did she want him to know that she'd been crying. He would ask why, and she wasn't at all sure she could explain without bursting into tears again.

Joseph's heart caught when he saw Rachel's face. At a glance, he knew that she'd been crying. Strike that. She'd apparently been sobbing her heart out. Her eyelids were inflamed and puffy. Blotches of red stained her otherwise pale cheeks. Her mouth was swollen.

"Sweetheart, what's wrong?" He stepped into the kitchen, closed the archway door, and dropped the bar into place. "Did something happen?"

"No, no, nothing." She flapped a slender hand and flashed an overly bright smile. "I just spilled the pepper, is all."

"The pepper?"

Joseph stared after her as she scurried away to the kitchen area. Over the years, he'd held his sister Eden in his arms more times than he could count, trying to soothe away her tears, and he instinctively knew that spilled pepper hadn't done that to Rachel's face.

"Lands, yes. I'm allergic. If I get a sniff, I'm sneezing and tearing up for hours."

Joseph didn't buy it. As he moved farther into the kitchen, he remembered Darby's description of Rachel right after the tragic loss of her family—a gaunt, terrified girl, hiding in the corner. Over time, she had put some weight back on and become a beautiful young woman, but in all the ways that counted, she was still hiding. Darby had just given her a much larger area to do it in.

"I have some wonderful news for you."

She turned from the range. "Really? What's that?"

He glanced behind her at the stove. No simmering pot demanded her attention. In fact, judging by the ambient temperature of the room, the fire in the box was dead out. Busywork, he decided, a way to avoid talking about whatever it was that had upset her.

"Darby is looking fit as a fiddle," he said. "Sitting up in bed, laughing, and—you won't believe this one—talking almost nonstop."

She smiled again, this time with a gladness and warmth that made her blotched cheeks glow. "That *is* wonderful news. Did you give him my best?"

"I did. But judging by his progress, I doubt it will be long before you can tell him yourself. Doc wants him to stay in bed for two weeks, but I won't be surprised if Darby is up and about long before that."

"That's my Darby," she said with a wet laugh. And then her eyes filled with sparkling tears.

Joseph moved toward her as if being tugged along by invisible strings. This wasn't the reaction he had expected. He'd hoped the news would please her. "Honey, what's wrong?"

She cupped a hand over her eyes and shook her head. "Nothing. I'm just being foolish."

In his opinion, anything that had her so upset couldn't be foolish. He grasped her wrist to draw her hand from her face. The pain that he saw in her blue eyes made him feel as if someone were driving a sharp blade straight through his heart. "Can't you tell me? Whatever it is, maybe I can come up with a solution."

"There is no solution." Her mouth quivered and twisted. "I just felt lonely today while you and Buddy were gone. It made me realize that you'll both be leaving soon, and then I'll be lonely all the time."

The blade through Joseph's heart twisted viciously.

"You see? I told you it was foolish. I've been alone for years. It's certainly nothing new. I can't think why I'm suddenly dreading it so."

Joseph had no problem figuring it out. He'd barged into her world and turned it topsy-turvy with a talking dog, dinner guests, a visiting toddler, poker games, and reading out loud. Rachel wasn't a solitary person by nature. Her life choices had been forced upon her by illness. Now that she'd gotten a taste of sociality, of course it was hard for her to contemplate a return to absolute solitude.

He caught her small chin and tipped her face up. "Are you by any chance thinking that once Buddy and I leave, we'll never come back?"

"Why would you want to? If I could leave, I'd never come back."

The fact that she wanted to leave and couldn't made his heart hurt even more for her.

"I'll be back for some of your great cook-ing, for starters. I also greatly enjoy your company. Do you have any idea how far it is from my house to yours?"

"No," she confessed thinly.

"Hardly more than a hop, skip, and jump. It'll be a lot closer for me to come here to play poker than to go clear to town. And what about Tom and Huck? I'll never find out what happens to those fool boys if I don't come over in the evenings to read."

"The books won't last forever. By the time Darby comes back, we'll probably have fin-ished both of them."

The stories wouldn't last forever; that was true. But Joseph was coming to believe that the feelings he was developing for her might. "There are lots of other books for us to read, Rachel. Until you introduced me to novels, I never realized how entertaining they are. I'm totally hooked now, lady. I can't imagine going back to never reading again."

"Truly?"

In all his life, Joseph had never wanted to kiss a woman so badly, not as a prelude to lovemaking, which was usually his goal, but to chase her tears away and make her smile again.

"Oh, hey, you've made a reader out of me for sure, and David, too, I think. And then there's Caitlin, who'll be coming to visit. Now that she's been here once, she'll be pestering you all the time. Mark my words. Also, don't be surprised if she asks you to watch after Little Ace now and again. She and Ace would like to go places without him sometimes—to have dinner in town or to a hoedown. David, Esa, and I watch him when we can, but we're not always available."

Joseph released her chin and stepped away before he gave in to his urge to kiss her. "Which reminds me. Bubba finished the ironwork to go over all your doors. There's plenty of light left. I should get started installing it."

"Oh, but I was hoping—"

"You were hoping what?" Joseph asked.

"Nothing. I was just hoping we might play cards or something."

"Maybe we can do that this evening. For now, I should work on your doors." He arched an eyebrow at her. "You can't very well have guests coming and going all the time without the proper setup. Now can you?"

*Guests coming and going all the time.* The words remained with Rachel long after Joseph left the kitchen. She'd been wallowing in dark despair before he returned a while ago, and now, with only a few words from him, she felt buoyant. Visits from Caitlin? Looking after Little Ace? Oh, how she hoped. But what truly lifted her spirits was knowing that Joseph would come to see her often.

In a very short while, she'd become unaccountably fond of him. He was like a ray of sunshine in her dismal little world that chased away all the shadows.

In order to install the ironwork, he had to go in and out a lot. His frequent use of the archway door kept Rachel running back and forth to lift the bar and drop it again after he left. She'd hoped to make a custard pie for dessert that night, but with so many interruptions, accomplishing that was nearly impossible.

"I'm sorry," he said as she let him into the kitchen again. "I don't mean to be a pest.

Working on both sides of the wall like this is a bugger."

He'd chosen to install ironwork over the porch door first, and Rachel knew that he had to climb in and out the window each time he came or went. "You, a pest? I'm the bothersome one. The job would be much simpler if you could just open the porch door and step outside."

He chucked her under the chin as he walked by. "If just opening the door was an option, you wouldn't be needing the bars."

He crouched down next to the exterior door and set to work, drilling through the wall with a handheld auger fitted with a one-inch bit. With each turn of the crank, the muscles across his shoulders and along each side of his spine bunched and flexed under his blue chambray shirt.

As Rachel went back to the table to roll out her piecrust, she found it difficult to keep her eyes off him. Hunkered down as he was, his thighs supported much of his weight, and with each shift of his body, she could see bulges of strength beneath the faded blue denim of his jeans. For such a powerfully built man, he moved with incredible grace, dropping easily into a crouch, leaning sideways with perfect balance, and then pushing effortlessly to his feet.

Watching him brought butterflies fluttering up from her stomach into her throat. She wanted to place the flat of her hand on his back to feel that wondrous play of tendon and muscle beneath her palm. She also yearned to trace the contours of his arms. Her own body was mostly soft except for where her bones poked out, so everything about his fascinated her. When he wasn't watching, she studied the sturdy thickness of his fingers, the width of his wrists, the distended veins on his sun-browned forearms, the breadth of his shoulders, and the way his torso tapered like a wedge down to his narrow hips.

As Rachel poured the custard into the pie dish, she found herself recalling how lovely it felt when he kissed her, and her cheeks went unaccountably warm. She tried to tell herself it was heat from the oven that had her face burning, but she knew better. It was looking at Joseph that was making her feel warm all over. She also felt deliciously excited, as if something wondrous were about to happen.

"I need to go out and shove the carriage

bolts through," he told her as he strode to the archway door. "You want to come drop the bar behind me?"

As Rachel followed him to the archway, even his loose-hipped stride drew her gaze.

"I'll only be gone a minute." He flashed her a grin as he slipped out into the dining room. "When I finish tightening those bolts down on the inside of the wall, I'll get to work on the ironwork over the front door and here. Then you'll be set."

As Rachel dropped the bar, she wished that he would forget the silly ironwork and just kiss her again.

When Joseph finished installing all the ironwork, he insisted on Rachel's coming to see Bubba's gift to her. When he opened the archway door, she could barely speak. A sturdy crisscross of bars now covered the opening into the dining room.

"Nobody will get past those without a key or hacksaw," he assured her. "Bubba has Pierce Jackson, the local locksmith, make all his locks. They're the same kind they use at the jail."

"Oh, Joseph, it's beautiful."

He chuckled. "I wouldn't go that far. I gave

it a scrub and touched it up with some stove black yesterday. It's made of scrap iron, like I said, and the pile has been sitting out in the weather for going on two years. All the bars were rusty."

She reached out a hand to touch the metal. "Thank you so much."

"Don't thank me, darlin'. Bubba did most of the work."

"And I deeply appreciate all his efforts. But it was your idea." She laughed incredulously. "I can't believe I'm standing here, Joseph. I can see into the dining room, and it doesn't frighten me at all."

His voice sounded oddly thick when he replied, "If it helps, that's all the thanks I need."

"Oh, *yes*," Rachel assured him, and she meant it with all her heart. "I feel as if I've been let out of jail." She no sooner spoke than the absurdity of the comment struck her. "Out of jail, but behind bars. How does that make sense?"

"It doesn't have to make sense to anyone but you."

Rachel turned to look at him. In that moment, she felt certain that she would never forget a single line of his face. "Thank you so much, Joseph. Looking out and not feeling afraid is a fabulous feeling, absolutely *fabulous*."

He handed her two large skeleton keys, pointing out the differences in the notches so she would be able to tell them apart. "This one's for the archway, and this one's for the ironwork over the porch door. I only had one key made for each so you can rest assured that no one else can get in." When she had studied the keys and nodded to let him know she had their shapes memorized, he handed her six more, all of which were exactly alike. "These are for the ironwork over the front door of the house. You can keep one, if you like, and give out the others to special friends like Caitlin. She'll be able to come in without a fuss that way, and once she's inside, with everything locked up behind her, you can let her into the kitchen through the archway."

Rachel tucked the two kitchen keys into her skirt pocket. Then she offered him one of the six front door keys. "You're my most special friend of all, Joseph."

His smile slowly faded, and for a long moment his gaze delved deeply into hers. "Thank you for that. It's a fine compliment."

She pushed the key at him. "Then take it, please."

He reached into his jeans pocket and plucked out a duplicate. "I already confiscated one. Once I board your window back up, I'll be needing a way in." He slipped the key back into his pocket. "I plan to use that front entrance a lot, by the way, even *after* Darby comes home. The next time you start thinking how lonely you'll be when Buddy and I leave, think again. We're gonna pester the daylights out of you, and that's a promise."

"A promise I hope you'll keep."

His eyes went so dark they looked almost indigo. "I never break a promise, darlin'. If I give you my word on something, you can count on it."

Rachel hurried away before he could see the tears in her eyes.

The following day, Joseph got up early, tended to chores while Rachel cooked his breakfast, and directly after he ate went to work on a new, much thicker wooden door for her archway. Using two makeshift sawhorses that he fashioned from boards he'd found in the barn, he set up shop in Rachel's back dooryard, only a few feet from the porch so he could keep a close eye on the house. So far, no attempt had been made on Rachel's life, but it was never far from Joseph's mind that the killer might simply be waiting for an opportune moment. He couldn't afford to forget that and let down his guard.

At around eleven, Joseph heard a creaking sound and glanced up to see the thick back door open a crack. His heart soared, for he knew what it had cost Rachel to lift that bar and disengage the deadlocks. He doubted she'd opened that door in years.

"Joseph?" she called. "Are you there?"

He knew very well that she'd probably just seen him through the peephole, but he answered, all the same. "Right here, darlin'. You've got your bars to protect you. Open on up and enjoy the sunshine. It's a gorgeous morning."

"Oh, no," she said, her voice faint and trailing shakily away. "A crack is fine. I thought maybe we might talk while you work."

Joseph grinned as he grabbed his tape measure. "'Drink to me only with thine eyes.'"

"You've read Jonson?" she asked incredulously.

*Uh-oh.* The lady knew her poetry. He used his square to mark his cutting line. "Actually, no. I just memorized certain lines of poetry to woo the ladies. I got them from Ace. He was always the reader in our family. Named his stallion Shakespeare, after a black, leather-bound volume my pa gave him. Damned fool actually *read* it, and I think he memorized half of it. Then he went on to read everything else he could get his hands on, and memorized great lines that he likes to spout all the time to make himself sound learned. I found only a very few to be useful."

"Meaning only a few to impress the ladies? For shame, Joseph Paxton. Poems are ballads for the soul."

"My soul is fine. I know plenty of poems, darlin'."

"Do you now? Recite something then."

"'Little Bob is a fool, for he don't go to school, and never at work is he seen. And because he don't look inside of a book is the reason he's so very green.' There's some poetry for you."

"That isn't poetry, Joseph. It's a child's rhyme."

"Go ahead. Make light of it. I'll bet you don't know any."

"'Come here, little kitten,'" she recited back, "'I know you love me. I shall put down my sewing, and then we shall see, how smart you will look, when you play and you caper, all over the room, with your round ball of paper.'"

"You like cats?" he asked.

"I love cats, especially kittens. They're so darling when they play."

Joseph filed that information away for later. One of his barnyard cats had recently given birth to a litter of kittens. "'There was an old woman. And what do you think? She lived upon nothing, but victuals and drink. And though victuals and drink were the whole of her diet, this naughty old woman would never keep quiet.'"

She burst out laughing. "Are you trying to tell me something?"

"Nah. If your new archway door comes out slantindicular because I measure wrong, it makes me no nevermind."

"Perhaps I should be about my business, then." She released a shrill little sigh. "I need to make bread sometime today. We're almost out."

"Don't run off. I won't mess up on my measurements. I was only joshing you."

"But what about the bread?"

"Make a pan of cornbread. That'll do us until tomorrow."

"Are you certain?"

"'Old mother Ro, she was always so slow that she couldn't even wink in a hurry,'" he said in a singsong voice. "'But dear little Dick, he is so very quick that he keeps all the folks in a flurry.'"

"I take it back. You do know your verse," she conceded.

Joseph let loose with a gloating chuckle. "Got you whupped, don't I? I know more rhymes than you do."

"You most certainly do *not*."

She launched into several more rhymes from childhood, and then she treated him to some lovely, far more serious poems by famous poets.

"I take it back," he conceded. "I'm flat outclassed. But, hey, book learning isn't the only kind of knowledge that comes in handy. I know a whole passel of things you'll never learn from a book."

"Such as?" she challenged.

"Never squat with your spurs on."

She burst out laughing. Joseph imagined how she might look, throwing her head back and squeezing her eyes closed with mirth. His lips curved in a pleased smile. Damn, but he loved to make the lady laugh.

"What other tidbits of wisdom are floating around in your brain, Joseph Paxton?"

"Some ranchers raise pigs, and some will even admit it. But either way, they're raisin' pigs."

She groaned. "I do not raise pigs. I just have a few kitchen hams and several sides of bacon fattening up in my pigpen. Surely you have something more impressive than that tucked away in your mind."

"Never smack a man when he's chewin' tobacco."

She snorted. "Either that, or be smart enough to duck. What else?"

"Never ask a barber if you need a haircut."

"Hmph. I can tell that you haven't asked that question in a while."

"You making derogatory comments about my hair, woman?"

"No, sir, I like your hair fine. I was just making an observation."

"Never follow good whiskey with water

unless you're out of good whiskey," he tried.

"So far, I am not unduly impressed with your store of knowledge."

Joseph thought for a moment. "About the time you get to thinkin' you're a person of some influence, try orderin' someone else's dog around."

"Oh, puh-lease. Surely you've got something better than *that*."

"If you're gonna take the measure of a man, take his full measure," Joseph retorted.

"I'm trying. But so far, I haven't seen a whole lot to measure."

Joseph grinned. He loved that she was plainspoken. When he stuck his foot in his mouth, she'd be likely to understand, at least. "Here's one for you to pay attention to, darlin'. If you're gonna speak your mind, be sure you're ridin' a fast horse."

She giggled again. And so it went. Joseph kept a sharp eye on the door. Over the course of what remained of the morning, the crack widened just a bit.

Miss Rachel was glimpsing a ribbon of sunshine for the first time in five years. Joseph had Bubba White to thank for that.

The next time a heifer died at Eden, he'd present the beef to the blacksmith and his family to express his gratitude.

It wasn't often that a forge and anvil could make a miracle happen.

Because he had promised David that he would ride with him over to the Pritchard place that afternoon, Joseph postponed eating lunch until the new archway door was completed. He had just finished sanding the extra-thick planks when Ace showed up to stand guard duty.

"Howdy, big brother!" Joseph called. "You got a strong shoulder I can borrow? I'll need help carrying this thing into the house."

Ace swung down off Shakespeare and sauntered over to peruse the door. "Jumpin' Jehoshaphat. You're never going to fit that thing through the window, Joseph."

"Don't have to. We can take it in through the front door."

Ace rolled up his shirtsleeves. "That's one thick mother. It's a door for a fortress."

"It is, at that." Joseph hooked a thumb at the back door. "Rachel needs barricades, not doors. I figure this will make her feel plenty safe."

"How much protection does she need?"

Not so long ago, Joseph had asked himself the same question. Now he simply accepted and no longer tried to make sense of it.

Once they got the door hefted up onto their shoulders, the two men grunted, huffed, and puffed their way around to the front of the house, whereupon the stout creation had to be lowered to the ground while Joseph used his key to unlock the ironwork that now covered the front entrance.

"I think I've ruptured a gut," Ace said.

Joseph chuckled. "That's a gambler for you. Never turned your hand to hard work."

Ace snorted. "If it weren't for my gambling, you would have starved to death as a young pup."

"That I would have. No aspersions upon your efforts to feed me intended. I was just teasing you."

Once the entrance was opened, they carried the door into the vestibule. Ace kicked the interior door closed behind him, and Joseph called that good enough until they had carried their burden to the dining room. What Rachel didn't know wouldn't hurt her, and he'd be back to lock up soon.

*     *     *

Rachel nearly jumped out of her skin when a deafening crash sounded in the dining room and vibrations rolled through the kitchen floor. She whirled to stare at the archway.

"Rachel?" Joseph called. "Don't shoot us, darlin'. It's just me and Ace with your new barricade. Time to open up. I need to install it."

Rachel had a bad moment. What would she have for a barricade while the installation took place? Nothing, she guessed, and the very thought sent her heart racing. She nevertheless gathered her courage and lifted the bar, opened the interior door, and quickly unlocked the ironwork. Then she scurried away to the water closet.

She'd no sooner moved the broken door to cover the doorway than Joseph said, "Honey, you're perfectly safe. Ace is even faster with a gun than I am. Like we'd let anyone get into the kitchen?"

Rachel inched the door to one side so she could peer out. The two men were already lifting her new barricade into position, and the sight of it calmed her. It was at least four inches thick, so heavy that both Joseph and

Ace strained to maneuver it. "My goodness, Joseph, it's *lovely*."

The comment set Ace to laughing. "Lovely? This door is stout, but that's about all I can say for it."

"What are you saying, that my handiwork is lacking?" Joseph asked.

Soon the men were volleying teasing remarks back and forth, their deep chuckles and laughter filling the kitchen. Their jocularity soothed Rachel's nerves enough that she was able to leave the water closet.

"There she is," Joseph called over his shoulder. "Slipping out to see the finished product. Almost up, darlin'. I just hope you don't bust a gut opening and closing the damned thing. It's heavy, and that's a fact."

Rachel stepped closer to admire her new door. It was three and a half planks wide and every bit as stalwart as the porch door that Darby had fashioned for her years ago. "Oh, Joseph, such a lot of work. You shouldn't have."

"Just took some elbow grease," Joseph assured her, "and I'm used to that. It felt kind of good to break a sweat, actually. I'm used to going from morning 'til night."

While the two finished tightening hinge

screws and shaving the door to fit, Rachel fixed lunch. When the door had been installed, she welcomed to her table the third guest in less than a week, and in the doing, she marveled at how Joseph's presence in the house had so greatly changed her life. Only a short time ago, she couldn't have imagined having even one visitor. Now guests in her kitchen were becoming a common occurrence.

"Caitlin's coming later," Ace said around a mouthful of salt pork sandwich. "She couldn't leave until Little Ace woke up from his midmorning nap. She's probably driving over now."

Rachel's heart lifted. "I will be glad to have her."

"She's bringing a bunch of fashion stuff. Recent periodicals with all the latest nonsense in them."

Rachel's heart soared again. She'd had no need to follow fashion, living as she did, and she no longer had any idea what might be in vogue. But a part of her still yearned to look pretty, regardless. Especially now, with Joseph around. She wanted him to— She aborted the notion, horrified at the train of her thoughts. She wanted him to want her.

Joseph caught her eye and gave her a quick wink. "Fabulous lunch, Rachel. You have magic in your fingertips."

Recalling how she felt every time he touched her, she thought it was Joseph who had the magic touch.

"It *is* good," Ace seconded. "Thank you for inviting me to eat."

"Feeding you is the least I can do," Rachel said, collecting her thoughts and forcing them to more practical matters. And as she spoke, she realized that she sincerely meant it. Ace had spent more afternoons at her house recently than he'd spent at his own, and she knew he had a ranch to run. He was also operating minus Esa, one of his full-time hands. "I deeply appreciate all the time you've taken away from your work to be here. Thank you so much."

"Hear that?" Ace gave his brother an arch look. "Some people *appreciate* me and have the good manners to say thank you."

Joseph swallowed and grinned. "What have you done that I should thank you for?"

"I helped carry in the door and install it."

"Oh, that." Joseph shrugged and took another bite of sandwich. "If I were to thank you for every little thing, you might get a big head and start expecting it. That wouldn't do."

Ace turned laughing brown eyes on Rachel. "Do you see what I have to put up with? I think I raised them wrong. Should have kicked their butts more often, I reckon."

Joseph flashed a broad grin and winked at Rachel. "Too late to correct the mistake now, big brother. Nowadays, I kick back."

Ace's expression turned suddenly serious. "You and David going back over to Pritchard's today?"

Joseph sat back on his chair. Not for the first time, Rachel noted how different the two brothers were, one with jet-black hair and brown eyes, the other blond and blue eyed.

"Pritchard's place will be one of our stops," Joseph replied.

Ace wiped his mouth and dropped his napkin on his plate. "You boys be careful. Jeb Pritchard's not just mean; he's crazy, to boot."

Joseph smiled. "We'll be fine, big brother. We were trained up by one of the best."

"Jesus!"

Joseph dived for cover, praying as he hit

the dirt that David had bailed off his horse just as quickly as he had. Jeb Pritchard was shooting at them. Even as the realization registered in Joseph's brain, another bullet plowed into the dirt right in front of his nose. No shotgun today. The son of a bitch had a rifle.

"You okay?" David called from behind a rock.

Joseph kept his head low, using a bush to hide himself. "I'm fine," he yelled back. "But I need more than this for cover." He scrambled sideways to get behind a log. When he felt halfway protected, he drew his Colt, wishing like hell that he had his rifle. No such luck. The weapon was still in the saddle boot, and Obie, being the intelligent animal he was, had galloped away to hide behind some trees. "What's that man's problem?"

Just as Joseph posed the question, Jeb hollered, "You ain't been invited onto my property, you cocky bastards. Until you are, I'll shoot every time I see your faces!"

David sent Joseph a bewildered look. "What's gotten into him? I'm the law, for God's sake. He can't just open fire on the law."

"Looks to me like he's doing just that." Joseph brushed dirt from his eyes. "Means business, too. He's not good enough to place his slug an inch from my nose just to scare hell out of me. I think the ornery old bastard just missed."

David checked his weapon for bullets.

"Why bother?" Joseph called. "He's out of range."

"Damn it," David bit out. "I need my Winchester."

"It's long gone. The horses are off behind the trees."

A bullet hit the rock where David was hiding, the lead making a *ker-chunk* as it sent up a spray of granite. David sank lower to the ground. "Damned horses are smarter than we are."

"I think you're right," Joseph bit out. "Let's pull foot. I don't know about you, but I'm not looking to die today."

"You think we can make it to the trees?"

"If we stay on our bellies and keep our heads down." Crawling away went against Joseph's grain. But, he rationalized, it was better to crawl and live to see another sunrise than take a slug between the eyes. "You ready?"

As Joseph slithered away from the log, Pritchard opened fire again. Geysers of dirt and pine needles shot up all around him. He picked up speed, pushing hard with his feet, grabbing earth with his hands, praying with every inch of ground he covered that his brother hadn't been hit.

When they reached the trees and relative safety, the two men pushed up onto their knees. The instant they came erect, another shot rang out, and David's Stetson went spinning away.

"Holy shit!" they yelled simultaneously and hit the dirt again.

A few seconds later, when they'd crawled beyond the reach of Jeb's bullets, David looked back at his hat. His blue eyes blazed. "That miserable sack of shit came within an inch of blowing my brains out. Now I'll have to buy a new Stetson. You got any idea how much those things cost?"

It had been a spell since Joseph had purchased a hat. "No, how much?"

"A small fortune, that's what." David brushed dirt and pine needles from his hair. "He'll pay. Now I've got reason to arrest the son of a bitch. He tried to kill a lawman. That's a serious offense!"

Joseph gazed through the trees at Pritchard's shack. "You're gonna need help to take that ornery polecat in."

Silence. Joseph looked back at his brother. David was eyeing him expectantly.

Joseph held up his hands. "Do you think I'm crazy? No way, son. You need a posse."

"And who will I deputize, a bunch of farmers who can't shoot their way out of a flour sack?"

Joseph sighed. "I had plans for later this afternoon."

"Your plans just changed."

## Chapter Fourteen

Jeb Pritchard stank up the whole jail and raised so much sand about being locked up that David threatened to shoot him to make him be quiet. Billy Joe Roberts, David's lanky young deputy, was as excited as a kid at Christmas to have an actual criminal in one of the cells.

"You reckon the Pritchard boys will try to break him out?" Billy Joe asked David.

David considered the question. "I hope not. I'd have to lock them up, too. The place already stinks to high heaven." He extended a hand to Joseph. "Thank you, big brother. That went fair to middling well, I think. Not a single shot fired."

Joseph chuckled as he shook David's hand. "I'm glad it went so well. With polecats like them, it could have gotten nasty."

He and David had crept up on the Pritchard place, using bushes as cover until they reached the house. Then they'd each taken up positions outside a door and entered simultaneously on the count of twenty. All four of the Pritchards had been napping, and before they could reach for their weapons, Joseph had had the barrel of his Colt .45 pressed to Jeb's temple.

"I kind of hope the Pritchard boys try something," Billy Joe said. "We could use some excitement around here."

"Not that kind of excitement, Billy Joe." David met Joseph's laughing gaze. "Just in case, though, I should probably stick around here tonight. No reading that book without me, you hear?"

Joseph gave his brother a mock salute as he turned to leave the office. "I'm gone to take a bath. Wrestling with that no-account left me smelling almost as bad as he does."

It took Joseph thirty minutes to reach the Hollister place. When he entered the barn to get Obie settled into a stall for the night, he saw that Ace had already done the evening chores again. Making a mental note to thank him, Joseph headed for the house. When he entered by the front door, the sound of voices and laughter coming from the kitchen area reminded him that Caitlin had come to visit.

"Pugh!" Rachel waved a hand in front of her nose as she let Joseph into the kitchen. "What *is* that smell?"

Joseph plucked at his shirt. "I met up with the south end of a northbound skunk. I'll be taking a bath, if you don't mind."

"Not at all." Rachel flapped her hand again. "Please do. We promise not to peek through the cracks when you lean the door over the hole."

The very fact that she was thinking about peeking through those cracks heated Joseph's blood. He shot her a questioning look. She gazed back at him, as innocent as could be. But her cheeks went pink. *Hmm.* At times when she'd been bathing, he'd been tempted to peek through those cracks a few times himself. So he knew how her mind was working. The realization gave him pause. The attraction he felt for her wasn't as one-sided as he'd believed.

Caitlin and Ace sat at the table. As Joseph sauntered over to greet them, he saw that he had interrupted a poker game. This evening, beans were the token of choice, the largest pile at the seat Rachel had just vacated.

"Uh-oh. I can see the lady's luck is still holding."

"Luck?" Ace shook his head. "The woman's a cardsharp."

"I am not," Rachel protested.

Caitlin was frowning over her cards. "I can't *believe* the awful hands I've been getting." She glanced up and smiled. "Come and join us, Joseph. Maybe you'll change our luck."

Joseph glanced around for his nephew. The toddler was fast asleep on the sofa in Rachel's small parlor. "Looks to me like someone ran low on steam."

"Ace let him play outside with the dogs," Caitlin explained. "They ran his little legs off."

Forcing himself not to study Rachel's delightful form and instead look at the cards, Joseph moved closer. When he saw his brother's hand, he winced and said, "Ouch."

"Do you mind?" Ace gave him a burning look. "Occasionally I like to bluff."

"You best say your prayers if you're going to bluff with a hand like that."

Ace threw his cards down. "Misdeal!"

"You can't call misdeal just because Joseph gave your hand away," Caitlin cried.

"Sure I can." Ace shot another glare at his brother. "Rachel's right. You stink. What *is* that smell?"

"You are a little odoriferous, Joseph," Caitlin agreed.

"Odor*iferous?* Where on earth did you learn a word like that?" Joseph asked.

"She reads occasionally," Rachel interjected.

Joseph cast her a sharp glance. She flashed a saucy smile and dimpled a cheek. In that moment, he sorely wished the guests weren't present. That bathtub was large enough for two. A vision of Rachel with soap bubbles slipping over her breasts filled his mind. His body snapped taut.

*God help me.* He marched away, determined to banish all such thoughts from his mind. She was a *lady*. She was *off-limits*. She was marriage bait.

Ace and Caitlin stayed after supper. Playing cards was impossible with two romping dogs and a lively toddler running about the kitchen, so the adults settled for chatting over coffee about nothing in particular.

Watching Rachel interact with Ace and Caitlin did Joseph's heart good, and seeing how gentle she was with Little Ace warmed him through and through. For a young lady who'd spent years in total seclusion, she was taking to company, and to children as well, like a duck to water. Joseph suddenly pictured her holding his child to her soft breast, a golden-haired angel gently stroking the gilded curls of a beautiful baby. And where had that come from? He didn't want a kid. He didn't want a wife.

In short, he didn't want these feelings.

"You ever seen an obedient dime?" Ace suddenly asked.

"Uh-oh," Caitlin said. "Here we go. Prepare yourself, Rachel. Once they get started on this, they just won't quit."

Rachel's eyes fairly danced as she met Ace's gaze. Then she glanced questioningly at Joseph. From his vantage point, it was a guileless look, but the question behind it— "Is this okay?"—only made Old Glory grow harder and throb more painfully. She looked to him for guidance. Knowing that made him ache to hold her in his arms. And how did that make sense? He wasn't in the market for a woman who looked to him for guidance. In short, he wasn't in the market for a wife, and she had "wife" written all over her.

Cheeks still rosy, she finally returned her gaze to Ace. "An obedient dime? No, I can't say I've ever seen one. Mine always jumped right out of my pocket."

Ace rifled through her cupboard for a wide-bottomed glass. Once back at the table, he placed a dime on the tablecloth and flanked it with two half-dollars, leaving about an inch between the coins. Then he perched the glass on the fifty-cent pieces.

"Without ever touching any of those coins," he informed Rachel, "I can make that dime come to my call."

"Ah, go on," Rachel said. "I bet you can't."

She glanced at Joseph again, her big blue eyes shimmering with emotions he didn't want to define. He was having enough trouble dealing with his own feelings, and he didn't need hers to cloud the issue. So why was she flashing those questioning glances his way, making him feel as if she counted on him to make decisions about everything outside her little world?

Because she'd come to trust him, he decided. And the realization brought him no joy. He didn't want her trust. He didn't want that responsibility. She was coming to count on him too much. And he was coming to want her to count on him *way* too much. That didn't fit into his life plan. He wanted to smoke at his table. He wanted to come home at the crack of dawn, drunk as a lord. He wanted to have no obligations to anyone, most especially a trusting woman with big blue eyes that made his heart ache. No matter how pretty she was. No matter how much he wanted her. Nothing about her fit—except the feel of her body against his. And that was Old Glory talking.

Joseph had learned years ago never to listen to Old Glory.

"How many beans is it worth to you to see me do it?" Ace asked.

Everyone burst out laughing. Rachel pursed her lips in thought. "Fifty," she finally wagered.

Ace sat at the table, called, "Come here, dime," and began lightly scratching the tablecloth with one fingernail. The dime walked out from under the glass, just as he had predicted. Rachel slumped in her chair, giggling helplessly as she shoved a mound of beans at him.

Not to be bested, Joseph fetched an egg

from the icebox. And why did he care about being bested? As he set up his trick on the table, he scolded himself for being such an idiot, but it didn't stop him from wanting to outshine his older brother in her eyes.

"You got any wine goblets?" he asked Rachel.

"What on earth do you need wine goblets for?"

"To show you an erratic egg."

She wiped tears of mirth from her eyes. "Out in the dining room." She handed Joseph the key to the archway ironwork. "You should find some goblets in Ma's sideboard."

When Joseph returned a moment later, he set the goblets on the table, rims touching, and put the egg in one of them. "Without ever touching that egg, I can make it hop from one glass to another."

"Oh, no, sir!" She flapped her hand at him. "No way." But her eyes told him that she believed he could do anything.

"What are you willing to wager on it?" Joseph asked. And, God forgive him, he wasn't thinking about beans.

She looked at her dwindling pile. "I don't have much left to wager with."

Joseph could think of several other things he'd love to win from her. "I'll take whatever you've got." *Those lovely breasts, for starters.* He wanted to taste her mouth, with no rules of propriety to forestall him. And he wanted to run his hands slowly over her skin, tantalizing her with the dance of his fingertips until she shuddered with pleasure. He wanted to see those blue eyes go foggy and blind with passion.

She nodded in agreement. Joseph bent and blew sharply into the goblet holding the egg, and just as he'd promised, the egg popped out into the other glass. Rachel's eyes went wide with amazement, then she burst out laughing again.

And so went the remainder of the evening. When the Keegan family finally departed, the hour had grown late and Joseph was exhausted. Not because he'd worked hard, but because he'd been wanting the forbidden for hours. *Rachel.* She was so beautiful. His fingers actually ached with his yearning to explore her body. When he glanced at her, his heart knocked.

*What in hell was wrong with him?* She was just a woman. Until now, any woman would do. Only suddenly he wanted her, and only her, with an intensity that made Old Glory burn. Even worse, she blushed every time he glanced her way, as if she were feeling the same. *No,* Joseph told himself. She was off-limits. It didn't matter if she was attracted to him. Down that path lay obligation—and marriage—and responsibility he didn't want.

Unfortunately, he also instinctively knew that other things also lay in wait if he followed his urges, namely pleasure such as he'd never experienced. He glimpsed the answering desire in her eyes whenever their gazes met and felt the heat between them whenever they moved close. He was drawn to her in a way that defied reason, and that scared the hell out of him. He would have willpower. He would ignore the urges of his body. And most important of all, he would pretend he didn't see that invitation in her eyes.

It was an innocent invitation—the reaction of an untried virgin to biological needs that she didn't understand. It was up to him to be strong and protect her from being compromised.

After locking the ironwork door, Rachel pocketed the key in her skirt and turned a radiant smile on him. Before he could guess what she meant to do, she launched herself at him.

"Oh, Joseph, *thank you*, thank you, thank you, *thank you*. This was the best day, *ever*."

Fiercely hugging his neck, she rained kisses on his face. For an instant, Joseph couldn't think what to do with his hands. Then, as if with a will of their own, they settled at her waist. She felt like heaven against him, all soft, feminine, rose-scented warmth, the fulfillment of an evening-long promise. The yearning for her that he'd been so determinedly holding at bay swamped him like an ocean wave, and he got all the same sensations that he'd experienced as a child playing on the California beach—a feeling of being knocked almost off his feet, then staggering to catch his balance on shifting sand. Oh, *God*, he wanted her.

All his fine principles about never trifling with a lady were forgotten as he settled his mouth over hers. It wasn't a thought or a decision. He just reacted to a need that had been growing within him all evening and had suddenly become bigger than he was. Caught by surprise, she gave a muffled bleep. Then she sighed, relaxed in his arms, and surrendered herself to him.

Joseph was lost. She had the sweetest mouth he'd ever tasted—her soft lips parting shyly, the tip of her tongue darting away from his for a moment and then hesitantly returning. *Fine silk, drenched in warm honey.* He wanted to taste every delectable inch of her. His pulse slammed in his temples. He ran his hands along her spine, then lowered them to the soft fullness of her hips to pull her hard against him.

At the back of his mind, warning bells went off. He shouldn't be doing this. She wasn't some working girl at the Golden Slipper who'd played the game countless times and made up the rules as she went along. This was Rachel, sweet, wonderful, innocent Rachel, who'd never even been kissed by anyone but him. But when he tried to make himself pull away, he couldn't. Instead, he deepened the kiss, thrusting deep, tasting and testing the most secret recesses of her mouth. She moaned and stepped up onto his boots to kiss him back with fierce, awkward hunger, taking her cues from him.

She was a quick learner, he thought dizzily,

a dear, untried, lovely student who had no idea of the danger into which he was luring her. *Rachel.* She felt perfectly right in his arms, as if she'd been fashioned just for him, and that sense of quiet awareness filled him again, even as he grazed his hands up her sides, feeling the soft ladder of her delicate ribs beneath his fingertips. *Right for him. All that he'd been searching for.* Dizzily, he assured himself that he'd never hurt her for the world, that this was only a kiss, a harmless kiss. He would stop soon. He would. And that was the last rational thought that went through his head.

And then her breasts were cupped in his hands. Her breath caught when his thumbs grazed her nipples through her clothing. She moaned and let her head fall back, offering herself to him with childlike trust. The change of position pressed her pelvis forward. He could feel her pliant warmth against his hardness. And the gift was too intoxicating to refuse.

He nipped lightly at her velvety skin, following the graceful column of her neck down to her collar, and then his fingers were at the buttons of her shirtwaist. As the blouse came undone, he trailed kisses in the wake of the parting fabric until he found the taut crest of one breast through the lawn of her simple chemise. She cried out and shuddered with pleasure as he drew on her nipple. Then she made fists in his hair to pull him closer. *Oh, yes.* This was better than anything he could buy. Better than anything he'd ever even dreamed of. *Rachel.* She was the taste that satisfied yearnings he'd never even realized that he had.

"Oh, Joseph!"

He spun in a slow half circle, with her feet riding on his boots. When he lowered her onto the bed and followed her down, he shifted to one side to avoid squashing her. He tugged at the ribbon laces at the front of her chemise to bare her breasts. They were as pale as ivory and as plump as little melons, the tips tinted a deep rose.

When he took one into his mouth, she arched her spine and cried out again. He caught the sensitive tip between his teeth, gave it a gentle roll, and then suckled her again. Her body quivered like a plucked bowstring. Running a hand down the front of her skirt, he made a fist over the cloth, pushed it high, and found the slit in her drawers. His fingertips were instantly drenched with hot, feminine wetness when he parted the soft folds at the apex of her thighs. His mouth found hers again. He kissed her deeply, passionately, as he homed in on the sensitive flange of flesh above her opening. She bucked her hips at the shock of sensation, but he rode her back down with the heel of his hand, lightly flicking and rubbing her, his only thought being to bring her to climax before he sought release for himself.

*Ruff-ruff-ruff.*

Buddy. The sound of his growling barks barely penetrated Joseph's brain.

But then it came again, a series of deep growls followed by three earsplitting yips. Joseph jerked as if he'd been touched by a red-hot brand. He broke off the kiss and stared stupidly into Rachel's dazed eyes. Felt her heat and wetness under his hand. Saw her bared breasts.

What in the hell was he *doing*?

He sprang to his feet. Bewilderment clouded Rachel's lovely features.

Grinning happily, Buddy scampered back and forth between Joseph and the bed.

Joseph grabbed for breath as if he'd just run a mile. He raked a hand through his hair.

"I am *so* sorry, Rachel. I don't know what came over me. I'm so sorry."

She pushed her skirt down and fumbled to close her bodice. Streaks of crimson flagged her cheeks as she sat up. "Please don't," she said softly. "It was as much my doing as yours. I started it, after all."

Joseph couldn't let himself off the hook quite that easily. Granted, she had initiated the embrace, but only with the most innocent of intentions. He was the one who'd taken it to another level. And, God help him, he was shaking with an urgent need to finish what he'd started.

Before he acted on that urge, he had to get away from her. This was *not* happening. He spun away to collect his bedroll and jacket from the water closet. When he emerged, Rachel gave him a bruised, hurt look.

"What are you doing?"

"I'll be sleeping in the dining room from here on out. I don't trust myself to stay in here with you."

She pushed to her feet. "But, Joseph, that's just silly."

Not silly. Had she no idea how devastatingly beautiful she was with her braid coming loose and her mouth swollen from his kisses? He wanted her so bad that he trembled.

"I'll be sleeping in another room, all the same. Do you mind letting me out?"

Joseph rolled his jacket, unrolled his jacket, and punched his jacket. He tried lying on his side. He tried lying on his back. He tried closing his eyes. He tried staring through the darkness at the ceiling. No how, no way could he drift off to sleep. Through the crack under the door, light from the kitchen spilled in a broad swath over the dining room floor to puddle against the wall. He couldn't help thinking that it was almost as golden as Rachel's hair.

What kind of man was he? Wanting her like this was wrong, and yearning to act on it was even worse. What if Buddy hadn't barked? Joseph kept coming back to that, furious with himself because he doubted that he would have come to his senses and stopped. He'd been that far gone.

Young women like Rachel were for marrying. Any man who would take her with no thought of making an honest woman of her wasn't worth the powder it would take to blow him to hell.

Did he want to marry her? Joseph mentally circled the question as if it were a coiled rattlesnake. He cared for her. There was no denying that. He had more feelings for her, in fact, than he'd ever had for any woman outside his family. But did he *love* her? It felt like love. Just a single tear, falling from one of her lovely blue eyes, had him scrambling to set her world to rights, and a single smile from her kissable lips made his heart soar. But couldn't that be only fondness?

And how the hell could he be sure that his feelings for her would last? Maybe he was letting Old Glory do his thinking for him again, and all these confusing emotions would vanish like a puff of smoke the moment he slaked his need for her.

A picture of her face moved through his mind. He didn't want to hurt her. She was too dear. He'd glimpsed pain in her beautiful blue eyes more than once. She'd already suffered enough without his adding to her heartache.

He heard the wood door creak open. The next instant, light poured into the dining room. He shifted his shoulders sideways and tucked in his chin to see Rachel standing behind the bars over the archway. She'd changed into a nightgown, pale pink and trimmed prettily with lace and ribbons. The lantern light behind her shone through the muslin, outlining every delightful curve of her body.

Joseph fleetingly wondered if one of the temptations that had so tortured Christ during his trial in the desert had been a beautiful woman in a nearly transparent gown.

"Joseph?" she called softly. "Are you still awake?"

He doubted he'd ever sleep again. "Yes, honey, wide awake."

"Can we talk for a bit?"

He almost groaned. "Only if you drape a blanket over your shoulders." *So I can't see your body.* "I don't want you taking a chill."

She spun away and returned a moment later wrapped in a blanket. He could still see the outline of her gorgeous legs, but at least the rest of her was hidden. He recalled the delicate pink of her nipples, and his body hardened.

She sat in the threshold, her back resting

against the doorframe, her knees hugged to her chest.

"So what do you want to talk about?" As if he didn't know. Every female he'd ever encountered intimately, in any degree, had wanted to talk about it afterward, especially if the intimate encounter had gone badly. Not that his intimate encounters usually did.

"Anything," she whispered, surprising him yet again. "I can't sleep."

He understood that problem. "Anything, huh?" He thought of a topic that had recently become dear to his heart. "You ever seen a courtyard?"

"You mean like in rich people's yards? It's a garden of sorts, isn't it?"

"Better than just a garden." Joseph punched at his jacket pillow again and lay on his side so it was easier to see her. "It's a room that's outside. Fancy ladies in big cities can go out in their nightclothes and sit in their courtyards of a morning to enjoy the sunshine and flowers. No one passing by on the street can see them."

She said nothing.

"Just imagine that, a room outside with an ironwork ceiling, made similar to your doors, and tall rock walls all around. You'd be even safer than you are in your kitchen. No shotgun can blow a hole through solid rock, that's for certain."

"Where did you see a courtyard?"

Joseph had seen courtyards in California as a boy. They hadn't been fortresses like he hoped to build for Rachel, but that was beside the point. "A number of people in California have them. They're really some pumpkins."

"Amazing. Too bad I'm not rich."

Joseph grinned. "Just imagine it, an outdoor room as safe as your kitchen where the sunlight comes down through the iron-bar ceiling and the birds and butterflies can come in."

She sighed wistfully. "With flowers all around," she added.

"Absolutely."

She sighed again. "It would be lovely. But there's no point in pining for things I can't have."

"It never hurts to dream a little," Joseph urged. "If *I* had a courtyard, I'd want a bird-bath and lots of flowers."

"Roses," she said. "I *love* the smell of roses."

Joseph had recently become fond of their

scent, too. Roses went onto his mental shopping list. He had no idea how to get any, but he felt confident that Caitlin did.

"And little stepping-stone walkways," she said dreamily.

Joseph's eyebrows lifted. Stepping-stones? *Whoa, girl. Don't get carried away.*

"And a fountain. If I were rich enough to have a courtyard, I'd want a fountain."

A fountain? That was way beyond anything he could give her. But at least he had her thinking about it and longing for an outdoor garden. "What other flowers do you like?"

"Lilacs," she said straightaway. "And violets. I adore violets. Tulips, too. Do you like tulips?"

Joseph liked all kinds of flowers. "I like tulips fine. What else would you enjoy about a courtyard besides the flowers?"

"The sunlight," she said fervently. "And feeling the wind on my face. Is there anything that smells lovelier than a summer breeze?"

She smelled lovelier than anything he'd ever known, all sweet and clean and dabbed with rose water. He studied her amber-limned features, imagining her sitting on a garden bench with sunlight igniting her golden curls and roses all around her.

"What would you say if I told you that you're about to get a courtyard?"

That brought her gaze to his. "Say what?"

"A bunch of folks hereabouts are going to start bringing wagonloads of rock for your courtyard any day now. The fellow that owns the quarry is donating the mortar mixings. And Bubba White has already started on the ironwork for your roof and gate."

Her eyes widened with incredulity. "You're serious."

"Dead serious. I wish I could take credit for the idea, but it was Sue Ellen White who came up with it. She talked it up at church and got a lot of other folks interested in helping out. 'Sunshine for Miss Rachel' is what they're calling it."

Her eyes went bright with tears. Then she covered her face with her hands.

"Sweetheart, don't cry."

"I can't help it," she said in a muffled voice. "A courtyard? Oh, lands, I can't believe it."

## Chapter Fifteen

The first wagonload of rock arrived the following morning, providing Joseph with a perfect excuse to stay outside most of the day, safely away from temptation. Since sexual frustration had his nerves strung tighter than a bowstring, he welcomed the opportunity to do some hard work.

Along about ten, Rachel cracked open the back door, clearly hoping to visit with him, but today he was farther from the porch. "I can't hear you, honey. I'd love to talk, but you'll have to open the door wider."

The door inched open just a little more. "Is that better?"

Joseph could hear her now, but he wasn't about to tell her so. "What was that?"

The crack widened. "Can you hear me now?"

"Come again?"

Finally her face appeared in the opening.

"Oh, *Joseph*." She beamed a radiant smile. "I can see *out*!"

"Imagine that." He mixed another batch of mortar in the wheelbarrow and began adding the second tier of rock to the courtyard wall. "You've got the bars to protect you, honey. Open on up and enjoy the morning."

"I'm good just like this," she insisted.

But soon she was sitting on the floor with the door opened wide enough to accommodate her bent knees.

"I can hear the birds, Joseph. Oh, lands, this is so wonderful!"

"If you'd open the door all the way, you might even see the little buggers."

She didn't find the courage immediately, but within a couple of hours she finally had the door flung wide. The look of utter joy on her face was something Joseph believed he would remember for the rest of his life. She said nothing. Instead, she just sat there, drinking in the sights and sounds for which she'd thirsted for so long.

At last she said, "Oh, Joseph, this is wonderful. Just *listen*."

Joseph paused in his work to cock an ear. At first he heard nothing, but then he realized that wasn't precisely true. He actually heard a multitude of sounds that were so commonplace to him that he mostly ignored them—the buzz of a fly, the raucous call of a jay, the wind whispering through the grass, the creaking of the oak as it shifted in the breeze.

"Pretty incredible, isn't it?" he asked.

"Oh, it's beyond incredible." She flung her arms wide. "The door is open, and I can breathe, Joseph. It's a *miracle*."

Her miracle came to an abrupt end when a new sound reached them, that of an approaching wagon. Buddy sprang to his feet and started barking. Rachel vanished lickety-split and slammed the door behind her. Squinting against the sunlight, Joseph saw that the driver was Charley Banks, and judging by the drop of the wagon, he had it loaded to capacity with rock. Way off in the distance, Joseph saw another wagon coming in as well.

Rachel's courtyard was about to become a reality.

Over the next two weeks, Joseph's days fell into a repeating pattern. As soon as he'd finished the morning chores and eaten breakfast, he went to work on the courtyard walls, stopping only to eat lunch or when Ace came over to stand guard duty. When the latter occurred, Joseph took care of errands in town, rode the Hollister land to check on Rachel's tiny herd of cattle, and then headed south to monitor his place. Darby was recovering nicely and beginning to grump about staying in bed, which told Joseph that the old foreman would soon be healed enough to come home.

That being the case, it was with a sense of sadness that Joseph saw the courtyard walls grow taller. Before he knew it, the project would be completed, Darby would return, and he would have no reason to stay on with Rachel.

Joseph tried to tell himself that he'd be pleased as punch to have his life back to normal again. Calving season was drawing to an end. He'd be free to go into town on Friday nights to play poker and pursue other pleasures. And, hey, he'd be able to sleep in a regular bed again. But somehow none of those thoughts cheered him. He had a challenging poker opponent in Rachel, and the idea of a two-dollar poke in the upstairs rooms of the Golden Slipper now held little appeal. There was only one woman he wanted. And unless he was prepared to marry her, he couldn't, in good conscience, have her.

One afternoon when Ace came over to lend a hand with the courtyard walls, Joseph blurted out his troubles.

He began with, "How do you know when it's the real thing, Ace?"

Slathering mortar over a section of rock, Ace sent Joseph a sidelong look. "When what's the real thing? If you're talking about gold, you bite it."

Joseph swore under his breath. "You know very well what I'm talking about. Why are you always so dad-blamed difficult?"

Ace chuckled. "The last time I even *hinted* at that, you damned near took my head off. Oh, no, little brother. You want to talk about it, you're going to say the word straight out."

Joseph slapped a rock into place on the wall with such force that the impact jarred his teeth. "What's in a word? It's the feeling that matters."

"Yeah, and if you can't put a name to the feeling, you have a problem."

Joseph added another rock, this time with a little less force. "All *right*, damn it. I think I may be in love with her."

"If you only *think* you're in love with her, you're not. There's no thinking to it when it happens. You can't breathe for wanting her, and the mere thought of losing her ties your guts into knots."

When Joseph thought of leaving Rachel to return home, knotted guts were the least of his troubles. His heart actually hurt. "I reckon I love her, then." He slapped another rock into place. "Only what if I'm wrong? What if my feelings for her fade? I've never had any constancy with women. You know that."

"Before he falls in love, what man does?" Ace wiped a speck of mortar from his lean cheek. "Love brings about changes of heart you can never imagine until they happen to you."

"What kind of changes?"

Ace mused over the question for a moment. "Well, for one thing, if you're really in love, you're ruined for all other females."

Joseph muttered none too happily under his breath again.

"And when you're truly in love, what you once regarded as a huge burden and responsibility, namely a wife and kids, suddenly is a pleasure. You *want* the responsibility, and when that first child comes into the world, instead of thinking of the scary stuff, you're so proud you think you'll bust."

"Little Ace is a fine boy. I don't blame you for being proud."

"I can tell you this. You've never felt love until you hold your own little baby in your arms. If he sneezes, your heart almost stops for fear he's taking sick, and you wake up in the dead of night to poke a finger under his nose just to make sure he's still breathing. And if by chance he's between breaths and you feel nothing, pure panic seizes you."

"Sounds like a bad case of influenza to me."

Ace grinned. "I reckon that's why we don't *decide* to fall in love. It just happens upon us. Later in the marriage, I reckon there are times when love does become a decision— along about the time your wife gets her monthly curse, and the sweet, angelic little gal you married suddenly snarls at you like a hydrophobic dog. When that happens, you *decide* to love her anyway and don't snarl back."

"When has Caitlin ever snarled at you?"

"Hasn't—yet. But she's been grumpy as all get-out a few times. In short, Joseph, your feelings for a woman do change after a

time. It doesn't stay fresh and exciting forever."

"I knew it."

Ace nodded sagely. "One day you wake
up, and you realize you know everything
there is to know about her. You've heard all
her stories. You know what she's going to
say before she says it. Your feelings
change, plain and simple. The excitement of
new love is gone."

"You see?" Joseph slapped another rock
into place with such strength that mortar
splattered in all directions. "That's exactly
my worry, that I'll make a commitment and
then wake up one morning with changed
feelings."

"It'll happen," Ace said with absolute certainty. "And that's the best part of all, the
changes that come with time."

Joseph gave his brother another sharp,
questioning look.

"When the excitement fades, the real love
takes over," Ace went on. "It's there from
the start, I reckon. It's what brings two people together. But in the beginning the real
love is overshadowed by all the excitement
and newness. When the excitement wears

off, you get down to the reality of love, and that's the best part."

"If the excitement goes, how can that be the best part?"

"Don't confuse excitement with passion. Caitlin still excites me that way as no other woman ever has—or ever will. I'm talking about in between those times, when you're troubled and she understands without your ever saying a single word. Or when you sit with her on the porch of an evening to watch the sunset, and you find that just holding her hand and being with her is the best part of your whole day. Love gets comfortable, sort of like your favorite pair of boots."

Joseph braced his hands against the wall and stared down at his Justins. He wouldn't trade them for a dozen new pairs and dreaded when they wore out. "So that's how I'll feel about Rachel in five years—like she's my favorite pair of boots?"

Ace snorted with laughter. "Not exactly, no. But something like that. I've never been good with words, Joseph. You know that. All I'm saying is, the new wears off, and the feelings change. For instance—have you ever seen a really, *really* pregnant woman who walks with her back arched and her feet spread wide to keep her balance, and thought she was the most beautiful female you'd ever seen in your life?"

Joseph shook his head. "No, I can't rightly say I have. Pregnant women mostly just look swollen up and awkward, if you ask me."

"Same here. I'd never seen a pregnant woman I thought was beautiful until Caitlin was big and pregnant with Little Ace. And then, let me tell you, my eyes were opened. In my opinion, she'll never be more beautiful than she was during the last weeks of her pregnancy. I think she's gorgeous now. Don't get me wrong. But she was flat *beautiful* then. Sometimes I'd look at her and get tears in my eyes."

Joseph saw a suspicious gleam of wetness in his brother's eyes even now. Old boots and pregnant women? A part of Joseph just didn't get it, but another part of him—the part in his heart that hurt at the thought of leaving Rachel—sort of understood.

"I don't want to hurt her," he told his brother. "You know what I'm saying? Before I say a word to her, I need to be absolutely sure that my feelings for her are real and lasting."

"You're a good man, Joseph. And knowing you as I do, it's my guess that you wouldn't be wrestling with all these questions if you didn't love the girl. That's part of it, you know, never wanting to cause her pain. When that becomes one of your biggest concerns, you're usually already gone coon."

Later that same afternoon when Joseph was riding in from a tour of Rachel's land, he encountered David on the road that led up to the house.

"Hey, big brother," David called. "What're you doing out here? I thought you had to stay close to Rachel."

"Normally do." Joseph drew Obie into a trot to ride apace with David's gelding. "Ace is spelling me for a bit. I went over to check on things at home. Then I rode the fence line over here and checked on the cattle. Darby runs fewer than twenty head, but they still require a look-see every now and again."

"How's Darby doing?" David asked.

"Chomping at the bit to be out of bed. He's looking real good. What brings you out this way in the middle of the afternoon?"

"The circuit judge came to town. He slapped Jeb Pritchard with a steep fine for shooting at us that afternoon when we rode over to his place, threatened him with a six-month jail sentence if he ever does it again, and turned the old bastard loose."

Joseph wasn't happy to hear that. "Damn it. After all we did to put the son of a bitch behind bars?"

"I hear you," David commiserated, "but once the judge rules on a case, it's out of my hands. I figured you needed to know." He gazed out across the pastureland. "Best be keeping a sharp eye out, just in case. If he's our man, he's fit to be tied right now and spoiling for trouble."

Joseph shook his head. "That's the flaw in circuit judges. They have no idea what's happening locally and make stupid rulings."

"Well, there's one bright note," David replied. "My jail smells a hell of a lot better with that old coot out of there." As they approached the house, David whistled. "You've flat been working, son. Looks to me like you've got that courtyard almost done. Before you know it, Darby will be back to full steam and you'll be free to make tracks."

"In another week, I reckon."

The knowledge that his time with Rachel was running out made Joseph feel as if a steel band were being tightened around his chest.

The last day of the courtyard wall construction, half the town showed up to add the finishing touches. Joseph had told Bubba about Rachel's list of courtyard appointments, and Bubba had passed the information on to Sue Ellen, who evidently had a habit of flapping her jaw almost as hard as she worked. Everybody and his brother seemed to know exactly what Rachel wanted, and they were hell-bent to see that she got most of it.

Bubba brought the ironwork. Sue Ellen came with a second wagon filled with cuttings from her garden. Ron and Diana Christian showed up with a beautiful bench that the sawyer had crafted after hours. In one of his rare moments of defiance against his skinflint wife, Harrison Gilpatrick arrived bearing rosebushes that he had already ordered from Sacramento for the spring planting season. Several ranchers and their wives brought yet more plants that they'd taken from their own yards. Jesse Chandler, the chimney sweep, and his wife, Dorothy, who ran the local candle shop, brought three birdhouses that he had made and she had decorated. Doc Halloway contributed a birdbath that he claimed he never used.

Joseph was overwhelmed by his neighbors' generosity. "Thank you. Thank you so much."

The responses Joseph received all rang with one common note, a generosity of spirit that nearly brought tears to his eyes: "It's nothing." "It's our pleasure." "We just pray she can come out and enjoy the sunlight." He only wished Rachel could find the courage to open her door and personally thank everyone.

But that was wishing for too much. She had already come a long way in a very short time. Having so many people in her dooryard was probably terrifying for her. Fortunately, no one had arrived with any expectations. They'd come to work, and work they did. After the ironwork was laid out over the enclosure, everyone helped lay the final tier of rock to anchor the bars. The bolts to the garden gate were set right into the concrete, making the stout barrier of iron as close to being impenetrable as the rock to which it was attached.

The women worked within the enclosure

on the aesthetic aspects of the courtyard. One of them came up with the idea of building small corner shelters atop the wall for nesting robins. Stepping-stones were laid out to wind through the flowers. Bubba's burly son, Eugene, dug a small pond—Sue Ellen's idea, in lieu of a fountain—and Charley Banks lined it with mortar and rock to hold water. Garrett Buckmaster donated some goldfish from his own fishpond. Clarissa Denny, the dressmaker, supplied the fish food, purchased at the general store. Beatrice Masterson, the milliner, brought strips of sod from her own lawn to add small sections of green grass. Shelby Templeton, the cobbler, and his wife, Penny, brought a sapling oak.

When all was done, Joseph teared up, an embarrassing moment for a man who'd always kept his emotions under tight rein. Caitlin hugged his arm and patted his chest. "It is beautiful, isn't it?"

Joseph had such a lump in his throat he could only nod. It was early in the season yet, so only the violets and crocus were in bloom, but the women had managed to make it look like an established garden, equal to anything Joseph had ever seen in

San Francisco. It went beyond beautiful. Every inch of that courtyard had been created with loving and caring hands.

Ace saved Joseph the need to speak. "As you all can see, my brother is struck speechless, and well he should be. This is, beyond a doubt, the prettiest little garden I've ever seen. Miss Rachel is going to love it." Ace motioned toward the closed door. "She's got a peephole, you know. I'm sure she's peeking out even as I speak. This is a beautiful gift. There are no words to thank all of you."

The courtyard was so packed with people that Joseph feared the newly transplanted flowers might be trampled. Everyone stepped carefully, though. Sue Ellen White smiled and waved at the door. "Hello, Rachel! Joseph did most of the work, but we hope you enjoy the little things we've added."

Others called out as well, saying they also had contributed very little but hoped she could enjoy the enclosure.

Rachel collapsed on a chair at the table and sobbed her heart out. All those people! For so many years, she'd felt alienated from everyone in town, convinced that they all

thought her insane. To have them band together like this to give her an outdoor garden touched her so deeply that she had no
words. She hadn't been forgotten, after all.
They simply hadn't known how to help her.

She was still weeping when she heard the
wagons begin to pull out. Soon she heard
footsteps inside the house. She tried to dry
her eyes, but the tears just kept coming.

A knock sounded on the archway door.
"Rachel, open up, darlin'."

She didn't want Joseph to see her like this.
Oh, *God*. It felt as if her heart was breaking,
only for happiness. He knocked again.

"Sweetheart, don't do this to me. I can't
get in."

She scrubbed at her cheeks again. "I'm c-
coming."

"Why are you crying?" he called. "Have
you seen that beautiful courtyard?"

Stifling her sobs, she went to the archway,
opened the door, and then struggled to insert the key into the lock with shaking
hands. The instant the iron barrier was un-
latched, Joseph swept into the room. He
took the key from her and locked up after
himself. Then he closed and barred the
wooden door.

"What is this?" He tucked the key back into her skirt pocket and drew her into his arms. "Don't cry, sweetheart. You should be happy."

It felt so wonderful to be held by him again. Over the last two weeks, he'd scarcely touched her—only an occasional, accidental brush of their fingertips, and he'd absolutely refused to sleep in her water closet anymore.

"Oh, Joseph, it's s-so b-beautiful."

"And that's to cry about?"

He cupped the back of her head in a big, hard hand. Rachel pressed her face into the lee of his shoulder and savored the feeling. She wished the moment might last forever, that he'd never pull away and leave her feeling alone again. He drew her over to the sofa and sat with her still held in his arms.

"Enough, darlin'. I hate it when you cry."

Rachel took a shuddering breath. Then she closed her eyes and sank against him. She loved having his well-muscled body curled partly around her, loved resting her cheek against his heat. She could hear his heartbeat, a strong and sturdy *thump-thump-thump* that was reassuringly rhythmic and even, not thready and erratic like her own.

They sat in silence for a long while, and then he gently set her away from him. "I'm sorry," he said huskily, "but if we stay close much longer, I'll do something we may both regret."

Rachel didn't believe that she would ever regret anything that happened between them. He lived by rules that were important in his world but weren't in hers. She ran a hand over his ribbed chest, pleasuring herself just by touching him. He caught her wrist and shook his head.

"Please don't," he said thickly. "I'm hanging on by a thin thread as it is."

Rachel didn't want him to hang on. "Darby will come home soon, and you'll leave," she whispered. "Is it so wrong for me to want this time with you, so wrong to want the memories only you can give me?"

His grip on her wrist tightened. "I want to give you more than memories." He took a deep breath, met her gaze with burning intensity, exhaled shakily, and said, "Will you marry me, Rachel?"

The question took her completely by surprise. She tried to free her wrist. "What?"

He kept a firm hold on her. "I spoke plain. Will you marry me?"

She shook her head mutely.

"You talk about me leaving? I don't think I can. I love you, Rachel Hollister. I want you as my wife. I want to give you my babies. I want to grow old with you."

Fresh tears sprang to Rachel's eyes. "Are you mad? I can't marry you, Joseph. What have I to offer you?"

"Everything," he said huskily. "Absolutely everything."

"I can't raise children, living as I do. What would I do, push them out through the wood safe to see them off to school?" She gestured with her free hand to encompass the kitchen. "A family can't live in one room."

"I'll remodel my place and make it one hell of a big room," he said softly. "And I'll build you another courtyard and a vestibule as well, a safe antechamber so you can look out through your bars before you let anyone into the house. The children can come and go through the garden gate."

Rachel shook her head. "No, Joseph. Children need their own bedrooms. A family can't exist the way I live."

"Sure it can," he insisted. "The water closet is another room. That doesn't bother you. The cellar is another room. That doesn't bother you, either. We could have a regular home, Rachel, you and I together, with bedrooms for our children."

He made it sound so attainable. It was true that the water closet didn't bother her, or the cellar, either.

"I'll make it work," he whispered. "I swear to you, darlin', I can make it work. No hallways to frighten you, just a big room like this with water closets all around, only they'll be bedrooms, with you in the big room, living as you do now, never needing to go outside unless it's to sit in your courtyard or work in your flowerbeds."

The thought of leaving her kitchen and moving to his place terrified Rachel. She shook her head again. "I can't leave here, Joseph. I'm sorry. I want to be with you more than anything. But I just can't leave here."

He sighed and lifted her clenched fist to trail kisses over her knuckles. "All right, then. We'll live here. I can modify this place, adding on water closets as we have babies."

Rachel gaped at him. "But you have your own ranch."

"And the land adjoins yours. Maybe Darby

would be willing to live at my place. It's only a house, Rachel. Only a piece of land. I'll sell out if I have to. What I can't do—what I absolutely can't do is go home and be apart from you. I've been wrestling with the problem for two weeks. I just can't do it, darlin'."

Fresh tears welled in Rachel's eyes. "Then don't go. Stay. We don't have to get married for you to stay."

"Oh, yes, we do," he retorted. "I have a set of standards, Rachel Hollister. We'll either do it right, or we won't do it at all."

Rachel wanted so badly to say yes. Oh, how desperately she wanted that. But the whole idea rocked her world. "I can't leave here, Joseph."

"I'm real clear on that, Rachel. I'm not asking you to leave here. I'm just asking you to make what's between us right in the eyes of God."

"But *how*? How would we even get married?"

"I'll bring the preacher here."

"Into my kitchen?"

He smiled. "You've got bars, sweetheart. He can stand in the dining room and say the words. Or we can do it in your courtyard, with him outside the garden gate. He doesn't have to be *in* your kitchen or *in* your courtyard for us to do the deed."

"What if our baby got sick?"

"I'd bring Doc out. You know Doc. Surely you trust him enough to let him inside."

Rachel did trust Doc. She focused on a button of Joseph's shirt. "I don't know. There would be so many problems, Joseph. I've never even considered the possibility of getting married."

He kissed her knuckles again. Then he forced her fingers to unfurl so he could trail the tip of his tongue over her palm. "I want you," he whispered. "I want to hold you in my arms and love on you the whole night long. It's a powerful kind of want, Rachel. So powerful that I'm not sure I'll be able to control it if I'm around you too much."

Jolts of sensation shot up Rachel's arm. With every flick of his tongue, she melted a little more. "Wh-what are you saying?"

"That you have to marry me. Otherwise, I'll have to stay away to keep from taking you." He nibbled at the base of her thumb. "I want to taste you like this all over. I'm dying, I tell you. Put me out of my misery and just say yes."

He tugged her toward him and began nibbling under her ear. Rachel's head went dizzy and her insides turned molten. Her lashes fluttered closed. She remembered how it felt when he'd kissed her breasts— how divine it was when he'd touched her in her most secret place. Her breath began to come in ragged little spurts that didn't quite reach her lungs. She wanted to experience all those feelings again more than she'd ever wanted anything.

"Oh, Joseph," she moaned.

"Say yes," he whispered urgently. "Trust me to make it all work, darlin'. It'll be perfect, I swear. Please, just say yes."

"Yes," she breathed. "Oh, yes, Joseph." She wanted him to open her shirtwaist again, to bare her breasts. "Yes, yes, yes."

He drew her into his arms, enfolding her in a fierce hug that almost crushed her bones. "You're sure?"

"Yes, oh, yes."

"Then I'll make the arrangements." He grasped her firmly by the shoulders and set her away from him. "I want it done as soon as possible. No folderol, no nonsense. We'll keep it simple and just get it done."

Rachel blinked and almost toppled off the sofa cushion. She watched in bewildered confusion as he pushed to his feet and started pacing. "We'll invite Caitlin and Ace, of course, and David, too. I know you've never met my little brother, Esa, but will you mind terribly if he comes?"

What Rachel minded was that he had left her. *Again.* She pushed at her hair, straightened her shirtwaist, and gained her feet. "I thought if I agreed to marry you that we'd— you know. If we're going to get married soon, I thought that we could finish this time."

He settled an implacable gaze on her. "We haven't even started yet. Trust me on that. And we won't, not until I've got a ring on that pretty little finger I was just kissing."

"But what harm is there in—" She broke off. "If we're going to be married, Joseph, why can't we be together that way a tiny bit early?"

"Because that's putting the cart before the horse. When I make love to you, you're going to be my wife, right and proper. I won't have it any other way."

Rachel searched his expression and knew he meant it. "But *why*?"

"Because it's the Paxton way. We're going to do this properly."

She could see that arguing with him would get her nowhere. "How long will doing it properly take?"

The following morning, Joseph opened the back door wide and led Rachel to the ironwork over the opening so she could look out on her courtyard. "It's perfectly safe," he assured her. "Nothing can get in but birds, butterflies, and bugs. Do you feel up to going out there?"

Rachel wasn't sure. "Oh, Joseph, I don't know. I'm fine standing here behind the bars, but—"

"You've got more bars out there, honey." He stepped in close behind her and encircled her waist with his arms. "I'll hold you close. How's that? If you start having a problem breathing, I'll carry you back inside."

Rachel had taken to carrying both keys in her skirt pocket at all times. He loosened one arm from around her and went fishing. When he plucked out the key, she shrank against him and closed her eyes. "Wait!" she cried.

"I'm right here," he assured her. "I won't let any harm come to you, Rachel. I swear it.

We'll go out together. I won't turn loose of you unless you want me to."

He reached around her to insert the key into the lock. The mechanism grated loudly as it disengaged. He dropped the key back into her pocket and pushed open the iron-work. Rachel felt like a bit of flotsam being carried forth by a wave. His chest was a wall at her back, his arms like steel bands around her, his legs pushing against hers to make her feet move.

"Joseph?" she said shrilly.

"I'm right here. One little step at a time. You're okay."

They were out on the porch. Panic washed through her in cold waves. She expected her lungs to freeze. But that didn't happen. He stopped at the steps and just held her close. She felt his heartbeat thrumming against her shoulder, felt his breath sifting through her hair to warm her scalp. She leaned weakly against him and closed her eyes, scarcely able to believe that she was outdoors and not suffocating.

"I love you," he whispered near her ear. "I love you as I never have anyone or anything. Please open your eyes, Rachel. Trust me."

She trusted him as she had never trusted

anyone. She lifted her lashes. A little bluebird came down through the ironwork roof
just then to light on the back of the bench.
Then, with a flutter of his wings, he sailed
over to the birdbath. Water flew as he
dunked his head and flapped his wings.
Rachel watched through a blur of tears.

"Oh, *Joseph*."

"Pretty wonderful, huh?" Then his body
went suddenly tense. "Oh, *shit*."

"What?" Rachel glanced up and all
around, but she saw nothing alarming, only
thick rock walls and stout iron bars to keep
everything but the smallest of creatures out.
"What is it?"

"The fish. When the mortar was set, I was
supposed to fill the pond and put them in. I
forgot all about them. I hope the little buggers didn't freeze last night."

Rachel's heart caught. "Where are they?"

"In that can by the bench."

"Oh, the poor things." Rachel broke free of
his embrace and hurried down the steps.
She was halfway across the courtyard before it struck her that she was outside. Oh,
God, *outside*. She staggered to a stop,
frozen in her tracks. Her heart pounded violently. But nothing else happened. She

could still breathe. She just felt a little dizzy and disoriented. "Joseph?"

"You're fine, sweetheart. You've got walls all around you. Look at them. Name me anything that can go through that rock."

The tension eased slowly from Rachel's body. She turned in place, looking all around, and there were walls everywhere. She let her head fall back to put her face up to the sun. The gentle warmth on her skin was beyond wonderful. She held her arms wide and turned again, filling her lungs with fresh, cool morning air. Oh, lands, it smelled so good.

She heard Joseph chuckle. She stopped spinning to face him. A smile curved her lips. She wanted to shout. She felt just that wonderful.

"Have I ever told you that you're the most gorgeous creature I've ever clapped eyes on?" he asked.

Rachel shook her head.

"Well, you are. I think I fell in love with you the first time I ever saw you."

It occurred to Rachel then that she'd never told him that she loved him back. She swallowed to steady her voice. "I love you, too, Joseph. I love you, too."

He said nothing, but that was all right because his eyes told her all she needed to know. "You gonna stand there all day or check on those poor fish?"

"Oh!" The bluebird skittered away as Rachel ran the remaining length of the courtyard. She picked up the can to peer inside. She saw a flash of orange. "They're fine," she cried. "There are three, Joseph. My goodness, they're so tiny."

"They'll grow. They're probably just babies."

"Whatever shall I feed them?"

"Clarissa Denny brought you a tin of food," he assured her. "The first order of business is to fill the pond so they've got a place to swim."

He set himself to the task of hauling water from the kitchen in a milk bucket while Rachel knelt to admire her violets. Joy creased her cheeks as she fingered the delicate purple blossoms. She'd thought never to touch a living flower petal again.

"You okay?"

"I'm fabulous. I've never been better."

After filling the pond, he set the fish loose in the water and scattered granules of food from the tin that he'd fetched from the porch. Rachel sat beside the pond to watch the fish eat. The sunlight played on the water, sparkling like diamonds. It had been so long, so very long, since she'd been outdoors.

The morning breeze drifted in through the garden gate, ruffling her hair. It carried with it scents that she'd almost forgotten—the smell of oak and pine, of grass and manzanita, and fresh air blowing in off the mountains.

"Oh, Joseph."

He sat on the garden bench, one boot propped on his opposite knee, his arms riding the top rail of the backrest. When Rachel glanced up, she knew that she'd never seen any man more handsome. When she said as much, he laughed.

"Yeah, well, you haven't seen many men in a good long while. Could be I'm homely and you just don't know it."

Rachel had more trust in her memory than that. Joseph Paxton was one good-looking fellow. She pushed to her feet and walked slowly toward him. A guarded look entered his eyes.

"Don't even think about it," he said.

Rachel stopped and put her hands on her

hips. "How do you know what I'm thinking about?"

He gave her a mischievous wink. "Because I'm thinking about the same thing."

She tapped her toe on the dirt. "Are you now?"

"I am, and thinking about it is all I'm going to do."

Rachel sighed in defeat and went back to admiring her violets.

The wedding took place three days later. Joseph meant for it to be a simple affair, with only the preacher, Darby, and members of his family in attendance, but somehow the word got out that Miss Rachel, presently the most popular lady in town, was getting married, and everybody and his brother came to witness the nuptials. Taking a head count through the garden gate, Joseph saw that everyone who'd worked on the court-yard was there, plus a few extras, and they evidently meant to stay afterward to cele-brate, for they'd brought sawhorses and planks to serve as makeshift tables, along with countless dishes of food.

Didn't they understand that Rachel was terrified of strangers? Joseph was afraid that the presence of so many people might force them to have the ceremony inside, and that wouldn't do. He wanted his bride to be standing outdoors in the sunlight when she gave him her hand in marriage. He thought about stepping outside to ask them all to leave but changed his mind when he saw Caitlin's redheaded brother, Patrick O'Shannessy, along with his lovely, newly pregnant wife, Faith, and their daughter, Chastity. Not all were strangers. Some were family who had reason and right to witness this wedding.

As that thought went through Joseph's mind, he saw a woman with a cane standing off by herself under the oak tree. She was dressed all in blue, her day gown mostly covered by a matching double-tiered cape. Atop her head she wore a blue Venice bonnet with a veil covering her face. Through the netting, Joseph had to stare hard to make out her delicate features. He inclined his head to her and smiled. She nodded in return. Amanda Hollister had come to attend her great-niece's wedding.

The knowledge filled Joseph with a sense of rightness that was multiplied a hundredfold when his bride emerged from the kitchen to stand on the porch. She wore a white dress that Caitlin had worked day and night to complete, a delicate, ethereal creation of satin and lace. Sunlight pooled around her like a halo. Joseph took one look at her and knew she was the most beautiful creature on God's green earth. Through the lace veil, she was smiling at him—a radiant, angelic smile made all the more brilliant by the sparkling tears on her cheeks.

A raucous clamor of bells rang out. Joseph was startled by the noise and glanced over his shoulder to find the source. Esa, shaking three cowbells, grinned from ear to ear. "I never thought I'd see this day, my brother Joseph tying the knot. We have to mark the moment."

Joseph winced. He'd been joking about ringing cowbells at Darby's wedding. What was Esa thinking? Only somehow it was the perfect touch, a dash of family craziness tossed in to make the most wonderful day of his life truly memorable. Years from now, when he remembered this moment, he would smile over Esa's idiocy.

Only his brothers weren't done. Oh, no. David unearthed his fiddle from behind the bench, Ace plucked his mouth organ from his shirt pocket, and the three of them filled the air with a blend of sour notes and clanging that sounded a little like the wedding march with church bells ringing in the background—if Joseph used his imagination.

Rachel clung to Darby's arm as he led her down the porch steps. If asked at that moment what her thoughts were, she couldn't have said. She had eyes only for Joseph, who stood waiting for her at the garden gate. In her mind, Bubba's iron bars had come to symbolize freedom and new beginnings, so it seemed fitting that Joseph should be standing in front of those bars. Joseph had made all of this happen for her, after all. Sunlight, fresh air, the scent of new violets, birdsong. He'd filled her life with so many wondrous things, and now he meant to fill it with still more—a future with him, the chance to love and be loved, and possibly to even have babies. Never had she felt so happy.

When the music began, Rachel thought it was so beautiful. *Music.* She'd heard not a single note in over five years. She moved slowly forward, taking her cues from Darby, her oldest and dearest friend, but keeping her gaze fixed on Joseph. He was so handsome. He wore a black, Western-cut suit jacket that showcased his muscular build, a black string tie dividing the starched points of his white shirt collar. Though she'd never seen him in anything but faded denim and chambray, he wore the finery with aplomb.

As Rachel drew closer to him, she glanced at his feet and almost burst out laughing. A woman might take a cowboy out of his jeans, work shirt, and Stetson, but never out of his boots. Though he had polished them up, he wore his Justins, scuff marks, gouges, and all. No spurs, thank goodness. If he accidentally dropped the ring, he might have to squat.

Through the veil, she met his gaze. The burning intensity in his blue eyes made her feel like the most loved woman on earth. Darby put Rachel's hand into Joseph's, then discreetly stepped aside to stand by Caitlin, the matron of honor. As best man, Ace stood at the other side of the gate, opposite his wife. David and Esa also stood nearby, the latter holding Little Ace.

Joseph gave Rachel's hand a gentle squeeze and placed it on the crook of his arm, his fingers resting warmly over hers.

Then he turned her so they faced the gate that opened from the courtyard into the surrounding backyard. Rachel leaned closer to him, needing to feel his solid strength as they made ready to say their vows.

Hannibal St. John, No Name's new preacher, stood just outside the courtyard gate, gazing solemnly at them through the bars. He was a tall, fine figure of a man with hair almost as blond as Joseph's. His earnest blue eyes were kind and understanding, which helped soothe Rachel's sudden attack of nerves when she saw all the people gathered in the backyard behind him. *Lands.* Joseph squeezed her hand again, as if he sensed her panic. *I'm here,* that squeeze said. *Don't be afraid. I won't let anyone hurt you.*

Rachel willed the tension away and tried to focus on the preacher.

"Dearly beloved," Hannibal said in a booming voice, "we're gathered together here today . . ."

St. John went on to give a short homily on the sanctity of marriage, but Rachel scarcely registered a word. No matter. She *knew* what marriage was all about. She'd been raised in a loving family by parents who'd taught her with their everyday actions. She also had Joseph to guide her if ever she should falter. *No hallways to frighten you, just a big room like this with water closets all around.* With a husband like that, how could she fail to be a loving, selfless wife?

"Do you, Joseph Simon Paxton, wish to take this woman, Rachel Marie Hollister, to be your lawful wife?"

Joseph squeezed Rachel's hand again and turned to look at her face through the veil. "I do," he said in a loud, certain voice.

Rachel didn't hear the rest of the ceremony. Somehow she managed to repeat her vows on cue, and Joseph got the wedding band on her finger as well.

When Hannibal St. John pronounced them man and wife and then told Joseph that he could kiss his bride, Joseph lifted her veil with shaky hands, drew her into his arms, and kissed her as if tomorrow might never come. Buddy barked, casting his vote of approval. Cleveland echoed the sound. Joseph's brothers hooted, whistled, and cheered. Weeping as if at a funeral, Caitlin rushed over to hug them both.

"Congratulations!" she cried. "Oh, you

make such a beautiful couple." Sob, sniff. "Our Joseph, married. I just can't believe it! Your mother will have fits when she learns it happened without her being here."

"I know," Joseph replied, "but I wasn't about to wait for her to travel all the way from San Francisco."

Rachel felt a large pair of hands settle on her shoulders, and the next thing she knew, she was being kissed by her eldest brother-in-law, the fearsome gunslinger Ace Keegan, who, she'd learned, wasn't really fearsome at all. Next, she was passed to David, who teasingly arched her back over his arm and pretended to kiss her deeply.

"Jealous, big brother?" he asked as he allowed Rachel to come upright.

"Hell, no," Joseph retorted.

Esa, who looked more like David than he did Joseph, approached Rachel shyly and thrust out his hand. "Us never meeting before this, I don't reckon it's appropriate for me to kiss the bride today."

Joseph piped in with, "If you're thinking on doing it later, little brother, you'd best think again. I'll let it pass today. Tomorrow I'll rip your ears off."

Everyone laughed. Rachel went up on her

tiptoes to kiss Esa's cheek. And then she found herself facing Darby. She loved every wrinkle in his craggy old face. He drew her gently into his arms. Beneath his shirt, Rachel could feel the bandage around his middle, so she returned his embrace with care.

He turned his nose against her hair, putting his lips just behind her ear. In a choked whisper, he said, "Be happy, little girl. That's only ever been my wish for you, that someday you might be happy."

"Oh, Darby." Rachel put her arms around his neck where she could hug him with no fear of causing him pain. "I love you so. Thank you, thank you, thank you for all that you've done for me. You're my best friend in the whole world, and you always will be."

"Not no more, sweetness. That gent over there who's now your husband will be your best friend from this moment on. He's a good man. You caught yourself a keeper."

Still hugging Darby's neck, Rachel nodded. "I did, didn't I? I can't believe how lucky I am."

"It's high time some luck came your way, darlin'. I only wish your ma and pa could be here today." He drew back to smile down at her. "They would be so proud and happy for you."

"I'm sure they are here, Darby," Rachel replied. Recalling Joseph's sentiments on such matters, she added, "If we believe in God and a life hereafter, we have to believe that they're here. They'd never miss my wedding."

Darby grinned. "Well, now, I suppose that's right."

Joseph joined them just then. He slipped a possessive arm around Rachel's waist. "All my brothers just informed me that they'll be standing in line to kick my ass if I don't treat this lady right," he informed Darby. "Are you gonna threaten me next?"

Darby chuckled. "Nah, I'll leave the ass-kickin' to them. I'm gettin' too old for all that shit."

Joseph smiled and shook the old foreman's hand. "I thank you for giving her away, Darby. You're like a father to her, so that was fitting."

Ace moseyed over to them. He curled a big hand over Darby's shoulder. "Good to see you back on your feet, old friend."

Darby pursed his lips and gave his head a partial shake. "It was touch and go there for

a bit. But I'm on the mend now, for sure."
He angled a glance at the garden gate, then
arched an eyebrow at Rachel. "How do I get
out of here, darlin'? There's a lady out there
I want to say howdy to."

Joseph knew to which lady the old foreman referred. "I'll let you out through the
house. Rachel might have trouble breathing
if we open the gate."

Darby nodded. "Nobody knows about
that better than me." He bent to kiss
Rachel's cheek. "I'll be back shortly, little
girl."

Using the key that Rachel had left on the
kitchen table, Joseph made fast work of
showing Darby out. When he returned to
the courtyard, he found his bride, slipped an
arm around her waist again, and raised his
voice to tell his brothers, "The show's over
now, everybody. You can all go home."

Moans and groans followed that an-
nouncement. Little Ace grabbed Joseph's
pant leg, chortling and grinning as if to say
the fun had just begun.

"My sentiments exactly," the child's father
called across the garden. "The party's just
started. Until we're all good and ready to
leave, you can just suffer."

"Oh, boy," Joseph said under his breath to Rachel. "All I want is for everyone to go so we can—"

"Hey, big brother!" David interrupted, jostling Joseph half off his feet with a shoulder jab. "Have a snort." He passed a jug under Joseph's nose. "I want to drink to your happy future."

"No, thanks. I want to keep a clear head," Joseph replied.

"Say what? It's your wedding day." David gave Rachel an imploring look. "Tell him, sis. He's supposed to celebrate."

"You're supposed to celebrate," Rachel informed her groom, pleased as could be that David had just called her sis. "One drink won't hurt."

Joseph sighed and took the jug. After taking a swallow, he passed it back to his brother. "There. I've celebrated."

Only Joseph's brothers hadn't finished with him yet. Ace approached next, insisting that Joseph have a celebratory drink with him. Next came Esa, and then the rotation began all over again. Several snorts later, Joseph had stopped arguing when the jug was passed to him, and Rachel thought he looked a mite too happy. He had doffed his suit jacket, the tie had vanished, and he'd unfastened the white dress shirt to midchest, revealing golden curls and a wealth of bronze skin rippling with muscle that made her want to call the party to a halt herself.

The next thing Rachel knew, a sawhorse table appeared in her courtyard and Caitlin was busy setting out food. Rachel suspected that someone had opened the gate when she wasn't watching, for the sawhorses hadn't been there during the wedding ceremony and none of the dishes belonged to her. She could only assume that they'd been brought by the women from town, who couldn't have passed them in to Caitlin through the bars.

Before Rachel could obsess overlong about someone unlocking her gate, David started playing his fiddle and someone outside joined in with a guitar. Joseph grabbed Rachel around the waist and began swirling her across the garden.

"Joseph, *no*," she cried. "I don't know how."

"Just move with me," he said. "Just let go and move with me."

Rachel looked up at his dark face, then into his sky blue eyes, and she loved him so much that she couldn't possibly refuse. So she let go, just as he'd asked, and danced with him.

Despite the chill in the air after the sun went down, the party went on until long after dark. Lanterns were lighted, both inside the courtyard and out, those outside hung from tree limbs and wagon tailgates to illuminate the area. It had been so long since Rachel had needed a wrap that she couldn't recall where she'd stowed her cape. To keep her warm, Joseph draped a wool blanket around her shoulders.

"I love you," he whispered.

Rachel doubted she would ever tire of hearing him tell her that. "I love you, too."

He leaned down to kiss her, whispering against her lips, "They'll leave soon. I promise."

Rachel couldn't help but laugh. "I don't mind their staying. It's been a lovely party."

"And they're dragging it out just to torture me," he tacked on. "Brothers. You can't live with 'em, and you can't live without 'em."

"I saw that!" David yelled. "No more of that stuff until we leave."

Joseph laughed and straightened away to look at David. "We were just talking."

"Yeah, right."

When Joseph wandered away to speak with someone, Caitlin sidled up to Rachel, cleared her throat nervously, and said, "It suddenly occurred to me that your mother died when you were quite young."

"Yes." Rachel looked up through the bars at the sky, fancying that her parents were up there somewhere, drifting among the stars, looking down. "I had just turned seventeen."

"Oh, *dear.*" Caitlin toyed with the buttons of her dress. "Would you mind stepping inside with me for a few minutes? I think we should have a little talk."

Joseph was chatting with Darby when he realized as he scanned the courtyard that his bride had vanished. He excused himself to go in search of her. When he stepped up onto the porch, he saw that the wooden door was closed. When he tried to open it, the thing wouldn't budge.

"Damn." He rapped his knuckles against the oak. "Rachel, you all right in there?"

Her faint reply was, "I'm fine. Caitlin and I are just having a little talk."

"About what?"

"Just things."

Just *things*? Joseph wondered about that. "What's wrong, little brother?"

Joseph turned a pensive frown on Ace, who stood on the top step behind him. "Rachel and your wife have barricaded themselves off in the kitchen. Rachel says they're having a little talk."

"About what?"

"Rachel said, 'Just *things*,'" Joseph replied.

"Uh-oh." Ace stepped up onto the porch. "Caitlin?" he called through the door. "Can I talk to you for a minute, sweetie?"

"Not right this moment," Caitlin called back. "Rachel and I are having a talk."

*"Shit,"* Ace said.

"What?" Joseph asked.

"They're having a little *talk*," Ace echoed unnecessarily.

"I know that much. What the hell's so important that they've got to hide in the kitchen and talk about it right now?"

Ace sighed and pinched the bridge of his nose. "Wedding night stuff, I'm guessing. And trust me when I say that Caitlin isn't the one to prepare your wife for her first bedding."

Joseph shot a worried look at the door. "She isn't?"

Ace leaned close so their noses were only inches apart. "Do you remember how long it took me to get that girl into bed?"

Joseph remembered Ace being as grumpy as a bear with a sore paw for weeks on end. After Ace got the problem settled, Joseph also remembered having to sit in the barn at crazy times of the day, unable to enter the house because the ropes of Ace's bed were creaking and the headboard was doing a double shuffle against the wall.

"I remember it being a tough time, but it all came right between you in the end."

"It came right between Caitlin and me, Joseph, but her first experience was a nightmare. She was *raped*, remember? Trust me when I say she isn't the person to tell Rachel what her first time is going to be like."

Joseph saw his point. He hooked a thumb at the door. "Well, get her out of there, then. Rachel's fine as things stand. *Eager,* in fact. I don't need Caitlin filling her head with horror stories."

"She won't. Caitlin has a kind heart. She's

just liable to paint a pretty grim picture of how bad the virgin pain is."

Joseph pounded on the door again. To his brother, he said, "God damn it, Ace. She's your wife. Get her away from mine before she causes all kinds of grief."

"How?"

"How what?" Joseph asked, impatience lending an edge to his question.

"How do you expect me to get her out of there?" Ace expounded.

"Tell her to come out. Just put your foot down for once. You wear the pants in the family."

Ace arched his eyebrows. "That isn't how it works. It's true that I wear the pants, but Caitlin wears the drawers. If I want in to them, I don't strut around like I'm the boss, issuing orders to her."

"Make an exception this one time. It's my wedding night."

Ace pounded on the door again. "Caitlin, sweetheart, Little Ace is crying and I can't make him stop."

Joseph rolled his eyes. "That is *so* weak. I can't believe it. My big, tough brother can't assert himself with a woman half his size."

They heard the bar lift. Ace smiled. "Worked, didn't it?"

The door opened and Caitlin appeared. When she saw her son happily romping with Buddy and Cleveland in the courtyard, she sent her husband a questioning look. "I thought you said he was crying."

"He suddenly stopped." Ace shrugged. "You know how little boys are, crying one minute, happy as bugs the next."

Rachel exited onto the porch after her sister-in-law. Joseph half expected her to give him an accusing glare, but instead she only smiled secretively and stepped close to hug his arm.

Joseph patted her hand. He felt the curve of her hip pressing against his and the soft warmth of her breast against his arm. The delicate scent of roses curled around him like tendrils of silk. God, how he wanted her. The need was so intense he ached.

He wished the public celebration would end soon so the private one could start.

## Chapter Sixteen

When all their guests had left, Rachel and Joseph adjourned to the kitchen, leaving Buddy outside in the courtyard. Rachel was a whole lot more nervous than she had expected to be. Caitlin, whose husband was wealthy, had given her a gorgeous gossamer negligee to wear tonight, one she'd ordered for herself but hadn't yet worn. It fell in voluminous folds to tease a man's eye.

Joseph strode slowly toward her. "What did Caitlin talk to you about?"

Rachel released a shaky breath. "About how wonderful tonight will be."

He gave her a dubious look. "And nothing else?"

Rachel shrugged. "She warned me that it may hurt dreadfully for a moment."

His eyes darkened with concern. "Are you worried about it?"

Rachel considered the question. "Not unduly. Caitlin assured me that after the first bit of pain, it's like dying and going to heaven if you're with the right man." She reached up to press her fingertips to his jaw. "You are definitely the right man, Joseph. I love you so much it pains me."

He dipped his head to kiss her palm. "And I love you so much that if this hurts you, it's going to half kill me."

"I know." And Rachel truly did. Joseph was nothing if not caring about her feelings. Indeed, she felt that he understood her better than anyone ever had. "And I can't imagine that it will be that bad. If it were, no one would ever go back for seconds."

A twinkle slipped into his eyes. "Do I hear an echo?"

Rachel recalled his warning to her after they'd shared their first kiss, that he wasn't the marrying kind, preferring instead to flit from woman to woman. She giggled. "Ah, yes, the buffet man. Sadly for you, you're now tied down to one lady."

"And happy to be tied down. I never thought it'd happen, but now that it has, I'm looking forward to seconds"—he nibbled at the inside of her wrist—"and thirds"—he trailed kisses along the cuff of her sleeve—

"and fourths, and fifths. I'll never tire of you."

All the folds of gossamer weren't concealing, after all. Horrified, Rachel couldn't lift her chin and stop gaping at herself. The gown was as transparent as glass. She could see her bosoms, her belly button, her nether regions, and even the freckle on her knee. What on *earth* had Caitlin been thinking? Rachel couldn't leave the water closet wearing this.

"Is everything all right in there?"

Rachel almost jumped out of her skin. The door still wasn't fixed, and propping it up over the opening left cracks, which she'd taken to covering with linen towels. It sounded as if Joseph was standing right outside.

"Caitlin bought me a special negligee for tonight," she confessed, "and I thought it was lovely until I put it on."

"What's wrong with it?"

"It's just—" Rachel couldn't think how to describe it. "It *isn't*."

"It isn't what?"

"It just *isn't*. Imagine if I stood naked behind glass, and there you have it."

"Hmm."

"I can't wear this, Joseph. It'd be *too* embarrassing."

"Then don't."

"I didn't bring another gown in with me."

She heard his boots thumping. Then came the scrape of a drawer opening. A moment later, he pushed a white Mother Hubbard through to her. Rachel hugged it gratefully to her breasts. "Thank you."

"You're welcome, darlin'. And no matter about the nightgown. I don't care what you wear."

Rachel sighed dreamily. To please him, perhaps she could wear the negligee, after all.

Joseph had resumed his seat at the table and, as was his habit, had rocked back on the chair to straighten his legs and cross his ankles. He had just finished stretching and folded his arms behind his head to flex and roll his shoulders when Rachel finally emerged from the water closet.

She wore nothing but a see-through shimmer of soft stuff that made her completely nude body look as if kissed with morning dew. His startled gaze dropped to her beautiful, rose-tipped breasts and then trailed in stunned amazement to the dark gold thatch of curls at the apex of her shapely thighs. His breath whooshed from his chest like air from a bellows, his entire body snapped taut, and somehow the teetering chair got away from him.

Just like that, over he went, hitting the floor so hard that it rattled his brains.

"Joseph?"

A vision of gossamer scurried across the room to stand over him.

"Oh, lands, are you all right?"

Joseph gaped at the pretty little breasts dangling and bouncing above his nose as she leaned over to look down at him.

"Sweet Christ," he said stupidly.

Hands aflutter, she knelt beside him. "Did you hit your head? Are you injured?"

Joseph couldn't rightly say if he was injured. He only knew one part of him was in fine working order. He rolled toward her to get free of the chair, hooked an arm around her neck to pull her to the floor, and straddled her hips as he came to his knees. "My God, you're beautiful. You are so damned beautiful."

Her cheeks went pink as he slid his gaze

over her breasts. "This isn't fair. You're fully clothed. I want to see you, too."

That was a request Joseph could deliver on. Buttons went flying as he jerked off his shirt, the tiny mother-of-pearl disks going *tick-tick-tick* as they struck the floor. He tossed aside the shirt and braced his arms to lean over her. His whole body jerked when she trailed her slender fingers over his chest.

"Oh, Joseph, you're pretty, too."

Pretty wasn't a word he would have chosen to describe himself, but coming from her, it would do.

With the first kiss, Rachel forgot all about feeling shy. *Silken caresses of lips and tongues.* Being in Joseph's arms eclipsed all her worries, allowing her to focus only on the sensations that his mouth, hands, and hard body evoked within her. He was lantern light and shadows, his sculpted torso gleaming in the amber illumination like burnished oak.

At some point, he swept her up into his arms and carried her to the bed, where he proceeded to make love to her just as he did all else: straightforwardly, thoroughly, and masterfully. She wasn't sure when he peeled her negligee away, only that he replaced the tease of netting with his hands and mouth, touching and kissing her in places she'd never dreamed he might, until her body quivered with delight and throbbed with need.

When he trailed his lips down her torso and settled his hot mouth over her secret place, she was too far over the edge to feel embarrassed, and soon his clever ministrations obliterated every rational thought in her mind. With every sweep of his tongue, her body jerked and quivered, a hot, electrical, urgent ache building within her until she arched upward, frantically seeking release.

With a fierce growl, he gave her what she sought with harder, quickening flicks of his tongue until the throbbing ache inside her shattered like thin glass, shooting shards of sheer ecstasy all over her body.

"Joseph?" Disoriented and suddenly uncertain, Rachel reached for him as he drew away to kick off his boots and remove his trousers. "Don't go."

"Not on your life, darlin'." He returned to her then, kneeling between her parted thighs. When their gazes met, she saw his

concern for her beneath the glaze of passion in his eyes. "You're as ready as I can
get you, sweetheart. If this hurts too much,
just tell me, and I swear I'll stop."

Rachel wasn't worried. No matter how
much it might hurt this first time, she
wanted it over with so he would never have
that worried look in his eyes again.

"Just do it," she whispered.

He slowly nudged himself into her, and
Rachel did indeed feel pain. She clenched
her teeth and clutched at his muscular
shoulders, braced for the invasion. Only it
didn't come.

"I'm hurting you," he whispered raggedly.
He started to withdraw. "I can't do this."

Rachel locked her bent legs around him
and bucked forward with her hips to finish it
herself. Pain exploded through her. It hurt
so much that it fairly took her breath.

"Oh, *shit*." Joseph gathered her into his
arms. His body was shaking, shaking horribly. "Oh, sweetheart. Why did you do that?"

She'd done it because he couldn't. Tears
stung Rachel's eyes. He would have
stopped rather than cause her pain. That
told her how very much he loved her, as
words never could. And the pain was reced-

ing now, becoming more a dull ache than an actual hurting.

"It's better now, Joseph." She trailed kisses along his jaw. "Make love to me. Make me feel as if I've died and gone to heaven."

He pushed up on his arms and moved tentatively within her. "How's that?"

Rachel's breath caught at the sensations that darted through her. "Good, very good."

He thrust with more force, magnifying the delight.

"Oh, *yes,* Joseph, *yes!*"

Joseph had never felt so drained in his life. His bride was an insatiable bed partner. Not that he was complaining. Holding her close, he lay on his side, facing the kitchen. Her soft, naked bottom was nestled against Old Glory, who'd given up the ghost and didn't stir even when she wiggled. Joseph tried to remember how many times they'd made love over the course of the night. One time blended together with another, creating a glorious blur in his mind. He could only say with certainty that he'd loved her well and thoroughly.

The kitchen looked as if a storm had come

along and rained clothing. He smiled and buried his face in Rachel's curls. Oh, how he loved her. Never in all his life had he imagined himself capable of loving anyone this much. She was so wonderful—and so brave—and so openly honest about her feelings. *I want to see you, too.* How many virgin brides faced their first bedding with such enthusiasm? *Oh, Joseph, you're pretty, too.* Was it any wonder he loved the girl?

Exhaustion settled over Joseph like a black blanket. He gave himself up to it, moving from consciousness into sweet, rose-scented dreams.

When Joseph awakened some time later, Rachel had left the bed. As he sat up, he realized that the day had long since dawned, the porch door was flung wide, and the iron-work was hanging open. He slipped from bed, drew on his trousers, and padded barefoot to the doorway. The sight that greeted his sleepy gaze—Rachel, strolling barefoot about the garden, wearing nothing but the gossamer gown—nearly took his breath away.

Weeks ago, he had tried to picture how

she might look in her courtyard, but his imagination had failed him on two counts. The garden was far prettier than he had envisioned, and the woman in it was even more beautiful. Her hair fell in a glorious cloud of golden curls to her narrow waist. Her body could have been sculpted in ivory.

Mesmerized by her, Joseph moved out onto the porch. She gave a tinkling laugh when she saw him. "Come look, Joseph. We have a rosebud."

The only rosebuds he was interested in were at the tips of her breasts, but he obediently followed the path of stepping-stones until he reached her side. After giving the rosebush due attention, he caught his wife around the waist and kissed her. She melted against him in eager surrender, then stiffened slightly and glanced uneasily around the courtyard.

"I'm not sure this is the place for this. I feel self-conscious."

Joseph nibbled the silken slope of her neck. "No need for that. Except for Buddy, it's completely private here." He skimmed his hands up her sides to cup her breasts and then lifted them to his searching lips. "Ah, Rachel, you're so beautiful."

She moaned and arched her spine. "Joseph?"

"It's all right. Trust me," he whispered.

She moaned again, and by the sound, he knew that he had won. He proceeded to make love to her in the sunlight on a patch of new grass—and then on the porch—and then on the kitchen table.

A man needed breakfast, after all.

Darby remained at Eden for a week after the wedding to give the newlyweds privacy, and Joseph made the most of each day. Because he couldn't take Rachel anywhere for their honeymoon, their activities were limited. They talked, they ate, they completed the few chores that they absolutely had to, and then they spent the rest of the time doing what they enjoyed most, making love.

Rachel continued to surprise Joseph with her unabashed enjoyment of physical intimacy. Most ladies in his acquaintance adhered to strict rules of social conduct that he suspected followed them to the bedroom. Such was not the case with Rachel. Joseph didn't know if it was because she'd been sequestered for so long, or if she simply possessed a free spirit. He only knew she never said no to anything.

One evening, upon request, she happily cooked his supper while wearing nothing but her apron. That ended with the meat scorching. Not that either of them cared about eating when the meal was finished. Another evening, they bet articles of the clothing they were wearing while playing poker. When Rachel lost her drawers to Joseph, he threw in his hand.

In all Joseph's life, he couldn't recall a time when he'd laughed so much. If ever he'd had doubts about getting married, they vanished during that week. Rachel was his companion, his wife, his lover, and his confidante. He loved to hear her giggle. He loved listening to the inflections of her voice when she read to him. He loved watching the myriad expressions that entered and left her beautiful blue eyes while they conversed about any subject. In short, he just loved the girl. She was everything he could have wanted in a woman, and she made him feel complete, as if he'd found the other half of himself. Even better, he knew that Rachel felt the same way. They were meant for each other, plain and simple.

Darby's appearance at the garden gate on Monday morning, a week and one day after their wedding, marked the end of Rachel and Joseph's honeymoon, but Joseph didn't expect it to end their happiness. While Rachel stayed in the kitchen behind her bars, Joseph let the old foreman into the courtyard, patted him on the shoulder, and invited him to join them for breakfast.

"That'd be good," Darby said as they followed the stepping-stones to the porch. "I have some news to share."

"What kind of news?" Rachel beamed a smile through the ironwork as she inserted a key into the lock. Pushing the bars wide, she beckoned Darby inside. "Something wonderful, I hope."

Darby swept off his hat and nodded. "I think so. I ain't so sure how you're gonna feel about it."

Rachel's smile faltered. She wore a pink shirtwaist tucked into a gray skirt with organ-pipe pleats at the back. Joseph suspected what Darby was about to say, and a premonition of doom came over him like a gray cloud.

"You're leaving," Rachel said softly. It wasn't really a question. The sadness in her eyes bespoke certainty. "Oh, Darby, not because I'm married, surely. You'll always be welcome here."

Darby slapped his hat against his leg. "I know that, honey. This isn't about me feelin' unwelcome. It's about me havin' a life of my own. You've got a husband to love you and look after you now. I'm not needed here like I used to be. I'm finally free to do other things and go where the wind takes me."

Rachel nodded. And then she smiled just a little too brightly. "Of *course*." She clamped a hand over the swirl of braid atop her head. "Oh, of *course*, Darby. How selfish of me. I never thought. I just never thought. Have you found another job, then?"

Joseph wanted to gather Rachel up into his arms and shield her from what Darby was about to tell her, but the rational side of him realized that he couldn't protect her from everything.

"Not another job, exactly, although it will mean me workin' somewhere else." Darby's larynx bobbed. "There's a lady I've loved for a good many years, and I've asked her to be my wife. I know it's a little late in life for me to be tyin' the knot, but I'm gonna get hitched anyhow."

Rachel's mouth formed an O of surprise. Then all the clouds of regret vanished from her eyes. She clapped her slender hands, laughed with absolute gladness, and threw her arms around Darby's neck.

"Married? Oh, Darby, that's so lovely. And it's never too late! I'm so happy for you, so very happy! Joseph, did you hear? Darby's in love."

"I heard," Joseph replied solemnly. He thrust out a hand to the foreman. "Congratulations, Darby. I'm happy as I can be for you. I truly am."

Rachel loosened her arms from around Darby's neck and fairly danced in front of him. "Who is she? Tell me all about her. Is she pretty? Is she good enough for you? When did you meet her?"

Darby moistened his lips. Then he shot a look at Joseph. "I met her years ago, honey, long before you were ever born. As for whether she's pretty or not, I think she's beautiful, and that's all that counts."

Rachel's smile faded again. "You don't act very happy about it, Darby."

He sighed and smoothed a gnarled hand over his hair. "That's because I'm afraid the news is gonna hurt you, and you gotta know I'd never hurt you for anything."

"That's just silly. I'm delighted for you. Why would the news hurt me?"

"Because the woman I plan to marry is your aunt Amanda."

All the color drained from Rachel's face.

"I'm sorry, honey. I know you've got hard feelings toward her. I'm not sure why, but there it is. You've got a right to your feelings, just like I've got a right to mine."

Rachel swayed on her feet. Joseph stepped in close to grasp her arm.

"Amanda," she whispered. "You're going to marry Amanda Hollister?"

"I've waited well over half my life to be with her," Darby replied. "I'm an old man, and time's runnin' out. Forgive me, little girl. I know you're gonna hate me for it."

Rachel squeezed her eyes closed. "Never that, Darby. Never that."

"For the last five years, I've made all my choices for you," the foreman went on. "I don't regret a single minute, mind you. Please don't be thinkin' that. But now that you have Joseph, I can make some choices for myself. I hope you can find it in your heart to understand."

Rachel wrapped her trembling hands around Joseph's arm as if she needed his strength to support her weight. "I do understand, Darby. You've given five years of your life to me. I shan't begrudge you a chance at happiness, no matter who it's with."

Darby's green eyes filled. He nodded and looked out through the ironwork at the garden. "I'll be stayin' on here for about a week, if that's okay. If you'd rather I didn't, I can sleep in Amanda's barn until our nuptials."

Rachel's nails dug into Joseph's arm. "This is your home, Darby McClintoch. You can remain here however long you wish."

Darby left without joining them for breakfast. The tension in the air was so thick it could have been eaten with a spoon. Rachel sank down on a chair at the table, braced her arms, and covered her face with her hands. Joseph sat across from her.

"I'm sorry, sweetheart." It was all he could think to say.

She didn't look up. "I want him to be happy," she said in a strained voice. "I truly do, Joseph. Only why must it be with *her*?"

Joseph chose his words carefully. "Can you tell me why you hate her so?"

She shook her head.

"There has to be a reason, darlin'." Joseph sincerely believed that. Rachel had such a loving and caring heart. He couldn't envision her hating anyone without good cause. "There just has to be."

"My dreams," she whispered raggedly. "It's something in my dreams. She was behind it. I know it. I just don't know for sure *how* I know it."

"Can you tell me about your dreams? Maybe if we talk about them, maybe if you can describe to me what you see in them, we can come up with some answers."

Long silence. Then, "*Blood*. I see *blood*. Everywhere, Joseph, everywhere. On the grass. On Denver's yellow fur." Her shoulders jerked. "Tansy's pink dress, drenched in blood. And Ma. Oh, *God*. Oh, *God*. No face. Pa's p-playing his fiddle, and she's d-dancing over the grass, laughing and smiling at him. But then she has no face."

Joseph's stomach rolled. "You mentioned once that you see Denver leaping up to bite the man's leg, and that the man pulls his revolver and shoots him between the eyes.

What else do you see, sweetheart? Picture his boot. Picture his leg. Is there anything special about the gun—or possibly the saddle? If you see his leg, if you see his hand holding the gun, you must see other things."

No answer. Joseph studied her bent head for a long moment. Then he sighed. "If it's this painful for you, honey, just let it go."

Still no reply. A cold, itchy sensation inched up Joseph's spine. "Rachel?"

She didn't move. Concerned, Joseph reached across the table and drew her hands from her face. Her lashes fluttered open, but even though she appeared to be looking at him, she didn't seem to see him.

"Rachel?" he whispered.

Nothing. He looked deeply into her eyes, searching for any sign that she heard him. It was as if everything within her had been snuffed out.

"Oh, Jesus."

Joseph carried his wife to the sofa and sat with her cradled in his arms. Morning came and went, and still Rachel didn't move or speak. She just lay there against him, limp, eyes open but unseeing, not hearing when he spoke to her. As the hours dragged by,

Joseph began to fear that she might never return to herself.

His fault. He'd pushed her into thinking of that day. He'd forced her to describe what she saw in her dreams. Her mother, without a face. He closed his eyes, so sorry for pressuring her that he ached.

It was nearly three o'clock in the afternoon when Rachel finally stirred. Pushing against his chest, she sat straight, stretched as if she'd just awakened from a long nap, and beamed a smile at him.

"My goodness. How long have I been asleep?"

Joseph glanced at the clock. "For a bit." Over nine hours, to be exact.

"Lands, just look at the time. I should have made bread today." She swung off his lap. "It's far too late for that now, Joseph. Will cornbread do for supper?"

Joseph's body was cramped from sitting still for so long. He worked his arms to get the achy cricks out, his gaze fixed on his wife. She didn't seem to recall their discussion, leading him to wonder if she even recollected Darby's news. If so, she gave no sign of it. Humming the wedding march, she tied on her apron and hurried about the kitchen.

"I am *so* hungry. I'd swear I had no lunch."

Or breakfast, either. A cold, crawling fear moved through Joseph. Rachel was not only hiding behind walls, but also behind memory loss. He'd never known anyone who could simply erase unpleasant memories from her mind, but that seemed to be what she was doing.

He wanted to confront her, to ask what she recalled of the morning. But fear held his tongue. What if he upset her and she went away from him again? Even worse, what if she stayed away next time? Joseph had heard of people going into trances. Sometimes they never came right again. He loved Rachel too much to take that chance.

And so he pretended with her that the events of the morning had never happened.

That evening when Joseph left the house to do chores, he went looking for Darby and found the old fellow resting in the bunkhouse.

"I still tire easy," Darby explained as he swung his legs off the bed and finger-combed his hair. "Do a little bit, then I gotta sleep."

"You lost a lot of blood, and you're still not completely healed yet." Joseph made a mental note not to allow Darby to overdo it during the week he planned to remain there. "Something happened up at the house this morning, partner. You and I need to talk."

Darby gave him a questioning look. Joseph briefly explained about his conversation with Rachel and how she'd blinked out on him when his questions upset her. "I don't think she remembers any of it," Joseph said in conclusion. "Not our talk—or your news about marrying Amanda."

"I'll be." Darby shook his head. "That's beyond strange."

It was the strangest thing Joseph had ever witnessed, and it made him scared to death of losing his wife. "I'm thinking it might be best if you don't make any further mention of your marriage."

Darby sighed and pushed to his feet. "I can't for the life of me understand what's going on in that girl's head. Amanda still loves her with all her heart. She came to your wedding, hiding behind a veil."

"I know. I saw her there, Darby."

"It's so sad. She'd give anything to hug that girl and cuddle her up. How did Rachel get it into her head that Amanda was behind the killings?"

Joseph had no idea, and he was coming to accept that he never might. He also realized that his first loyalty had to be with his wife. "I know that it'll pain Amanda that I've asked this, but when next you see her, please tell her that I don't want her coming around here again, veil or no. If Rachel were to recognize her—well, I just don't know how she might react. That trance she was in today scared the bejesus out of me. I never want it to happen again."

The following morning when Joseph went out to milk the cows and feed the stock, he found Darby in the barn, saddling up his gelding, Poncho.

"Where are you off to so early?" Joseph asked.

"Thought I'd ride fence line," the old foreman replied. "Maybe count cows if I don't tucker out before I get around to it."

Joseph hadn't been out to check on the cattle since his marriage. The livestock grazed for feed and had water aplenty, so during his honeymoon he'd let them fare for themselves. "How about trading jobs with me? That's a lot of fence line to ride."

"It is, at that, but I'm no invalid, son."

"I never meant to imply that," Joseph replied. "But those cows are my worry now. If you'll stick close to the house to keep an eye on Rachel, I'll be happy to get out for a while, truth to tell."

"All right, then."

Darby started to loosen the saddle cinch. Joseph brushed the old man's hands aside and handed him the milk bucket.

"I can lift my own saddle," Darby protested.

"Never thought for a minute that you couldn't." Joseph quickly swept the saddle from Poncho's back and settled it over a stall rail. "The cows are bawling to be milked. I'll take care of your horse and saddle my own."

Muttering about bossy young pups, Darby sauntered away to do the milking.

After finishing the chores and eating a breakfast that Joseph handed out through the garden gate, Darby took up squatting rights under the oak tree, his rifle resting across his outstretched legs, which were comfortably crossed at the ankle. As Joseph left to ride fence line, the old fore- man yelled, "No need to worry while you're gone. I won't get caught with my back turned twice."

Joseph nodded. He had every confidence that Darby would keep a sharp eye out for trouble. He rode close to say, "Been a week since I counted the stock. I'll be taking my dog along to help sniff them out."

Darby lifted his hat in farewell. "Have a good ride."

It was a beautiful April morning, and Joseph had every intention of enjoying it. He was never happier than when he was in the saddle, especially when the mount be- neath him was Obie. The stallion, sired by Ace's black, Shakespeare, had his daddy's fine conformation and even gait. Joseph had never owned a horse who gave him a smoother ride, and Obie was steady and trustworthy, to boot, never spooking, al- ways responsive, and as sure-footed as any animal Joseph had ever seen.

During the ride around the perimeters of the property, Buddy did what he did best: running with his nose to the ground to sniff out cattle. Into copses, over rocks, into gullies, the dog maintained an easy lope, never seeming to tire of the hunt. By noon, when Joseph took a break for lunch, the shepherd had routed out ten of Rachel's eighteen head.

"Good boy." Joseph made over the dog for a few seconds. "It's been a spell since we worked. But you haven't lost your knack for it."

Buddy happily growled in reply.

The dog kept a sharp eye out for treats as Joseph lifted the flap of his saddlebag. "Yes, Rachel sent you lunch. Same as she sent for me. Spoiling you, isn't she?" Joseph sat in the shade of a tree to eat. After laying out Buddy's food on the grass, he tucked hungrily into his own, appreciating every bite. "Damn, but that girl has the magic touch. No bread for sandwiches, so instead we get biscuits. But mine's still good enough that I could go for seconds."

Joseph unfolded another cloth and gave a satisfied sigh when he saw turnovers, fried golden and still slightly warm from the skillet. He sank his teeth into the gooey peach center and closed his eyes in pure pleasure.

Buddy barked and pranced with his front

feet, his lolling tongue dripping drool as he eyed the dessert.

"This is people food," Joseph protested. "Besides, she only sent two."

The dog pranced again and licked his chops. *Ruff!*

Joseph groaned and handed over the second turnover. "All I know is, you'd better work for it this afternoon. We've got a lot more fence to ride and eight more cows to find."

Joseph reached the creek around two in the afternoon. He'd ridden through there several times since Darby had been shot, but never without an eerie sensation crawling up his spine. Jeb Pritchard's place wasn't far away as a crow flew—or as a horse walked, for that matter—and Joseph couldn't turn his back to the mountain of rocks without half expecting to take a slug in the back.

Today was no exception, which was why, when Buddy suddenly started to bark, Joseph leaped from his horse and hit the dirt with his weapon drawn. Joseph squinted to see into the deep shadows cast by the projections of stone that reached toward the sky like gigantic arrowheads.

"Buddy!" he yelled.

But the red-gold dog was already gone up the steep hill. Joseph could hear him up in the rocks barking excitedly. Then came a shrill yelp and silence. Joseph was on his feet and running before common sense could make him think better of it.

"You rotten old son of a bitch!" he yelled as he charged for the rocks. "If you hurt that dog, I'll tear you apart with my bare hands." Joseph took cover behind a boulder. "Buddy?" he called.

He heard nothing but the wind. His heart squeezed with fear for his dog. He wanted to race up there with no thought for his own safety, but with the ebb of that first rush of rage, he knew how stupid it would be. So he went slowly, darting from one rock to another, trying to shield himself as he ascended the hill.

After Darby's shooting, he and David had scoured this area and found the place where they believed the sniper had hidden to take aim. It was an opening of about forty feet across, encircled by boulders, which offered a broad view of the flat and creek below. When Joseph reached it, he searched the ground for any sign of disturbance to indicate that a man had recently been hiding there, but he saw nothing, not even a turned blade of grass.

Believing that they'd found what they sought, Joseph and David hadn't climbed any higher that other afternoon, so Joseph was surprised as he pressed upward to find that the mountain wasn't all rock as it appeared to be from below. There were grassy openings aplenty between the clusters of stone.

Joseph was about halfway to the top when he heard the thundering tattoo of a horse's hooves. At the sound, he almost ran back down the hill to jump on Obie and give chase. But Buddy was above him somewhere, and Joseph strongly suspected that the shepherd might be badly hurt. He had to find his dog. He could track the horse later.

Joseph found Buddy lying before what looked like the opening of a cave. As Joseph approached, he had eyes only for his dog, searching for blood, dreading what he might find. To his relief, Joseph saw that the shepherd was still breathing. He holstered his gun, dropped to his knees, and gently ran his hands over red-gold fur to check for wounds. No blood that he could see.

Bewildered, Joseph made a second pass over the dog's body, this time parting the animal's coat, thinking that perhaps a puncture wound might not bleed heavily enough at first to soak through the thick fur. *Nothing.* Turning his attention to Buddy's head, Joseph soon found what he was seeking: a small gash along the dog's temple.

"Bastard," Joseph muttered. "I don't know what he hit you with, partner, but he flat snuffed your wick."

Buddy whimpered and shuddered. Joseph's temper soared. The dog didn't have a mean bone. How could anyone do this?

And why?

When Buddy's eyes came open and Joseph felt confident the dog was going to be all right, he turned a more observant eye to his surroundings. Not just a cave, after all. A long wooden box lay nearby, and it was still wet. A portable mining sluice?

Buddy pushed up on his haunches. Joseph ran his hands over the animal's fur. "Sorry about that, my friend. I didn't know anyone was up here. Next time I call you back, maybe you'll think smart and do as I tell you, huh?" Joseph carefully scratched behind the dog's ears, avoiding the small gash. "You did good, though. Damned good. It looks to me like you've sniffed out more than cows today."

Joseph pushed to his feet and approached the mouth of the cave. He couldn't see very far inside, but what he did see confirmed his suspicions. Tracks and an ore cart. This was a mine—a gold mine, if Joseph guessed right. Only whoever had been doing the digging had taken great pains to keep his activities hidden. At day's end, Joseph suspected even the portable sluice would vanish inside the cave. To the eye of a casual passerby—if anyone ever happened to have reason to come up here, which was doubtful—they would see only an opening in the rock.

Joseph stepped deeper into the cave. After his eyes adjusted to the dimness, he saw a lantern, a miner's light, and all manner of other paraphernalia lying about. Joseph grabbed the miner's light, struck a match to illuminate it, and tossed away his Stetson to don the headgear.

"Just what do we have here?" he mused aloud. His voice bounced back at him, echoing and reechoing. That told him that the cave ran deep. "Well, well, well. Suddenly it all makes sense."

Joseph's excitement grew apace with his footsteps. *Gold.* Who would have thought it? But it wasn't beyond the realm of possibility. No Name itself was a mining town that had gone bust so quickly that the folks who'd swarmed there hoping to get rich left for better digs before giving the community a name. But then there was Black Jack, Colorado, where fortunes had been made in the foothills of the Rockies, a fellow named Luke Taggart topping them all. Joseph had heard stories that the man had more gold in just one bank than Midas could ever conceive of.

But that was the stuff dreams were made of. Years ago, folks around No Name had settled down to a more grueling reality, scratching out a living on the land, very few of them doing well. Ace's railroad spur had changed that immensely, making it easier and far more profitable for cattle ranchers to get their stock to auction in bustling Denver. Even so, the mind-set of folks had remained the same. To put bacon on one's plate, nobody looked at the dirt hoping to find gold.

They prayed to see sprouts of grass hay or alfalfa if they had water, and wheat or oats if they didn't.

The light that blazed from Joseph's head-lamp played over the rock walls of the tunnel. He could see where someone had chipped at the rock until it played out, and then had moved deeper. Occasionally he saw traces of gold, but nothing to shout about. Then he rounded a corner and saw where someone had blasted with dynamite. Now he was in business. Tresses had been built to support the tunnel, and as he moved deeper into the bowels of the mine, the air became ever colder and thinner.

Someone had been chipping away at this rock for a spell, Joseph decided. One man, possibly two, all under cover of secrecy. His boots slid on the obliterated pieces of stone, left behind by a weary digger who had exhaustively removed possibly tons of rock to some other location to hide the goings-on here. *Years,* Joseph concluded. Small extractions of gold, over time, had occurred here. In a regular mine, countless men swung picks to break out the ore, and dynamite was used whenever they needed to go deeper, ever in search of the mother lode. But this person or persons hadn't been able to search for the precious metal aggressively for fear of discovery. A little here, a little there, day in and day out, week after week, and year after year.

Joseph rounded a corner in the tunnel. "Sweet Christ."

The miner's light played over a wall of solid rock that was ribboned with gold, some of the veins thicker than Joseph's wrist. The sight fairly boggled his mind. He couldn't recall how much an ounce of pure ore was selling for right then. *A lot.* Enough that a greedy man or men might kill to keep a rich vein like this a secret.

The thought made Joseph sick. *No face.* Five years ago, a family had come here to picnic along a creek on their own land. Father, mother, sisters, and brother, they'd had no inkling that they were so close to a deadly fortune. Had Denver, Rachel's beloved dog, run up here, much as Buddy had, with her little sister, Tansy, at his heels? Neither child nor dog would have understood the significance of this find if they had come upon it.

But greedy men often had no sense. With a fortune hanging in the balance, what might they do to protect their treasure from discovery? Even though Tansy probably hadn't realized the significance, she would have seen enough to go back down to the creek where her family was picnicking and mention what she had seen to her father.

So they had slaughtered the Hollisters. All of them except Rachel, who, by some miracle, had lived. Joseph believed in God with all his heart, and in that moment of revelation he also believed with utter conviction that God had put the projectile of that one bullet slightly off, possibly by sheer divine will, so that it glanced off her skull. God, in all His wisdom, knew, even then, that Rachel Hollister would be the salvation of Joseph Paxton, a young man who didn't want a wife, wasn't looking for a wife, and believed he didn't need a wife. Only he had, and somehow God had saved her—out of all the members of her family, he'd somehow saved Rachel, for Joseph.

Tears burned in his eyes. Tears of absolute, mindless rage. *No face.* His sweet Rachel had seen her mother's face blown away while she danced over the grass on a sunny afternoon. *Holy Mother of God.* Marie Hollister, who'd read her Bible the night before she died and marked her place with a ribbon so she could live her life according to Scripture, observing every code of decency, had died a violent, senseless death right before her daughter's eyes. And for what? For gold. So a selfish bastard could line his filthy pockets.

Joseph leaned against the cold rock. He'd never clapped eyes on any of Rachel's family, but he'd seen that vacant look in her eyes and held her in his arms while she was overcome by the horror of their deaths. *Jeb Pritchard.* That stinking, immoral, hell-bent *bastard.* He'd killed his own wife. Why hesitate to spill more blood? Now Joseph knew how the fools could afford to buy whiskey and nap in drunken stupors on a spring afternoon. They'd done their labor, and it didn't involve cows. Their whiskey money was a crow's flight away, deep in the bowels of a cave.

Joseph didn't need to see any more. He exited the dig, gathered his injured dog in his arms, and hurried down the hill. The circuit judge could hang up his hat. Jeb Pritchard was going to pay for what he'd done.

# Chapter Seventeen

Darby was still lounging under the oak tree when Joseph returned to the Bar H. Joseph drew up near the tree to dismount and set his dog down. Buddy wasn't his usual energetic self. He just sort of stood there, looking around.

"What's the matter with him?" Darby asked.

"He got beaned a good one."

"Beaned?"

Joseph quickly gave Darby a recounting of the afternoon.

"I'll be damned. Gold, you say?" Darby shook his head. "I knew there was a cave up on that hill, but I paid it no nevermind. Nosin' around in places like that's a good way to get snake bit or come nose to nose with a badger."

Joseph normally avoided caves himself for the same reasons. "Somebody went nosing around in there. Some time ago, if I'm any judge. Mining on the sly, you can't move a lot of rock at once, and a considerable amount of digging has taken place up there."

"And you reckon it was Pritchard?"

"Who else? Jeb's been in a snit about that creek since way back in seventy-nine. He had reason to be down there, walking the property, trying to figure out how to alter the course of the stream back onto his land. At one point or another, he came across that cave, realized there was gold in there for the taking, and started helping himself. Chances are his boys have been aiding him in the endeavor."

Darby narrowed his eyes. "And on the day of the killings, the Hollister family chose a picnic spot just a little too close to his treasure."

"And one of the children wandered up into the rocks," Joseph added. "My guess is that it was Tansy, the five-year-old. Pritchard knew the game would be up if the little girl realized the significance of what she'd seen and blabbed to her daddy."

Darby shook his head again. "So, to make sure that didn't happen, Pritchard opened fire on the whole family." His eyes glittered with anger as he met Joseph's gaze. "Hangin's too good for the bastard."

"I totally agree," Joseph replied. "But we've got to abide by the law, all the same. Otherwise, we're no better than they are."

"So what's your plan?"

"I need to ride into town and talk with my brother. He's wearing the badge. He needs to make the decisions about how to best handle it, I reckon."

Darby drew his watch from his pocket. "How late you think you'll be?"

"I should be back in a couple of hours. My guess is David won't want to make a move tonight. Not enough daylight left to get organized and ride out there before dark. We're going to need manpower this time around, if for no other reason than to help search the property. If Pritchard's been filching gold from Bar H over the last several years, there'll be evidence of it somewhere on his place."

Darby closed his watch. "I promised Amanda I'd come see her tonight. If I run a little late, she'll be sure to understand."

Joseph caught hold of Obie's reins and prepared to remount. "I appreciate you looking after my wife for me, Darby. If she should ask where I went, it might be best if you tell her I had business in town."

"No details." Darby nodded. "I gotcha. As for thankin' me, son, there's no need. I love Rachel, too. Watchin' after her ain't a chore."

David rocked back on his office chair to prop his boots on the edge of his desk. Frowning pensively, he said, "So you were right all along. It was Pritchard."

"It sure looks that way to me." Joseph paced back and forth in front of the window. "I can't think of anyone else who might have had reason to be in that area and come upon that cave. Can you?"

David sighed. "It's not beyond the realm of possibility that Amanda Hollister knows about it. She worked on the Bar H for years."

"Are you back on that again?"

David held up his hands. "Not really, no. I'm inclined to think you're right about it being Pritchard. I'm just trying to look at it from all angles."

"If we find nothing at Pritchard's place to implicate him, we can consider other angles then."

"Jeb isn't gonna sit on his porch having a smoke while we search his place," David pointed out. "He'll raise holy hell and possibly start shooting at us again."

"I've considered that," Joseph said. "We're going to need reinforcements. A small army, if you can round one up."

"Most men hereabouts are willing to stand in as deputies when I need them. I'll send Billy Joe out to ride from house to house while I go knocking on doors here in town. What time in the morning do you want to join up with us?"

When Joseph got back to the Hollister place, Darby pushed to his feet and walked out to meet him.

"David's rounding up a posse," Joseph said. "I'll meet up with them on Wolverine Road at ten tomorrow morning. We'll descend on the Pritchard place en masse. If Jeb sees a huge group of riders, maybe it'll discourage him from getting trigger-happy."

"I hope so." Darby hooked a thumb toward the house. "Don't go makin' a widow of that girl, son. You'll flat mess up my plans."

Joseph chuckled. "I have a few plans of

my own that I don't want messed up, so I'll do my best to stay safe."

Darby's green eyes twinkled. "I just want to enjoy my last years with someone special. If you're home to stay, I think I'll go callin' on her for a bit." The old foreman returned to the tree to collect his rifle and a handful of wildflowers. "Just a little nonsense I picked while you was off gallivantin'."

Joseph grinned. "A little nonsense, huh? Looks to me like you're thinking sharp. Most ladies love flowers."

Darby nodded. Then he squinted up at Joseph. "How long's it been since you gave some to Rachel?"

"I gave her a whole courtyard full of flowers."

"That don't count. You gotta pick 'em, son. Makes a gal melt every time."

An hour later, when Joseph finished the evening chores, he walked a wide circle around the house to collect any wildflowers that Darby had missed before he went indoors to greet his wife.

The following morning shortly after Joseph left to run some unspecified errands, Rachel went out in the courtyard to tend her garden. Each little task brought her joy: watering the roses and counting the tiny buds, carefully plucking weeds from around her violets, admiring the cheerful and showy blooms of the crocus, and feeding her three fish, which she could have sworn had already grown a bit. Though the air was crisp, requiring her to drape a blanket over her shoulders, she smelled spring on the breeze, and, oh, how wonderful that was.

"My roses have six buds, Darby. *Six*."

The old foreman, who stood guard outside the gate, came to peer through the iron bars. "Well, now, ain't that somethin'?"

"It *is*, it surely is." Rachel beamed a smile at him. "And just look how my violets are flourishing!"

"Pretty as can be," he agreed. "And just lookee at that. You got a barn swallow checking out that birdhouse yonder. Could be she'll make a nest inside."

Rachel watched the small bird hop in and out of the hole. "Oh, wouldn't that be grand?" She held her arms wide and twirled in a circle. "He's given me heaven right here on earth, Darby. You just can't know how much I love that man."

"I think I've got an inklin'. And I'm happy for you, honey. So very happy."

Rachel tugged the blanket back around her shoulders. Sobering, she asked, "How are you feeling? I'm so selfish, only thinking about me. Is your wound healing fine?"

"I'm feelin' stronger every day. And you're entitled to be just a little selfish for a spell, darlin'. That's how it's supposed to be right after gettin' married, more so for you than for most."

They chatted a while longer before Rachel went inside to check on her rising loaves of bread. She'd just returned to the garden to laze on her bench in the sunshine for a bit when she heard a horse fast approaching. Buddy started to bark rather furiously, which she decided was just as it should be. Someone was coming, and it was the dog's job to raise an alarm. Rachel wondered who might be calling. Someone from town, possibly, bringing something more for her courtyard? Harrison Gilpatrick was supposed to bring her some tulip bulbs, and Garrett Buckmaster had promised her some pond lilies. She was greatly looking forward to receiving both.

A little over a week ago, Rachel might have

rushed into the house to bar her door and hide at the sound of an approaching horse. But she'd come to feel quite safe inside her courtyard. As Joseph was fond of reminding her, the walls out here were made of stone and almost a foot thick. No one could get in. Only she and Joseph had a key to the gate. If anything alarming happened outside the courtyard, she'd have enough advanced warning to escape into the house.

Rachel no sooner thought that than she heard Buddy snarl. It was so unlike the dog to be unfriendly. She turned on the bench to stare at the gate. The dog let loose with another snarl, prompting Darby to say, "Silly fool pup. You need to learn the difference between friends and foes. Mind your manners." Then, "Buddy! Get back here!" Darby whistled. Then he cursed. "Joseph will have my head, you dad-blamed mutt. You're supposed to stay here today!"

Rachel pushed slowly to her feet. She felt frightened suddenly without knowing why. No, that wasn't precisely true. *Buddy.* He was a friendly fellow, always ready for a pat on the head from friend or stranger. It wasn't in his nature to snarl at anyone—or to ignore Darby's calls.

She heard the horse slowing to a trot out front.

"Howdy, Ray," Darby said. "What brings you out this way so bright and early?"

"It's the boss, Darby. She's gravely ill. Came on her real sudden like. I sent one of the men for Doc Halloway, but she's asking for you."

Rachel shot up from the bench. *That voice.* Her heart was pounding hard, and an awful coldness trickled over her skin like ice water. *That voice.* Black spots danced before her eyes. *Oh, my God.* It was the voice in her nightmares. Her breath suddenly hitching, she stumbled backward toward the house. *Him—it's him.* She fell on the steps. Scrambled back to her feet. The world swirled upside down and then came right again. Oxygen, she needed oxygen. She hugged a porch post to hold herself erect, fighting frantically for breath. Staggered away, trying to reach the doorway. Fell into the house, her legs so watery that they would no longer support her weight. *Him, him, him.*

Sprawled on her belly, she grabbed the ironwork to swing it closed. Dragged herself to her knees and tried desperately to fit the key into the lock, only in her panic she couldn't hit the hole. Her numb fingers lost their grip on the metal bow, and the key fell to the floor. With a sob, she twisted sharply at the waist to seize hold of the thick wooden door, shifting out of the way to pull it closed. The portal slammed shut with a loud thunk. Pulling herself to her feet, she engaged the deadlocks. Then, with violently trembling hands, she dropped the bar into place.

*Him.* If she lived for another hundred years, she would never forget that voice. Panic swamped her. She staggered to a corner, dropped to her rump, and pressed her back to the walls. *Him.* He'd come to kill her. She knew it. *Oh, God.* She needed Joseph. *Joseph.* Thinking of him calmed her somewhat. She was safe inside her kitchen, just like always. She had the shotgun to defend herself. She wasn't sitting unsuspecting on the grass along the creek this time. Oh, no. This time, she could fight back.

The thought sent her crawling across the floor to the gun rack. She struggled to her feet, still dizzy from lack of breath. Shells, she needed shells. She pulled so hard on the ammunition drawer that it came clear off the runners and crashed to the floor. She grabbed handfuls of ammunition and shoved it into her skirt pockets. Then she wrested the gun from its niche. With violently trembling hands, she managed to break open the barrels, load both, and snap them back into place.

On weak legs, she made her way to the wood safe, flung open the door, and dropped to her knees to peer out. *Joseph.* She had a wonderful life to look forward to now—a husband who loved her, the possibility of children and happiness and laughter. She wasn't about to die and miss out on all that. Oh, no. She would be ready. He wouldn't have such easy pickings this time.

She tried to listen, but her breathing was so ragged that it was hard to hear anything. She gulped and tried to hold her breath. Was that a horse trotting off? She gulped again and closed her eyes on a silent prayer. Then she peered out the wood safe again.

"Darby?" she called softly. "You there?"

No answer. Had he left? *No, no, no.*

"Darby," she called just a little louder.

What if *he* was out there? The thought had her slamming the door of the wood safe closed. As the latch dropped, she pressed her back to the wall. *Okay.* She was fine. Darby wasn't answering, but she was safe. Her familiar kitchen was just like always, everything locked and barred closed. No one could get in. She was just fine. Let him try to come in one of the doors. Let him just *try*.

Time passed. Rachel's heartbeat slowed. Her breathing became regular again. More important, she was able to think more rationally. *Ray.* Darby had called the man Ray. She would tell Joseph when he got home. Joseph would go after him. Ray would be removed from the face of the earth. That was a good way to think of it. *Removed.* She'd never have to worry again. Joseph would go after him, and from now on she'd be safe because she finally knew his name.

A gray fog clouded her vision. Rachel blinked, tried to focus. *No,* she told herself. No more running away in her mind. She had to hold on to his name. *Ray.* And he worked for Amanda Hollister.

The gray fog grew thicker. Rachel blinked, passed a hand over her eyes. *No.* After the grayness came blackness. She knew that all too well. It had come over her the first night when Joseph had knocked on her door to tell her Darby had been shot. She had to be strong this time. She had to keep her head. Her life might depend on it, and she needed to live so she could have Joseph's babies. She had to live because he had given her so much to live for. She couldn't let herself succumb to the blackness when that awful man might be out there.

*Ray.* She knew his voice, and now she knew his name. A terrible pain lanced through her head. She rested the shotgun across the bend of her lap and drew up her knees to rest her throbbing brow on them. Images pelted her. Horrible images. *No face.* Her ma, falling—falling—falling. Her head bouncing on the grass when she landed on her back. *No face. Blood—everywhere blood.* Visions of crimson-soaked pink flashed through Rachel's mind. *Tansy's pretty little dress.* And then red on yellow. *Denver, her loyal dog, lying limp on the ground.* And Daniel. A picture blinked. *Daniel, with a chicken drumstick still caught between his teeth and a reddish-black hole suddenly appearing between his blank blue eyes.*

The blackness tried to move over her, but

Rachel kept fighting against it. *Ray.* She would forget his name if she gave in to the blackness. She'd wake up and she wouldn't remember anything. She couldn't allow that to happen, not this time. Oh, how it *hurt.* Remembering *hurt* so much, and it was horrible beyond comprehension. But she had to do it. For Tansy. For her ma. For Daniel. And for her pa, who'd used the only weapon he had, his beloved fiddle, to try to protect them. He'd sprung up from the grass and charged the shooter, shattering the string instrument on the man's shoulder.

Rachel raised her head, staring blankly at nothing, her mind replaying events that she had blacked out for years. She and Daniel had been arguing over the last piece of chicken in the basket, and Daniel, being stronger than she, had wrestled the drumstick from her hand. Grinning impishly, he'd sunk his teeth into the meat. *Kaboom.*

Rachel shuddered and closed her eyes. *Oh, God.* Daniel's head. Blood, all over the blanket, even before he fell. Blood, splattered all over her. Rachel remembered staring stupidly at the blood, not understanding where it had come from, and then seeing Daniel fall as if a gigantic force had struck him. She had scrambled to her knees, screaming, "Daniel? Daniel!"

Rachel's stomach convulsed, and she gagged, bringing up only gall to wet her skirt. *Daniel.* The blackness edged close again. She shoved it away. Joseph's voice whispered in her mind. *You mentioned once that you see Denver leaping up to bite the man's leg, and that the man pulls his revolver and shoots him between the eyes. What else do you see, sweetheart? Picture his boot. Picture his leg. Is there anything special about the gun—or possibly the saddle? If you see his leg, if you see his hand holding the gun, you must see other things.*

Rachel gagged again, bringing up more than bile this time. But she scarcely noticed because she was seeing Denver, her wonderful, loyal Denver, throwing himself at the man's leg, seeing the man reach for his gun, seeing him point the barrel at her dog's head. *Push past it. Don't think of poor Denver. See the man's leg, his boot, the saddle.* And there it was, the horror that had skirted at the edges of the blackness for so long, a brand on the rump of the sorrel horse, an H within a circle.

Rachel started to shake so violently that

she could barely hug her legs. Her family's brand, only altered. The Bar H ranch had always used an H underscored by a bar to brand their animals. When Amanda had left the family fold, she had altered that brand, keeping the H but encompassing it with a circle. It had been different enough from the original Hollister brand to be legally recorded, enabling her to use the first letter of her surname to mark her horses and livestock, just as she always had. *The Circle H.* And Rachel had seen it on the rump of the killer's horse. For all these years, she'd blacked it out, but it was there in her mind now, like a photograph hanging on the wall. He'd been riding a Circle H horse.

As a very small child, Rachel had adored her aunt Amanda. No one had understood her so well. Mannie, Rachel had called her, still so young that she couldn't say Amanda. In her mind's eye, she could see herself racing toward her aunt, much as Little Ace ran toward Joseph now, her arms spread wide, her heart swelling with love. She had wanted nothing more than to feel Mannie's arms around her.

Rachel had loved her mother. No doubt about that. But she had adored Amanda, who'd never scolded when she got her dress dirty and who'd always seemed to take pleasure in her mischievousness as Rachel's mother never could.

A sob jerked through Rachel's body. *Mannie*. Long after Amanda had left the Bar H, Rachel had frequently gone to see her. Her aunt had always been ready to drop everything and spend time with her. Once, she might show her the new foals. Another time, she might take Rachel into the house for milk and cookies. When Rachel had had problems, she'd always been able to count on Mannie for solutions. Mannie, her best friend.

Rachel's mother, Marie, had always understood. Looking back on it now, Rachel wished she could give her ma just one more hug for being such a wonderful mother. They'd been so different, Rachel and her mother, Marie always fussing about every little thing, Rachel ever ready to traipse through the pigpen with no thought for being a lady. Whenever Rachel had had a problem that her mother couldn't solve, Marie had sent Rachel to town on silly errands—to buy special ribbon for a dress, or to pick up a book that Marie was yearn-

ing to read, or to purchase some pepper-
mint to satisfy a sudden craving. And while
in town, Rachel could slip over to visit Mannie, her father none the wiser.

*Love.* It was strange how it went every
which way and doubled back on itself.
Rachel had loved her ma very much, but it
had been only Mannie who could chase
away her tears and make her laugh. There
was no explaining it. Her ma had just
shrugged, saying that Rachel and Amanda
were kindred spirits, one the very spit of the
other. Sometimes it made Rachel feel guilty,
for on some level she'd always known that
no one loved her as much as her ma did.

When Rachel had first started growing
breasts, she was so upset that her mother
sent her off to stay all night with Katy, a
childhood friend. Only Rachel didn't go to
Katy's, and her mother had known she
wouldn't. It had all been a plot to fool
Rachel's pa, so he'd never guess that his
daughter was off with Mannie, getting her
head filled with all manner of nonsense.
Rachel and Mannie had talked grown-up,
female talk about the unwelcome growths
that were appearing on Rachel's chest, and
by morning Rachel had been able to look at

herself in the mirror and shrug. *Teats.* Cows had them. Mares had them. And Rachel was growing some, too. It was necessary because, someday, she'd have babies, and she'd need teats to feed them. Until then, they were just *there,* and she had to put up with them.

Rachel's ma had somehow understood that nobody could communicate with Rachel better than Mannie. And so it went until that fateful day along the creek when nearly everyone Rachel loved had died.

Remembering, Rachel clenched her teeth against the pain. Losing all of them would have been unbearable no matter *what*. But to grab her brother and then look up to see a CIRCLE H on his killer's horse? Rachel had *known* that brand. Every time she visited Mannie, she would see it—on the cows, on the horses, and even on Mannie's saddles. It was so familiar, a variation of the brand that had been in her family for generations, a trademark that signified *Hollister*.

For years, Rachel had been unable to write the letter H. Now she knew why, and a murderous rage roiled through her. *Mannie*. It had been the worst kind of betrayal. Her aunt hadn't been there that day to fire the rifle. But she had hired it done.

*That* was what Rachel had been running from for the last five years. *Mannie,* her beloved aunt, had paid someone to slaughter all of Rachel's family—and even Rachel herself. It was too horrible to accept.

She raised her head, feeling weak and shaky, but also stronger. Mannie had betrayed her, but Joseph never would. She couldn't huddle forever in a corner, afraid because one wicked woman had broken her heart and destroyed her ability to trust.

An odd smell reached Rachel's nostrils. She blinked and focused, staring for a moment at a table leg. What *was* that smell? She sniffed. Then she set the shotgun aside and pushed to her feet. The smell was really strong, and it grew stronger as she circled the kitchen and came to the water closet, which Darby had added on to the house after her parents' death. *Kerosene?* Rachel stepped fully into the enclosure. Kerosene, definitely kerosene. She knew the scent so well. For five years, all she'd had for light were kerosene lanterns and an occasional candle.

She heard a faint whoosh. Spun in a full

circle. What was that? She stepped back out into the kitchen. *Whoosh, whoosh, WHOOSH.* She spun again, her eyes bulging from their sockets, her ears straining to hear. *Kerosene, igniting.* She'd heard the sound a thousand times if she'd heard it once. After touching a match to a kerosene-soaked wick, a whoosh always followed. Only now it wasn't a wick that had been lighted.

Rachel moved to the center of the kitchen, knowing even before she saw smoke squeezing up through the floorboards that someone had set fire to the house. A crackling sound surrounded her. *Oh, dear God.* He didn't plan to force his way into her sanctum. He meant to incinerate it. With her *inside.*

## Chapter Eighteen

If this doesn't beat all," David said. "They're gone?"

Joseph scanned the area, taking in the Pritchard shack and the outbuildings. Not a sign of any human movement. Pigs rutted in the hog pen. A chicken high-stepped across the yard. A cow bawled in the barn. But he saw no sign of the Pritchards anywhere.

"Sure looks like they're gone to me." Joseph swung down off his horse. "That'll make our job easier. Let's get it done before they come back."

David dismounted. Turning to the group of men behind them, he began giving orders, sending one bunch of deputized volunteers to the barn, another to search the rest of the outbuildings, and still another to walk the property.

"We're looking for mining equipment," he

barked. "Or anything else connected with mining, possibly even gold. There has to be evidence here somewhere." To the men who were about to walk the grounds, he added, "Be watchful for recently turned earth where something might be buried." To the men about to search the barn, he yelled, "Look in the stalls, under the tack room floors, up in the hayloft. Leave nothing unturned."

When the search parties had been dispatched, Joseph and David descended on the house. As Joseph stepped onto the porch, a loose board rocked under his boot. He jerked the plank free to look under it. *Nothing.* But they'd only just started. They would find the evidence they needed to see justice done. Every last one of the Pritchards might soon be swinging at the end of a rope.

*Tansy.* As he entered the Pritchard shack, he kept remembering Rachel's face as she had described the child's blood-soaked dress. And her mother, with no face. Rage roiled within him. How could these filthy excuses for human beings have done such things? It went beyond evil. To sight in on a little girl and pull the trigger? Joseph shuddered as he upended beds, opened cupboards, rifled through drawers. *Bastards.* He wanted to find enough evidence to see them hang. Nothing less.

David stepped on a loose floorboard and dropped to his knees to rip at the planks like a madman. As Joseph went to help him, his nostrils were filled with the stench of the men who frequented the house.

They ripped up half the floor. David had just jumped down to search beneath the remaining planks when a shout sounded from outside. It was Charley Banks. "We found it! Gold! A bunch of gold!"

David and Joseph raced outside. Charley stood outside the barn doors, holding up two partially filled burlap bags. Joseph could see by the strain on the man's face that the sacks weighed a great deal. He and his brother ran across the pocked yard.

"Are you sure it's gold?" David demanded.

Charley dropped the bags at his feet and reached into his shirt pocket to extract a chunk of yellow. "It's gold, all right." He turned the piece of ore in the sunlight. "Christ almighty, that must be a thick vein."

Joseph had seen the vein, and Charley was right; it ran deep into the rock. The tension eased from his body. The Pritchards were finished. Justice would be done. The blood on a little girl's pink dress would be avenged. And perhaps, somewhere along the way, Rachel would finally find peace, knowing that her family's killers had been punished.

David opened both bags, stared at the contents, and cursed vilely. Turning to Joseph, he said, "You had it right all along, Joseph. Those filthy bastards slaughtered the Hollisters."

Following that pronouncement, Joseph heard a shout. He turned to see Jeb Pritchard and his boys riding in on sweaty horses. Jeb swung down from the saddle before his sons even got their horses reined to a stop.

"So it was *you*!" he cried. "You cut our fence wire and chased our cattle off our land!" He turned a fiery gaze toward his house, saw the dismantled porch, and shook his fist. "What in God's name have you done? You come in here and tear apart our home? What's the matter with you?" He sent Joseph an accusing glare. "Enough of this *bullshit*. I ain't done nothin' wrong. My boys ain't, either. You've bedeviled me for *weeks*. I'm thinking you learned nothin' from what happened to your pa. Hanged, he was! And for somethin' he didn't do! Now you're hell-bent to do the same to me and mine!"

For just an instant, Joseph wondered if he'd been wrong. He disliked Jeb Pritchard. The man was so filthy that Joseph could have scraped the crud from his skin with the dull edge of a knife blade. But did Jeb's failure to bathe regularly make him evil?

Then Joseph's gaze shifted to the burlap bags at Charley's feet. Hard evidence didn't lie. Pritchard had been caught red-handed. Bags of gold, hidden in his barn. That hen nesting in his bathtub hadn't laid two bags of golden eggs.

"Hands behind your back," David ordered. "And I'm warning you, Pritchard, if you give me a moment's grief, I'll shoot you and dance on your grave."

Men surrounded Jeb's sons. Alan started to reach for his gun.

"I wouldn't if I were you," Joseph warned him.

Charley Banks jerked the thin younger man off his horse and none too gently pulled his arms behind his back while Garrett Buckmaster tied his wrists.

"You'll regret this!" Jeb cried. "And, by God, you'll fix all that you tore up. You got no right to come onto my land and destroy what's mine."

"We found the gold in your barn, Jeb," David said coldly.

"What gold?"

"*That* gold." David pointed to the bags. "And I'll venture a guess that we haven't found the half of it."

"You're crazy. Gold in my barn? You think I'd wear shoes with holey soles if I had gold stashed away? And where would I get it? Huh? Ain't like it grows on trees."

"I found the mine," Joseph inserted. "You didn't kill my dog, by the way, and it's lucky for you."

Just as Joseph spoke, he heard a distant barking and turned to see a red-gold ball of fur streaking through the trees. Buddy, in a flat-out run, barking every inch of the way. As the dog skidded to a stop, Joseph cried, "When are you gonna learn that stay means *stay*?"

Buddy lunged at Joseph's boots, snapping and snarling. Then the dog whirled, ran off a ways, and stopped to look back.

"What's gotten into you?" Joseph asked.

The shepherd dashed back, circling Joseph, nipping at his calves, and barking wildly. Buckmaster laughed. "Damn, Joseph. Dog needs lessons on the difference betwixt people and cows. He's trying to herd you."

When Buddy ran off again, Joseph gazed thoughtfully after him. "He got knocked into a cocked hat yesterday. Maybe his brains are still rattled." Only even as Joseph spoke, he looked into his dog's intelligent amber eyes and doubted his own words. "What's wrong, boy?"

The shepherd wheeled in a circle, then darted back toward the trees—and home. Joseph knew it was crazy, but his gut told him that the dog was trying to tell him something. "I gotta go," he told David.

"What?" David cried incredulously. "We aren't finished here yet."

Joseph was already racing for his horse. "Something's wrong at home. I gotta go!"

Joseph swung up into the saddle, turned Obie, and urged him forward into a run. Buddy barked and took off through the trees, his white paws moving so fast his legs were a blur. Feeling just a little foolish, Joseph leaned low over Obie's neck, guiding the stallion to follow the dog.

When they reached the fence line that divided the Bar H from Pritchard's land, Buddy sailed over the four strands of barbed wire as if they weren't there. Joseph nudged Obie with his heels. The stallion's powerful muscles bunched to leap, and over the wire they went.

As they neared the creek, Joseph saw the smoke—a huge mushroom of roiling grayish black reaching ever higher into the blue sky. *Oh, Jesus.* He became one with his horse, bent legs supporting his weight, torso parallel to Obie's back, his cheek riding the animal's sweaty neck. *Rachel.*

Joseph's heart almost stopped beating when he saw the house. The place was a blazing inferno, flames leaping far higher than the oak tree. He was out of the saddle and running before Obie skidded to a complete stop. He saw Ray Meeks, Amanda Hollister's foreman, racing back from the spring, water sloshing from the bucket he carried.

"Help me!" Ray yelled. "You gotta help me!"

But Joseph knew it was already too late. The entire house was afire, the heat rolling from it so intense that it seared his face.

*Rachel*. He dropped to his knees and screamed, "No! No, God, *no-oo-o!*"

And then he heard wild barking. Buddy was at the courtyard gate, frantically trying to dig under it. Joseph staggered to his feet. Since his marriage to Rachel, he'd had duplicate keys made for the kitchen doorways and courtyard gate so he could let himself in and out. Digging in his pocket as he ran, he pulled out the three skeleton keys. Which one went to the gate? He was so terrified that he couldn't remember their shapes.

He reached the ironwork, shoved in one of the keys, and sobbed with relief when the lock turned. The metal was so hot that it blistered his hands as he jerked it open. "Rachel? Rachel!"

He ran into the courtyard, looking everywhere for her. The plants were already scorched. A birdhouse hanging from an iron bar burst into flame and exploded like an Independence Day firework. Joseph threw up an arm to protect his face, knowing that Rachel couldn't have survived this, not even if she'd come out into the courtyard. He moved toward what had once been the porch, yelling her name, wanting to throw himself into the flames and die with her. But something inside the burning house exploded just then. The force of it knocked him clear off his feet and backward.

He lay sprawled on the ground for a moment, dazed and disoriented. Then he rolled onto his knees. As he came erect, he saw Buddy in a corner of the enclosure digging at the dirt. Joseph scrambled over on his knees. Not dirt. A pile of wet blankets. Joseph prodded the hot wool, felt firm softness underneath. *Rachel.*

He grabbed her up in his arms, blankets and all, lunged to his feet, and ran from the courtyard with his shoulders hunched around his burden. When he reached the old oak, he dropped back to his knees, pulled away the blankets, and saw her pale, soot-streaked face.

"Rachel?" He grabbed her up into his arms again. "Don't be dead. You can't be dead. Rachel!"

Her body jerked. Then she coughed. Joseph made a fist in her wet hair and cried like a baby. "Oh, sweetheart. I'll never leave you again. I swear to God, I'll never leave you again."

"Joseph," she croaked. "Tried—to—kill

me. Wet the bl-blankets in the p-pond." She coughed again. "Saved myself."

Then she looked past his shoulder and he felt her whole body tense. Joseph knew it had just dawned on her that she was out in the open. He quickly drew the blanket back over her face. "You're all right, honey. You're all right. I'll get you somewhere safe. I'll get you somewhere safe."

She turned her face against his shirt, her hands knotted on his arms. Joseph was about to reassure her again when Buddy let loose with a low, vicious snarl. Joseph darted a surprised glance at his dog. The shepherd's hackles were up. Turning, Joseph saw that Ray Meeks was staggering toward them. The closer the man came, the more viciously Buddy growled.

Such behavior was completely unlike Buddy. Joseph felt his wife trembling against him. Was she terrified by the openness, as he'd first thought, or by the man? He spoke softly to his dog and told him to sit. Buddy obeyed and stopped snarling, but Joseph could tell the animal was ready to attack if Meeks made a wrong move.

"Ah, Jesus, Joseph, I'm so sorry." Tears trailed down the man's cheeks, leaving pale tracks. "I am *so* sorry. Amanda took gravely ill. I promised Darby that I'd look after Rachel while he went to be with her. And I *tried,* I swear to you. I only went as far as the barn to unsaddle my horse and give it some water, and I never took my eyes off the house the entire time."

Wariness tightened every muscle in Joseph's body.

"I don't know how they sneaked in on me like that. The first I knew they were here was when I saw them riding away, and then flames started shooting up from the house. I tried my damnedest to put the fire out, but they'd doused the whole place with kerosene." Ray held out his hands, which looked to be charred. "I tried, partner. I put everything I had into saving her. I'm so sorry."

Meeks had missed his calling as an actor. If Joseph's wife and dog hadn't been telling him different, he would have believed the man was sincere.

"Who rode away?" Joseph asked, stalling for time. He had never in his life been afraid to draw down on another man, but he held Rachel in his arms. He was fast enough to take Meeks out. He had every confidence in that. But he couldn't slap leather with Rachel in the line of fire. "Who set fire to the place?"

Ray passed a sleeve over his tear-filled eyes. "I can't be positive. They were some distance off and riding fast. But it looked like Jeb Pritchard and his boys."

Meeks glanced at the sodden lump of wool in Joseph's arms. "I'd give my right arm to undo this. I'm so sorry about your wife. I should never have gone to the barn."

Joseph prayed that Rachel wouldn't move. Meeks had tried to kill her and clearly believed that he'd been successful in the attempt. Joseph bent his head. He needed to put distance between himself and Rachel before Meeks realized she wasn't dead and went for his gun. Only what if Rachel cried out when Joseph tried to move away from her?

Before Joseph could think what to do, he heard the sound of approaching horses. Meeks turned to squint into the distance. When he recognized the riders, his blackened face went pale.

Amanda Hollister and Darby McClintoch rode in. Despite her palsy, Amanda swung out of the saddle with the skill and grace born of a lifetime on horseback. She quickly jerked her rifle from its boot, turned aching blue eyes on Ray, and said, "I dumped the tea in a potted plant."

Ray licked his lips, gave a shaky laugh. "Pardon me?"

"What was in it?" Amanda's whole body was shaking. "Arsenic? You were so worried about making sure I drank it that I grew suspicious. Then I noticed an odd taste. While you had your back turned, I dumped it out. You thought I'd swallowed it all when you left to come here for Darby. You figured I'd be dead by the time he reached my place, that I'd never be able to say I hadn't sent for him."

Joseph looked back and forth from Ray to Amanda, not understanding any of the exchange. *Poisoned tea?*

"You killed my nephew." Amanda raised the rifle to her shoulder. "You murdered his wife and Daniel and little Tansy. Shot them down in cold blood. I never wanted to believe it was you. The very thought broke my heart. God forgive me, it was so much easier to lay the blame on Jeb. So I turned a blind eye and told myself that my son, my long-lost child, couldn't have done such a heinous thing."

"Put that gun down, Ma." Meeks laughed again. "You aren't going to shoot me."

It hit Joseph then, like a fist to his jaw. Ray's eyes. The first time Joseph met the man, he'd experienced an odd sense of familiarity and asked Ray if they'd met before. Now Joseph knew what it was about Ray that had struck a chord in his memory. *His eyes.* He had Rachel's arresting blue eyes and her fine features as well.

"Now you've killed my Rachel," Amanda went on, her voice beginning to shake as badly as her body was. "I loved that girl like my own. How could you do this?"

Ray held his hands out to his sides and retreated another pace. "You're talking crazy. Arsenic in your tea? You're my mother. I love you. Why would I do such a thing?"

"That's a good question." Amanda curled her finger over the trigger. "Stand fast, Raymond. If you take another step, I'll drop you in your tracks."

"This is insane!" Ray cried.

"Is it? I noticed that someone had been in my desk last week. Then I discovered that my will was missing. I thought I might have misplaced it. But then it reappeared in the drawer, right where I always kept it. Even then, I didn't want to believe what my common sense was telling me. What a sentimental old fool I was, hoping against hope that my boy was everything he pretended to be. But the truth was, you took the will to get legal counsel to see where you would stand if I married Darby. I'm sure you learned that everything I own will become his, leaving you with nothing."

Amanda shook her head sadly. "You wanted it all. Didn't you, Ray? A little gold here and there wasn't enough to satisfy your greed. Getting my little spread after I died wasn't grand enough for you, either. You wanted the gold, you wanted this ranch, you wanted *everything*. And time was suddenly running out. I was days away from marrying Darby. You had to stop that from happening, and you had to kill Rachel, as well, to take possession of this ranch. Joseph had found the mine. You knew you'd be able to do no more digging without running the risk of getting caught."

"You gave me up!" Ray yelled. Swinging an arm to encompass the ranch, he cried. "It should've been mine. I had as much right to it as Henry, maybe more! You worked harder to make a go of this place than his father ever did. But what did I get? A tiny little spread where I'd have to scratch out a living for the rest of my life. Oh, yes, and the gold! Some compensation that was, none of it really mine to take, and me taking a huge chance every time I came over here to chip rock."

Ray moved back another step. "You talk about your family. What about *me*? Then, to add insult to injury, you decide to get married when you're seventy years old with one foot already in the grave. I've worked that meager, parched piece of land for almost eight years, waiting for you to die so it'd be mine, and you were going to take even that from me."

"What happened in the past is over. I eventually found you, didn't I? And I didn't willingly give you up. My father forced me to do it."

"A lot of comfort that is to me. I got cheated out of everything, even the Hollister name!"

"It's no excuse, Raymond. You've wrongfully taken human life. You have to pay for that."

"Hang, you mean?" Ray shook his head. "No way. For once in your life, be a decent mother and just let me go."

"I can't do that," Amanda said sadly.

Ray went for his gun.

"Don't, Raymond!" Amanda cried. "Please, for the love of God, don't."

Joseph rolled sideways to cover Rachel with his body, but before he could draw his weapon, Amanda Hollister fired her rifle. Ray's blue eyes filled with incredulity. He dropped his chin to stare stupidly at the blood blossoming over the front of his gray shirt. The revolver fell from his hand.

"You shot me," he whispered.

And then he dropped facedown on the dirt, shuddered, and died.

The rifle slipped from Amanda's trembling grasp. On unsteady legs, she made her way to her son, dropped to her knees, wrapped her arms around his limp body, and started to sob.

"God forgive me. My baby boy. God forgive me. God forgive me."

Darby knelt beside her. As he laid a hand on her heaving back, he sent Joseph a tortured look. There were no words. Amanda Hollister had just killed her own son. Joseph sorely wished that it hadn't been necessary. But sadly it was. Ray had gone for his gun. He wouldn't have hesitated to shoot. Amanda had done what she had to do to keep her son from hurting any more innocent people.

Nevertheless, the memory of this day would haunt her for the rest of her life.

## Chapter Nineteen

Rachel came slowly awake. Nearby she heard the crackling of a fire, which terrified her for a moment, but then she felt Joseph's big, hard hand curled warmly around hers and she knew that she was absolutely safe. She slowly lifted her lashes. His darkly burnished face hovered above hers, his beautiful blue eyes cloudy with tenderness.

"There she is, finally coming around," he said softly. "I thought you were gonna sleep until sometime next week. I tried to tell Doc not to dose you with that much laudanum, but he wouldn't listen."

Rachel only dimly recalled Doc's being there. She glanced uneasily around. She lay on a dark leather sofa in a strange room. A fire crackled cheerfully in the hearth of a large river-rock fireplace. "Where am I?"

"My place. Don't panic. Every window in this section of the house is boarded over, inside and out. Esa and David's handiwork. And Ace blocked off the hallway just beyond the water closet. It's not quite as good as your kitchen, but almost. We brought in a bed before he blocked the hall. We have the place trimmed down to one room, more or less." He smiled and lifted her hand to trail silky lips lightly over her knuckles. "When I built this house, I think I was building it for you and just didn't know it. I made the kitchen and sitting room all one area."

Rachel turned onto her side to better see his face. Moving made her hands hurt. When she glanced down at her knuckles, Joseph said, "You kept them out from under the wet blankets to hold them close around you. The heat from the fire was pretty intense and blistered the backs of your fingers."

Rachel sank back against the pillows. It all came back to her then—the fire, throwing blankets into the fishpond and draping them around herself to stay safe from the flames, smoke, and heat. "Oh, Joseph." She gave him a questioning look. "Ray's dead, isn't he?"

He nodded, his expression going solemn. "Amanda shot him."

Rachel squeezed her eyes closed. "Poor Mannie."

"Who?"

"Mannie. It's what I've always called Aunt Amanda. Ray was her son?"

Joseph kissed her knuckles again. "It's a long story," he said.

"Tell me," she whispered, and so he began. Much later, when he finally stopped talking, Rachel said, "So that's why my pa always said Mannie had brought shame upon the family name. Because she had a child out of wedlock."

Joseph nodded. "I guess she never stopped pining for the baby boy she gave away. When she had the falling out with your father and left the ranch, she hired a detective to try to find her son."

Rachel sighed. "I remember when Ray came to work for Mannie. She was always patting his arm and smoothing his hair. I wasn't that old back then, about fourteen, I think, but I thought it was odd. I decided that she probably just liked him a lot."

"A whole lot. He was her son, and she loved him."

"But she never told anyone?"

Joseph ran a hand through his hair. The

strands fell back to his shoulders, glistening like threads of spun gold. "Darby rode over a bit ago. He has the whole story now, straight from Amanda, and he wanted me to hear it first so I might explain it all to you."

Rachel searched his gaze. "Is it bad?"

"Let's just say your aunt Amanda isn't entirely innocent in all of this. But let me start from the first. All right?"

Rachel nodded.

"Years ago, when Amanda was still a fairly young woman, she had a secret place on the Bar H where she often went to be alone. Your great-grandfather Luther Hollister and your grandpa Peter didn't treat her very well. They never quite forgave her for getting pregnant. When their coldness toward her got to be too much, she'd go to her secret place, a cave that she'd found up in the rocks near the creek. One afternoon, she took a lantern with her to see how deep the cave went, and she discovered that there was gold in the rock.

"To spite her father, who'd already informed her that he had cut her out of his will and meant to leave her nothing, she kept the gold a secret, never telling anyone. It was her one little bit of revenge. In her defense, I have to also add that Amanda never thought there was a lot of gold. She had no way of knowing how deep into the rock the vein went, and generally speaking, this area hasn't proved out to be rich, No Name being a perfect example. Keeping the discovery to herself was more an act of defiance, her only way of striking back at two men who had made her life a misery. She'd not only been forced to give up her baby, but she'd lost the only man she ever truly loved."

"Darby."

Joseph reached to smooth Rachel's hair. She so loved the feel of his touch that she turned her cheek into the palm of his hand.

"Yes, Darby. There's been a lot of sadness in her life. Finally locating Ray was one of the few things that ever went right for her, or so she thought. He had been adopted by a Kentucky farmer and his wife, mainly so he could help with the work around their place. Ray had a terrible childhood, according to the story he told Amanda, getting whipped for the least infraction, sometimes not getting fed as additional punishment." Joseph sighed and shrugged. "Who knows the real story? Maybe he was horribly abused, maybe he wasn't. He could have made it all up to make Amanda feel even more guilty for giving him up as a baby."

"So he could control her," Rachel whispered.

Joseph nodded. "We'll never know. But Amanda did feel terrible for him. She had so little to offer him, really, a small spread that made barely enough to keep the wolves from her door. He was her son, a Hollister by birth, and, in her mind, deserved so much more. She saw no point in legally claiming him as her child. She had no other children to contest her will. At that time, your father had the family ranch and was doing well. She knew he wouldn't care who got her meager little patch of land. Claiming Ray as her child would have caused a scandal that might have reflected on her loved ones." He smiled and trailed a fingertip over Rachel's mouth. "Namely you. She saw no point in causing a bunch of gossip that might hurt you. So she just made Ray Meeks her sole beneficiary so he would get what little she had when she died."

"Which wasn't much," Rachel observed.

"No, not much. So to make up for it, Amanda told Ray about the cave on her family's land. If he was careful, he could sneak in and chip out some gold now and again. Small compensation, in her mind. She had no way of knowing that Ray would discover a veritable fortune inside that cave, enough gold that he would kill to protect the secret."

Joseph stared at the fire thoughtfully. "The day your family was killed, I believe one of you children went up into the rocks and came upon the cave."

Memories flashed through Rachel's mind in a dizzying rush. "Tansy," she whispered raggedly. "I remember that now. She went traipsing off right before lunch, and Ma sent me and Daniel to find her. She was already coming back down the hill when we came upon her. I remember her saying that she'd found a dark, scary place, and had seen a spook looking out at her. She was fanciful and often told whoppers. Daniel and I pretended to be interested, but we didn't take her seriously." An awful pain moved through Rachel's chest. "We went back down to the creek and had lunch. Daniel and I were still eating when the first shot rang out."

"It stands to reason that Tansy's spook was Raymond Meeks," Joseph said thickly.

"Tansy had seen the cave and possibly his mining paraphernalia. He knew she would probably tell. He couldn't take that chance, so he rode down the hill and opened fire on all of you, his hope being that Estyn Beiler, the marshal back then, would think it to be a random act, some drunked-up plug-ugly who happened onto your land and decided to do a little target practice."

Rachel felt sick, physically sick.

"Only that wasn't how it went. Instead, Amanda Hollister was the prime suspect. If all of you had died, she was next in line to inherit everything. She was the only person who really stood to gain by your deaths—or so everyone believed. You can bet Ray Meeks sweated bullets, terrified that Beiler would start digging and discover that another person stood to gain as well, namely Ray because he was the sole beneficiary of Amanda Hollister's will."

Rachel cupped a hand over her eyes.

"You okay?" Joseph asked softly. "We can let this go, honey. I know it has to be difficult for you to hear."

Rachel lowered her hand. "No, no. I need to know, Joseph. Then I just want to put it behind me if I can."

He sighed and resumed talking. "Ray left you for dead that afternoon, not realizing that the bullet glanced off your skull. He was probably in a hell of a snit when he heard you survived. It wasn't as if he could finish the job, not without raising suspicion again. You went into seclusion, making it almost impossible for him to try to kill you and make it look like an accident. One good thing came of it for Ray, though. With your father dead, all the hired hands quit, and only Darby was left to work your ranch. By exercising a little caution, Ray was able to go to and from the mine with scarcely any risk of being seen. That's a big spread, and Darby couldn't be everywhere at once."

"So he contented himself with that and worked the mine for all these years."

"Precisely. It wasn't an ideal situation. He had to do all the picking and digging and hauling on the sly. But judging by what I've seen, it was very profitable. Maybe he hoped to eventually play the mine out, pull up stakes, and live like a king somewhere else. I only know that he left you and Darby alone for a good long while."

"Until Darby rode up into the rocks, searching for a stray."

"Ray apparently believed that Darby had seen the mine. A fortune was at stake. So Ray shot him in the back. When Darby came riding into my place, my first thought was that he'd taken a stray bullet. But Darby insisted it was too much to be a coincidence and believed he'd been shot by the same person who murdered your family."

"And you came to my house to look after me." Rachel smiled sadly. "Something lovely to make up for all the bad, that. I met you."

He lifted her hand to nibble at the base of her thumb. "Yeah, and just for the record, Mrs. Paxton, I'm as thankful for that turn of events as you are. But I want to finish this." He smiled and winked at her. "Contrary to what Ray evidently thought, Darby hadn't seen the mine. And the new marshal, David, was as baffled as Estyn Beiler had been five years ago, with no real clues to solve either shooting incident. It's highly unlikely that Ray would have done anything else to arouse suspicion if Buddy hadn't seen or heard him up in the rocks yesterday, raised sand to alert me, and then taken off up there.

"I'll never know how that dog knew that

Ray Meeks was a polecat, but somehow he did. He wasn't barking a friendly hello, like he normally does. Buddy knew the man was dangerous. When I called him back, he didn't listen. He just charged on up the hill, and Ray hit him in the head with something to shut him up. When I went looking for my dog, I found the damned mine."

"And the secret was out."

"Essentially, and Ray stood to lose a veritable fortune in gold. Even worse, everything else was going to hell in a handbasket as well. His mother had suddenly up and decided to get married. He realized that Darby, as her husband, would have legal right to her property and could probably contest her will, cutting Ray out cold. They were planning to marry in less than a week. He panicked and hatched a plan to kill his mother and you both. He hoped to make Amanda's death look natural—she is old, after all, and Doc might have thought her heart just stopped. And your death could appear to be the murder it actually was, with all the evidence carefully laid by Ray to implicate the Pritchards.

"It was a pretty clever plan, actually. He apparently eavesdropped on Darby's conversation with Amanda last night and knew of my and David's decision to round up a posse to search Jeb's property at ten this morning. Sometime last night, Ray sneaked into Jeb's barn to plant a couple bags of gold. Then bright and early this morning, he cut Jeb's fence wire, herded the Pritchard cows off the property, and then went by Jeb's place to tell him that his cattle were running all over hell's creation. When we got to Jeb's, no one was there. Then Buddy came racing in, acting deranged and trying to make me follow him." Joseph's eyes went bright with wetness. "I'm so glad now that I had the good sense to pay attention to that dad-blamed dog. He knew you were in danger."

Rachel shivered, remembering. "Right after Ray showed up, Buddy started snarling. When Darby scolded him, he ran off and wouldn't come back. I didn't know he was going to find you, but I'm ever so glad he did. If you hadn't come—"

Joseph laid a finger over her lips. "Don't say it, Rachel. It's a miracle you survived. Right after I entered the courtyard, a birdhouse exploded from sheer heat. I've never seen anything like it."

"Buddy saved my life by going for you, Joseph. I can't leave that unsaid. He knew Ray meant to harm me. Somehow he *knew*."

"Maybe dogs can smell evil in a person just like they smell fear. When I reached your place and got you out of the courtyard, I would have believed Ray's story in a heartbeat if it hadn't been for Buddy snarling at him. If not for that, everything Ray told me would have played into what I already believed, that the Pritchards were behind everything. I knew Jeb and his boys had been gone from their place when we got over there. Then Ray said he'd seen them riding away from your house right before it went up in flames. It all fit, and I would have believed him, I think." He sighed. "I feel bad about that now. Jeb's dirty and unlikable. I almost made a terrible mistake, something I never would have forgiven myself for, all because I don't like the man."

Rachel glanced around. "Where is Buddy, by the way? I owe him a big thank-you hug."

"I figured he deserved a treat and let him go home with Ace tonight so he can play with Cleveland until he drops."

Rachel laughed softly. "Good. He does deserve a reward. When he comes home, you need to kill a steer so I can feed him steak until it comes out his ears."

"What about me? Don't I get a reward?"

Rachel pushed up on an elbow to hook an arm around his neck. "Oh, yes, but I've something better in mind for you."

Rachel smoothed his hair, kissed him just below his ear. "It's over, Joseph. It's finally, truly over. From this moment forward, I don't want to think about Ray Meeks ever again. I want to concentrate on our life together and on making you happy."

"I can go for that," he said with a growl. "You sure you're feeling up to it? You had a pretty horrible experience today."

A nightmarish experience, and Rachel wanted to put it completely, forever behind her. "I feel fine, thank you. I just need you to help me think about something else."

Within seconds, he went from serious to passionate, tearing at her clothing, laving her body with kisses. Rachel forgot about the fire—forgot about Ray Meeks—forgot about Mannie.

She was alive, and that had to be celebrated.

Later when they lay satiated in each other's arms with only a film of sweat separating their naked bodies, Joseph whispered, "Shit."

"What?"

"I just ripped your shirtwaist, getting it off you."

Rachel tasted his ear, wanting him again. "It's okay. I didn't like that shirtwaist very well, anyway."

He nibbled just below her jaw. "It was your *only* shirtwaist. Every other stitch of clothing you owned went up in flames."

Rachel realized he was right and burst out laughing. "Oh, dear. I guess I'll have to run around the house stark naked."

"Hmm. Now there's a thought. Stupid me. I was thinking more along the lines of going shopping to get you new clothes."

She nipped the underside of his chin. "Shame on you."

He grinned and kissed her. Against her lips, he whispered, "No worries. I'll get you one of my shirts to use as a nightgown for tonight, and tomorrow I'll go shopping." He trailed his mouth toward her breasts. Then he went still and let loose with another curse.

Rachel grinned and ran her hands into his hair, trying to direct him to where she desperately wanted to have his mouth. "What now?"

His wonderful hands cupped her breasts. "Ace boarded off the hallway. I forgot to get any of my clothes out of the bedroom."

Rachel started to giggle. She was still laughing when Joseph thrust himself deeply into her. Suddenly all thought of laughter abandoned her. *Heaven on earth.* Caitlin had told her exactly right.

Some time later, Rachel stood before the fire, her only covering a blanket from off the sofa. A loud crash of breaking glass came from the back of the house. She smiled and turned to warm her backside. *Joseph, breaking through a window again.* Except for it being in his house instead of hers, it seemed they'd come full circle, with one small difference.

This time, she wouldn't shoot at him when he reached the kitchen. The man had his fine points and was definitely a keeper.

# Chapter Twenty

*Three months later*

Rachel sat in her new courtyard on a bench fashioned for her by No Name's only sawyer, Ron Christian. It was a gorgeous July afternoon, and she had nothing better to do than enjoy the sunlight that poured down through the iron bars to warm her skin and make her roses and violets bloom.

*Heaven.* Jesse Chandler, the chimney sweep, had built her another trio of birdhouses, and his wife, Dorothy, a gentle, softspoken blonde who made gorgeous candles, had decorated each of them. Harrison Gilpatrick had defied his wife yet again to bring her several more rosebushes, and the first spring buds had now matured into gorgeous full blooms. The patches of lawn were a brilliant summer green. Her new school of goldfish loved their new pond. Everything in Rachel's world was absolutely right. Joseph had seen to that.

Just as he'd promised, he'd created a safe world for her at his ranch. She had everything she could possibly need at her fingertips within her living area: a water closet, a brand-new washing machine, retractable clotheslines to dry the laundry, and designated areas for comfortable living—a kitchen, a dining room, a bedroom, and a parlor—the only remarkable difference being that now her area was larger because, without knowing it, Joseph had built his house just for her, combining his kitchen, dining area, and sitting room into one large open section. In the days since her near brush with death, he had added on a vestibule, just as he'd promised, and Bubba White had fashioned more ironwork for the doors, ceiling, and gate, making her feel absolutely safe.

Everyone had worked so hard to create this world for her, and Rachel loved it. She truly did. The courtyard was even larger than the first one. Joseph had slaved from dawn to dark building the walls, taking them out much farther from the house this time so she wouldn't perish in the event of another fire. The thought brought tears to her eyes. So much love, and so much *work*.

When she thought of all the hours of labor that had been invested, she didn't know how to tell Joseph that she no longer needed any walls.

Directly after Ray Meeks' death, Rachel had needed the barricades, just like always. Boards over the windows. A shotgun within easy reach. No doors that opened onto the outdoors. Only somehow, over the weeks that followed the fire, something within her had inexplicably healed, and she awoke one morning wanting the boards off the windows so she could see out. And once outside in her courtyard, where before she had always felt so miraculously free, she suddenly felt imprisoned, all that was within her yearning to see the world beyond the walls.

She didn't know what to do. Joseph had spent a small fortune adding on to the front of his house to build her a vestibule. And he'd neglected his ranch to build these fabulous, impenetrable walls of rock for her. How could she tell him that she no longer needed or even wanted them?

She heard a conveyance pull up out front. No urge came over her to run into the house to hide. The demon that had haunted her dreams for so very long no longer existed.

Maybe it was Doc, coming to check on her again. Or maybe it was someone from town, bearing yet another sweet gift to make her little world more beautiful.

Only she wanted the real world now. She wanted to go walking through the fields with her wonderful husband. She wanted to go horseback riding and lie on her back in a shady place, watching the clouds drift by and listening to the birds.

Rachel had prayed for so long to get well. For *years*. And she had despaired, convinced she never would. But that was before Joseph. Before Buddy. Before Joseph's wonderful family. Maybe she would pretend to be sick a while longer. She'd lived in a dark cave for so long. She could surely do it for a few more months. Then everyone who had worked so hard on this beautiful courtyard might not feel quite so deflated when she informed them that she no longer needed it.

"Rachel?"

That voice. It was one that Rachel had adored all her life. She sat frozen on the bench for a moment. Then she twisted to look over her shoulder. There, gazing at her through the bars, was Aunt Amanda.

"I'll go if you want," she said shakily. "I'll understand if you hate me. I truly will. But I had to at least try to see you one more time."

Tears filled Rachel's eyes, nearly blinding her. "Mannie."

"Yes, it's me. I'm a little worse for wear, I'm afraid." She curled a shaky hand around a bar. "I won't stay but for a minute, sweet girl. Only for a minute. I just want to say that I'm so very sorry. I loved him, you know. My Raymond." Amanda grabbed for breath and shakily exhaled. "Sometimes when we love a child so very, very much, we're blinded to his faults. I won't lie to you. Deep down, I think I always knew. But I couldn't *believe*. Does that make any sense?"

Rachel tried to nod, but the muscles in her neck seemed to have turned to stone.

"As a mother," Amanda continued, "I couldn't believe it of him. So I found others to blame, and I pretended he was all that I wanted and needed him to be, the wonderful son that I had lost and found again."

Rachel pushed slowly to her feet. Her throat had closed off, and she couldn't speak.

"I just need you to know that I never

stopped loving you. *Never.* I was an old fool, and you and your family paid the price for it. I can never undo that. I will never forgive myself for the pain I've caused you. I just hope that someday, when you hold your own little boy in your arms, you'll come to some sort of understanding and finally be able to forgive me. There's no love like the love a mother feels for her child. *Nothing* compares. And when that child goes wrong, it is so very hard to stand back and see him for what he really is, without the love clouding your vision."

Rachel moved slowly toward the gate. Struggling to reclaim her voice, she finally managed to say, "I don't hate you, Mannie. I love you with all my heart."

Amanda raised her chin in that prideful way she had. "What?"

And suddenly Rachel knew why she was finally well. The imagined betrayal—the terrible hurt of it—had never happened except within her mind. Mannie had had nothing to do with what had occurred on that horrible day. Her only crime had been to love her son too much and to remain loyal to him to the last.

"I said I love you," Rachel repeated more

firmly. "I always loved you best, more than anyone. I always loved you best." She reached into the pocket of her new skirt and withdrew the key to the gate. "Please, Mannie, come in. Let's talk for a while."

"Oh, no. I know how you are about doors opening onto open places, sweetheart."

Rachel sighed wearily. Then she shoved the key into the lock and opened the gate. "How I *used* to be."

Once Amanda was inside the courtyard, Rachel led her to the garden bench, and after a time, when they'd healed all the old wounds and clarified all the misunderstandings, Rachel said, "Joseph went into Denver last week to confer with a lawyer. We've talked, and I've decided that I don't want the Bar H. My great-grandfather was a stupid old codger, and Grandpa Peter was just as bad. You worked that land all your life, and it rightfully belongs to you. We're in the process of deeding it all to you."

Amanda's eyes filled with tears. "I appreciate the thought, darling, I truly do. But I'm too old to give a damn about any of it at this age. I just want to be with my Darby during my last days."

"Poor as church mice? No." Rachel's

voice rang with firmness. "There's a fortune in gold on that land. I want you to live out your last days with your Darby, but I want you to do it wanting for nothing, which is just as it should be."

"Joseph needs more land than he's got," Amanda argued. "Such foolishness. You're the young folks. You need the ranch and the gold far more than Darby and I do."

"Leave it to our children," Rachel replied.

"I could do that, but here's a better idea. Fifty-fifty, dear heart. You and I, the Hollister women, splitting the profits from that mine." Amanda chuckled and looked up through the bars at the sky. "My father is surely rolling in his grave. I always thought that part of the reason he never forgave me for getting pregnant was the fact that I was a female. It saved him from having to leave any of his precious wealth to someone in a skirt."

Rachel giggled. And suddenly Amanda's idea struck her as being absolutely right: a way for Mannie to finally have her revenge, with the last of the Hollister line, two idiotic females in skirts controlling it all.

"We'll be rich, Mannie."

"Richer than my father ever dreamed of being," Amanda replied with a satisfied sigh.

"Is it a deal, then? Darby can work the ranch as long as he feels up to it, but you and Joseph will actually own it and manage it. And the gold will be divided equally between you and me. Darby and I will build a grand little house over there and live out our last years like a king and queen, working only when and if we please. What we don't manage to spend before we die will go to your children, although I have to warn you that I've always had a hankering to see far-away places. Maybe we'll spend it all traveling."

Rachel hoped so. No one deserved to see far-away places more than her aunt Amanda. "It's a deal," she replied.

And they shook on it.

As they moved on to talk about other things, Rachel felt like a child again, confessing her troubles to always understanding Mannie.

When Rachel had told her the entire story about no longer needing any walls, Amanda threw back her head and chortled with laughter. Flicking Rachel an apologetic glance, she wiped tears of mirth from under her eyes and said, "What a pickle."

"I already know it's a pickle. Joseph will want to strangle me when he finds out."

Amanda laughed some more.

"It's not funny, Mannie. I'm well, and I can't tell anyone. Joseph has been so wonderful. You just can't know. He's created a safe world for me here, doing everything within his power to make me happy. How can I tell him it was all for nothing?" The back of Rachel's throat burned. "I always thought I'd be so happy if I got well. Now I just feel awful and wish I were sick again."

Amanda shook her head. "Sick again? Rachel Marie, bite your tongue. Where is the man?"

Rachel jumped up from the bench. "Why? You aren't going to tell him?"

Amanda laughed. "No, but you are. Right now, this instant. Where is he?"

"Out in the fields. I think he's plowing."

"Well, then. Plowing means he hasn't turned dirt everywhere yet, and you can still find some grass. Run out there and make best use of it."

"The best use of grass?" Rachel asked, completely baffled.

"Yes, the grass. Where's your head at, young lady? By the time you finish with him, he won't care about the damned courtyard. He'll only be delighted that you're well. How can you think otherwise?" She glanced around the courtyard. "You got a lovely garden out of it. Be thankful for that and count your blessings."

"But what of all the people from town?"

Amanda rolled her blue eyes. "They wanted to give you sunshine. Do you think caring hearts like that will nitpick? They are going to be happy as can be that you're well."

Rachel cast a dubious look at the gate. "Oh, Mannie, I've never been so scared in my life."

"Pshaw." She flicked her fingertips at the gate. "Off with you. Are you the daughter of my heart or not? Sometimes you have to dig deep for courage, girl. Start digging."

Rachel ran over to hug her aunt. "Oh, Mannie, I have missed you so."

Amanda gathered her close for a long, tight embrace. Then she pushed Rachel away. "Go on. Give the man something to smile about. You can tell me about it later."

Rachel let herself out the gate. *Deep breath.* And, oh, that felt so wonderful. She was *free*. After five long years in prison, she was absolutely free. Way off in the distance, she saw Joseph shuffling along behind the mules, his strong shoulders braced to control the plow as it dug deep into new earth.

"Joseph!" she called.

He didn't look up.

"Joseph?" she called again.

Her voice must have carried to him on the summer breeze, for he drew the team to a halt and looked up. Rachel ran faster, her arms held wide. She saw him pull the gear off over his head and start toward her, haltingly at first, as if he couldn't quite believe his eyes, and then surging into a flat-out run, as if every second that passed might be their last.

They collided in the pasture between the house and the field. Rachel locked her arms around his strong neck. "I'm well, Joseph. I'm well! I didn't know how to tell you."

She babbled on about the courtyard and the vestibule and all the boarded-up windows and how terrible she felt for not needing them anymore. And then Joseph locked an arm around her waist, dropping to his knees and taking her down with him.

"You're well? You're well and you couldn't tell me? Sweet Christ, woman. Like I care about that damned courtyard?" He caught her face between his hands. Dirty hands, ingrained with the soil that provided their livelihood. "Being out here doesn't bother you? You can breathe?"

Rachel took a deep breath, just to show him. "I'm so sorry, Joseph. I didn't realize. Not until the courtyard was almost finished. And then I felt so *awful*. All that work for nothing. I didn't know how to tell you, and I just—"

His hungry mouth cut off the rest of the sentence. The next thing Rachel knew, she was on her back in pink clover, with the most wonderful, handsome, sexy man on earth braced on his arms above her.

"I love you," he whispered raggedly as he trailed kisses down her throat. "It's a miracle, Rachel. A miracle. We won't have to shove our kids out the wood safe to send them to school."

Rachel snorted with laughter. And then as his hot mouth found one of her breasts, she forgot what she was laughing about. *Joseph.* She loved him as she'd never loved anyone. As he shoved up her skirts and thrust himself deeply into her, Rachel drank in the blue sky above them, reveling in the wondrous feeling of a summer breeze flowing gently over her bare skin.

Joseph's gift to her.

When their passion was spent and he collapsed beside her, Rachel whispered, "It's a good thing the grass is tall. I'll bet anything that Mannie stayed to watch."

*"What?"*

Rachel giggled and then told him about her aunt's visit. "She still hadn't left when I ran out here to tell you."

Joseph jerked his pants up. "You mean I was flashing my bare ass at your aunt?"

"Oh, I doubt that. I think the grass is tall enough to have covered you."

"You *think*. You don't know for sure. You just *think*? I've a good mind to turn you over my knee and paddle your bare butt."

"Hmm. That sounds fun."

He grabbed her and wrestled her across his lap. Rachel shrieked and burst out laughing when he threw up her skirts and playfully pinched her bottom instead.

Laughter. Wrestling with her husband in the grass, with clover forming a pink blanket all around them. If she lived to be a hundred, she doubted that life would ever get better.

Everything, absolutely everything, was perfect just as it was.

# EPILOGUE

Tucker stared long and hard at the last page of Rachel Hollister's diary, feeling oddly empty inside, as if the last few pages of her memoirs had been dribbles of water, spilling from inside of him, leaving nothing. Such an incredible story, with such happiness at the end, the kind of happiness he had never experienced and wasn't sure he ever would.

He turned to look at his mom. On this, the fifth afternoon of their diary reading, she was smiling dreamily, staring at the curtains over her kitchen bay window, as if remembering something.

"What are you thinking?" he asked.

Mary Coulter shrugged and grinned. "About your dad. About the first time I ever saw him. About our courtship." She sighed. "What a glorious thing true love is. It only gets better with time. Comfortable, like Ace tried to explain to Joseph, and ever so precious after all the excitement wears off. I nag at your father to change his shirt, and I chew him out whenever he messes up, never sparing any words. But I love him more now than I ever dreamed possible when we were young and just starting out."

She patted Rachel's diary. "It's so good to read something like that. They lived and loved so long ago, but even then they found a happy ending. Isn't that wonderful?"

"How can you know that?" Tucker asked. "Maybe Joseph woke up one morning and his feelings had changed. Maybe the excitement all wore off." It had happened to Tucker more times than he wanted to count—a sizzle, thinking he'd found the woman of his dreams, and then the inevitable fizzle. "They got married so *fast*. What was it—a month after they met, maybe? They barely knew each other."

His mother looked at him as if he were an alien and rapped him sharply on the forehead with her knuckles. "They were together almost constantly for all that time. Trust me, they knew all the things they needed to know about each other, and the love they felt was real."

Tucker shook his head. "Ten years later, I'll

bet Joseph Paxton was sweating behind a plow, wishing he'd never bitten off all that responsibility. A wife and kids and bills to pay. The romance doesn't last. If you buy into that, you're in for a big fall."

Mary smiled. "I knew you'd say that." She turned on her kitchen chair and plucked something off the counter behind them. "Read that, you doubting Thomas. It's Joseph's last letter to Rachel, shortly before he died."

"What?" Tucker was so into the story by now that he reverently took the yellowed paper from his mother's hand. Unlike the paper in the diary, these sheets looked familiar, lined in blue and from a tablet, much like the sheets of paper he'd used to do his lessons in grade school.

His mother's eyes shone. "He was ninety-four when he wrote that letter. It's dated 1952. Your grandma Eden received it from one of Joseph and Rachel's children, and she saved it in the family Bible. I've never read it without crying. It's so beautiful."

*My darling Rachel:* the letter read in spidery, faded ink, clearly written by an old, palsied man. *I fear that I may leave you soon.*

"He died a year later," Mary whispered reverently. "He knew his time with her was almost over, and he wanted her to know all the things in his heart. Isn't that beautiful? She passed on about a year after he did, but she had this to sustain her."

As Tucker read on, his throat got tight, and he wasn't the sentimental sort.

*You have given me so much. When I first met you, I thought I was opening up the world for you, but I was so wrong. You were the one who opened up all of my windows so I could see the beauty beyond the glass. Holding Little Joe in my arms, watching him grow into a man. Then Paul, Peter, Mary, Sarah, and John. When did we start giving them biblical names? We never reached our goal of replicating the twelve apostles, my darling, but each one is so very special.*

*I am afraid now as the end draws near, not of dying, but of growing so weak that I'll have to leave you. I feel the time coming close. But even though I will leave you in the flesh, I will never leave you in spirit. I'll be a ghost to haunt you, my sweet Rachel. I will be the scent of roses in the summer breeze. I will be your comfort in the shadows. I'll be the creak you hear when the house settles at night. I am going to stay with you as long as you remain here, a good ghost who can't bring himself to depart for heaven until you can go with me. I have unfinished business here, the other half of my heart. Heaven won't be heaven if you aren't there with me. I guess I'll be one of those disobedient spooks I once told you about, refusing to follow all the rules, only I won't be an evil one. Just the spirit of a man who isn't complete without his Rachel beside him.*

*Fortunately, I won't have to be a spook for long. You'll join me on the other side soon, and then we'll go to heaven together. I swore once that I would never leave you again. I meant it. I will never, ever leave you, my darling. You can go to the bank on that. And I know that God will allow me to keep that promise. I will be the wind in your hair. I will be the bark of Buddy's great-grandson many times removed. I'll be the softness of a rose-bud against your sweet cheek. I'll be the warmth of the blankets around you at night.*

*When I'm gone and you cry for me, dry your tears and feel my presence. I'll be right there beside you, unable to touch you as I did in this life, but there all the same.*

*I love you, sweet Rachel. I always will. My body may die, but that which is between us never will.*

*Your loving husband, into eternity,*
*Joseph*

The signature blurred in Tucker's vision, for he feared that he would never write such words to a woman. Maybe true love—the genuine article—had died out in modern times. Or maybe he was just unlucky. He'd never found anyone who meant a fraction as much to him as Rachel had meant to Joseph.

"Isn't that incredible?" Mary whispered.

It was, indeed, incredible. Tucker saw the proof, right there in his hand, that true love could actually happen. At least it had way back in the 1800s. Maybe women had changed, becoming more selfish and self-serving. Or maybe men had changed, becoming more focused on physical pleasure than meaningful relationships. He didn't know. He only knew that nothing so precious and lasting had ever come his way.

"When I was younger, I used to hope that your father might one day write a letter like that to me," his mother whispered.

Tucker turned to study Mary's sweet face. Her eyes were closed, and her smile glowed with happiness.

"But now that I'm older, with so many years behind us," she added, "I no longer need him to write the words. He loves me just that much, and I love him just as deeply. We'll go on, and one day we'll be at the last of our lives, as Joseph was when he wrote this letter to Rachel, but even though our bodies are dying, what we feel for each other never will."

Tucker had a lump in his throat. And a yearning. He'd seen his sister and brothers find such happiness in their marriages. They'd found the magic. What was wrong with him that he hadn't found it, too? Soon he'd turn thirty-fire. His good years were almost gone. God, he'd be forty before he knew it.

What did he have? Only one half of a veterinary practice. Rather than talk about that with his mother, he asked, "Do you think they're still there in Colorado, living near No Name?"

"Rachel and Joseph?"

"No, their descendants. Paxtons and Keegans. They must still be there."

Mary thought about it for a moment and then nodded. "It's a branch of our family that we've never kept in contact with, but they surely must be. People like us, who have bits and pieces of the past hidden away in their attics."

Tucker had a sudden yearning to go there—to No Name, Colorado.

Maybe there he would find the magic that eluded him in Oregon.